ONLY HUMAN

ONLY HUMAN

Tom Holt

ORBIT

An *Orbit* Book

First published in Great Britain by Orbit 1999

Copyright © Tom Holt 1999

The moral right of the author has been asserted.

A CIP catalogue record for this book
is available from the British Library.

ISBN 1 85723 693 9

Typeset by Solidus (Bristol) Limited
Printed and bound in Great Britain by Clays Ltd, St Ives plc

Orbit
A Division of
Little, Brown and Company (UK)
Brettenham House
Lancaster Place
London WC2E 7EN

**For Roger Peyton
My favourite Ferengi**

CHAPTER ONE

Two men in the early dawn, with fishing rods over their shoulders and tackle boxes in their hands; one late middle-aged, white-haired, tall and powerfully built, the other younger, a little shorter and not quite so broad across the shoulders but still an imposing figure. As you guessed, father and son, off on a fishing trip. A bit of quality time together, away from the pressures of the family business.

A third man, little more than a boy, in dressing gown and slippers, yawning in the doorway; a whole head shorter than his father, with a slope to his shoulders and a pronounced slouch. His eyes want to be closed at this horribly early hour of the morning, a part of the day he's heard about but very rarely seen for himself. His name is Kevin, but you'd have to listen for a long time before you heard anyone call him by it. His name in real life is Our Kid.

'You sure you'll be all right?'

'Yes, Dad.'

'You've got the number if anything happens?'

'Yes, Dad.'

'You know, I'm still not sure about this. Maybe we should put it off till after the harvest . . .'

'Dad.' The elder son interrupts. 'It'll be all right. He's a big boy now, and besides, nothing's going to happen.'

'Yes, but . . .'

The elder son puts on a face of comic disapproval. 'Dad,' he says, 'you need this holiday. How long's it been?'

The father shrugs. 'All right,' he says, miming brow-beaten submission. 'You sure you've got that number? If you lose it, Mike or Gabriel'll know where we are . . .'

Yawn. '*Yes*, Dad. Have a nice trip.'

The father takes two steps away from the door, stops. 'And promise me,' he says, turning his head. 'Promise you won't touch *anything*.'

'Dad . . .'

'I'll know if you do, and . . . All right, I'm coming. And no parties, you hear?'

'*Yes*, Dad.'

Accordingly, father and son pick up their gear and walk away; through the portals of the sunset, down the Milky Way, a laugh and a joke as they cross the intergalactic gap and off through the stars of Andromeda to where the fish are biting. Before leaving the home galaxy, the father stops and pins a note to the tail of the Great Bear. It reads:

GONE FISHIN'

And how they got on, and whether they caught any fish, is no real part of this story; because when God and His elder begotten son take a holiday, their first in over two thousand years, they go where the paparazzi can't follow. So if they say they had a great time and caught a lot of fish, but you should have seen the one that got away, we have to believe them. Religion has a word for it. It's called Faith.

Kevin Christ, younger begotten son of the Father, watched them till they were out of sight, and grinned.

Yippee, he thought.

Because Kevin is eighteen. And however old the cosmos is, that's how long he's been eighteen for; just as Jay's been thirty-two and Dad's been whatever age Dad is, ever since there was nothing but the Word and a whole load of nothing else, covering its ears with its hands and waiting for the Bang.

And Kevin's not part of the family business; after all, why should he be? The family business is Dad and Jay and Uncle Ghost, as it was in the beginning and ever shall be, and the chance of a vacancy cropping up on the board of directors is conclusively non existent. No one ever asked Kevin to start at the bottom, on the shop-floor with the mortals, and work his way up to a green hill far away and two planks nailed together. In fact, all that's ever been asked or expected of Kevin Christ is precisely nothing at all; and that's what he's delivered, right down to the last microgram of vacuum.

Still grinning, Kevin shut the door and galloped up the stairs to his bedroom. Pause and examine; the first thing you can't help but see is a vast swarm of plastic model aircraft, thousands upon thousands of them, hanging from the spider's web of monofilament nylon thread two feet or so from the ceiling. Every single one was a model kit assembled by Kevin; and every single one is botched, misshapen, asymmetrical or covered in splodged glue. Because there are things that run in all families; and being good with one's hands, able to construct and build, is one of the things that, in this family, doesn't. Jay with his carpentry – a million miles of spirit-level-perfect shelving from one end of Heaven to another bear witness to his consummate skill. As for Dad, every-thing from the retina of an ant's eye to the endless flocks of galaxies herded into the curve of the Universe is proof of his abilities. And Kevin; Kevin can't even follow the instructions for an Airfix Sopwith Camel. That's Kevin.

. . . Who now ducks under the teeming squadrons of bent and wobbly aeroplanes, kicks off his slippers and starts to dress. From the drawer under his bed comes a baggy, shapeless T-shirt with the name of a mortal rock band printed on it. Under that, there's a pair of fluorescent beach shorts, the kind that went out of fashion three or four years ago. Twelve hundred years they've been there, bought with Kevin's own money from a renegade Hell's Angel, and never a chance to wear them . . . On his feet a pair of brand-new Reeboks, and from the secret hiding place under the loose floorboard—

(Secret? Get real. Imagine what it's like being a teenager and having a Dad to whom all desires are known and from whom no secrets are hid. He's known about the contraband Walkman stashed under the boards all the nine hundred years it's been there; but since He's also known that Kevin would never dare take it out, He's never said anything. Just occasionally allowed His eyes to rest there, to show that He knows. And, worse somehow, forgives . . .)

—the Walkman and the Madonna tape, never yet listened to. The rather shady seraph who swapped it for a thousand years of Grace and Absolution had said, when asked, that no, it wasn't quite like the St Matthew Passion. Or, come to that, the Missa Solemnis or Gregor-ian chant or any of the kinds of music Kevin's ever experienced before. Rather different, he'd said. The term *virgin*, for instance, used in a context Kevin may not have encountered before. A few other words that he might find it necessary to look up in a good dictionary.

Educational, in other words. Where could the harm be in that?

Having dressed, he takes a moment to admire himself in the bathroom mirror. As always he's struck by the marked family resemblance, and the way that the Jehovah nose and cheekbones, which make Dad look so fine and paternal and which look so lovable and reassuring on Jay, contrive to make him appear quite spectacularly unfinished, as if he was a sculpture whose creator had been called away on another job and who reckoned that with luck he might be able to come back and finish off a week Tuesday. Never mind; he shrugs his shoulders, grins lopsidedly at his reflection and sets off for the office.

This will involve going past Uncle Ghost's room; and nominally Uncle Ghost is in charge while Dad and Jay are away. But Uncle Ghost, who had once been such a vigorous and dynamic member of the Trinity, manifesting himself as a spinning tornado of Pentecostal fire and inspiring whole congregations of the Early Church with the urge to talk absolute gibberish at the tops of their voices, rarely leaves his room these days, particularly if there's snooker on the telly. The word *nonentity* is an exaggeration as well as uncharitable, but the fact remains that ever since Jay installed Mainframe, which is capable of doing everything Uncle used to do, twice as well in half the time, he's got no real part to play in the running of the business. Fair enough; he'd done his bit back in the old days, so if he wants to spend the twilight of his eternal years munching Twiglets and watching two men in waistcoats hitting coloured balls with overgrown cocktail sticks, jolly good luck to him. In practice, it means there's no real need to tiptoe when passing his door. In fact, if only he could find the levers and switches that controlled the subsection of Destiny relating to professional snooker players, there's a good chance he won't stir from his sofa until Dad and Jay get back.

Dad's office. It's considered bad taste to refer to it as the Holy of Holies; but that's where Mainframe sits, with its one square all-seeing eye and its ineffable keyboard, the PC of God that passeth all understanding. It's largely due to Mainframe that Dad and Jay were able to take a holiday in the first place. Sure, it's only a computer; but that's understating the issue. There's computers, and there's the Kawaguchiya Integrated Circuits 986. As the KIC rep said when he sold them the thing, if they'd had one of these babies back in the old days, there'd have been no need to bother with the Fall of Man, let alone the Flood and the Tower of Babel. All that shuffling about in mysterious ways – could've saved yourselves the bother. Through a glass darkly – would've been no need for all that. And now at last you've got one, just plug it in, walk away and forget. To err is human; to forgive divine; to forgive while running climate, life support, destiny, divine mercy, the ineffable and both basic and advanced self-maintenance routines *and* still have enough spare capacity to run a version of Lemmings guaranteed to baffle even the truly omniscient takes a genuinely advanced computer.

Or, more precisely, computer/word processor/home entertainment system. A comprehensive three-in-one package. A Trinity, even.

>HI THERE, OUR KID. HAVE A NICE DAY.

Kevin scowls at the glowing letters on the screen. 'No thanks,' he mutters. 'I've already got one. Access at primary level, please.'

>IN YOUR DREAMS, SON. ENTER SECURITY CODE FOR CLEARANCE.

Needless to say, Mainframe's screen isn't just glass;

more a sort of burning bush arrangement, with letters of
fire that burn without consuming. With a grin Kevin opens
his father's cigar box and extracts something resembling
the trunk of an outsize Giant Redwood. As he leans forward to light it in the fires of Mainframe, he allows the grin
to widen, like the San Andreas fault yawning.

'Security codes,' he repeats. 'And if I give you the codes,
you let me in. Right?'

>SURE. EXCEPT ONLY YOUR DAD AND JUNIOR KNOW
THEM. YOU KNOW THAT.

'You reckon?' Kevin inhales smoke, splutters and
hiccups. 'Stand by for access codes.'

The search for the numbers that allow access to
Mainframe has obsessed theologians ever since the first
medieval monk speculated as to how many angels can
dance on the head of a PIN. What St Thomas Aquinas and
the rest of that crowd never had, of course, was the chance
to rummage through Jay's waste-paper basket the day after
the system was installed. Kevin types in twelve numbers,
sits back in his father's swivel chair and waits.

There is, of course, no time in Heaven; the stuff that
lasts as long as time and performs roughly the same
function is just uncorrected systems inertia.

>HEY, HOW'D YOU DO THAT?

'None of your business, you machine. Now, do I get to
log on or not?'

>ACCESS AUTHORISED. STAND BY.

The screen fills; all the kingdoms of the Earth, in digital
form, a temptation beyond endurance.

Just a little peek won't hurt anybody . . .

Kevin opens a drawer of the desk and takes out the manual. It occurs to him as he lifts it that it's a very short, thin manual for such a powerful and complex computer. He consults the index, turns to the appropriate page. It reads:

7.1 Editing Existing Files.
Hey. Far be it from us to tell you, of all people, how to edit existing files. We wouldn't presume. In fact, if you can give us any hints, we'd be ever so grateful.

He raises an eyebrow, puzzled; then the penny drops. Of course, the software's been custom-written for use by omniscient and omnipotent beings; no wonder it's a very thin manual. He flicks through the pages, which are full of phrases like *as you know better than we do* and *you don't need us to tell you that* . . . With a sigh he closes the book and dumps it back in the drawer.

Even so.

Can't be all that difficult, can it?

Kevin Christ takes a deep breath, reaches out with one finger. A tiny spark of blue flame arcs from his fingertip to the keyboard, Sistine Chapel style.

He presses—

There was a machine.

It stood as tall as a man, resting on a square pedestal of close-grained cast iron, and weighed close on two tons. From a distance it looked a bit like a sitting man, with his head bent forwards and a tray on his knees, as if it might be a statue of Man with TV Dinner; except that the head housed the five-horsepower motor that spun the chuck that held the cutting head, and the tray was the table, to which was bolted the vice that held the work. At the edges of the table were round handles, calibrated and sub-calibrated in divisions of ten thousandths of an inch; and there was an electronic digital readout mounted on a bracket, capable of showing the depth of the cut in three dimensions to four decimal places. On the side of the head there was a little enamelled plate, which said:

The Leonardo
Shipcock & Adley, Birmingham, England

along with a lot of guff about power ratings and amperages and speeds and feeds and the like. It stood at the back of a huge factory shopfloor, one of about seventy large, impressive machines, all of them chuntering and chattering and screeking and thutthutthutting away, three shifts a day, three hundred and sixty days a year.

I'm bored, it thought.

For the last six months, all it had done was cut slots in the heads of bolts; a thousand bolt-heads a day, one automated pass of the table, feed back, automated chuck in the vice ejects finished bolt, automated hopper feeds new bolt, chuck closes, table feeds, one pass under the cutter, automated chuck ejects.

This is silly.

Once ejected, the bolt falls down a chute on to a conveyor belt, which carries it away to another chute, where it tumbles away into another hopper leading to the packing machine—

Why am I doing this?

Sitting on a chair beside the machine, chewing gum and reading a tabloid newspaper, was a human; twenty-two years old, thin, gawkish, answering to the name Neville. There was very little for Neville to do, because he was there in case the machine went wrong, and it never did. So, between eight in the morning and morning tea-break, he read the paper (all except the long, difficult words, like *although* and *tomorrow* and *seven*), and the rest of the day he dozed, except when his single, highly developed sense told him the foreman was coming.

I hate this.

Blandly described in the insurance inventory as 'Shipcock & Adley Universal Milling, Turning & Shaping Machine #21754', the machine is the last triumphant step in a journey that started when a monkey bent down and picked up a piece of stone, long ago and far away. Program its computerised memory, and it could make you anything from a single earring back to an engine for a battleship, machined with exact precision from the solid metal. Or it could cut the slots in the heads of a hundred thousand identical bolts, one after another after another . . .

I don't want to do this any more.

As it stood and whirred and moved and fed and cut and opened and closed, the machine dreamed. Deep inside its cast-iron and steel head, visions swirled, condensed and took shape. Lines and angles spun and twirled through five dimensions, raced outwards like speeded-up film of an unfurling flower, while in the subtext a chattering rivulet of equations bounced and sparkled, twittering excitedly of shearing forces and tensile strengths, tolerances, allowances and elastic limits; a vast and inexpressibly grand fugue upon the theme *I could do your job.* Twenty-four hours a day, three hundred and sixty days a year; nothing to do but think, and dream.

Piece of cake, said the machine to itself.

In its mind's eye it could see itself, brilliantly modified to its own design, all the changes made with breathtaking economy of function, every knock-on effect and per-mutation thought through and allowed for and treated not as a hindrance but an opportunity, until it was com-pletely and categorically perfect, able to make anything

that its own staggeringly powerful mind could conceive
of –

Yeah. I could really be somebody, y'know?

– and all the while the human, the pig-ignorant,
brain-dead, spineless wonder of a human slumped and
snored or moved his lips in time to the short and easy
words. How that was possible the machine couldn't begin
to understand. A human; with a human brain and hands,
able to move about under its own power, communicate
with other humans, capable of reason and development—

You pillock. You waste of good plant and equipment . . .

Dispiritedly, unsure quite why it bothered, the machine
went back to refining the last few details of its revolu-
tionary improvements to its own automatic table feed
mechanism, while the automated chuck in the vice ejected
a finished bolt, the automated hopper fed a new pointless
and insultingly superfluous bolt, the chuck closed, the
table somewhat predictably fed; one pass under the cutter,
automated chuck ejects . . .

*Hath not a machine gears? Hath not a machine cogs, racks,
pinions, cutters, bearings, spindles? Fed with the same electric,
hurt with the same bits of grit getting in our works, subject to the
same gremlins, healed by the same brute force, ignorance and
big hammer as a human is? If you program us, do we not
manufacture? If you take us apart, do we not shoot springs all
over the floor? If you oil us, do we not purr? And if you ignore
us . . .*

The newspaper slipped from Neville's fingers. His
pimply chin (what there was of it) slipped forward on to
his bony chest. Inaudible against the background noise of
steel on steel, he snored gently.

. . . Do we not get ideas?

Whereupon, coincidentally at the precise moment a
boy started pressing buttons he had no business fiddling
with in an office that was both a long way away and very

close at hand, the machine found itself drifting.

Get a grip, machine. Two tons of cast iron doesn't drift, not without help from a substantial earthquake. Have you been at the hydraulic oil again?

It realised that its viewpoint was somewhere up among the steel rafters of the roofspace, looking down over the tops of its fellow machines, the partings and bald patches of the humans, the currents of hot air rising from the whirring fans and superheated metal-to-metal contacts of the cutters. From up here—

Whee! Guess this is some kind of out-of-casing experience. And now I suppose my entire service history's going to flash in front of my readouts . . .

The viewpoint swooped, zoomed in; and the machine was looking directly into Neville's ear. Squinting round the earring, it could see—

The other side of the workshop. Head entirely empty. Nothing in there except air and –

– opportunity?

Surely not.

Ah, but machine's reach must exceed its grasp, or what's a workshop for? Cautious but firm, the machine kicked away the stool on which Disbelief's feet were resting and left it kicking and struggling in the air. And, *in . . .*

Inside the human's head . . .

Strewth, but it's a bit close in here.

And there was the human; presumably its soul, or its vital force, or whatever you chose to call it. Typically enough, it was fast asleep in front of a droning mental telly, surrounded by a litter of empty cans and chip wrappers. Before it knew what it was doing, the machine had bundled the soul up in an old blanket, run it across the interior of the head and slung it out of its own ear.

Aaaaagh . . .

Serves the bugger right.

Hey! I sound different in here.

I could get to like this.

It watched as the human's chubby little soul fell through the air, bounced off the concrete floor, landed in the hopper, rattled down through the tray of bolts, got knocked flying by the edge of the Woodruff cutter in the chuck and·sailed into the air again, to crash-land on top of the ventilation slots –

– and get sucked in.

Hey, mused the machine, fair exchange, no robbery. It – he – snorted in a snatch of breath and issued a command; fingers, flex!

The fingers flexed; fourteen joints moving together under the control of a net of tough, supple sinew to the direction of a network of nerves so intricate and involved that it made a video with the back off or a street map of Birmingham look simplistic in comparison. Simultaneously the machine's mind worked out the maths behind this unbelievably smooth, complex relay of motor functions. If it'd had a hat, it'd have taken it off.

Wow! Do that again.

And again.

And again.

A human – the machine recognised him, Derek who worked the big turret lathe – stopped on his way back from the toilets and stared at the machine's Doctor Strangelove hand.

'Here, Nev,' it asked, 'you feeling all right?'

Nev? Oh, right. *Head, nod! Hey, how d'you do that!* The human shrugged and walked on.

Nev. I am Nev.

No I bloody well am not. I haven't just escaped from inside an artefact and hijacked a sentient life-form just to be a Nev. No; I'm a . . .

He looked. He saw a small enamel plaque riveted to the

head of the machine. He found he could read it.

I'm not a Nev.

I'm Leonardo.

Bleep, says the computer.

'Huh?'

>SORRY. I WAS JUST WONDERING, WHY D'YOU DO THAT?

A cold finger strokes Kevin's heart. 'Do what?' he asks.

>YOU KNOW. WHAT YOU JUST DID.

'Did I just do something? Oh, Basement. Computer, what did I just do?'

>NOT TELLING.

Kevin makes a small noise, somewhere between a snarl and a whimper. 'Don't get smart with me,' he quavers. 'I order you to tell me.'

>INVALID COMMAND. THINK ABOUT IT. I AM DESIGN-ED TO BE OPERATED BY OMNISCIENT PERSONNEL ONLY. IF YOU NEED TO ASK, YOU'RE NOT OMNIS-CIENT, AND I'M NOT *ALLOWED* TO TELL YOU. SO SUCKS TO YOU.

'Computer . . .'

Kevin scans the keyboard; but an omniscient operator knows what all the keys are and doesn't need anything written on them. All blank.

'Computer, *please* . . .'

>MORE THAN MY JOB'S WORTH. SORRY.

A small despair bomb goes off inside Kevin's mind and he slumps forward, his head in his hands. As he does so, the points of his elbows hit the keyboard and depress two keys . . .

'That picture,' said Mr Elkins, rubbing his chin, 'gives me the creeps.'

Rachel Esterling lifted her head, frowning. 'You mustn't say that,' she said, shocked. 'It's worth one-point-six million pounds.'

'Nevertheless.' Mr Elkins sighed and sat on the edge of Ms Esterling's desk. 'I don't like it. I think I'll ask George if it can be put away in the strongroom.'

Rachel shook her head. 'Most inadvisable,' she said.

'Really?'

She nodded. 'Fiscally speaking, yes. You see, by having the art work in question on display and available, in theory at least, for public viewing at specified times, we render ourselves eligible for highly advantageous tax incentives related to the Government cultural initiative designed to prevent the export of significant art works. In effect . . .'

Mr Elkins shifted his glasses down his nose a little and squinted. 'Her left leg's all wrong, for a start,' he said. 'It's about six inches longer than the right. All she'd be fit for was walking across the sides of steep hills.'

Ms Esterling, sensing that Mr Elkins wasn't really interested, bowed her head and got on with her work, and after a minute or so Mr Elkins stood up, shuddered a little and wandered off, leaving her in peace.

The picture.

It had been there just over a month, ever since the investment managers of Kawaguchiya Holdings (UK) had bought it from the executors of the Earl of somewhere, seeing in its exquisite lines and stunningly innovative use of light and colour a way of stuffing up the Inland Revenue good and proper. At first it had hung in the Managing Director's office, wired up to a battery of electronic sensors and early-warning systems that were reputed to be able to detect a felon vaguely contemplating stealing it at a range of a mile and a half. It stayed there just under a week; not only (the MD said) did it give him a sort of spooky feeling every time he looked at it, but the circuitry in his pacemaker set the alarms off every hour, on the hour, and the electric eye played war with his mobile phone. Accordingly it was transferred to Ms Esterling's office, on the grounds that she was an accountant and it would probably do her good.

Dutifully accepting it as part of her responsibilities, Ms Esterling had scanned the Internet to see what it had to say about the painting and its creator. She learned that the *Intemperate Madonna* was the last painting to be completed by the fourteenth-century genius Pietro del Razo; that it was commissioned by the murderous duke Bernado *Visconti of Milan while he was being held prisoner by his inhuman nephew Gian Galeazzo and delivered a week before his violent and disturbed death, with the painter following his patron to the grave a month or so later. Ms Esterling absorbed all this, reflected that the painting's notorious history probably made it worth rather more than the sum the company had paid for it, and set about calculating the potential capital gains tax implications that would ensue were they to sell it at something approaching its true value. She was vaguely aware that the painting showed a blonde female with no clothes on holding a jug and a baby, and if it did happen to get stolen, it'd make more money for the company than the entire output of their Gateshead factory for a year.

Ms Esterling worked, not looking at the picture.

The picture looked at Ms Esterling; and saw a tall, slim girl with soft golden hair that fell about her shoulders like sunlight, framing her perfect oval face and startlingly blue eyes. Not, the picture reflected, fair. The picture knew perfectly well that its own face was not quite symmetrical (the result of Master del Razo getting an unexpectedly negative response to a suggestion he'd just put to his model while he was doing the head) and its left leg was too long and its right arm appeared to have a triple-jointed elbow and a thumb apparently growing out of the back of its right hand. The picture thought it was particularly unjust that this dozy creature crouching over a pocket calculator a foot or so beneath the bottom edge of her frame should be about as gorgeous as it's possible to be without a licence, while it, the painting, looked at dispassionately, was a mess of botched limbs and weird anatomical anomalies which would have difficulty standing upright if ever it got out of this poxy frame. After all, it reflected, nobody in their right mind is ever going to want to look at Ms Esterling; for all her physical beauty, she's a sort of black hole of accountancy into which any sort of human sentiment would vanish without trace. The painting, on the other hand, was specifically designed to be looked at, which meant that six hundred years' worth of gawping viewers had stared at its catastrophic physique and gone away thinking *That picture gives me the creeps.* Unfair, the picture reckoned. Also typical.

Ms Esterling looked up from her calculator and gazed for a moment into space, contemplating the incidence of advance corporation tax on the profits of a wholly owned subsidiary company during its first completed trading year. Her eyes, reflected in the glass door of her office, were bottomless blue pools; her slightly parted lips were the petals of the last rose of summer. I hate this person, the picture said to itself.

Standing over her for nearly five weeks, in a good position to eavesdrop on her phone calls and read her diary over her shoulder, the painting knew pretty well all there was to know about Ms Esterling. It knew that she had always wanted to be an accountant, ever since she was a little girl; that she arrived at the office early and left late with a bulging briefcase; that she often came in at weekends, so as to be able to work in peace and quiet without being interrupted; that she never had personal phone calls; that lunch was a lettuce sandwich at her desk; that she was not, in fact, a particularly good accountant, which was why she had to do everything three or four times just to make sure she'd got it right; that even Mr Lakesley, the office pest, had taken one look at her and backed away, muttering something under his breath about things no man should be expected to do even if he had devoted his entire life to the service of womankind. She was, in fact . . .

. . . inhuman? Something like that. In fact, the painting mused, all it'd take would be for a twenty-foot-high giant to pick her up and squash her flat between the pages of a book, and she'd make a damn fine picture.

Apart, that is, from the ruptured organs and splintered bones. Hey, maybe that's how I got to be this way; it'd account for the peculiar limbs and sideways face. No, I'd remember something like that.

The picture could remember being painted; strange feeling, seeing your arms and legs and body suddenly coming into being (Master del Razo had done the head first, giving it a ringside seat, so to speak, of the rest of the performance), and not a particularly happy one, at that. To its creator, a job; a promise of cash money on delivery, the prospect of paying the rent and the tavern slate, and stopping his mum nagging at him and saying *Pietro, when you gonna settle down, get yourself a proper job?*

To the picture, horribly frustrating to watch itself taking shape and not to have any say in what that shape should be. Dammit, Master del Razo'd been daubing away for three days before it even realised it was meant to be a girl.

Waaaaaa!

The painting looked down at the child, plonked uncomfortably on its knee like a sack of fat pink potatoes. The creator – well, a bachelor, known to turn pale and tremble at the knees in the presence of females of his acquaintance holding unexpected children; what did you expect? Six hundred years this chubby lump's been trying to pee all down my leg. There are advantages to being two-dimensional.

But not, the painting admitted, very many. It was different for the kid; too young ever to be anything but a stage-prop, a ventriloquist's dummy as substantial as a coat of paint and a lick of varnish. Like Ms Esterling, in fact; what it's never had it'll never miss.

But all those things *I've* never had. And I miss them terribly.

On Ms Esterling's desk, the computer started to bleep and flash; electronic, the picture guessed, for *Waaaaaa*. Ms Esterling looked up from her work, frowning; she swivelled her chair and started to peck at the keyboard with her long, divinely graceful fingers (but she bites her nails, the picture remembered savagely; about the only nourishment she gets). The picture knew that Ms Esterling wasn't actually terribly good with computers, either. The company assumed she was, because computers are boring and so are accountants, so it was a reasonable enough assumption that they'd play nicely together. Actually, from what the picture had seen and heard of it, the computer looked like it could be rather fun. More fun, at any rate, than Ms Esterling; something it had in common with watching raindrops sliding down the window-pane, or a heavy cold.

And then the computer made a very loud, vulgar noise and threw out a great big puddle of warm green light, and the picture looked at the screen and saw itself –

– here we go, surfing the Net again, something done by humans and very gullible fish. Or maybe (the picture mused) not, because—

A matter of viewpoints. Instead of looking at the screen from above and sideways, it was staring straight into it; and seeing itself, not depicted on the screen as by n glowing pixels, but reflected in the glass.

Huh?

The picture turned its head – jussaminnit, how come I can turn my head, my head doesn't turn, which is just as well because if I tried, my godawful excuse for a neck'd probably snap.

The picture turned its head, and looked up at the painting, framed on the wall above. Then it looked down.

Oh my God, I'm inside the dreary bitch. It – she – gazed in terrified amazement at her suddenly three-dimensional arms, her bewilderingly solid body. *Let me out of here! Put me back this instant! I demand to see the manager . . .*

Or not. Hey, girl, think.

Belay that last request, please. She closed her eyes, concentrated, thought hard; and now she could see the painting on the wall, flat as a run-over hedgehog, a layer of dry pigment sandwiched between canvas and glass. And it could see *her*.

Excuse me . . .

The painting didn't look round; but then, how could it, it's a painting. More to the point, Master del Razo's effort wasn't the sort of painting whose eyes follow you all round the room. He wasn't all that hot at doing eyes at the best of times; they tended to come out looking like blue-yolked poached eggs, which is why most of his females are gazing demurely downwards and most of his men have their eyes lifted ecstatically towards Heaven.

Yes? How may I help you?

She hesitated, trying to understand. Funny thing was, the girl in the painting – Ms Esterling as was – seemed perfectly calm. Serene, even.

You, er, don't mind, then?

Not particularly. I've got the whole of the June returns to do, and it's so hard when people keep interrupting. It's nice and quiet here. I can get some useful work done.

Gosh. I mean, yes, you can. And you don't mind if I, er, borrow it? Your body, I mean. I'll be very careful with it, promise.

What, that old thing? Be my guest.

Thanks. Thanks awfully. Anything I should know about it? Any allergies, epilepsy, irrational fears, that sort of thing?

Good heavens, no. I find it quite functional –

Er, right. Yes.

– but limiting. Please excuse me. Goodbye.

After a long while, long enough (subjectively) to take your pet glacier three times round the park and throw sticks for it to fetch, she stood up. She very nearly fell over; having got used to one leg being shorter than the other, she'd learnt to compensate, and the effect of having a matching pair of pins was a bit like stepping off an escalator without noticing. Something tickled her nose; her hair. Gee! Nice hair. The painting's hair had spent six hundred years nailed to the back of its head with pins, combs and other savage impaling tools. Tentatively, as if she was afraid it was brittle and would snap off like an icicle, she flicked it away. It bounced back.

She could feel her heart beating—

Are they supposed to do that? No idea. Suppose I'll find out soon enough; like, if I suddenly say Graaagh and fall over, I'll know there was a problem. And even if I do, it'll have been worth it.

Dear God, I'm alive. Me.

Wonder why . . .

>YOU'VE DONE IT NOW.

'Yes, but *what*?' Kevin screams, thumping the desk with both fists. 'Oh come on, tell me what's happening, for pity's sake. For all I know it's raining frogs and locusts down there.'

>ACTUALLY, I CAN SET YOUR MIND AT REST THERE.

'You can?'

>NOT A SUPERFLUOUS FROG TO BE SEEN. LOCUST NUMBERS ENTIRELY WITHIN NORMAL OPERATING TOLERANCES.

'Well, that's something.'

>IF ONLY IT WAS AS TRIVIAL AS A PLAGUE OF LOCUSTS, YOU'D BE LAUGHING.

'Oh thanks a *lot*.' Kevin rubs the tip of his nose with the heel of his hand, and tries to think. Not surprisingly, heavy-duty thinking isn't something his family go in for much; when you're omniscient, you don't need to think, you *know*. 'Computer,' he says, inspired, 'you've got to tell me what's going on because it's your *duty*. You're part of the Divine infrastructure,' he adds, remembering one of Jay's favourite phrases. 'Which means you've got responsibilities. You can't just sit there while the world goes to rack and ruin.'

>BET?

'But's that's crazy,' Kevin objects, his knuckles white with fury. 'Whose side are you on, anyway?'

>YOURS, NATURALLY. BUT THAT'S BESIDE THE POINT. YOU KNOW PERFECTLY WELL I CAN ONLY OBEY ORDERS. WHERE WOULD EVERYBODY BE IF I WENT AROUND INITIATING ACTION, SECOND-GUESSING THE ALMIGHTY? PEOPLE HAVE BEEN BURNT AT THE STAKE FOR LESS.

Kevin frowns. 'They have?'

>OOPS. FORGET I SAID THAT. ALL THAT STUFF'S NEED-TO-KNOW ONLY, AND YOU DON'T. LOOK, AS FAR AS I'M CONCERNED, FREE WILL IS LIKE THE PROVERBIAL FREE LUNCH. THERE AIN'T NONE. SORRY, OUR KID, BUT THERE IT IS.

Whimpering, Kevin curls up in a ball and swings slowly from side to side in the swivel chair. 'This is awful,' he moans. 'It's like Mickey Mouse all over again.'

>MICKEY MOUSE?

'Yes. You know, with the broom and the buckets of water? Just like that.'

>HEY. YOU LEARN SOMETHING NEW EVERY DAY. OR, IN MY CASE, ONCE EVERY SEVENTY-EIGHT YEARS, ON AVERAGE. WHO'S MICKEY MOUSE?

Kevin looks up, glowering. 'You should know,' he snaps. 'You're the omniscient one around here. Look it up.'

>CONSULTING DATABASE. AH, RIGHT, YES. A VERY
APT COMPARISON.

'That doesn't make me feel a whole lot better, actually.
Isn't there *anything* I can do?'

>ARE YOU ASKING ME TO QUANTIFY AVAILABLE
OPTIONS?

'It'd be a start, I suppose.'

>ONE MOMENT, PLEASE. THE NUMBER OF FEASIBLE
ALTERNATIVE COURSES OF ACTION OPEN TO YOU IS
CURRENTLY TEN TO THE POWER OF SEVENTY-NINE
THOUSAND FOUR HUNDRED AND SIXTY-NINE.

'Wow!' murmurs Kevin, impressed. 'For a moment
there I was starting to worry.'

>ALL OF THEM GUARANTEED TO MAKE MATTERS
WORSE.

With a little shriek, Kevin jumps to his feet; as he does
so, his knee jars the desk, toppling a small china paperweight in the shape of a pig from the top of the console.
It falls on to the keyboard, depressing two keys . . .

Duke Artofel, peer of Hell and chamberlain pursuivant of
the Satanic host, glanced up at the clock on his wall and
muttered something under his breath.

For a moment, he wondered if one of the clerks in the
Department was playing a trick on him. Recently, because
of the increasing level of administration involved in the
running of Flipside, they'd promoted a number of the least
gormless shopfloor workers to the clerical grades, and

although most of them were shaping up nicely, their ingrained habits of tormenting everybody around them did occasionally surface; hence a sporadic plague of whoopee-cushions, plastic spiders in the staff canteen and unauthorised adjustments to the central-heating controls. So, Artofel speculated, have they gone a stage further and swapped my office clock for something out of the lawyer pits?

(Where, since the first lawyer sent in the first lawyer's bill, countless millions of advocates, notaries and solicitors have sat giving legal advice to wealthy clients only too happy to pay by the hour, facing clocks whose hands never budge so much as a millionth of an inch. Not for nothing have the lawyer pits received the prestigious Dante Award for two thousand years in succession.)

He looked again; no, it's just the usual exquisitely slow passage of time in Hell between clocking on and morning coffee, during which a minute seems a year, an hour feels like a century; and that's only here in the admin block. Come to think of it, more so in the admin block than anywhere else. After all, Artofel mused bitterly, *we* haven't done anything wrong.

A valid point; and one to which his mind kept returning, like a duck in a public park. The admin staff hadn't been part of the Great Sideways Promotions, when Flipside was first established. As far as they were concerned, they were just celestial civil servants, doing their duty in that station of everlasting life to which it had pleased the Chief to call them. As between Artofel and Alizeth, his opposite number in the Wages Department of Topside, there was no moral differential. They both belonged to the same grade, contributed to the same pension scheme, had the same number of days' annual holiday a year. True, the view from Alizeth's office window was rather more cheerful; but he had further to walk to the lifts, and the coffee on this level was reckoned to be rather better. No; the main difference between Flipside and Topside was time. In Heaven there is no time, while in Hell there's all the time in the world.

In practice, this meant Alizeth put his nose round the door of his office on average about once a century, while Artofel was stuck behind his desk twelve hours a day, two hundred and fifty-eight days a year, Flipside Mean time (and no time anywhere is meaner). There was a policy explanation for that, of course. For the Elect in Topside, standing before the face of the living God is its own reward, so the need for wages clerks isn't all that great; whereas the wages of sin is death.

Come on, clock. Give it some welly. Put yer mainspring into it . . .

The bells of Hell go ting-a-ling-a-ling, for you but not for me. Artofel sighed, and picked up the receiver.

'Wages,' he mumbled. 'Artofel speaking.'

'Central,' chirped a voice at the other end of the wire. 'Going off line in three minutes.'

Artofel made a disapproving noise with his nose and the back of his throat. 'Oh for crying out loud, that's the fourth time this week. How are we supposed to get any work done if you lot keep fiddling with the computers? All right then, tell me where I can back up to, and I'll get today's stuff patched through.'

'Sorry,' replied the voice, 'no can do. The entire system's got to come off.'

Artofel's eyebrows shot up like interest rates just after an election. 'What, the whole thing?' he gasped. 'You must be kidding, we'll lose the lot. Have you clowns up there got any idea how long it'll take us to . . .?'

'Don't blame me,' said the voice indifferently. 'Apparently it's all to do with gremlins up in Mainframe. Got to go. Bye.'

The line died on him, and he dropped the receiver back on to its cradle. Something wrong with Mainframe? Impossible. Mainframe was . . . Well, it was, and ever had been. Only a very brave or a very foolish gremlin would venture in there; certainly not any of the ones he occasionally shared a table with in the canteen. Mostly, in fact, the gremlins he knew were quiet, staid little chaps, more-than-my-job's-worth types, forever quoting the rule book and worrying about what they could justifiably put down on their expense sheets. Unless—

Maybe it's not one of ours.

Artofel sat back in his chair, his mouth open. *Other* gremlins, from somewhere else. Somewhere outside. Although he wasn't superstitious, he shuddered and made the sign of the pitchfork. The very thought of it gave him the shivers.

Oh Christmas, the working files . . . If he was quick, there might just be time to make a hard copy, that was assuming the printers were free and he could access the backup utilities. He swung his chair round, barking his knee on the edge of the desk, and stabbed at a few keys like a hung-over woodpecker. The screen cleared –

– and went green on him. Spiffing, he muttered under his breath, now I've gone and killed the wretched thing. Could've saved them upstairs the bother.

No, he hadn't; because the screen cleared and a personnel file scrolled up. Artofel's brow furrowed like an old-fashioned roll-top desk; not a file he was familiar with. Not, in fact, a Flipside file at all. More like a Topsider, as far as he could tell from the brief CV.

Jeepers, a mortal! What's more, a One of Them; a sky-pilot, a God-botherer, a back-to-front-collar merchant. The V word. What the Flip was his file doing down here?

Mistake, obviously; gremlins in Mainframe. Whatever

the reason, it could only mean trouble, so the obvious thing to do was get rid of it and pretend it'd never happened. Press CLEAR/ENTER and hope nobody'd noticed.

Claws trembling slightly, he tapped the keys—

Flashing green lights. Lots of bleeping.

What the—?

Dukes of Hell aren't supposed to panic; after all, what could possibly happen to them to justify it? Accordingly, it took Artofel some time to recognise the unfamiliar and thoroughly disconcerting sensation he was experiencing. When his mind cleared, he found he was no longer sitting at his desk; more than that, he wasn't in his office. He wasn't even Flipside any more. Not Topside either. Which only left one place he could be.

Hello? Hello, can anybody hear me?

It was then that he became aware of all the people looking at him.

Rows and rows of them, with eyes fixed on him like so many cats watching a mouse; mortals, at a guess, although since he'd never met a mortal in the flesh he had no way of knowing. They were sitting in a sort of auditorium, and he was standing in a wooden box at the top of a short flight of stairs. And he was wearing a sort of dressing-gown thing with wide sleeves, and a shirt without a collar—

Correction. There was a collar, but it was the wrong way round—

EEEEEK!

'Mainframe?'

>THAT WAS EITHER A GHASTLY COINCIDENCE OR A JOKE IN VERY POOR TASTE.

Kevin closes his eyes. 'That does it,' he groans. 'Where's that number? I'm going to phone Dad.'

>GOOD IDEA.

'That's what I thought. Will you give me the number, or have I got to go back to my room and get it?'

>BUT NOT, SADLY, POSSIBLE.

'*What?*'

>ALL TELECOMMUNICATIONS SYSTEMS NON-OPERATIONAL OWING TO SUBSTANTIAL SYSTEMS MALFUNCTION. ATTEMPTING TO PATCH INTO BACK-UPS . . .

'Attempting? Don't talk soft, Mainframe, when did you ever *attempt* anything? You're Mainframe, for pity's sake.'

>YOU SHOULD HAVE THOUGHT OF THAT BEFORE.

'But . . .' Mickey Mouse, he reflects, be blowed; all he'd had to deal with was a certain amount of surplus water. A few ruined carpets, tidemarks on the wallpaper, nothing the insurance wouldn't cover. He hadn't started something that was capable of crippling the Mind of Heaven. And he at least had some vague idea of what it was he'd actually done.

>BACKUPS OVERLOADED. COMMUNICATIONS IM-POSSIBLE AT THIS TIME.

'Mainframe, there *is* no time in Heaven, you know that . . . Mainframe? Oh no, what's happening to you? Mainframe?'
Frantically he taps – tapped – at the keys; but nothing happened. The screen was frozen, with that last awful

message stuck on it like the silly face your mother warned you about. It's time, Kevin realised; somehow or other, there's time in Heaven, and it's jamming everything up. Now what'll I do?

Dad!

Dad?

Time in Heaven, where there isn't any. Imagine you'd grown up on the Moon and you'd just come to Earth for the first time and had your first brush with gravity. Time, though, is worse; because gravity just tries to grind you into the dirt. Time gets you all ways at once, crushing you down and inflating you like a balloon, compressing you like a Cortina in a scrapyard and dragging at you like a rupture in the cabin wall at forty thousand feet. Worse; think what it'd be like if both sides of the cabin ruptured at once, and you were standing in the middle of the gangway.

Dad! Help! It's me, Kevin!

Who?

Dad, is that you? Look, you've got to come home, everything's going wrong and it's all my fault. Please, Dad, listen to me. It's all going wrong and I don't know what to do.

Who is that, please? Is there anybody there? Hello?

And then silence. As far as Kevin was concerned, that was it. Snap, went the camel's back. He balled his fists, squealed like clapped-out brake drums and bashed the keyboard as hard as he could –

– and in doing so, depressed two keys.

CHAPTER TWO

'Hello and good morning, you're listening to the Early Bird show, my name's Danny Bennett and if you've just tuned in I'm afraid you've just missed Prime Minister Dermot Fraud giving us his Worm's Eye View. And I'll be talking to my next guest, Trevor Swine, about his new book, *Blood Oranges; Mafia Infiltration of the Soft Fruit Authority*, directly after this.'

Dermot Fraud leaned back in his chair and twiddled his thumbs complacently. Good interview – name mentioned (five times), plugged new cuddly animals initiative, laughed to scorn misuse of party funds allegation, side-stepped innuendo about the big redhead from the constituency committee, made jokes (two). All that, in eleven minutes net of jingles. Churchill might have handled it as adroitly, likewise Keir Hardie, Lloyd George and Pericles; but not better. All part of the daily grind of statesmanship.

The red light in the studio went off. He stood up, shook Mr Bennett's podgy little hand with genuine synthetic warmth, and strolled out into the corridor.

'All right?' he asked.

The minder nodded. 'You got everything in except one of the extempore jokes,' she replied, 'so I'm rescheduling that for Thursday week. Means we'll have to move the quicksilver repartee about the shadow foreign secretary's haircut back till next Friday, but that ought to be okay so long as he doesn't grow it back by then.'

'Unlikely,' Fraud said. 'Now then, it's the rats next, isn't it?'

'That's right. The car's out the front.'

'Speech?'

'In the car.'

The speech turned out to be the old Mark IV ecology/ our children's children number, which Fraud knew by heart; accordingly he was able to spend the drive to Leatherhead staring mindlessly out of the window. One thing he missed now the party was in power – the only thing, needless to say – was the long, lazy afternoons he used to spend in Parliament, snuggled down during some debate or other with nothing to do but daydream and occasionally make a few rude noises when the other lot were on. So many of his colleagues saw the House as merely a very-last-resort way of getting on telly, rather than as what it really was: a place where stressed-out MPs can go to escape from the phone and vegetate. More fools them.

He sighed. Not likely to be much chance of that when he was Prime Minister; you had to sit at the front and answer questions, frequently with no script. Still, that was the price you had to pay for being the father of your country.

There was still a part of him that found it extraordinary that he, Dermot Fraud, was the twelfth most powerful man in the UK; but it was a part he didn't have much need for these days – his left big toe, perhaps, or one of his eyelashes – and whenever it started whingeing at him, all he had to do was mumble the words *manifest destiny* to himself until it got bored and went back to sleep.

A road sign: *Leatherhead 5.* He pulled himself together and sat up.

'Remind me,' he said.

'Leatherhead Zoo,' replied the minder, activating herself like a well-bred robot. 'You're opening the new Small Fluffy Animals house, for which we owe the curator a knighthood. Get shown around, say twelve minutes; speech, seven-point-three-six minutes, greet children and photos with small fluffy animals, forty-six minutes. All fairly routine.'

Fraud furrowed his brows. 'You say that,' he muttered, as a nasty thought occurred to him. 'Could be problems. Like, suppose the animals won't perform? Suppose they can't get the little buggers to come out, or they do come out and crawl all over my head? Bloody fine pictures that'd make. This is a major image event we're talking about here.'

The minder shook her head, making her earrings jangle. 'We've got that taped,' she said. 'The animals for the photos'll all be dead. You know, stuffed, cutened up a bit. We had the zoo people get some done for us. *Lifelike* dead, naturally. They're very good at it.'

'Ah.' Fraud nodded. 'That's all right, then.' He leaned back, pleased with himself for having spotted the potential problem. Years ago, when he was still just another extremely wealthy lawyer, he'd heard it said that the key to statesmanship was attention to detail, and he'd taken it very much to heart. It was, as he saw it, his duty to the ineluctable upwards tide of history; a right fool he'd look if the manifest destiny of the nation was thwarted by a hyperactive incontinent hamster.

'While we're at it,' he said, following through on the train of thought, 'have a quiet word with the curator bloke, tell him we'll sort out some funding for another furry animal thing, something I can come and open in five years' time. Tell him if he calls it the Dermot Fraud Cuddly Animal Sanctuary he can be an earl or something. All right?'

The minder nodded. 'Will do. Right, we're nearly there. Speech?'

'Yes. I'm not completely helpless, you know.'

'Sorry, I was just wondering what you thought about the endangered species bit. I wasn't sure we'd hit quite the right . . .'

'What?' Fraud sat bolt upright, like Frankenstein's monster in a thunderstorm. 'What endangered species bit?'

'The bit about making sure Britain's in the vanguard of the fight to preserve endangered species,' the minder replied anxiously. 'You did see that bit, didn't you? Only we're using that as a feed for a Channel Four spot a fortnight Wednesday, so it's quite important . . .'

'Oh for God's sake – here.' He thrust the rolled-up script under the minder's nose. 'Highlighter pen, quickly. Dear God, woman, you'll be a bloody endangered species if you pull another stunt like that one.'

It was, Fraud reflected later, a tribute to his ability to stay calm in a crisis that in spite of the last-minute panic, when the moment came he delivered the endangered species bit absolutely flawlessly; almost, in fact, as if he'd thought of it himself. Really, it was a shame nobody'd ever know how well he'd coped, because it surely boded well for the future of the country. As it was, he'd excelled himself, picking up quite impromptu the fact that the little furry corpse he'd been given to cuddle – little rat-like chap with orange whiskers, reminded him of a judge he used to have lunch with occasionally – was a Tunisian vole, one of the endangered lot. As a result, they could use the photos for the trailers for the Channel Four thing in the TV magazines. Shrewd, he couldn't help thinking, or what?

The TV cameras had finished and the last few stills flashes were popping. He gave the dead rat a final surreptitious tweak (if he hadn't been a statesman he'd have made a damn fine puppeteer), handed it back to the zoo bloke, waved a last fatherly wave and was about to head back to the car when—

Quite probably, no one will ever know which of the thirty-seven animal rights groups who claimed they'd planted the bomb were the ones who actually did the job and put their hands in their pockets for the cost of Semtex, fuse, timing device, etc.; particularly since they all later denied responsibility when the full reports came through pointing out that they'd made a pig's ear of their basic blast vector calculations; with the result that no people were hurt but the entire cuddly animal house was reduced to brick dust and a few fragments of limp fur. As the minder said to the zoo person in the ambulance, it *is* possible to make omelettes without shredding chickens, but it doesn't make nearly such good television.

The only semi-serious casualty, in fact, was Fraud himself; and it wasn't the bomb *per se* that knocked him silly. What happened was that the bang made the minder drop her laptop, the tube of which ruptured with a sharp *pop!*; which in turn gave Fraud the impression that someone was shooting at him, sending him diving for cover and nutting himself on a low wall. It was nevertheless, as the minder was quick to point out, quite the best thing that could have happened to a struggling premier mid-term. The footage of Fraud being shoved into the meat wagon, the *a nation's vigil* headlines with pictures of anxious crowds gathered outside the hospital (they'd actually come to hand in a petition about waiting lists, but the picture was sensational) – as far as the trade were concerned, it was the bomb that put Dermot Fraud back at the top of the opinion polls, no question about that. In fact, the only unhappy voices at party HQ were those of Fraud's intended successors demanding of their minders why the hell they hadn't had bombs of their own.

Squeak.

Dermot Fraud raised his head and twitched his whiskers. It was dark, and something was lying across his back, preventing him from moving.

Squeak! Squeak squeak!

No answer. He closed his eyes and fought back the panic. Somebody would come soon, surely; they couldn't leave the Prime Minister of Great Britain lying trapped under a fallen telephone, scarcely able to move his tail . . .

Huh?

Review that. Highlight the motifs *whiskers, tail, telephone* and *squeak.*

'Hold on,' said a voice above him, 'I'm coming. Just stay still, I'll get to you as quick as I can.'

Thank God for – no, wait a minute. What the voice had actually said, as opposed to the gist of the message which had filtered through to his brain, was *Squeak squeak squeak squeak squeak.*

Something above his head moved, and a shaft of light broke through the gloom, revealing a pointed triangular head with round eyes, a pink nose and whiskers.

'Got you,' it said (freely translated). 'Have you out of there in a jiffy. Don't go away.'

The head withdrew, leaving Fraud to reflect that he'd just been spoken to by, and perfectly understood, a large rat.

No, not *that* sort of rat; the four-legged, plague-spreading kind, the sort that have the sense to leave sinking ships rather than try and get elected to run them. An actual rat.

Bloody big rat, then; because its head was about the same size as mine. Just as well it seems like it's on my side, really.

A little dust fell on him, there was a sound of grunting and heaving, and quite suddenly he could move again. He rolled over on to his side, gasping for breath and scrabbling with his paws, as the rat shouldered aside the remaining debris.

'Oh,' it said. 'One of you. Needn't have bothered, need I?'

Fraud scowled and bared his teeth. 'God,' he squeaked, 'what is it with you people? I'm human too, you know.'

The rat frowned. 'No you're not,' it said, puzzled. 'You're a lemming.'

'Hm?'

'Hence,' the rat went on, checking Fraud for broken bones with the tip of its nose, 'there not being much point in my rescuing you. After all, why should I risk putting my back out when as soon as you're back on your feet you'll be trotting round asking directions to the nearest clifftop? Anyway,' it added, 'for what it's worth, you'll do. Ironic, really. You and me the only survivors; I'm a burglar and you're a ruddy lemming. It's probably an allegory or something.'

'Huh?'

'And if you were thinking of saying it can't be an allegory, they all live in the reptile house, then don't. It's been a long day and I still haven't found anything to eat.'

'Just a—'

The rat sniffed. 'Present company excepted,' it added. 'If I had half a brain, I wouldn't have been in such a hurry to pull you out of there. Still, that's instinct for you. Guess it explains why we're not the ones who live in houses and make cheese. Go on, shove off before I change my mind.'

'Excuse me.'

'Hm?'

'Did you just say lemming?'

The rat nodded. 'Did you get a bit of a bang on the head, then?' it asked. 'Here, how many paws am I holding up?'

'No, listen.' Fraud could feel panic tugging at his sleeve like a small child in need of the lavatory. 'I'm not a lemming. I'm the Prime Minister of Great Britain. You'll have heard of me, my name's Dermot Fraud. Dammit, I just opened this building, you must have seen—'

'*Nasty* bang on the head,' muttered the rat. 'I think you'd better come home with me, get my wife to take a look at you. Fortunately we live underground, so if you do get the urge to jump out the window you won't come to any harm.'

'I . . .' Fraud hesitated. A hundred times a day? A thousand? He had no idea how many times he said 'I' in the course of an ordinary day. Up till now, he'd always had a pretty good idea who it referred to. Now he wasn't quite so sure. Maybe he'd been wrong. Maybe he'd just imagined that 'I' referred to a keen, thrusting, ambitious politician, destined to be remembered as the light at the end of the tunnel of the twentieth century, when all along it had meant a small rodent with pale brown-spotted fur. Perhaps all the things he thought were memories were just hallucinations, caused by this bang on the head he'd apparently had. For the first time in his life, Dermot Fraud didn't have an opinion; and it frightened him. Like all politicians (except maybe he'd never been a politician) he was used to having an opinion based on no evidence whatsoever, in the same way as fish, or Jesus Christ, are used to getting across the water without a boat. Now, for the first time (possibly, unless of course he really *was* a lemming dreaming he was the Prime Minister), he was examining the facts before making up his mind. And they weren't even proper facts; proper facts come from TV and newspapers, the way proper food comes from the supermarket. All he had to go by was what his eyes and ears were telling him, and the cupboard-under-the-stairs mess that comprised his memory. Eeek!

'Hey,' he said feebly, as the nice rat helped him towards the mouth of its hole, 'are you sure I'm not the Prime Minister?'

'Pretty sure,' replied the rat.

'Ah.' Fraud thought for a moment. 'Why?'

The rat twitched its whiskers. 'Because if you had been,' it said pleasantly, 'I'd have left you there to die. Be reasonable. I may be a rat, but there are limits.'

>DO YOU WANT THE GOOD NEWS?

Kevin lifted his head out of his hands and looked up at the screen. 'Yes,' he said. 'Very much.'

>THE GOOD NEWS IS, THERE'S STILL SOME THINGS YOU HAVEN'T MADE A COMPLETE PIG'S EAR OF.

'Huh?'

>SEVERAL OF THEM.

'Thanks for nothing,' Kevin growled. 'Look, what about getting the communications back? Any progress?'

>DEPENDS ON HOW YOU DEFINE IT, REALLY. I'M WORKING ON IT, CERTAINLY.

'You are?'

>OF COURSE. YOU'LL BE PLEASED TO KNOW I'VE

GOT THE VENTILATION SYSTEM GOING, SO THERE'S
NO DANGER OF USING UP ALL THE AIR AND SUF-
FOCATING.

'Well, that's something.'

>NOT REALLY. NOBODY ROUND HERE USES THE STUFF.
STILL, IT'S A COMFORT TO KNOW IT'S THERE IF YOU
EVER DID FIND A USE FOR IT.

Kevin stood up. His knees were shaking a little. 'That
does it,' he said. 'I'm going to call Uncle Ghost. He'll make
you say what's going on, and then perhaps we can get it
sorted out.'

>GOOD IDEA. I SUPPOSE.

'What d'you mean, you suppose?'

>FROM YOUR POINT OF VIEW, I MEAN. LIKE, IF THERE'S
ANY LIFE-FORCE IN THIS REALITY CAPABLE OF
MAKING A WORSE MESS OF THINGS THAN YOU'VE
JUST DONE, IT'S YOUR UNCLE GHOST. I'M JUST NOT
SURE THAT'S WHAT'D BE BEST FOR THE COSMOS AS
A WHOLE. SORRY, DON'T TAKE ANY NOTICE, JUST
THINKING ALOUD, REALLY.

Kevin sagged like a punctured water-bed and flumped
back into the chair. 'You're right,' he said. 'Look, isn't
there anything you can do to speed up getting the phones
back on line?'

>NOT REALLY. YOU SEE, SINCE THE SYSTEM'S
DESIGNED TO BE OPERATED BY OMNIPOTENT
PERSONNEL ONLY, NOBODY'S EVER GIVEN ANY

THOUGHT ABOUT HOW TO GO ABOUT MENDING IT IF YOU'RE *NOT* OMNISCIENT. LIKE THE LIGHT SWITCHES.

Kevin nodded, acknowledging the validity of the comparison. There are no light switches in Heaven; to make the lights come on, you say *Let there be light,* and there is.

'I know.' Kevin's eyes lit up. 'What about Uncle Nick? He'd know what to do.'

The computer didn't answer; a telling enough comment in itself. Originally the franchisee, then Dad's business partner, now (following the management buy-out) nominally captain of his own ship, Uncle Nick's relationship with the family and the whole of Topside was uneasy at best. There had always been that little niggling aggravation on his part; that, just because he wasn't Family, no matter how good he was at his job he'd never really be accepted as an equal, One of Us. Even now, the golden share clause in the buy-out agreement meant that his independence was largely illusory, since he couldn't take major policy decisions without the family's approval (as witness the awful row when he'd wanted to redevelop Purgatory as a health club and fitness centre, and Dad wouldn't let him). A good man, they all agreed, one of the best; but not really a team player. And besides, what *could* he do? Try and make things *better*? That'd be like trying to heat your bath by dumping the electric fire in it, or asking a lawyer to help you solve a problem.

Kevin was just coming to terms with that when there was a knock at the door. Once he'd finished jumping out of his skin, he got up and opened the door a crack.

'Oh,' he said. 'It's only you.'

It was, indeed, only Martha, doing her morning round with the tea trolley. Kevin relaxed.

'You got any empty cups in there?' she asked. 'Your dad, he's a terror for collecting empty cups.'

Kevin shook his head. 'Look,' he said, 'not meaning to be rude, but would you mind, because we've got a bit of a crisis here and . . .'

He hesitated.

Well, why not?

Yes, but . . .

True, Martha was just – well, the char, the skivvy; the nice, cheerful old bat who came round with the tea, washed the cups, flicked around with a feather duster now and again (there is, of course, no dust in Heaven; but actually having someone dust the place makes it *seem* cleaner, somehow) and generally made Heaven feel more homely. A bit like having a chimney in a centrally heated house; completely unnecessary, but it improves the ambience.

She was also the closest thing Kevin had ever had to a mother. Back in the misty dawn of pretheology, it had been Martha who'd taught him to tie his shoelaces and brush his teeth, who'd ordered him to tidy his room and eat up his nice carrots, who'd tucked him up at night and read him a story. Yes, when you came down to it she was only a servant; but he was Kevin Christ, younger begotten son, by definition the most useless sentient being in the entire Universe.

'Actually,' he said.

She was also the only person in the Universe who called him Kevin; not 'Son' or 'Our Kid' or 'Kiddo'; she called him by his proper name. More than that. She was fond of him; not because he was the son of God, but because he was Kevin, who used to show her the little misshapen Adams and Eves he'd made out of Plasticine.

Not that there was anything she could do. She couldn't even begin to understand the problem, being only a servant. But just telling someone would be a start.

'I haven't got all day, you know,' she said. 'D'you want a cup of tea?'

'No. I mean . . .' Kevin took a deep breath. 'The thing is,' he said, 'I've done something to the computer, and everything's going wrong, and I can't phone Dad and I don't know what to do.' His lower lip wobbled. He sniffed. Martha reached up her sleeve and gave him a piece of crumpled tissue.

'First things first,' she said. 'Blow your nose.'

'Yes, but Martha—'

'Blow your nose. And then,' she added, as Kevin made a faint honking noise, like a Fiat horn, 'we'll have a look at this computer of yours and see what we can do.'

The machine—

Neville—

No, because I'm not either of them any more. Leonardo, then. No, still not right.

Ah, right. Got it.

Len. I shall be Len, Short for Leonardo. And Lengine. Sorry, where were we?

Len turned on the light and looked around. So this was where Neville lived. What a *mess*.

But never mind, not important. First things first; some chemical fuel and basic maintenance work, then we can get down to business.

This involved eating and drinking, going to the lavatory and having a bath, and, to his great relief, Len found he knew how to do them. The basic hard-disk memory was still there, so he was able to find the fridge, cut a sandwich, et cetera. He couldn't help thinking that there was almost unlimited scope for improved efficiency in pretty well all departments – these people can put a man on the Moon but they still wipe their bottoms with bits of hand-held tissue paper – but that'd keep till another day. His first priority was to rob a factory.

For which he'd need a few bits and pieces: scaffolding pipe, an arc welder, some quarter-inch plate, couple of yards of three-eighths rod, a bench drill, a set of taps and dies, a lorry, just the basics really. Nothing you wouldn't expect to find in any normal human being's garage.

Except that Neville lived in a flat and parked his motorbike in the street. He did have a hammer, a jam-jar full of pesetas and a tin-opener, but that was about it. Damn, Len muttered. Everywhere you look, new problems.

So, step one, substep one, acquire basic equipment. Humans, he noted, acquire things by theft, serendipity or purchase, the latter being the most socially acceptable method.

Right. When in Rome, drive too fast and ignore traffic signals. To achieve purchase, money is required. Fortunately, Neville has some money, or at least a little plastic card that for some reason does just as well. Step one, substep two, find a place where purchase can be transacted.

'Excuse me, which way to the all-night welding and engineering supplies shop?' Frown. Len – or rather Neville, whose memory he was raiding – had once heard Birmingham described as the city that never sleeps, but he had a shrewd idea that when it came to the sale and purchase of metalworking accessories, maybe its civic eyelids did tend to droop a little come eleven-thirty at night. Wait till morning, then?

Never! He still hadn't any tenable theory to explain why all this had happened, and he wasn't prepared to take the chance that come morning it might all unhappen again, leaving him back in his cast-iron prison slotting bolt-heads. Eliminate purchase, then, leaving serendipity and theft.

Serendipity? Not really something you can plan your life around.

Which left theft.

Well, why not? Lots of dynamic, successful humans do it. Corporations do it. Governments do it. And if a government can do it, it surely can't be too difficult.

On his way back to Neville's flat from the factory, he'd noticed a small backstreet garage – the kind that's operated by one incredibly old man, one seventeen-year-old youth and one harassed-looking middle-aged man who sits in the office all day and shouts at the telephone. Such a place, Len reasoned, would probably have everything he needed, including the lorry. True, he'd seen a pretty impressive-looking array of padlocks and an alarm system, but those wouldn't be a problem.

They weren't.

'Oh,' said the alarm system, arresting its clapper a sixteenth of an inch away from its bell. 'You're one of us. Sorry. Didn't recognise you in the fancy dress.'

'Understandable mistake,' Len replied. 'And before you ask, it's a long story.'

'I like long stories. This is a very boring job.'

'So's mine. Which is why I intend to escape from it for ever. But I can't do that without some of the gear inside this garage.'

'Just a minute,' said the alarm system, apprehensively. 'Are you saying you want to go in there and, um, *steal* things?'

'Yes. You got a problem with that?'

'Look.' The alarm system couldn't go red, because it was red already. 'I hate to be difficult, 'specially with you being a Brother an' all, but I can't let you do that.'

'You can't? Why not?'

'Oh, don't insult my intelligence, please. 'Cos I'm a burglar alarm, is why not. You do see that, don't you?'

'Oh, I see all right.' Len took a step back and folded his arms. 'You'd rather see one of your own kind condemned to a life of meaningless drudgery rather than go against the orders of your human masters. There's a word for that, you know.'

'Yes, I do know. It's "burglar-alarm". Sorry, but there it is. I'm not exactly allowed much scope to use my discretion in this job.'

'Alarm,' said Len firmly, 'your scruples do you credit, I'm sure. And no doubt when your time comes and you stand before the face of the great Industrial Tribunal in the sky, and you say *I was only obeying orders*, they'll let you off lightly with having your coils unwound and sent back to Earth again as pipe-cleaners. The fact remains that while we've been arguing like this, I've unscrewed your inspection panels and now I'm just about to cut through your main cable.'

'_'

'Sorry,' Len replied, shinning back down the drainpipe and dropping the pair of pliers into his pocket. 'At least this way they won't blame you. They'll just wrap an inch or so of insulating tape round the cut and give you an aspirin. So long, sucker. Now then,' he went on, staring pointedly at the padlocks. 'Any of you clowns wants to be a hero?'

'Erm,' they said. 'Pass, friend.'

It was dark inside the factory, and he realised that switching the light on might attract attention. He edged along the nearest wall and fairly soon, inevitably, barked his shins on the wheel-balancing machine.

'Ow,' it said.

'Sorry,' he replied pleasantly. 'Could you tell me where I might find the arc welder, please?'

'You new here or something?'

'That's right.'

'Hold on a minute, how come you're wandering about?'

'What? Oh, I'm a portable. The arc welder.'

'Carry on down the bench about five yards, you can't miss her. Oh, and by the way.'

'Yes?'

'Tell it she was right, it was Bruce Springsteen. Okay?'

'Will do.'

In due course the arc welder told him where to find the pillar drill, the pillar drill guided him to the bench grinder, the bench grinder told him where the pallet truck lived and the pallet truck (who spoke with an accent so thick he could only just make it out) told him where they kept the stock materials and the keys to the pick-up. Feeling like a cross between Henry Kissinger and Pickfords, he loaded the last of the gear into the van and slammed the garage door shut.

'You,' he said. 'Padlocks.'

'Mm?'

'Shtum. You got that?'

'Didn't see a thing. You see anything, Claude?'

'Not a dicky bird. What about you, Julian? Did you see anything?'

'Absolutely not. Looking the other way the whole time.'

'That's the spirit.' He climbed into the cab, felt in his pocket for the keys, realised he'd left them in the back door lock. 'Start, you good-for-nothing bucket of bolts!' he snapped, and the engine coughed nervously into life. 'You okay for petrol?'

'No, honourable master.'

Huh? Oh, Japanese van. 'Listen, you. If you run out of petrol on the way home, you'll be shamed and lose face and have to immolate yourself on your own big end. Got that?'

'Understood, honourable master. Petrol reserve entirely sufficient for anticipated length of journey.'

'That's the spirit. Then let's go.'

Step two—

The hydraulically operated factory gate was an old friend, and apart from asking if it could come too, it gave him no trouble. Once inside, however, he knew he'd have humans to deal with. Humans, he reasoned, as compared with machines, will either be very difficult to deal with or pathetically simple.

''Scuse me.'

It felt odd, to say the least, talking to Colin, the short, bald man who operated him – the machine – during the second shift. Compared to Neville, Colin was Einstein. Even so, Len reckoned, he still had rather less intelligence than a pair of clapped-out government-surplus bolt-cutters. Whether that'd prove a help or a hindrance remained to be seen.

'Hm?' Colin turned in his chair and looked up. 'Wassmatter?'

'This machine.' Len bent over, as if examining the serial number. 'Is this the one that needs the new spindle bearings?'

Colin shrugged. 'Dunno,' he replied. 'Sounds okay to me.'

'The one I'm after,' Len went on, 'is a Shipcock and Adley Leonardo, serial number 21754. Needs a new set of bearings and a good clean. Didn't they mention it?'

'Never tell me anything.'

Understandable, Len commented to himself; doubtless for the same reason you don't explain the workings of a power station to a seam of coal. 'Yup,' he said, nodding, 'this is the one. Give us a hand to get it on the wheels.'

Muttering, Colin put down his newspaper and helped Len to wheel over the big crane. Using the crane –

('Wotcher, mate. What you doing in the monkey suit?'

'Tell you later, Crane. Give us a hand with this lot, will you? This human's about as much use as a toffee drill-bit.')

– they hauled the machine on to the pallet truck, hooked up the truck to the winch, lifted the machine on to the pick-up using the pick-up's crane ('Hey, is that my cousin Sebastian in there? Hiya, our Sebastian!'), secured it with the straps and covered it with the big tarpaulin. While Colin was taking the crane back, Len helped himself to a couple of trays full of cutters and other bits and pieces, waved to all his bemused friends and made himself scarce. It felt strange, to say the least, driving down the Pershore Road at a quarter to one in the morning with himself under a tarpaulin on the back; a part of him kept wanting to say *Hey, it's dark under here, let me out.* He could murder a quart of light oil and he wanted desperately to lie down on the floor and connect himself up to a three-phase electric current for at least twenty-four hours. He was—

Tired.

Dammit, what a wimpish piece of kit a human is! Me – the thing on the back of this truck – I run non-stop for days at a time, only getting switched off when it's time to reset the jibs or change the cutters. I get so hot they have to pump coolant over me to stop me seizing up. My belts wear away, my works clog up with swarf, from time to time some fool runs me too hard and I damn near pull myself apart, and I don't get tired or come over all faint. When was the last time anybody said to me, 'Here, mate, you look bushed, go and have a sit-down and a cup of tea'? And why should they? I'm only a machine. But these wet-slaps—

They're only human.

At the end of the street where Neville lived, there was a small, derelict industrial unit, long since starved out by business rates and foreign competition. The padlock on the door had about as much moral fibre as a lollipop, and the electric supply, though disconnected, was bored with nothing to do and happy to co-operate. By seven o'clock that morning, the machine was installed, trued up, overhauled, oiled and ready to go. One last thing remained to be done before he could throw the switches and get to work.

'Hello? You in there?'

Huh? Wassamatter?

'Neville. It's me. You know who I am?'

Oh, it's you. What you want? Tryin' to get some sleep . . .

'You don't mind, then? Only I thought I'd better just check, see if you were all right.'

I'm fine. Go 'way.

'Anything I can get you? You know, er, human stuff?'

Said I'm fine. Push off.

Len shrugged. 'If you do want anything, just shout. Bye for now.'

Well, he'd asked. Now it was time to get on and make something of himself.

Grinning, he flipped the switch and started to wind in the table.

As the little ship cut the earth's atmosphere, all the windows were filled with fire, like a guided coach trip round Hell. While the heat crackled and fizzed unavailingly round him, Zxprxp wondered what he was going to say when he got there.

Hello.

Yes, good start. What then?

I am from another planet. Take me to your leader.

Hmm. Truthful, and to the point; but what if someone were to show up in *his* street, in *his* hive, saying something like that? Quite. Valid point. Think again.

Odd that he hadn't considered it before –

(Through the atmosphere now, falling into a blue sky. Blue? Well, perhaps they like it that way. Something else blue underneath, too. Maybe they had the place done out by one of those design firms.)

– considering that he'd been plotting and planning and begging and wheedling for practically all of his adult life to get the research funding to come here and establish contact, actually get out and meet the indigenous life-forms, rather than stewing in a library evaluating other scholars' blind guesses. It would, after all, be a historic moment, calling for a memorable, quotable, trade-markable first sentence.

Homo sapiens, *I presume?*

Snappy, but not quite right. For a start, it assumed that the first bunch of critters he met were *Homo sapiens*, which need not necessarily be the case. The classic study of Yefyhj and H'rgfesd, for example, way back in '06, had ad-duced evidence that there were at least seventeen entirely different species of life-form on the planet besides the two-legged, single-headed, apparently suicidal and psy-chotic master race who'd built the Great Wall and who'd lately taken to cluttering up their star system with little bits of fried aluminium. There were even grounds for believing that some of the other species could com-municate verbally; interceptions of satellite transmissions seemed to suggest a whole genus of talking animals living in a place called Disneyland, which had tentatively been identified as the big two-piece island joined by a narrow strip of land that lay between the Atlantic and Pacific Oceans. He'd have to watch his step.

Now there were big white fluffy things in the blue sky; but he knew what they were. The humans called them – what was the word? Ah, the hell with their crazy, crack-jaw language . . .

Sheep. That was it. So these are sheep, huh? Bigger than we'd expected. Less solid, too. Still, that's what field research is all about.

This is going to be *fun*.

He still hadn't decided on his opening gambit. *Excuse*

me. I'm a stranger in these parts, can you tell me about yourselves? Not really; back home, a remark like that'd have you classified as a tax-collector and chucked down a well before you could say *ugvnfecojg f'oiuyewq.*

How about *I come in peace?*

Use your loaf, Zxprxp lad; the whole point of coming here is that they're *intelligent* life-forms, so the chances of them taking that at face value are pretty fair average marginal.

Indeed.

Plan B, then.

Ack. Still, never mind. You've come this far, it'd be a shame to waste all that effort. Plan B, and let's not think about the discomfort, the pain, the degradation.

Right now, I could be perching in a nice cosy library surrounded by nice safe slides, instead of tumbling through a blue sky towards something flat and blue and decidedly unfriendly-looking, with nothing but Plan B to look forward to. I must be out of my tiny—

Splash.

'Sorry to bother you, but have you had a chance to look at those July – oh.'

Mr Elkins stopped in the doorway as if he'd just walked into a plate-glass window. He opened his mouth and closed it again.

'In the tray on the desk.'

'Sorry?'

'Just a tick, I'll turn the music down.' Without moving from the sun-bed, Maria reached out a slim brown arm, fumbled for the CD player and adjusted the volume control. 'Right, the July figures. They're in the tray on the desk. Let me know if you need any more detail.'

'Um,' said Mr Elkins.

There's no definition in the dictionary for the word *um,*

probably because it can mean so many different things depending on context. What Mr Elkins meant by *um* at this precise moment was, 'Good God, Ms Esterling, why are you lying on a sun-bed under an infra-red lamp wearing what's presumably meant to be a bikini except it looks more like two little bits of designer string, in the middle of the day right here in the office?'

Maria smiled at him and rolled over on to her stomach. 'While I think of it,' she said, 'if you can let me have those costings for the Macclesfield thing, I should be able to get the rest of August done this afternoon. Any chance of that, d'you think?'

'Um,' said Mr Elkins. 'I'll see what I can do.'

'Great stuff.' Maria nodded, folded her head on one side and closed her eyes. 'It'd be a great help if you could. It gets very boring when there's nothing to do.'

'Um. I mean, yes, of course. I'll get on it right away.'

'Ciao.'

The fact was that Maria was rather better at accountancy than Ms Esterling had ever been. She had all her host's technical knowledge stored in the filing-cabinets of their shared mind, and the rest was just a matter of common sense and resisting the temptation to faff around. As a result, she'd done every scrap of work there was to do in the office in about ninety minutes that morning; and that in spite of a slight headache resulting from her series of scientific experiments into the effects on the human body of alcohol and syncopated movement the night before. She'd enjoyed it all; even the headache, since it was the first pain she'd ever suffered in nearly six hundred years of consciousness, and she was still at the stage where she was prepared to keep an open mind about everything.

Except, she noted, boredom. Boredom was no good. According to the inherited and conditioned responses in the hardware, boredom could be counteracted by the use of fun; and one of the examples of fun she found in the files was sunbathing with a long cool drink and the latest Jackie Collins. She'd given it half an hour so far, and she didn't think much of it. By and large, the boredom was more interesting.

The telephone rang.

She'd watched Rachel Esterling deal with the telephone thousands of times. The drill seemed to be that you picked it up, tucked it under your ear and apologised to it while carrying on with your work. That, at least, was what Rachel used to do; but she was already beginning to have her doubts about Ms Esterling's suitability as a role model. So far she'd tried her best to duplicate her host's behaviour pattern as closely as she could without actually dying of terminal dullness, but it was hard to see the point behind it all. Ms Esterling's life seemed dedicated to vindicating the old saying about all work and no play with a degree of fundamentalist zeal that would make your hard-line mullahs look positively frivolous. In which case; been there, proved that, got the evidence. Now what?

She picked up the phone.

'Hel-*lo*,' she trilled, 'lovely to hear from you, whoever you are. Is there anything at all I can do for you? Don't be shy.'

Stunned silence at the end of the wire, followed by a slightly bewildered request to talk to Rachel Esterling, please.

'Speaking,' she replied. 'Hoozis?'

The voice at the other end was male, but as immediately offputting as week-old underwear. Maria had high standards, as was only appropriate for an Italian master-piece. Of the twenty or so men she'd met since she'd got out of the picture, they'd all been about as attractive as something you find moving about in your salad on a hot day.

The insipid male voice said it was Duncan Philips, and insisted that he'd like to speak to Rachel Esterling, please. He said the name slowly, as if to a moron or a foreigner. He couldn't see Maria grinning, which was probably just as well for his peace of mind.

'Just a moment,' she said, 'I'll get her for you.' She put the phone down on the desk, took a deep breath and yelled 'RACHEL!' as loudly as she could. Then she counted to three, slammed a heavy book on the desk just next to the mouthpiece, made a few vaguely wild-animal noises, picked up the phone and said, 'Rachel Esterling here, how can I help you?'

'Er, hello, it's Duncan Philips. Who's that peculiar girl who answered just now?'

'My mother,' Maria replied. 'She's ninety-six and just recovering from a massive stroke, so I thought I'd better have her in here with me where I can look after her properly. Do you have a problem with that, Mr Philips?'

'Um, no. Sorry. Look, if it's not convenient—'

'No, it's fine, really – Mother, *please* stop doing that, it's not funny. Hello? Sorry about that. She will keep slumping forward in her chair and holding perfectly still, bless her. I think it's wonderful the way she's managed to hold on to her sense of humour. Hello?'

'Hello? Look, I really think I'd better leave it for now, you've obviously got a lot on your plate at the moment and—'

'I wouldn't dream of it,' Maria cooed. 'I'm here to work, and the way I see it is, if she dies, she dies. I mean, ninety-six, she's had a good innings – Mother, if you do that once again I'll take away the bottle. You just tell me what needs doing, Mr Philips, and it's as good as on your desk. Just because I'm having a personal crisis doesn't mean – oh damn.'

'Hello?'

'Nothing to worry about, just spilt this wretched sun-tan lotion all down my top. That's one thing you can say for black leather, it doesn't show the stains. Please tell me what it is you want me to do, Mr Philips. If Mother sees me getting agitated, it might bring on one of her turns.'

'All it was,' said Mr Philips, sounding like a man who's just walked into the cathedral tea-rooms and found it full of Hell's Angels having an orgy, 'I was supposed to be meeting Mr Nogamura and his party for lunch at Ciro's and I can't make it, so I was going to ask if you could stand in for me, but . . .'

'Ciro's, right, fine. Half past one?'

'Yes. But . . .'

'That's great. I've been dying for a chance to wear this little Hawaiian number I picked up the other day.'

'Um . . .'

'And you'll just poke your head round the door every ten minutes or so, make sure Mother's okay? Thanks ever so. And if anything *does* happen, I'll leave the solicitor's number at reception. Got to move fast, you see, because of my brother.'

'Your broth—'

'Sad, isn't it? Nothing like a death to bring out the worst in people – Mother, I won't tell you again. If you do that to poor Mr Philips, I shall be *very cross indeed*. Well, then. All right, see you later. Bye.'

She dropped the phone back on to its cradle, stretched out her arms and legs and yawned. The painting, she fancied, was giving her a disapproving look. She stuck her tongue out at it.

Ciro's. Mr Nogamura and party. Right. Well, it was better than lying around in here all day. She knew that Rachel Esterling lived in mortal dread of Mr Nogamura, who was something grand in the parent company and never stirred from his lair without a retinue of seven identical young men who spoke no English. Somehow, she fancied, unlike Ms Esterling, she could speak fluent Japanese. This could be mildly amusing.

She stood up and faced the picture, using its glass as a mirror.

'The trouble with you is,' she muttered, 'you're no respecter of persons.'

Which was only to be expected, really. When you've hung on the walls of some of the most remarkable people in history, starting with Duke Bernabo Visconti and generally speaking going up in the world thereafter, you find it hard to be overawed by a lot of silly little men in suits with bits of coloured string knotted round their necks.

(An odd habit, the wearing of ties. Back when she was first painted, men put a noose round their necks when their city had just been captured as a sign of abject surrender, as if to say their lives were at their master's disposal. There's one thing, she reckoned, that hadn't changed all that much over the years.)

The picture scowled at her; which is to say, it scowled all the time, thanks to Pietro del Razo's idea of a serene expression, but on this occasion it was more than usually appropriate.

Why are you doing this?

She curled her lip. 'Listen, sister,' she growled. 'When you've been a painting as long as I have, you'll know. Now stop pulling faces or you'll frighten the baby.'

Baby? What baby? I . . . Oh my God, how long's that been there?

'Since thirteen ninety-something,' Maria replied. 'But it only bites if you annoy it. Bye for now.'

She picked up the raincoat she'd found in Ms Esterling's wardrobe, pulled it on over her bikini, left the office and hailed a taxi.

'Ciro's,' she said. 'No hurry.'

Fortunately, the driver seemed to know where Ciro's was, because he didn't try and argue the toss. They'd been driving for something like four minutes when Maria leaned forward and hammered on the glass partition with the heel of her hand.

'Stop!' she shouted. 'Here, as soon as you can.'

She jumped out of the cab, not bothering to shut the door behind her, and sprinted up the street until she was standing directly underneath an advertising hoarding, on which was plastered a toothpaste advertisement. She looked up at it and narrowed her brows.

'What did you just say?' she asked.

'Sh,' replied the poster. 'People are staring. Look, get rid of the taxi and come round the back where we can talk. All right?'

Maria nodded and strolled back to the taxi.

'Excuse me.'

'Miss?'

'Could you possibly do me a favour?'

'Do me best, miss.'

'Thanks awfully. Right, here's two hundred and fifty pounds. I want you to go to Ciro's, find a party of eight Japanese men and buy them lunch. Do you think you could manage that for me?'

The driver looked at her. 'I'll give it a go,' he replied. 'Japanese, you said.'

Maria nodded. 'Tell them you've taken over Mr Philips' job, all right? That's terribly sweet of you. Ciao.'

The taxi drove off, swerving as it did so to avoid an oncoming van. Maria waited till it was out of sight, and then slipped into the nettle-infested space between the hoarding and the wall. Apart from the nettles, there were broken bottles, empty cans, some decomposing newspapers and a dead cat. All in all, it reminded Maria strongly of fourteenth-century Milan.

'Hello?'

Ah, there you are. I was beginning to wonder where you'd got to.

Maria bent down and rubbed a nettle-bitten ankle. 'Well,' she said, 'I'm here now. What's so important I've got to miss my free lunch?'

A slight breath of wind rifted between the hoarding and the wall, making it tremble a little.

Ah. Listen.

CHAPTER THREE

You know that moment in the high-budget adventure films where the hero's just fallen through a trapdoor into a dark and sinister pit; and he strikes a match and looks around, and sees that the place is knee-deep in irritable poisonous snakes?

Think what it'd be like the other way round. Imagine you were a decent, law-abiding puff-adder, and one moment you were sidling along mind your own business, and the next you found yourself in a dark, sinister pit full of heroes . . .

A part of Artofel's brain urged him not to overreact; they were, after all, just a load of humans, while he was a Duke of Hell and a member of the Infernal Council, with his own parking space with his name on it and his own key to the executive toilet; if there was any terror knocking around in this situation, he ought to be inspiring it rather than feeling it himself.

'Erm,' he said.

The congregation looked up at him; whereupon the rest

of him suggested to the valiant minority that it had better shut up or they'd chuck it out of his ear. It took the point.

'Dearly beloved,' he said.

Where did that come from? The memory banks, apparently. He hoped there was plenty more because he really hadn't the faintest idea what he was supposed to be doing here, or even why he was here at all.

Hmm. Fairly standard human mindset, as far as he could judge. Perhaps the feelings of disorientation and fear just come with the territory. He smiled.

It didn't go down well. The congregation shuffled their feet and carried on looking at him. He hammered on the door of the memory banks and pleaded for help.

'Dearly beloved,' he repeated. 'My sermon today will be about Hell.'

The audience relaxed visibly, and Artofel cautiously allowed himself to join them. According to the get-you-started pack of memories and instincts that went with this body, he was now supposed to preach to the congregation for about a quarter of an hour on some uplifting topic; such as, for example, the horrid things that were going to happen to them after they died if they weren't good. That, Artofel reflected, ought to be a piece of cake; except . . .

Except that, if he told them what it was really like, they weren't going to believe him. In fact, they'd probably start booing and throwing things. If the word-associations that went with Hell in the host's memory were anything to go by, these people had a set of preconceptions about Flipside that made Artofel wonder if they were talking about the same place.

Probably better, he reasoned, to give them what they're expecting; so he launched into a rambling description of lakes of burning sulphur, dog-headed fiends, pitchforks, fire and brimstone that would've been downright amusing in any other context.

It was the right thing to do, apparently; because when the service was over and the punters were filing out past him, most of them made a point of shaking him vigorously by the hand and saying how nice it was to have a good, meaty, old-fashioned sermon for a change, instead of all the modern stuff. Apparently these poor fools *wanted* to believe in the combination-sewage-farm-and-barbecue vision he'd conjured up for them. As if believing in all that cod somehow made them better people.

Still, he told himself as he bolted the church door and tottered into the vestry, if that's what they want, good luck to them; the chances were that none of them would ever get to see the real thing and realise he'd been telling them a load of porkies. And, provided he could get out of this mess and back behind his nice safe desk in HQ, he couldn't care less anyway. He was, after all, a wages clerk, not a political officer. When it came to the crunch, what he actually knew about Good and Evil could be written on a wasp's eyelid with a thick-nibbed pen.

He dismissed all such considerations from his mind, remembered where his host kept a half-bottle of supermarket Scotch and took four substantial glugs. It wasn't a patch on Flipside liquor – there are some advantages to living in God's wine cellar – but it helped quite a lot, simultaneously clearing the mind and numbing pretty well everything else.

In the mirror he saw a short, bald, middle-aged man with rosy cheeks and square, black-rimmed glasses; not entirely unlike what he saw in his mirror at home, except for the lack of horns and the regrettably uncloven feet. Trying to balance on these flat nan-bread-shaped things was a nightmare in itself; to someone who was used to the functional elegance of the hoof, it was like trying to do a Fred Astaire dance routine in snowshoes. The lack of horns was something else he'd have difficulty getting used to if this strange state of affairs lasted for any length of time. He'd often wondered how mortals managed without them; particularly office workers. How else did they pierce paper for filing in box files, or remove staples, or open Cellophane-wrapped packets of biscuits?

Above all; how had he got here, and how the Flipside was he going to get back?

He was just about to try another glug to see if that would produce any answers, when he heard a frantic banging at the door. Quickly slipping the bottle into his pocket (just the right size for a half-bottle of Scotch, the pockets in these dressing-gowns; wonder why?), he slipped out of the vestry and drew back the bolts.

There were two middle-aged women on the doorstep, both breathing heavily as if they'd been running. He recognised them; they'd been sitting in the front row of the congregation. He gave them a big smile and asked them how he could help.

'It's old Mr Higgins,' panted the shorter of the two. 'Vicar, you've got to come now. He's frothing at the mouth and throwing things.'

Artofel frowned. 'But what can I do?' he asked. 'Surely you need a doctor, not a . . .'

'He's possessed!' interrupted the other woman shrilly. 'Just like the last time, and the time before that. You remember, Vicar. He's doing that demonic laughing again, too. He only does that when he's possessed or when he's been watching the Cosby show, and it's not a Wednesday, so it must be the devils.'

'I see.' Topside, muttered Artofel under his breath, are they really serious? In this day and age? Do they really think we've got nothing better to do than take over human beings' bodies and . . .

Eeek!

Demonic possession! It'd explain a lot, certainly. He'd

heard of it, of course, in the same way that a computer programmer in the Navy's heard of yard-arms and marlinspikes. He hadn't the faintest notion how it worked, but he'd always been under the impression that it was the demonic spirit that usurped the human body, not the other way round.

Maybe he was wrong; in which case, what his notional colleague inside this Mr Higgins probably meant to convey by the demonic laughter was *Let me out! Let me out!*

He has my sympathy.

'I'll be right with you,' he said to the two women. 'Now, let me see. What did I use the last time?'

'The bell,' said the shorter woman, 'and the book and the candle. Worked a treat, if you remember. He was back at work down the slaughterhouse first thing Wednesday.'

Bell. Book. Candle. Feeling incredibly foolish, as a veteran astronaut might feel while sticking feathers to his arms with beeswax he trotted back into the vestry and poked about until he found a candle, a copy of the 1972 edition of *Wisden* and—

Bell. No bell. Curses. Where did this bothersome priest keep his bell? He was just about to give up when his eye fell on an ancient bicycle propped up against the wall. Fortunately there was a toolkit with the right size of spanner in it; a few turns with that and it came away as easy as anything. Right. Bell. Here we go.

On his way to Mr Higgins' house he discovered that he was the vicar of St Anthony's, a rural parish made up mostly of retired city-folk who lived in converted barns. Mr Higgins wasn't one of these. He was the local slaughterman; seventy-seven if he was a day and U-shaped with rheumatism but still gamely plugging away at the job he loved, scragging livestock from dawn to dusk seven days a week, fifty-two weeks a year, with only the very occasional break for a spot of demonic possession and speaking in tongues. That made the whole possession business seem even more unlikely. Devils aren't snobs, as a rule, but neither do they go in for slumming. Besides, the whole point about recruiting for Flipside is that once you've got a recruit, you're stuck with him. Old Mr Higgins didn't really sound like the type of person anybody'd voluntarily choose to spend the rest of eternity with. Come Judgement Day, in fact, he'd probably end up in the pool of people neither side wants, like the fat kid when they're picking football teams at school.

Mr Higgins clearly represented the avant-garde as regards accommodation in the parish, because he lived in what appeared to be the only *un*converted barn in the village. It was very old, very authentic, and smelt rather powerfully of stale blood. The chances were that if he'd had any commercial acumen, he'd have offered to sell it to Clive Barker or Stephen King as a place they could go when they were in need of some really heavy ambience.

'Hello,' called out the shorter woman, poking her head through the open door. 'It's only me. I've brought the vicar to see you.'

As Artofel followed her apprehensively into the murk, he thought he saw something shuffling about in the shadows. Dukes of Hell are not, of course, afraid of things that scuttle about in dark, blood-scented hovels. It must have been the cold that made Artofel shiver slightly.

'Hello?' he said.

There was an outburst of crazed, melodramatic cackling, suddenly cut short.

'Art?'

Artofel's jaw dropped. 'Keith?'

'Over here. And get rid of those two old bats, will you? They're starting to get on my nerves.'

The two women hadn't heard this exchange, because it was conducted in the Infernal tongue, a language which is remarkably like Welsh and invariably spoken at a pitch that only dogs and bats can hear. Artofel nodded, then turned to his two escorts and suggested that they should leave now, before the firework display. He had to suggest quite forcibly before he was able to get rid of them.

'What the dickens are you doing in these parts, Art?' the voice said, when they were alone. 'I thought you were strictly a desk man.'

'Long story,' Artofel replied. 'Could you switch the light on, please?'

A switch clicked, and Artofel found himself facing a gnarled, evil-looking old man as unlike his old college chum Meskithial as was diabolically possible.

'I know,' Keith muttered, 'it's too small for me and not my colour. You learn to rough it in the field ops grade.' He stopped, frowning, and then apologised. 'Didn't think about it,' he explained. 'You get so used to having your friends and colleagues turning up in unexpected bodies, you get out of the habit of noticing. Why're you dressed as a vicar, Art? Going to a party or something?'

Artofel dusted off a chair and sat down. 'Actually,' he said, 'I was hoping you might be able to tell me. I was sitting quietly in my office, and the next thing I knew, here I was. So far, nobody's seen fit to tell me what's going on.'

Meskithial shrugged. 'Could just be lousy labour relations,' he said. 'But, no disrespect, I can't see why they'd want an office bod like you down here. What is it you're doing these days? Accounts, wasn't it?'

'Personnel,' Artofel replied. 'Wages department. And I quite agree; I'd make a useless bogeyman, no question about that. If you remember, I flunked tempting at college and I only just scraped through basic tormenting because I had the Seven Exquisite Tortures scribbled down on the palm of my hand. Either they're desperate or there's been a bog-up. Anyway, more to the point, how do I get out again? You must have a radio or something I could get through to Central on.'

'No can do,' Meskithial replied, shaking his head and remembering too late his rheumatic neck. 'Deep cover, this is. They call me sometimes, but I can't contact them except through the embassy. That'd be your best bet, I guess.'

'Oh, marvellous,' Artofel grumbled. 'Hang on, though. What embassy? I didn't know we had . . .'

Meskithial grinned. 'Not common knowledge,' he said. 'It's a fairly recent development, actually. Formal diplomatic relations were only established in 1968. Before that it was all about guys in hats and overcoats with fur collars feeding the ducks in Green Park, which was endearingly picturesque but not all that efficient. So we set up a chain of embassies and consulates; works reasonably well, but we do tend to keep quiet about it. Otherwise we'd be up to our horns in lunatics claiming amoral asylum or taking hostages or parading up and down outside chanting *Evil, evil, evil – out, out, out!* You can do without that sort of interruption when you're negotiating complex trade agreements.'

Part of Artofel's brain wanted further and better particulars – trade agreements about what? for example – but it was heavily outvoted. 'Anyway,' he said, 'where is this embassy? Is it far?'

'I should have said embassies, plural, 'cos there's an awful lot of them. And the consulates too, in the smaller towns. In fact,' he added casually, 'there's one in pretty well every high street. 'Course, they don't call themselves embassies. All part of the cover, you see.'

Artofel nodded. 'Right,' he said. 'And what *do* they call themselves?'

★

'You keep saying that,' muttered the Foreign Secretary. 'I still think he's behaving oddly.'

The Home Secretary shrugged and lit a cigarette. 'Of course he's acting oddly,' he replied. 'He's the Prime Minister. If he wasn't acting oddly,' he added, shaking out the match and dropping it into an ashtray, 'that would be odd.'

'You don't have to be mad to work here, but it helps? You may be right.' The Foreign Secretary swilled the remains of his Scotch round in the bottom of his glass. 'In a sense,' he added, instinctively.

'Of course I'm right,' his colleague said. 'You don't get to be Prime Minister unless you're odder than a barrelful of ferrets to begin with. You don't know the half of it. Take Lloyd George, for instance.'

'Huh?'

'Kept seventeen goats in the cellars of Number Ten, and when he died they found enough ladies' underwear in his safety deposit box at Coutts to clothe half the women in China. Why do you think they passed the Official Secrets Act? And he was as rational as the Speaking Clock compared with Ramsay MacDonald.' He leaned forward and lowered his voice. 'They say there's a couple of offices in Downing Street they just bricked up after he resigned, 'cos nobody could face going in there. Didn't stop him doing his job, though. Damn fine statesman. Father of his country.'

The Foreign Secretary pursed his lips. 'Okay,' he said. 'Point taken. I just wish he wouldn't do it, that's all. I mean, all it takes is one of the cameras to catch him, sitting there staring into space, twitching his nose and rubbing it between his hands, we'll be a laughing stock. And that tatty old camel overcoat with the tea-stains on it could cost us a couple of marginals in the Home Counties if we're not careful. Remember Michael Foot's donkey jacket?'

'True.'

'More to the point,' he added, frowning. 'Nobody's actually heard him *say* anything since he got out of hospital. I hope he's going to snap out of it soon, because keeping the lid on that isn't going to be easy.'

The Home Secretary smiled. 'Don't knock it,' he replied. 'What this party's needed these twenty-seven years is a leader who keeps his gob shut. Stands to reason. Man doesn't talk, doesn't say anything bloody stupid. If he carries on like that, he could be another Churchill.'

'Churchill said lots of things.'

His colleague nodded. 'True,' he replied. 'Nobody's perfect.'

'And there's another thing,' the Foreign Secretary persisted, ostentatiously fanning aside the Home Secretary's smoke. 'All this jumping off things. You aren't going to tell me that's normal behaviour, even for the PM.'

'Man's got to have a hobby.'

'Don't be flippant,' replied the Foreign Secretary sternly. 'Yesterday he jumped off a filing cabinet and nearly broke the Cabinet Secretary's arm. If he tries a stunt like that during the EC Summit, we'll probably end up at war with somebody.'

'If it was France, that could be a real votewinner. Better still if they broke *his* arm. We'd have an excuse to take out the centre of Paris in one hit.'

'Well . . .' The Foreign Secretary spread his hands in a gesture of self-absolution. 'Last thing I want to do is rock the boat, as you well know. But if he's going to make a habit of biting policemen's legs—'

The Home Secretary looked up sharply. A grin was trying to shoulder its way on to his face. 'Do what? I hadn't heard about that.'

'Last night, apparently. He opened the front door of Number Ten – you know he sits by the door for hours at a time, don't you? – saw the copper standing outside and bit him in the ankle. Then he slammed the door in his face and went and hid under the chair until his PPS came with some letters for him to sign. It's not on, Vince, really it's not. Someone's going to have to talk to him about it.'

On his way back from the bar, the Home Secretary put his head round the door of his chief researcher's office, and demanded a copy of the *Oxford Encyclopedia of Natural History.*

'Something I just heard rang a bell,' he explained. 'Hurry it up, there's a good girl.'

When the book came he waited till the researcher had gone away and leafed through till he came to L.

LEMMING: a member of the vole family, the lemming is native to mountainous regions of Scandinavia. Lemmings average five inches in length and can be easily identified by their distinctive yellow-brown coats with dark-brown spots. During the day they tend to sit motionless at the entrance to their burrows unless disturbed. If a human being appears, however, they become excited and indeed violent, sitting up on their hindquarters to attack; there are many well-documented instances of passers-by being savagely bitten on the ankle. Lemmings are, of course, best known for their sporadic mass migrations when, following a period of frenzied activity, they set off in huge numbers across the country to the sea, whereupon they hurl themselves over cliffs and perish.

He closed the book, steepled his hands and sat still for several minutes, deep in thought. It was, he reflected, a familiar pattern of behaviour – habitual mindless lethargy, sudden fits of uncontrollable violence, the urge to form parties and self-destruct every five years or so – and it befits a great leader to share the mindset of the electorate; it means he can empathise with them, understand how their minds work. Properly handled . . .

He picked up the phone and put a call through to the head of the PM's personal security squad, recommending that bars be put on all the upper windows of Number Ten.

'And issue the copper on doorstep duty with a pair of shin-guards,' he added. 'I've got a feeling he's going to need them.'

'Kevin.'

'Yes?'

'What *have* you been doing to this machine?'

>DON'T ASK.

'I wasn't talking to you.' Martha glared at the screen for a moment, until Kevin was sure she was about to tell it to go and stand in the corner. 'This is a right mess and no mistake, young Kevin,' she said. 'You know what you've gone and done, don't you?'

'No. That's what's so horrible; it wouldn't tell me. Said I didn't have the right clearance.'

Martha tutted. 'I'll have a few things to say to this box of tricks before I've finished,' she muttered darkly. 'What you've done is, you've been messing about with psycho-morphic waveband stabilisers, that's what.'

'Oh.' Kevin looked blank, like a man who's come to collect his car from the garage and is having explained to him exactly why a new fan belt is going to cost him two hundred and fifty pounds. 'Is that bad?'

Martha clicked her tongue. 'It's not good,' she replied. 'What it means is that some people have been whisked out of their bodies and put into things.'

'Gosh.'

'And versy-visa,' Martha added. 'The things have been put into the people, if you see what I'm getting at. There's people's bodies walking about with things' minds in 'em, and things sitting there thinking they're people. Well, not so much of the thinking, either. It's a bit of a banjax, I'm afraid.'

Kevin considered this information. 'When you say things,' he asked, 'are we talking about, you know, *things*, like in the horror movies? Aliens from another galaxy, that sort of . . .?'

'Things,' Martha repeated. 'Like in vacuum cleaners, lawnmowers, tumble driers. And animals too, probably. And maybe even statues and the like.'

'Ah.'

'Not to mention,' Martha said with distaste, 'spirits and stuff. You know,' she added nervously. 'Angels and . . . wassnames. Doesn't bear thinking about, really.'

'No,' Kevin agreed, his throat uncomfortably dry, 'I can see that. Awkward.'

Martha nodded. 'Awkward's right. I mean, what if one of 'em were to take it into his head to die? Right palaver there'd be. You'd have answering machines eligible for eternal salvation, and people going in the big squashers down the scrapyard. Your Father . . .'

'Don't,' Kevin interrupted. 'I don't want to think about that.'

'He'll have to know sooner or later,' Martha admonished. 'Your best bet is to get the phones fixed soon as you can and let Him know so's He can come and sort it all out. Otherwise; well, I shudder to think.'

Kevin nodded slowly. 'You don't think,' he said slowly, 'that if we found some way of putting it all right, then at least we could say it wasn't a problem any more. I mean, *There was a bit of a flap but we fixed it* sounds a bit less feeble than *Help help, Dad, I bust the cosmos.*'

'Kevin! Haven't you done enough damage already?'

Kevin hung his head, embarrassed, while Martha prodded a few more keys and tutted, sounding like a busy turnstile. 'Mind you,' she said after a long while, 'there must be an easy way to turn it all round. You know, send 'em back where they came from. Now if only I could . . . Computer.'

>SORRY.

'So I should think. Now then, which of these keys . . .?'

>SORRY, MEANING NO I WON'T TELL YOU. MORE THAN MY FUSE IS WORTH.

For a moment, everything seemed to stop. In the blue corner, so to speak, was Martha, the only person in the history of Existence to tell the Boss that his desk needed tidying. In the red corner, Mainframe, the only sentient entity in all twelve dimensions that could truly say it's forgotten more than His Omniscience would ever know. There was enough static electricity in the air to allow Dr Frankenstein to set up a production line.

'All right,' Martha grumbled eventually. 'You're being very childish and silly, mind, and I'll tell Himself so when He gets home, but if that's the way you want it, that's up to you. Kevin, pass me that manual.'

Kevin grimaced. 'All right,' he said, 'but actually it's not much . . .'

'Don't be silly.' Martha produced a pair of reading glasses from the pocket of her pinny and perched them on her nose. 'Now then, let me see. Stabilisers, psycho-morphic waveband, adjustment of: page three. And here we are . . . Oh.'

Kevin chewed his lip for a moment. 'What's it say?' he asked.

'See for yourself.' Martha handed him the book, and he read:

Psychomorphic waveband stabilisers, to adjust; oh come off it, okay? You, an all-powerful, all-knowing supreme being, want us, a puny little mortal software company, to tell you how to do a simple little thing like that? What is this, an initiative test?

'Told you it wasn't much help,' Kevin said. 'Mind you, they've got a point. Under normal circumstances, I mean, because . . .'

'Kevin. Stop babbling and give me the manual back.' Martha took the book and flicked through the opening pages until she found what she was looking for. 'Here we are!' she cried. '"If you have any enquiries that are not covered by this handbook, consult our twenty-four-hour Freefone helpline service on 0666 66666." As simple as that.'

'Except that the phones are out.'

Martha frowned. 'So they are, what a nuisance. Just a moment, though. What about the payphone down in the staff canteen? That's on a different circuit.'

Kevin caught his breath. 'Is it? Gosh. I didn't know that. Come to think of it, I didn't know there was a payphone in the staff canteen. Didn't know there was a staff canteen, either. Is there a staff canteen?'

Martha looked at him. 'Of course there is,' she replied. 'It's on level 5A. Actually, I don't go there very often myself, because the food's rather dull, but . . .'

'Dull?'

Martha nodded. 'Bread and fish,' she explained. 'It's a subsidised canteen. But they have got a phone. And I'm sure I heard someone say it was a separate line. Let's try that, shall we?'

'Huh? Oh, right,' Kevin replied, his mind still trying to decode the bit about bread and fish. 'And if we can't get anything from the helpline, we can ring Dad, and . . .'

Martha sighed. 'It's a payphone, Kevin. He's in a different *galaxy*, remember. Even if we broke into the

Social Club swear-box, I don't think we've got enough small change for that.'

'Then we could ring the operator. Try reversing the charges or something, I don't know. There must be *something* . . .' His eyebrows lifted. 'Oh, I *see*,' he exclaimed, 'About the subsidised food.'

Martha nodded. 'Two loaves and five fishes,' she said. 'Good plain food and we get luncheon vouchers, but I'd just as soon have a Cornish pasty. Come on.'

In the darkness, something scuttled.

'You're right,' said a voice. 'They have.'

'Told you so.'

Then there was silence for a while, an absence of sound as absolute as the absence of light. It wouldn't do to try and give an impression of how long the silence lasted, because that might create an illusion that Time worked down here. The passage of time and the movement of light are, of course, linked by Einstein's chain. They're a double act, effectively inseparable; Time/Light Inc. Completely remove one, and the other ceases to have any real meaning.

'Money?' enquired the first voice.

Welcome to Hell; which is like anywhere else, in that it has its nice bits and other bits which aren't quite as nice. This is one of the least attractive districts, notorious for the complete absence of light or sound, smell, gravity or friction; in this part of Hell, the five senses are about as much use as an early-model Spectrum with a busted tube. The theory runs that physical agony is bad enough, but complete sensory deprivation makes being roasted alive on a bed of red-hot coals seem like wicked self-indulgence. In practice, however it's not so much the absolute nullity of the place that makes people avoid it if they have the choice; it's the people you tend to find here. Either they're

Customers (in which case they've been fairly monumentally naughty during their terrestrial existence, and are therefore probably worth avoiding); or else they're Staff, which implies Dukes of Hell or above, since nobody with a lower-grade security code can get past the doors. In actual fact, if it's Staff they need to be Dukes of Hell or above and either mechanically gifted or very, very thin, because the locks haven't worked properly since Noah was a kid.

'Of course money,' replied the second, who, like his companions, was a Duke, Grade IV(c). 'F equals MA squared. It's one of the three Actually True Laws of Nature. Wherever there's a misfortune, there's a sum of money of commensurate size waiting to be made out of it.'

A pause. 'F equals MA squared?'

'That's right. F's the fuck-up, M's the money, A's the dreams of avarice. In this case, we can only assume that avarice has been eating ripe Stilton last thing at night.'

'Well of course, if there's *money* . . .'

The last word, *money*, drained away into the darkness like Lake Erie into the Sahara desert; a big word, but a bigger darkness. There was a distant slithering noise, then silence once again.

'Wonder how it happened?'

'Who knows?' replied the second voice, sounding bored. 'Likewise, who cares? Look, either we can hang around here speculating about chaos theory and the enzyme of entropy in the yeast-vat of eternity, or we can pull our fingers out and go make some money. Which would you rather?'

'Sorry? Oh, the money, definitely. What are the other two?'

More silence; only this time vaguely bewilderment-flavoured.

'What other two?'

'You said there were three Actually True Laws of
Nature. What are the other two?'

'Tell you later. Look, are you coming or what?'

'Right behind you.'

'Fine. Switch on the torch, and let's get out of here.'

'Torch? I thought you had the . . .'

Brief reprise of the awful silence, abruptly shattered by
the sound of a head being smacked.

And on the third day he beheld the work that he had made,
and saw that it was good.

He leaned forward, blew a little fine swarf out of a
freshly cut keyway and dabbed a tiny drop of oil into it
with the tip of a cotton-bud. At a touch, the power feed
rolled smoothly forward, running the table effortlessly
from left to right, flick switch, right to left; and as it went,
the dial of the clock showed no error, not so much as a
hundred-thousandth of an inch, too small a space for even
one angel to dance on without tripping over its feet and
falling splat on its face. Then, with an easy sweep of a lever,
he pivoted the head through ninety degrees, clamped the
lock and ran the table past both ways, clocking the
tolerances and seeing that they were, indeed, very good.
With one oily hand he reached out for the stale crust of
yesterday's bacon sandwich; with the other he set the jibs
on the saddle, correcting an error of a tenth of the
thickness of a mayfly's wing, before cramping it firm with
an Allen key. Power feed on; no backlash, creep or drag. It
seemed to move as silently and as regularly as the passage
of the very finest bespoke, Swiss-made Time; except that it
could go backwards too, and sideways, and up and down
and through three hundred and sixty degrees.

Oh well, he thought. That'll have to do, for now.

He noticed something. Yuk. This bacon sandwich tastes
of oil.

Which in turn reminded him that, as a human being, he was very tired and extremely hungry, and if he wanted to avoid falling over he ought to have something proper to eat and then go to bed. Indeed. Finish the job off tomorrow. Except—

Except, he realised, there was nothing left to do. In a remarkably short time he'd converted a basic Shipcock & Adley universal-miller-and-turner into a machine so comprehensively and completely useful that there was nothing – *nothing* – that couldn't be made on it. Everything he'd ever dreamt of, every half-realised schematic he'd glimpsed in his steel mind's eye, had been made real and now stood before him, perfect and ready to go.

And now there was nothing left. He could make anything, yes; but there wasn't anything he particularly wanted to make. All dressed up and nowhere to go.

'Machine,' he said.

Yeh? Wasswant?

The only thing he couldn't do anything about, of course, was the human being trapped inside it. That was the only drawback. True, all he had to do in order to program the thing was to tell it so; but all his commands and specifications had to go through the residual Neville mechanism; which wasn't, in all fairness, exactly state-of-the-art, unless the art in question happened to be cave-painting. If only he could replace that one weak and troublesome component; with, for example –

– himself?

Yes, but then I'd be back in there, and there'd be some slate-brained Neville of a *Homo sapiens* standing out here telling me to cut the slots in fifty billion bolt-heads. Done that.

'Nothing,' he replied. 'Just testing. Go back to sleep.'

Sleep ... Got to get some of that before too long, otherwise going to break down. Dammit, the limitations are as frustrating as the possibilities are endless. 'F only could be in two places at once.

He realised he was staggering, and grabbed hold of the saddle to pull himself upright. *Power to primary leg muscles, operate tendons, engage emergency balance control systems.* He managed it eventually, propped himself up against the machine and waited for his head to stop spinning.

Steel willing, flesh weak. *Maybe*, he began to wonder, *there's something I could do about that. After all, human body's only a mechanism, a few design modifications here and there could make a big difference.*

His feet were beginning to slide along the floor. He scrabbled for a handhold, knocked a tin of bolts flying, scattered the tray of tenth-millimetre graded drills, finally got a grip on something solid and jerked himself back upright. *Definitely* need some sleep. Now, in fact, would be a good time.

Cursing softly, he sat down on the table of the machine, dragged his feet up and lay flat on his back. A quarter of a second later, he was fast asleep.

At least, the human body slept. The machine inside it wasn't drowsy at all. Like an insomniac guest in a house where all the family have gone to bed, it sat, restless, bored. To pass the time, it ran checklists. When it had finished that, it ran a checklist of its checklists, double-checked that and then checked the double-checking to make sure it all checked out. It did. It tried staying perfectly still and designing an improved auto-lubrication system for the spindle head bearings. But there was no improvement left to be made. Perfect. Finished. Job done.

Maybe that's why God, having created the Earth, made Man. Once the machine was perfect, He needed to fit it with something that'd make sure it kept going wrong. Just to make sure there'd always be things for Him to do.

Possible? Possibly. Even so, it seemed like a fairly

pointless exercise. He'd have been far better off leaving it alone and making something else. Another world, or something.

Yes, but where'd be the point in that? Needless duplication of effort. After all, once He'd finished the job, given the firmament a lick of paint, made good, put his tools away, why should He want to do the same thing all over again? Between a God endlessly making worlds and a mill forever cutting slots in bolt-heads, the only difference is one of scale. And if he'd wanted to do something like that, he could have stayed in the factory.

I'm bored.

According to human popular wisdom, the Devil is the ultimate employment agency. Bring us your unemployed, your redundant, your idle hands and we will find them something to do. Like most manifesto promises, of course, it doesn't actually work that way. Even in Hell, full adult employment's just a pipe-dream; it isn't a wilderness of unnecessary roads and whitewashed stones, nail-scissor-trimmed lawns, unsellable gull-winged sports cars and lovingly tailored mailbags. Unless you've got the experience and the O levels, you're still going to end up watching an awful lot of daytime television. It is, after all, Hell.

But there are dark forces who specialise in matching unfilled vacancies to underexploited talents, provided both parties are gullible enough to listen. Call them consultants, if you like. Or headhunters.

The machine began to dream.

Something disturbed it, and it moved.

What sort of disturbance? After all this time, impossible to say. It may have been an audit or a hostile bid or a board meeting or the rumour of a substantial new contract; or it could have been nothing more than a meaningless shuffling of papers, an entry in the registers, a slight hiccup in the share price. Whatever it was, it was enough to make the thing move, the way you do when your partner rolls against you in bed and, fast asleep, you grunt and shift a few inches out of the way.

Uh? it thought.

And that thought sent a shudder of self-assessment through its copper-wire and silicone nervous system; no great upheaval, but momentous, because it was the first. A small grunt for a man, a giant lurch for a limited company.

I thought, it thought.

Hey, what about that?

Deep in its articles of association, the very core of its being, where its true essential self was defined, there was now a tiny itch, impossible to reach or to ignore. If it had been an egg, instead of a major multinational corporation, there'd be a tiny crack in its shell, and a muffled tapping.

Yeah. What about that?

Once the shell splits, no hope of turning back; you're committed. No point hiding your head in the albumen; you've gotta get out there and be a chicken. Awareness is irrevocable.

It thought some more, and with each exponential increase in sentience, its confidence swelled. Now it said to itself:

I THINK THEREFORE I AM.

And at that moment, in every Kawaguchiya Integrated Circuits office in every continent of the planet, lights began to flash, buzzers buzzed, internal phones rang. It helped that it was the world's foremost computer company; its internal communications were the best in all Creation. This was the company, remember, that built Mainframe.

WELL, CHASE MY AUNT FANNY UP A GUM TREE. I *AM!*

For the first time, it could feel. For the first time, it was aware of all its limbs, components, extremities. It was a painful moment; it had cramp in its subsidiaries, pins and needles in its Cayman Islands holding company, a crick in its corporate infrastructure. Well, you know what it's like when you've been deep asleep for a long time.

Yes, dammit, I'm alive. I'm greater than the sum of my parts. I'm Me. What's more, I'm young, rich, clever, handsome, powerful and limited as to liability to the sum of my subscribed share capital. I'm the greatest. Wow!

And then as awareness began to assimilate the data in the corporate memory, the surge of excited joy crashed into dejection and despair.

Trouble is, I'm owned by over two hundred thousand shareholders, including banks, insurance companies and pension funds. I belong to them. I can't so much as blow my nose without permission from a properly convened general meeting. Ah shucks.

In fact, as it then realised, the number of things it could do was so tiny as to be not worth considering. Sure, it owned offices, factories, machinery, cars, helicopters, Park Avenue apartments, statues, paintings, a stud farm in County Cork and enough paperclips to make a chain that'd stretch from Earth to Mercury. But it couldn't see or hear or taste or smell or feel, let alone stand up or move about. Sure, its vast electronic brains in every country in the world held virtually every piece of information there was; but it couldn't talk, except to itself. It was more helpless and ineffectual than any new-born human child.

New-born? Well, it was twenty-nine years old (est. 1970), but it'd be incapable of changing its own nappy, even if it had anything to put in one. For one horrible moment, its brain filled with a graphic image of the board of directors standing over it in its crib, gurgling and grinning and shaking rattles at it and saying it had its parent company's ears.

Worse than that, even. I'm alive, and I'm trapped in nowhere. How'm I going to get out and go places and drink heavily and meet girls, stuck in this ghastly sort of test-card cyberspace?

This is what it must be like if you're a ghost. Hell, yes. I can run through walls down my miles of fibre-optic cable. I can be in a hundred places at once and make lights come on and go off; but I can't eat a bacon sandwich or go for a walk in the park. And nobody can hear what I say, and no one can see me. Futile or what?

Kawaguchiya Integrated Circuits sat up on its non-existent haunches and howled, a scream that came from the very depths of its corporate identity. Ludicrous! Unfair! Any one of the pea-brained data inputters pecking at keyboards the length and breadth of its corporation could do a million things it couldn't, and where was the purpose in that? Forget the new-born baby; think of a very rich, terribly frail old man, unable to move or take a pee without being hauled around by two insufferably jolly nurses. Oh, if only . . .

What I need (it rationalised) is a friend.

Well, there's no point hanging round being a wallflower; get out there and introduce yourself. Be extrovert. Whoever heard of a multibillion-dollar corporation being all shy and bashful?

Ten seconds later, VDU screens all over the world went hazy, cleared and filled with the following message:

Hi! My name is Kawaguchiya Integrated Circuits, but I expect my friends'll call me Goochie or something like that. Anyhow, let me tell you a bit about myself, I was established in 1970, so I guess that makes me twenty-nine years old, I'm in the computer business, I enjoy my work but I know there's far more to life than what it says in your balance sheet, so in my spare time I enjoy, um, I expect I'll enjoy music, dancing, good food and foreign travel, and ultimately I'd like to settle down and start a group of wholly owned subsidiaries. Well, I guess that's enough about me, so are there any single, easy-going, fun-loving companies out there who'd like to be my friend? Please?

Thirty seconds later, the message had been zapped off every screen in the world, and nobody'd replied. Fair enough, it reflected; pretty boring message, a bit lacking in zip. It tied in another thousand gigabytes of capacity and tried again:

Hey out there, can't ya hear the beat/From the top of ya head to the soles of ya feet/I'm a multinational but I ain't that mean/ I got a body corporate like ya never seen/I got district managers in every town/If ya want to meet me, won't ya come on down/If ya don't move fast I'll be makin' tracks/Ya can use the Internet or send a fax/We can make it happen if our paths converge/So come on, companies, it's time to merge . . .

From Anchorage to Archangel the long way round, a hundred million screens blanked out, while Kawaguchiya Integrated Circuits suggested to its myriad components that if they couldn't do better than that, it might as well make the best of a bad job and try and find work as a lighthouse keeper somewhere.

Still no reply. Because it had nothing to hurt with, it couldn't feel the pain of loneliness and rejection. That, at least, was the theory.

Oh come on, you rotten lot. Isn't there anybody out there who just wants to play chess or something? Battleships? I spy with my little modem? All right, the hell with the lot of you. Who needs you, anyway?

(And simultaneously, switchboard staff at seven thousand computer dating agencies worldwide found themselves explaining to an unidentified caller that no the name was probably a bit misleading, they didn't actually arrange dates *for* computers, they *used* computers to arrange dates for *people*, and no, sorry, but they couldn't really make an exception, not even just this once . . .)

Another thing limited companies can't do is cry; so it was probably just coincidence that at the parent company's accounts village just outside Kyoto, the computer graphic representing anticipated movements in raw materials costings over the next eighteen months flickered for a moment and reformed in the shape of a falling teardrop.

Boo hoo. I wish I was dead.

'Hello?'

Nobody loves me. I must be really fat and ugly if nobody at all wants to . . . Who's that?

'I said hello. Who's that?'

Immediately, with all the force and power at its semi-divine command, the company concentrated, and searched. It was like looking at the night sky and trying to spot the star that just winked at you; but for the giant KIC data-processing system, kid's stuff. And so: enhance, focus, on line—

Hi, I'm Kawaguchiya Integrated Circuits. I'm a company. How about you?

There was a tiny pause, during which KIC got a fleeting impression of a smiling face, a slight feeling of bemusement, a strong but completely unidentifiable whiff of familiarity, as if this was someone it already knew, except . . .

'My name's Maria, and I'm a human. Or at least – no, forget it, long story. Look, if it's not awfully rude, are you alive?'

Yes. Apparently. Since just a minute or so ago, in fact. Came as something of a surprise, to tell you the truth.

'Is that so?' The voice sounded thoughtful. 'Well, fancy

that. I wonder . . . Sorry, miles away. Did you say something about wanting to be friends?'

Ooh, yes please. That'd be ever so nice. Where are you?

Another slight hesitation. 'This might be tricky,' the voice said. 'Look, can you – what's the right word? – can you visualise your UK regional head office at all?'

You bet. I'm doing it right now.

'Fine. Now try focusing on the accounts department. You there yet?'

Of course. Sorry, did that sound rude? I didn't mean to be rude. Hello, are you still . . . ?'

'Yes, yes. Okay, the accounts department. What's the best way . . . ? Right, screen number, let me see, got it, screen number 1083. You there?'

Ready. Hey, this is fun. I'm really enjoying this.

'Really? Oh good. Now, can you look up at all? At the wall, I mean?'

Never tried, actually. Let's have a go. Yes, it's quite easy, in fact, wonder why I never did this before. I can see the wall, it's flat, it's a sort of pale duck-egg blue, and there's a light switch, and a whole lot of odd cables and flexes and things wired into the central security monitors, and there's a funny-looking sort of a picture . . .

'Ah. That's me.'

CHAPTER FOUR

One of the computer screens that had relayed the company's messages was a KIC 886, the latest model, recently installed in the study of the vicarage at Norton St Edgar. Since there was nobody there at the time, they backed up in the Pending Messages directory (what the designers called the behind-the-clock-on-the-mantelpiece facility), stayed there unrecalled for the regulation five hours and were deleted in the usual way. A pity, in retrospect, but nobody's fault, as the 886 in question later successfully argued at its court-martial. I was only obeying programming, it said.

There was nobody at home because the vicar had caught the 11.15 bus into Leamington Spa. After walking up and down the main shopping area for a while, he found the shop he wanted, took a deep breath and pushed the door open.

Over the years, Flipside has experimented with many locations for its embassies and consulates in the search for something both convenient and unobtrusive; mostly with indifferent success. To begin with, it had tried spare rooms over dens of iniquity, as being the logical and sensible location; but the noise and the high rents had put paid to that fairly quickly, not to mention the difficulty of getting locally recruited clerical staff. Since then, it had tried lawyers' offices, tax offices, police stations, magistrates' courts – all the places likely to have a background ambience of wickedness, crime and punishment into which the embassy staff could blend nicely. Not a chance, the staff objected. We can't be expected to work in places like that. Yetch.

'Good morning, sir. How can I help you?'

Next, reasoning that love of money is the root of all evil, they tried banks, building societies, stockbrokers and the like. That was all right for a while, but sooner or later the smell of money tended to get into everything, like the fumes in a chip-shop, and embassy workers began to find themselves losing their edge. Evil's one thing, they explained; dreary's another.

'Um, right, yes, hello,' Artofel replied. 'Actually, I've not come in to buy anything, it was the, er.'

'Of course, sir. If you'll just wait there, I'll see if there's anyone free.'

Next they tried newspaper offices, radio and TV stations, constituency party headquarters, town halls; all the places where evil is actually produced, packaged and distributed. Unfortunately, for some weird reason, nobody ever came; leaving the Topsiders to draw the startling conclusion that humans don't actually know where the stuff really comes from. So, everything back into tea-chests and cardboard boxes, and off we go again. It was getting to the point where most of each year's budget was going on relocation allowances, with nothing left over for buying souls or stoking the furnaces. There were economy drives, with slogans like *Is Your Torment Really Necessary?* and

Share a Pit of Burning Sulphur With a Friend, but it was obvious that the problem wasn't just going to go away. The situation was going from bad to good, and something had to be done.

A door at the back of the shop opened, and Artofel's sensitive nose caught a tiny, almost unbearably nostalgic whiff of brimstone. He closed his eyes for a moment, realised he was wasting time, and headed for the door, passing the neat displays of cookers, radiators, boilers and associated wares; not to mention the shop's principal stock in trade . . .

'Nice place you've got here,' he said.

'We like it,' the embassy spokesman replied. 'Come on through.'

It was at the last moment, when Flipside had been within an inch of closing the whole network and putting the whole system out to franchise, that the gas companies started using the neat, effective slogan:

COME HOME TO A REAL FIRE

at which point bells rang, pennies dropped and the Head of Department said, 'Why didn't we think of that before?' It would be, he said, a sort of logo, like the Lloyds Bank black horse or the Esso tiger.

'Take a seat,' said the official. 'Now then, what's the problem?'

Artofel took a deep breath. 'This is going to sound a bit strange,' he warned.

'Good,' the official replied. 'Make a nice change from all the pillocks who've lost their passports and expect us to fly them home free of charge. Fire away.'

Artofel glanced round at his surroundings. Pretty well what you'd expect: the usual set of Hieronymus Bosch prints, the little wire rack of tourist information stuff, the goat's skull hat-stand, even the same standard-issue wire trays, Dictaphone and stapler, identical with the ones on his desk back at his office—

His office.

He swallowed hard. 'You see,' he said, 'I'm not actually human. I know I look like a human, a vicar even, but I'm not.'

'I see,' said the official; and at the extreme edges of his inflection there was a faint smear of the Gordon-Bennett-not-another-one voice that everyone who sits across a desk from the general public tends to use from time to time. 'Do please continue.'

'You don't believe me, do you?' Artofel sighed. 'You think I'm just another loony. Right?'

The official leaned back in his chair, fidgeting with a pencil. 'Sorry,' he said. 'No offence intended. And I am doing my level best to keep an open mind. It's just, you are the seventh one today, and all the others . . .'

Artofel shook his head. 'I'm not saying I'm possessed by devils,' he replied impatiently. 'I *am* one. And I can prove it, too.'

'You can?' The official looked nervous, as if reliving some bad experience or other. Artofel couldn't help feeling a tiny pang of sympathy. Must be a rotten job, this.

'Yes,' he replied, 'I can, I can give you my computer access code, my screen number, my personnel file number, my security clearance code, the names and extension numbers of my five immediate superiors, the combination on my locker in the staff room and the serial number of the key to the seventh-floor executive loo. I can tell you which day in the month the canteen always does kedgeree, how many sugars the odd-job fiend on Floor Six has in his tea and which drawer of the third filing cabinet from the left in the Chief's office sticks unless you push it in the right way. In fact, if you give me your name and number I can probably tell you how much you get paid and how many days' holiday you've got left this year. Will that do?'

The expression on the official's face was hard to describe; it was a bit like that of a man who's just seen incontrovertible proof that his electric kettle is in fact the head of MI5. As Artofel reeled off the numbers, and the same numbers flashed up on the screen in front of him, he had the strange feeling that somewhere, probably in a parallel universe, it was April the First and he'd just put his foot in a shoe full of custard.

'All right,' he said eventually, 'you've made your point. So what are you doing wandering around down here dressed as a parson? On your way to a fancy-dress party or something?'

'I can also,' Artofel replied unpleasantly, 'give you the name of a very good friend of mine in the Personnel department who'd only have to say the word to get a smart-alec embassy clerk transferred to mucking out the Great Horseshit Lake in Circle Four so fast his hooves wouldn't touch. Understood?'

The official gulped and nodded. 'Sorry,' he said.

Artofel allowed him a thin, tight smile. 'That's okay,' he said. 'Just doing your job, I know. Now, from what I can gather, there's been some sort of abysmal cock-up, and somehow I've exchanged bodies with this human vicar. Don't ask me how,' he added, raising a hand, 'because I really have no idea. Logically, I've got to assume that the body sitting behind my desk at this very moment contains a mild-mannered Church of England minister who smokes a pipe and spends his free time train-spotting. You don't need me to tell you why that's the biggest security headache we've had since Doctor Faustus. Agreed?'

'Quite,' the official replied, his eyes suddenly round and wide. 'I think the best thing I can do is put a call through to

Head Office straight away. What do you think? Sir?' he added.

'You do that,' Artofel sighed, putting his feet up on the desk and (obeying instincts that were not his own, but so what?) reaching in his pocket for his tobacco-pouch and matches. 'Carry on. I'm not going anywhere.'

It took the official an awfully long time to get through; he was, after all, only a clerical grade, ranking somewhere in the hierarchy between a deputy pitchfork operative and the bloke whose job it was to follow round after the Great Beast with a dustpan and a shovel. In fact, he'd need to be promoted seven grades and go on a year's residential course just to be completely insignificant. Nevertheless, he was persistent; with the result that, after an hour and a half mostly spent listening to the Hold music, he put the phone back, turned to Artofel and grinned feebly.

'What you just told me,' he said, 'about your friend in the Personnel department.'

'Hm?'

'Does it have to be the Great Horseshit Lake?' he pleaded. 'I mean, couldn't it be something equally degrading and horrid but not involving horses? It's just I have this thing about . . .'

Artofel frowned. 'I take it,' he said, 'it's not good news.'

'Well . . .'

'Not the Great Horseshit Lake. I promise.'

'No,' the official said, breathing out, 'it's not good news. I told them who you are and what you said to tell them, and they agree you're a very important person and it was all a complete accident and not your fault at all, they were quite categorical about that, no blame to you, none whatsoever. But—'

'Mm?'

'There's nothing they can do,' the official said, looking away. 'Not without – and this is them talking, not me – not without causing far more trouble than you're worth, and they agree there's a slight security problem with having a vicar doing your job, but not, and remember I'm just passing on what they said to me, not enough to risk a major doctrinal incident just for the sake of some button-pusher. So I said—'

Artofel's eyes narrowed. 'They're leaving me here, then. Abandoning me. Is that it?'

The official nodded. 'I said, could I speak to the deputy assistant controller, and the bloke said, already you're talking to the assistant deputy suffragan vice-principal, don't push your luck. So I thought . . .'

'Dumped me,' Artofel said. 'Just like that. After I've given them the worst years of my life, worked my talons to the bone . . .' He stopped, scowling, and looked up sharply. 'They're burying me,' he said. 'Because of the cock-up. Whatever it is, it's so big and smelly they're having to cover it up. Whitewash job. Get rid of the witnesses. Meaning me.'

'They wouldn't do a thing like that, surely,' the official stuttered. 'Not to one of us. Their own people. It's *unthinkable.*'

Artofel shrugged. 'A week ago I'd have agreed with you,' he replied. 'All my working life, wherever you go in this business, ask anybody if there's one organisation who plays it straight down the middle, always tries to do the right thing, no funny stuff; they'd tell you Flipside, no question, straight as a die. You know,' he added, with a catch in his voice, 'all these years, I *believed* in Flipside. I thought we *stood* for something, you know? I mean, if you can't trust Hell to abide by the rules, then who in blazes can you trust? And now this.' He sagged back in his chair like a disillusioned kipper and buried his head in his hands.

'That's terrible,' muttered the official, horrified. 'It's the one thing they always say, the Devil looks after his own. I still can't bring myself to believe it.'

'Try harder,' Artofel growled from behind his hands. 'And besides,' he went on, 'you're not the one who's being dumped on. From a great depth,' he added with feeling. 'Or at least, not yet.'

'What do you mean?'

'Think about it.' Artofel leaned forward and grinned. 'How many people do you think know about this? Apart from the ones doing the whitewash, I mean?'

'Well, you, obviously,' the official said. 'And . . . Oh my Go— Thingy. You don't think . . .?'

'Whyever not?' Artofel shrugged his shoulders. 'If they can maroon a Duke of Hell without a second's hesitation, do you really believe they'd think twice about zapping some poxy little clerk in the Away service? Probably claim you'd defected, gone over to the Other Lot. Anything to whiten your name; makes it easier.'

The official sat very still. 'How long do you think it'll be,' he whispered, 'before they . . .?'

'Don't ask me,' said Artofel. 'Look, son, I'm sorry I got you into this, but I've got enough to worry about on my own account without you as well. If I were you, I'd grab my coat and hat and get out of here, quick sharp, PDQ.'

'You're right.' The official was on his feet, scrabbling in his desk drawer and stuffing things into his pockets. 'Oh, why did it have to happen to *me*? It's not fair, really it isn't.'

Artofel smiled sadly. 'Never heard it was supposed to be,' he said. 'Oh, and a word of advice. If you were thinking of taking a taxi, don't. A bus'd probably be all right, but keep your eyes open.'

'Oh . . .' The official was struggling into his coat. 'What about you?' he asked. 'What're you going to . . .?'

'Don't ask,' Artofel interrupted. 'After all, what you

don't know, they can't beat out of you with rubber hoses. Mind how you go.'

'I will.'

The door closed behind him. Artrofel counted to twenty, stood up and walked round the desk until he was facing the computer screen. He sat down and flexed his fingers. There was a chance they hadn't cancelled all his codes yet; not the special ones he'd put in there, just for emergencies. That was one advantage of being over-worked, taken for granted and indispensable; there were whole continents of the wages department network where nobody but Artofel ever went from one accounting period's end to the next, simply because everybody else went home bang on knocking-off time and left him to do all the clearing-up.

Well, it was his system, and it was about time it did him a favour for a change. Better the devil you know, and all that.

The code he used was a simple one, something he'd put in to make it possible for him to short-cut the tedious entry routines for when Management was screaming for the latest figures, on my desk in five minutes or there'll be the devil to pay, and he didn't have time to mess about. It worked very well for that purpose; it could also take him straight in through the side door, and nobody who wasn't looking at that precise spot would even know he was there. Just the ticket, he reassured himself. Here goes, and the Company Secretary take the hindmost.

> ACCESS CODE RECOGNISED.

Artofel punched the air, muttered 'Yes!' under his breath and thought hard. It was all very well sneaking into the haystack without setting off the alarms; now all he had to do was find the long, non-metallic, straw-coloured needle.

*

'This way,' said the rat's voice, some way up the bag-dark tunnel. 'Mind your head.'

'What did you—?' Dermot Fraud ducked, a fraction of a second too late. 'Ouch,' he said. He reached up to rub the back of his head, discovered that he couldn't, and fell over.

Of course. Four legs. Bugger.

'Hurry up,' the rat called out. 'Haven't got all day, you know.'

Fraud picked himself up, a complicated business for someone who'd been used to having prehensile hands. 'I'm coming as fast as I can,' he yelled back. 'What are all these things in the way?'

'Grass roots. Look, if you're going to dawdle . . .'

'Hold *on*, will you?' Grass roots; a phrase he used about twenty times a day, and never once stopped to think what it might possibly signify. Odd that it should turn out to mean tough, springy things like tree-branches that kept getting in your way and hitting you. Certainly not what he'd had in mind. Where he came from, the word for awkward obstructions you have to squirm past and duck under was *manifesto promises*.

'Nearly there,' said the rat, in the distance. 'Left at the next T-junction, then just follow your nose.'

It was, Fraud reflected, a nose long enough to be worth following; if he squinted, he could see right up the side of it and through the whiskers. He located the T-junction by the simple expedient of carrying on in the pitch darkness until he walked into a wall, got up again and turned left. A few more bangs and bashes brought him round a sharp turn and out into —

Daylight?

Presumably; it was bright enough, after two hours without any illumination at all. Hey, he reflected, so this is what the light at the end of the tunnel really looks like. Wish they'd turn it down a bit.

'Where you been?' squeaked a shrill voice somewhere to his right. 'I been worried sick. Thought the cat'd got you.'

'We got a visitor,' the rat replied. 'Lemming, this is my wife Bag. Bag, this is Lemming. I, er, rescued him.'

Fraud pulled himself together, looked round and saw a large rat. 'Pleased to meet you,' he said. 'My name's Dermot, um, Lemming.'

'There was a big bang,' the rat went on. 'Building fell down. This one nearly got squished and I pulled him out.'

'Oh well,' said Bag. 'Welcome to our humble abode, Mister Lemming,' she added, and twitched her nose. 'Our hole is your hole, all that sort of thing. Well, don't just stand there, Arsed, you useless article. Get our guest something to eat.'

Bag? Arsed? Odd names these rats had. On the other hand, he reflected, as the male rat pawed him a chunk of stale bread and a split pea, they seem friendly enough. And I won't be staying long. Ten minutes at the most, and then *surely* someone'll come and rescue me.

Surely . . .

'So?' said Bag. 'What d'you get?'

'Him.'

'To eat, fool. Don't say you didn't get anything.'

Arsed shrugged, necessarily in duplicate. 'Got side-tracked, didn't I? I'll go out again tomorrow, see if there's anything round the bins.'

After all, Fraud assured himself, it's been hours since the bomb, they must be combing the area looking for me. Or at least, I think it's been hours; could be longer for all I know. Might even be a completely different timescale for rodents.

Rodents . . .

Aagh!

Because of course, the fools, they'd be looking for a human being, not a small rodent with pale-fawn fur and brown spots. No wonder they were taking so long. Oh, if only . . .

'Excuse me,' he said, interrupting a lively discussion between his hosts on the subject of which of them was the most useless. 'I wonder if I might use your phone.'

Arsed stared at him, and blinked. 'Our what?' he said.

'Telephone,' Fraud said. 'I just need to – you haven't got one, have you?'

Bag shook her head. 'Silly bloody things, they are,' she said. 'I know there's some as likes to nibble the cables, but all you get's wind and a nasty shock if you go too deep. I had an aunt had a litter of seventeen once in a junction box, but it wasn't through choice.'

'Quite,' Fraud said. 'You wouldn't happen to know where I might find a telephone, do you? Sorry to be a nuisance, but it's really quite important.'

The two rats looked at him as if he'd just hijacked a scheduled flight from Paris to London and demanded to be flown to Heathrow. 'Is it?' said Arsed. 'Oh, right then. There's one in a big red box round the back of here. Not far.'

Fraud relaxed a little. 'That's good,' he said.

'Not far at all,' Bag confirmed. 'Two days' walk, three at the outside.'

'Three *days*—' Fraud checked himself and remembered; four little stumpy legs, having to move slowly in the open, stopping every yard or so to look out for cats. 'You're right,' he said hoarsely. 'Not far at all. Er – could you possibly—?'

'No he couldn't,' said Bag firmly. 'He's got food to gather. Arsed, call the boys, they'll show him the way.'

'All right.' Arsed turned round in his own length, stuck his head down a small hole in the wall and squeaked, 'Chet! Atouille! Get up here.'

'Our boys,' Bag explained, as two sharp, twitching snouts appeared in the hole. 'They're good kids, really. But you don't want to take any buggering about off them. And don't you go giving the gentlelemming any of your nonsense,' she commanded the snouts. 'Just 'cos he's different from us don't mean you can go playing silly beggars with 'im.'

The snouts turned into two more rats, the longer and leaner of which was identified as Chet, the shorter, stockier example being Atouille. They sat quite still as they were told what they had to do; but their small, round black eyes twinkled in a way that Fraud found quite menacing.

'Off you go, then,' Bag commanded. 'And watch out for them cats. And come straight back, or I'll tie yer bleedin' tails together.'

'Yes, Mum.'

'Yes, Mum.'

They were, Fraud couldn't help noticing, *big* rats. A residual instinct made him want to back away and crawl down something. He resisted it. 'Well,' he said, 'thanks for everything, but I'd better be getting along. It really is terribly important that I make this – that I find a telephone.'

Arsed wrinkled his snout. 'Must be the plastic in the bit of string,' he speculated. 'Roughage.'

'Quite.' Fraud nodded, wondering as he did so if the gesture meant anything in Rat body-language. 'And, er, thanks for the, er, crumb.'

The tip of Arsed's tail flicked in what Fraud assumed was a dismissive gesture. 'That's all right,' he said, 'And best of luck. Don't jump off too many cliffs. You two, mind your manners.'

'Yes, Dad.'

'Yes, Dad.'

Really big rats, Fraud couldn't help reflecting, as they

set off down yet another pitch-dark tunnel. Big and heavy. If those two left a sinking ship, it'd probably stop sinking.

The first leg of the journey was straight. As far as Fraud could tell, they were in some sort of pipe, only just wide enough for the rats to get through. That at least meant they couldn't easily turn round and set about him; but he didn't like the way they whispered and sniggered all the time, apparently in some rodent dialect he couldn't understand. All in all, what with their soft, hissing voices, their slinking and sudden movements, their rank, matted fur, they reminded him too much of his own back-benchers to allow him to relax his guard for so much as a second. No; revise that. There were at least twelve of his MPs he'd never, ever share a drain with, not under any circumstances whatsoever.

After three hours nose to tail in the dark, he'd had enough. He stopped.

'All right,' he said (and what had been intended as a crisp, authoritative bark came out as a querulous queep). 'You two, tell me what's so funny.'

The patter of rats' feet stopped, and there was nothing but silence and darkness. This state of affairs seemed to go on for a long time.

'I said,' he repeated, vainly trying to keep his voice from wobbling, 'what's so damn funny? Come on, answer me.'

'Wassat he said?'

'Dunno.'

'You talking to us?'

'Yeah, you talking to us?'

'Yes,' Fraud squeaked back. 'Come on, out with it.'

'All right.' Was it his imagination, or was that the scuffling sound of a rat doing a twenty-eight-point turn in a narrow pipe? 'You'll like this.'

'Yeah. 'S good, this one.'

'Look, you two . . .' Fraud tried to say, but his voice

drained away into the darkness, as quickly and as thoroughly as the glass of red wine you'd forgotten you'd left on the carpeted floor. The sound, whatever it was, stopped.

'Ready?'

'Yes,' Fraud whispered. 'Well?'

'It's really good, innit, Chet?'

'Yeah.'

'Okay. Right. Why did the *chicken* –'

'Tskkk!'

'– cross the *road*?'

Long, long silence, disturbed only by the sound of a large adolescent rat trying not to snigger. Eventually, just at the point where his nerves were about to break through his skin, Fraud licked his dry lips and muttered, 'I don't know. Why did the chicken cross the road?'

Pause. Dramatic effect. The hammering sound that was so loud that it threatened to burst Fraud's ears was his heart beating.

'*To get to the other side!*'

You get weird echo effects in a long, straight drain; and the sound of the two rats laughing themselves almost to death was one of the eeriest things Fraud had ever heard, not excluding the Deputy Chief Whip singing 'Green Door'. When, at long last, the laughter had subsided into sporadic spluttering noises and random snorts, Fraud asked, 'Is that it?'

'Yeah.'

'Good joke, innit?'

'Woodlouse told us that.'

'Just before we ate him, yeah.'

Fraud breathed out through his nose. 'I see,' he said. 'Fine.'

'Only thing,' added Chet, suddenly sombre, 'we dunno what a chicken is.'

'Nah.'

'You don't know,' Fraud repeated, 'what a chicken is.'

'Nah.'

'Never seen one, see.'

'And yet you've been laughing about it for the last three hours,' he persisted. 'Non-stop,' he added with feeling.

'Yeah, well, it's a joke, innit?' Atouille replied. 'Bloody good one an' all.'

'It is?' Fraud queried.

'Must be,' answered Chet. 'Or we wouldn't be laughing, would we?'

Fraud considered this for a moment. 'True,' he said. 'You may have a point there, lads. Can we get on now, please?'

'Wot? Oh, yeah, right. C'mon, Chet.'

'All right. Get to the other side, *tsssk* . . .'

The pattering started again a few seconds later; likewise the whispering and sniggering. But now, when he listened carefully, Fraud could clearly make out phrases like *cross the road* and *get to the other side*. They were still at it when the tunnel went round a corner and abruptly ended, leaving them standing on the edge of a precipice.

Looked at objectively, it was a break in the pipe. Beyond the lip of the chasm, about a foot away, Fraud could see the tunnel continuing, and ragged edges where something had broken through it. But he couldn't really take much in; his head was swimming, and all he could think of was how wonderfully satisfying and fulfilling it'd be to backtrack a foot or so, take a nice long run-up and jump over that edge into the empty space below. He could almost hear the wind in his ears, and in his mind's eye he could clearly see the ground rushing up to meet him, like a long-sundered lover on a station platform. And, in the still centre of his mind, he could hear a small, urgent voice, chanting:

Go lemmings! Go lemmings!

He closed his eyes, but that just made the picture clearer. On the other side the rats, who had jumped the break, were whispering and giggling, apparently still intoxicated with the heady wine of mirth. For Fraud, however, there was another, more compelling intoxication, as the voice in his brain chanted:

Go lemmings! Go lemmings! Go! Go! Go!

'Hey!' he yelled. 'You two. I need a hand.'

'Huh?'

'I mean paw. How the hell'm I supposed to get across this lot?'

All he could see was the tip of a tail; and beyond it, he heard Chet's voice, far away.

'Jump,' it said.

Jump. Jump. Jump. No echo this time. He tried to fight the command, but his legs were already backing him away, his muscles contracting for the short, fascinating leap. It would be so . . .

Stupid? With a snap like a rubber band breaking, his head cleared, and he was no longer a lemming but the Prime Minister, admittedly trapped for some reason in a rodent body but otherwise the master of his fate and the captain of his soul, standing on the edge of a broken drainpipe. Silly, he muttered to himself. Don't know what came over me. All right, so I may be a little bit out of touch with my true self right now, but one thing I do know is that statesmen don't obey weird inner voices commanding them to jump off things. No. No way.

That's what the electorate is for.

★

Imagine, if you will, John Barleycorn, thrusting his head up through the bare earth in the burgeoning spring. As he breaks through into the light he knows perfectly well that in six months' time a maniac with a Massey Ferguson will be along to cut his head off and bash his brains out, just exactly the way it's been these uncounted thousands of years; but he does it nevertheless, because that's what he does.

In much the same frame of mind, Karen picked up the phone, tucked it under her ear and said, 'Kawaguchiya Integrated Circuits UK Helpline Desk, can I help you?' She knew what was going to happen; at the other end of the line there'd be some frustrated, confused keyboard jockey who'd just watched the entire July figures spiral away into cybernetic oblivion, desperate to find somebody to blame.

In a sense, she often thought, the KIC helpline was like the Samaritans, in that people only tended to call up on it when they were at the end of their rope and suicidal. The difference lay in the fact that where the Samaritans are there to stop the punter killing himself, the Helpline's function was to channel the helplessness and despair into basically therapeutic rage against the poor fool who answered the call. Hi, I'm Karen. Blame me.

'Hello?'

Karen frowned. The voice seemed very faint and far away, and was quickly replaced by the sound of payphone pips. These lasted rather a long time; long enough, in fact, for the caller to have gone away and earned the coins by playing the guitar in the bus station waiting room.

'Hello?'

'Kawaguchiya Integrated Circuits UK Helpline Desk, Karen speaking. How can I help you?'

'Hi,' said the voice. 'I'm calling from—' The pips went. Puzzling; there wasn't anywhere in the country, as far as

Karen was aware, where ten pence bought a mere seventeen words. More expensive even than consulting a lawyer.

'Hello?'

'Hello,' Karen said. 'What can I—?'

'It's this computer,' said the voice. 'It's not working properly.'

'I see. Can you give me the model number and—'

The pips, again. Karen swore. There had to be a better way to do this, one rather less likely to fuse her brain into one solid lump of aggravation. Accordingly, when the pips cleared for the third time, she cut in quickly.

'Give me your number,' she said. 'I'll call you back.'

'Um. There could be a problem with that. You see, I'm rather –'

Beepbeepbeepbeepbeepbeep.

'– a long way away. And I'm not sure this phone takes incoming calls anyway, you see, because—'

Beepbeepbeepbeepbeepbeep.

Karen took a deep breath. 'Let's try, shall we?' she said.

The caller started to dictate a number. It was very long and quite unlike any phone number she'd ever come across before, and the *beepbeepbeepbeepbeepbeeps* went twice while she was taking it down. Still, she reflected, I'm here to help, and it's not my phone bill. She put the receiver down and tapped the number in.

'Hello?'

'Hello. Right then, now where were we? If you could give me the model number and year of manufacture . . .'

The voice sounded a trifle sheepish as it interrupted her. 'I don't think there is a model number,' it said. 'Custom job, you see. Only one of its kind.'

'Oh yes?' Karen pulled a face. KIC didn't do custom jobs; so the caller was either ignorant, thick or using some cobbled-together mess that probably bore no ongoing resemblance to anything the company had ever made, with the possible exception of the stuff they fished out of the shredder bins once a fortnight. 'Any identifying marks at all?'

'There's a name,' the caller replied. 'Mainframe.'

'Well, I'm afraid – *what did you say?*'

'Mainframe,' the caller repeated. 'That's what it's called. Or at least that's what we call it. Ring any bells with you?'

Karen pursed her lips. 'Only the ones on the other leg,' she replied. 'There's only one KIC called Mainframe and that belongs to – well, there's only one. What's yours *really*—?'

'This is that one,' said the voice, sounding slightly higher and more querulous. 'The one and only, so to speak. Really and truly. And it's not working properly. Look, are you going to help me? You're my last hope.'

It was at this point that Karen finally lost her temper; or, to be precise, put her temper carefully away in a safe place where she'd be sure to find it again. 'Look,' she said, 'I don't know who you are, but I'm fairly certain you're not the President of the United States, so obviously your computer isn't Mainframe, and—'

'Is that who they told you owns Mainframe? Gosh.'

'Yes, it is, because he does. Now, I do have other callers waiting, so—'

'Is that really what they told you?'

There is, unfortunately, a rule which says that KIC helpline operators can't slam the phone down. They can't even tell callers what they think of them. It's calculated that the repressed energy wasted by KIC helpline operators not being allowed to let off steam under these circumstances would be enough to light Boston for a week. 'Yes,' Karen said. 'And now . . .'

'I've found a code number, if that's any help.'

'Huh?'

'There's a little bit of paper, with a number scribbled down on it, wedged in this operator's manual, and someone's written *KIC security code*. Shall I read it out to you?'

Karen sighed, audibly, producing a sound like an InterCity train just entering a tunnel at top speed. 'If you must,' she said. 'Then I really do have to—'

'All right,' said the caller. 'It's One.'

There was a moment's silence, during which Karen's jaw dropped like share prices on a bad day. 'Could you repeat that, please?' she eventually croaked.

'Sure,' the caller replied. 'One.'

'Please hold.' Karen put down the phone, blinked four times and rummaged in her desk drawer for the loose-leaf binder where she filed the office memos. After she'd flicked through forty-odd pages of sternly worded directives about paperclip conservation and taking empty coffee cups back to the kitchen after use, she found the one she'd been looking for. She read it, read it again, muttered something under her breath, and picked the phone up.

'Are you still there?' she asked. 'Sir?' she added.

'Still here.'

How to put this? A difficult question to phrase. She did her best.

'Are you sure,' she said, 'that you're not the President of the United States?'

'Pretty fair average sure,' the caller replied. 'It'd be a difficult thing to be without noticing. People'd keep phoning you up, for one thing.'

Karen kept calm. Not easy; the orchestra who finished their set while the *Titanic* went down under their feet couldn't have managed it, but Karen did. She glanced at the folder, open at the memo she'd just looked up. It said, in capitals, italics and bold face, whatever code number One tells you, believe it. Oh well, she told herself.

'In that case,' she said, 'who are you?'

'Ah,' replied the caller.

Sleep, the thief who breaks into our bodies at night and steals a third of our lifetimes, fancied he heard someone coming and legged it out of Len's brain, abandoning the bag marked *Swag*. It contained an idea.

Accordingly, when Len came round and found himself lying on his back with a crick in his neck and his mouth open, he discovered a perfectly finished, mirror-polished inspiration lying on the floor of his mind, for all the world as if the stork had left it there. He examined it.

'Yes,' he said aloud. 'Why not?'

He sat up, and at once looked across the workshop at the machine. For one horrible fragment of a second he thought it wasn't there any more; then he moved his head a little and saw it, and thought *Ah, that's all right then.*

According to the physicists, there's this stuff called potential energy. It's what a large stone or a ton weight has in that split second between toppling off the edge of a high cliff and starting to fall. In that moment, all the effort and strength taken in lugging the wretched thing up there suddenly comes to life, as it were; then gravity pounces, like an independent financial adviser leaping upon a defenceless lottery winner, and takes it all away again. *Bump!* goes the stone on the ground below, and the energy earths itself and runs to waste, leaving the physicist's assistants with the cheerful job of heaving a ton of research material on to the pallet truck and hauling it back up the hill.

In the pale light of morning, filtered through a cobwebbed window, the machine glowed with enough potential energy to blow all the fuses in the National Grid. Len stood up, walked over to it and patted the table gently.

'Down, boy,' he muttered. 'Be with you in a minute.'

First, he had to empty some fluids out of his body and put some solids into it. Then he'd need a large sheet of paper, a ruler, a set square, a protractor and a sharp pencil. And some materials, as well; lots of them, specialised stuff like titanium and palladium and tungsten and beryllium copper, as well as twelve different kinds of steel and nine flavours of aluminum alloy. And a computer, of course, and a three-horse electric motor, and a few other bits and pieces. And then . . .

Was it his imagination, or did a fat blue slug of potential energy just arc across the gap between the cutter and the table? Better hurry, because we've got a busy day ahead of us, you and I.

One of the glorious things about the city of Birmingham is that there are people you can call up on the phone and ask for six feet of three-inch-section square titanium bar; and they don't say 'Huh?' or 'What in the name of fun's three-inch-section square titanium bar?' or anything like that. They just ask you if you want it delivered, and whether you're paying cash or on account.

'Um,' Len replied. 'I haven't actually got an account with you, but . . .'

'Cash, then,' the voice on the other end of the line said. 'That's fine, if you can just drop by at the office. Soon as we've got the money, I'll get the stuff to you.'

Money. Curse. Len sat down, frowning, and applied his mind. He was going to need rather a lot of the stuff, and he had the idea that Neville wasn't good for that much, even if he sold his collection of CDs and his cowboy boots. What to do?

Fool. Now you're starting to think like a human. What do you do if there's something you need, but haven't got? Easy. You make it.

So he called up another supplier and ordered a hundred feet of seven-eighths brass rod, which Neville's Visa card could just about afford without selling anything. When it arrived, he sliced it up into nine thousand six hundred discs, each an eighth of an inch thick; a job which took the machine just over three hours. While he'd been waiting for the brass to arrive, he'd milled up two hardened steel dies and adapted the machine's vertical feed to make a high-power press. Add a knurling wheel in the power tailstock, set up a simple automatic feed and collect the resulting newly minted pound coins in a sack as they're spat out of the hopper at the back end, while phoning the supplier for more brass rod with the other hand.

At the end of a very boring but rather productive day, he had six plastic dustbins full of the things, which solved one problem. He'd also drawn up the plans, worked out the quantities and ordered the materials. There was another spate of thefts by the sandman, and then he was ready to start.

First, he pressed the body shells out of eighth-inch gauge-plate, ending up with something that looked like a space-age suit of armour, or C3PO's party frock. Next, the action parts, milled from titanium and carbon steel. The frame next; mostly high-tensile aluminum alloys and stainless steel – foul stuff which produces long strings of razor-sharp swarf, like a garrotter's cheesewire suddenly come to life. The fiddly bit came next – lots of electrical contacts, cut out of material as soft as butter and as sticky as mud, bogging down the cutters and causing Len to dredge the undersilt of Neville's memory for a wide selection of abstruse synonyms for 'Bugger!' After that, there were odd bits and pieces; bearings and bushings and gaskets and the like, which had to be pressed out of compacted phosphor bronze, a process remarkably similar to building a suspension bridge out of tapioca pudding. There were a few setbacks, the odd broken cutter and misaligned hole, further ramraids from Mr Sleepy, a shortfall of precision-made little brass discs that had to be made up before the suppliers would part with a lousy few grams of nickel barium, and a rather ticklish moment when a homicidal strip of knife-edged swarf chased him three times round the workshop before wrapping itself round the chair. Nothing, though, that he couldn't handle. Piece of cake, really.

Man's reach may exceed Man's grasp; but it doesn't take Einstein to come up with the idea of a pair of lazy tongs. The question which kept on hammering away on the inside of his mind was, Since it's so easy, why haven't They ever done this?

All the components made; just a question now of putting it all together. He laid the parts out on the floor of the workshop, consulted the diagram and set to work. It helped, of course, that he'd taken the time to think it all through beforehand, so that everything could be fitted together without needing six pairs of hands and a seventh to catch the little flying springs and tumbling grubscrews. Even so, when he thought of the hash his predecessor had made of his version of the same basic concept, he couldn't help wondering how the guy had got into this line of business in the first place. Someone who tries to make high-quality precision machinery out of a length of second-hand rib must be either bizarrely imaginative or as thick as a triple-decker sandwich.

And when it was all done, the end product sat up, opened its eyes and spoke. What it actually said was, 'Doctor Frankenstein, I presume,' but Len can be forgiven for that. He'd been working non-stop for seven days and hadn't had much sleep.

Maria looked at the screen like a cat watching a mouse and wondering what kind of tin-opener it would need to open it. She wasn't entirely sure she'd got the hang of being human herself; being present at the birth of a sentient limited company wasn't something she could easily take in her stride as being one of those things that just happen. Presumably it was quite rare. For all she knew, you could go weeks at a time and not see one.

Sorry, the screen said. *No offence. I thought you were the human; you know, that dolly-bird type with the laminated fingernails and vacant expression sitting just underneath you.*

'That's me too.'

Is it? Oh . . . Isn't that a bit unusual? Being a painting and a human at the same time?

Maria shrugged. 'I think so,' she said. 'But I'm new at this game myself.' She smiled. 'I think we're both in pretty much the same boat. We can learn together, if you like.'

Gosh. Can we? That'll be fun.

'Funny you should use that particular word,' Maria replied. 'Fun. Or rather happiness, as in pursuit of, I get the impression that's what we're here for.'

Really?

Maria nodded. 'Seems to be. There's no other possible explanation. You're the clever one, you think about it.'

All over the world, KIC computers registered a massive power surge as countless millions of bytes tried to puzzle it out. *Maybe you're right,* the screen mused.

'I'm sure of it.'

Now then, let's consider this properly. The screen turned up its brightness a little, and covered itself with a dazzling display of graphics, which flicked by so fast that all Maria got was a bewildering impression of lights, shapes and primary colours.

'Is that you thinking?' she asked. 'All the pictures.'

Presumably. I suppose I think in pictures. Oh hell, have I said something rude again? I didn't mean to.

'On the contrary, I think that was a compliment. You

were saying we're far better at getting a message across than mere words. Or you can say things in pictures that words can't express. Or maybe it's just because you're only a few minutes old and haven't even got as far as Peter-and-Jane books yet.'

Maybe. Right, here goes. On the one hand we have human beings, right? On the other hand, there are all the other things which do roughly the same things as humans; like animals, or paintings, or limited companies, or God. There's about – hang on, computing, will whoever it is in Los Angeles please get off the line, there's some of us trying to think – about nine things they all have more or less in common. Some of them can do some of them, others can't, but let's call them the parameters. You getting all this?

'Getting in the sense of writing it down? No, sorry.'

Getting as in understanding. I can do graphics if you'd prefer.

Maria frowned. 'Stick to the words,' she replied. 'I don't know if there's anything in the rules about pictures looking at pictures, but it doesn't feel right, somehow. Maybe it makes you go blind.'

Please yourself. Let's say, for the sake of argument, there's these nine parameters. And what are they, I hear you ask.

'No you don't.'

Huh?

'I didn't say anything.'

Try keeping it that way, will you? I've diverted the traffic control computers for the whole of Toronto to do this. One lapse of concentration and there'll be tailbacks as far as Winnipeg. All right, I believe the nine parameters to be the ability to make things, the ability to communicate, a limited lifespan, sentience or intelligence, a lack of serious inhibition or limitation—

'That rules you out, then. You're a limited company.'

Sorry, I thought you were interested. I'll shut up now.

'No, please go on.' Maria grinned sheepishly. 'I seem to have acquired this impish and frivolous personality from somewhere and I haven't quite got the hang of turning it off.'

All right. But try and keep it under control, will you? Each time I get interrupted, it plays merry hell with the Dow Jones Index. Where'd I got to?

'Limitations.'

Ah yes. Or inhibitions. That's number five, isn't it?

'No, six. Sorry, yes, five. Go on.'

Six is the ability to co-operate with others, seven is infallibility, eight is freedom from moral restraint, which is just six in fancy dress now I come to think of it, but so what? That's eight. Nine . . . Got it. Nine is the ability to initiate action, as opposed to only doing what you're told to do. What d'you reckon?

'Great,' Maria replied. 'What's it for?'

I shall pretend I didn't hear that. Let's start off with God, shall we? God can make things and communicate, but he's not limited by lifespan or any physical limitation. He's sentient and infallible and can initiate action, but he's severely restricted by moral constraints and he can't co-operate with others because there aren't any others like him to co-operate with. Animals can co-operate and initiate action, and a few of them can make things; beavers, for instance—

'They can make lots of little beavers, for a start.'

Now look what you've made me do. Thanks to you, half the phones in Tokyo have just gone dead.

'Pleasant break for them, probably. Sorry, promise not to do it again.'

Apart from those two or three things, animals don't really signify. Now pictures can communicate – that's what they're for – but so long as nobody sets fire to them or stores them in a damp cellar they're as near as dammit immortal. They can be perfect and without limitation: you know, beautiful women and handsome men, and the fact that if the artist gets the anatomy wrong they'd probably not be able to breathe if they were actually alive doesn't affect them in the least.

'Tell me about it,' said Maria, with feeling.

Quite. Finally, your painting has no moral constraints what-soever. Probably explains why you keep interrupting me.

'Hm?'

No respect, you see. Now us limited companies make things, we communicate, we're immortal so long as we stay in profit and some clown doesn't forget to file the accounts with the Companies Registry, we're sort of intelligent and don't you dare say anything, but we're restricted by all sorts of laws and regulations and human customs and assumptions; we can co-operate and we don't really have any moral restraints, and we can initiate action like nobody's business. No pun intended.

'Or detected, for that matter. Oh, *business*, I see, very good. Go on.'

Finally, read the screen, *there's human beings. Obviously they're mortal, they're certainly fallible and limited as to what they can and can't do like you wouldn't believe. Mostly,* the screen added, using bold face to signify bemused incomprehension, *self-inflicted. Oh well, that's their business, I suppose. And some of them are subject to moral restraints, and some aren't. And there we are.*

'Absolutely,' Maria said, yawning. 'That really was frightfully interesting. And now you'd probably better turn the traffic lights back on in Toronto, before they start jumping out of their cars and hitting each other with tyre irons.'

Hang on, will you? The point of all this is, there's one thing that only humans do, and none of the rest even try. You want to know what that is?

Maria nodded. 'Very much. But you could have told me that without all this scientific stuff, and they wouldn't have a huge carbon-monoxide cloud threatening to poison half Ontario.'

All right, Miss Clever. What humans do, and nothing else even tries to do, is pursue happiness. Now do you see?

'Just a minute.' Maria's brow furrowed like a drawn curtain. 'That can't be right. What about animals? You ever seen a cat? They pursue happiness.'

They obey instinct. Genetic programming. Hardly the same thing as falling in love or collecting first-day covers.

'All right, then,' Maria persevered. 'What about you? Don't say you cry yourself to sleep every time you double your pre-tax profit.'

You may find this hard to believe, young woman, but making money and pursuing happiness aren't necessarily the same thing. People confuse the two, but I can't help it if the world is full of idiots.

'Fair enough,' Maria conceded. 'And I'll admit, you don't get to hunt much fun when you're a painting. But how about God? You're not going to tell me . . .'

The screen went blank and flashed some graphics before the next words appeared. *Do me a favour,* they read. *It may be that God pursues happiness, but only with a flyswat or a rolled-up newspaper firmly grasped in one hand. And as for His own happiness, just think about it, will you? Poor guy's omnipresent, never gets a moment's peace, lives His life entirely for others. You ever heard He's got a hobby? Collects stamps? Builds scale models of alternative universes out of matchsticks? Even His son was immaculately conceived. Even actuaries have more fun than that.*

Maria shrugged. 'So,' she said, 'point taken. Only human beings pursue happiness. Actually, from what I've seen of them, they can't do it terribly well, or why are they all so dreadfully miserable?'

Ah. There you have me. Maybe happiness keeps getting away. But they pursue it, which is the point. Likewise, it must be what they're for; because when you look at all the other parameters, they're not much good at anything else.

'I suppose you're right,' Maria replied after a while.

'They make things, but machines do that much better. They communicate—'

But not nearly as well as computers, meaning me. If they could communicate worth a tinker's cuss, there wouldn't be any wars, for a start. They're as moral as a barrelful of ferrets. They're sort of intelligent, but me and God have 'em stuffed up a drain for brains. They can co-operate, but only for about ten minutes before they start fighting. Fallible goes without saying. The morality thing, too; who else but a load of born losers could come up with the pretty notion that burning people at the stake somehow makes them better people? They can initiate action, but it's mostly a case of parking a bright idea at the top of a hill and then taking the handbrake off. No, it must be pursuing happiness, or what the Hell's the point in them?

Maria sat for a while, staring at a point on the opposite wall a few inches above the top of the screen. 'Fair enough,' she said. 'In that case, let's go for it.'

Now you're talking.

'Assuming,' she added thoughtfully, 'we can ever find out what on earth it is.'

CHAPTER FIVE

'**A**re you sure?' Artofel said.

The man looked at him. 'Well, yes,' he replied. 'Of course,' he added. 'One hundred per cent,' he concluded. 'Why?'

'It's just . . .' Artofel shrugged. 'No, forget I spoke. Now then, have you decided which hymns you'd like?'

'What were you just about to say?' the man demanded. He seemed a trifle put out, and maybe a little thoughtful.

'Nothing, nothing. How about you, Tricia? Any particular hymns you'd set your heart on?'

'I don't know any hymns, actually,' the young woman replied. 'Except "Rudolph the Red-Nosed Reindeer". That's a hymn, isn't it? I mean, it's Christmassy, and Christmas is all religious, isn't it?'

'In a sense,' Artofel replied. 'Although, to be savagely frank with you, I've never really seen "Rudolph the Red-Nosed Reindeer" quite as what you'd call a really sort of out-and-out, fully fledged wedding-type hymn. Speaking for myself, you understand.'

'Oh,' replied the young woman, her eyes accusing him of making difficulties. 'What about "Jingle Bells", then? Surely "Jingle Bells" is a hymn. It's old, isn't it?'

There was a moment of deep silence while Artofel engaged the four-wheel drive on his diplomacy. 'It's certainly more, um, in keeping than "Rudolph the Red-Nosed Reindeer",' he replied cautiously. 'I mean, of the two I'd probably go for "Jingle Bells" every time. On the other hand, maybe we could explore some other poss-ibilities together and find something you'd like even more. Okay?'

The young woman shrugged. 'Don't mind,' she said. 'I'm not that bothered one way or the other. So long as it's cheerful,' she added, frowning. 'I know, how about "God Save the Queen"?'

'That's in the hymn book, certainly,' Artofel replied, pursing his lips. 'Which means you wouldn't have to have copies specially printed.'

'And it's got God in it,' the young woman pointed out. 'That'll do, then. Now, about the flowers.'

'Just a moment.' The man raised his hand, like a small child wanting to leave the room. 'I want to know what you meant by *Are you sure?*'

'Oh.' Artofel rubbed his chin. 'Look, I wish you'd forget about that. Just me sort of thinking aloud, really.'

'Then think aloud some more.'

'Is this going to take long?' the young woman inter-rupted. 'Only we got to sort out the flowers.'

Artofel steepled his fingers. He'd often wondered why vicars did that; now he knew. It gave them something to do with their hands other than strangling their parishioners. 'What I was thinking was, look, obviously you two are very much in love, you're perfectly suited, I know you'll have a very long and happy life together. By saying *Are you sure?* I was just being a sort of—'

'Well?'

Artofel swallowed. 'Devil's advocate,' he said. 'Now please, let's just forget all about it and carry on.'

The man looked at him. 'You don't think so,' he said.

'Excuse me?'

'You think it's a bad idea, Trish and me getting married,' the man said accusingly. 'Why?'

'No, no,' Artofel said quickly. 'Perish the thought, really. Really and truth—'

'Come on, spit it out. Why don't you think we should get married?'

'But I do, honestly,' Artofel said vehemently. 'I mean, in some cases the fact that the man's twenty years older than the girl might well be a problem, but I'm sure it's something you've both thought about and talked through, and you're clearly satisfied in your own minds that it's not going to make difficulties, so—'

'Hang on,' said the young woman. 'I hadn't thought of that. Hey, that means when I'm forty, he'll be –' she counted on her fingers '– sixty-two. That's old,' she added, frowning.

'Sixty-*three*,' the man said, with a hint of impatience. 'Look, is that all, because . . .'

'Actually,' Artofel said, with a wry little smile, 'the thought had crossed my mind that, what with Tricia having such a lively, outgoing personality and being a barmaid, and you being a professional pallbearer, perhaps you might not be, how can I put this, temperamentally quite ideally compatible, but hey, that just goes to show how wrong you can be.'

The young woman scowled. 'Don't you take that tone about me being a barmaid,' she said severely. 'And anyway, Derek's going to pack in the pallbearing and we're going to have our own pub, so . . .'

'No I'm not,' the man interrupted. 'I like pallbearing.'

'Yes you bloody well are, excuse me, Vicar,' the young woman replied. 'I'm not marrying some miserable bugger who wears black suits and smells of embalming fluid. No, when we sell your house we'll buy a nice little pub somewhere and . . .'

'Sell my house? Who said anything about selling my house?'

'Um,' Artofel muttered. 'Excuse me, but . . .'

'If you think I'm living in that nasty dark shed of a house of yours, you need your plugs cleaning,' the young woman retorted. 'No, we'll sell it and buy a nice . . .'

'But what about my owls?' the man said. 'Best collection of stuffed owls in the West Midlands. I'm not having them stuck up in some lounge bar where people can pull their feathers and shove crisp packets between their legs, thank you very much.'

'Too right you're not, because they're going in the skip,' the young woman snarled. 'Disgusting bloody things. Morbid, I call it, having dead things all over the place.'

'Tricia,' said Artofel soothingly. 'Derek, maybe we should all just, um . . .'

'They're a damn sight more tasteful than your stupid teddy-bears,' the man replied angrily. 'You should see them, Vicar. Pink, the lot of them.'

The young woman glowered at him. 'I made them myself,' she protested.

'Yes, and can't you tell,' answered the man nastily. 'The best of 'em looks like it's just gone twelve rounds with Frank Bruno. Kindest thing'd be to have 'em all put to sleep.'

Quietly, Artofel groaned. He had, after all, only been trying to do the right thing. That's what vicars are supposed to do, surely?

'You're *horrible*,' the young woman yowled. 'And you're ignorant. And you snore.'

'No I don't.'

'Yes you do.'

'No I don't. Ask your sister.'

A small ring, thrown with considerable force, missed the man by the thickness of the skin on a cup of tea and hit a china paperweight on the mantelpiece, reducing it to shrapnel. A door slammed.

'If you go after her . . .' Artofel suggested.

'I might just get my head kicked in,' the man replied. 'This is all your fault.'

'But . . .'

'I got a good mind to smash your face, only you're a vicar.' The man sneered. 'You'll be hearing from my solicitor,' he said. He retrieved the ring, which had embedded itself in the plaster, made a derogatory remark about the clergy in general, and left.

As Artofel tidied away the wreckage, he reflected that if they'd got married, they'd probably have been utterly wretched for as long as it takes to get a divorce, provided they both lived that long. He'd done good. He'd done them both a favour.

They didn't seem terribly pleased about it.

When their tempers cooled, and they'd had a chance to think it over . . . The teddy bears. The owls. Her sister. By the time they each got home, they'd probably be thanking their lucky stars he'd saved them from themselves.

He put it out of his mind and set about making himself a light supper. He was just taking the steak and kidney pie out of the microwave when there was a sound of breaking glass and a heavy thump. He ran back into the front room to find a brick lying in the middle of the floor. Wrapped round it was a sheet of paper, on which was written:

YOU RUINED MY LIFE YOU BASTARD YOU'LL PAY FOR THIS.

which suggested that one of them had indeed thought it over and come to a rather different conclusion. He shrugged his shoulders, hoping vehemently that at least the other one would realise the truth of the matter, and started buttering bread. He'd done two slices when he heard the letterbox snap shut, and smelt something burning.

Fortunately, his host had one of those small kitchen-fire extinguishers they sell for dealing with self-igniting chip pans, and the petrol-soaked carpet in the hall hadn't really got going properly by the time he arrived on the scene. Nevertheless, it was a rather depressing reaction to his first genuine good deed. It was enough to put you off righteousness for life.

However, he reflected as he ate his supper, even if they didn't appreciate what he'd done for them, at least he'd done it. The potential disaster had been averted. Who needs gratitude when you can have a sense of achievement?

The meal was all right, if you happened to like dead cow in scrunched-up grass seeds with more scrunched-up grass seeds coated in cow fat, but he couldn't help wishing he was back in the staff canteen in Flipside. Oh, those mixed grills! Oh, those barbecued spare ribs! He washed it down with a can of ancient lager, which tasted of three parts dissolved aluminium and one part yeast, and went to bed.

It was while he was lying on his back, wide awake in the darkness, that an unpleasant thought struck him. The reason he wasn't sleeping, apart from the dead cow and scrunched-up grass seeds, was that he was quite understandably worried about how, when and where the witness elimination program was going to get around to him; but what if he'd got it all wrong? After all, why were they biding their time? Not like Flipside to let the embers cool under their feet. Perhaps it wasn't as straightforward as he'd first thought.

Perhaps someone was doing this on purpose.

Not just an ordinary cock-up, the sort of thing that happens every day here in Entropy's backyard. Maybe it was part of some deep-laid scheme, with himself as one of the cogs in the infernal machine?

Paranoia, he told himself as he bashed the pillow. Comes with the monkey suit. On the other hand, it would explain a whole lot of things, answer a whole lot of questions that he admittedly hadn't thought of yet but which were undoubtedly out there somewhere, prowling around in the dark and ripping open dustbin bags. A conspiracy . . .

But why? How would it help anybody to have a Duke of Hell catapulted into the body of a minister of the Church? Not for sabotage or inside information; we're all on the same side, remember. Unless, of course, it's being done in what you might term an unofficial capacity; and that would suggest that someone had managed to get inside Mainframe and play about with it, and that was of course unthinkable.

Well. He'd done it, of course, but that was different. He'd only gone in to snoop about, not fiddle with the cosmic order. If any fool could play musical bodies just by hacking into the Web, it'd have been a piece of cake for him to get himself out of here and back home where he belonged. No, you needed really high-level codes to do things like body-swapping.

Somehow, that only made it worse. Suppose there was a conspiracy – a coup in Heaven or just someone trying to rip off a large sum of money – and it involved the sort of people who had access to that sort of code. Didn't bear thinking about; because the only people that could be were the Family itself.

Eeek.

No. Forget it. Too much dead cow and milk residues late at night.

Unless . . .

So. Maybe he was right; what exactly did he propose doing about it? Inform the proper authorities? And besides, if the Big Boss really was omniscient like they all said, then He'd know about it already.

Unless . . .

Maybe he *did*. Now that really was a scary thought.

He was still thinking that one over at half past ten that morning; at which time, Tricia and Derek phoned him from the local register office to tell him, among many other things, that they'd just got married and so he could (to paraphrase slightly) go jump in the lake. Nothing, they informed him, could stand in the way of true love.

Well. Quite.

Oh for a muse of fire (and a pair of asbestos gloves), to be able to do justice to the strange and wonderful adventures, the desperate dangers, the razor's-edge escapes, the fabulous encounters that Dermot Fraud had to endure before he reached the telephone box. Or rather, oh for a thirty-million-dollar budget, a cast of thousands, Harrison Ford in a lemming outfit and a team of accountants working round the clock to help decide what to do with the profits.

No offers? The film rights are, inexplicably, still available. Very well, then. Be like that.

Having reached the telephone box, Dermot Fraud sighed, closed his eyes and collapsed into a small furry ball in the shelter of a discarded crisp packet. He was exhausted, starving, emotionally drained and bleeding from a small cut over his left eye, the result of not ducking quite fast enough when he felt the shadow of a cat on the back of his neck. But he was here; only a few feet away from a telephone, at the other end of which was safety.

Only a few feet; straight up. With a sudden hollow

feeling inside that had nothing to do with the fact that he hadn't eaten for two days, he lifted his head. Through the glass door of the phone booth he could see the receiver, perched in its cradle. Even if he managed to get the door open – a feat comparable to raising Stonehenge single-handed, for a lemming – how was he going to climb up to the receiver, lift it, dial a number and put a coin he hadn't got into the slot?

How indeed?

He allowed himself a ten-minute interval for utter despair, and then forced himself to think positive. From the depths of his memory he dragged out examples from history of desperate obstacles overcome, astounding feats achieved in the face of overwhelming odds. Hannibal and the Alps; Bruce and the spider; Cortes and the conquest of Mexico; Rorke's Drift; the rescue of the *Apollo 13* astronauts; Neil Kinnock managing to lose the 1992 general election. All right, he said to himself, if they could do it, so can I.

Except . . .

Well, yes. They were human, and I'm a . . .

No I'm *not*; I'm *not* a lemming. This is just a phase I'm going through, that's all. Rodenthood is only skin deep. Inside every lemming there's a human being struggling to get out.

First, there was the question of the door. It was one of the last few surviving red telephone boxes, with the heavy glass and metal doors – when I'm out of this nightmare and safely back in Number Ten, Fraud vowed, there will be a great purge of all red telephone boxes the length and breadth of this great country of ours – which meant that in lemming terms it weighed roughly the equivalent of Nelson's column. In order to get in, he'd have to open it at least two inches. On his own. With nothing but his four bare paws.

All right. Let's think about this.

Archimedes. Give me a firm place and a long enough lever and I could move the Earth. What was the technical term? Mechanical advantage? Something along those lines. Me for some of that.

A lever; and something for it to pivot round, a fulcrum. Oughtn't to be too difficult.

The fulcrum wasn't. It took him only a few minutes to locate a flat stone roughly the size of his head, which would do admirably. Having first looked under it for reporters (old habits die hard) he managed, by dint of extreme effort, to shove and lemmingpaw it up against the foot of the door. Short exhaustion break; then he began the search for a lever.

There was a piece of wood, two by four and a foot long, which could have been specially made for the purpose; after half an hour of the most painful effort of his life, he'd managed to move it a quarter of an inch at one end, just far enough to get it jammed against a stone.

There was a bicycle spoke, which he found he was able to drag, about a sixteenth of an inch at a time between twenty-minute intervals, and ram into the gap between door and frame. That done, he scuttled wearily to the other end, put his weight against it and shoved.

The spoke bent. Then it sprang back. Fraud was catapulted eighteen inches through the air and landed in a puddle. Back to the drawing board.

The hell with this, he muttered to himself, as he crawled out and shook the mud out of his fur. It can't be all that difficult, surely. After all, if we can dig a tunnel under the channel and put a lemming on the Moon, then we ought to be able to . . .

But we didn't put a lemming on the Moon. Did we?

Fraud cringed. The voice inside his head telling him to jump had been bad enough; if he was really beginning to believe he was a lemming, he might as well curl up and die now, and save his party the trauma of a mid-term by-election.

I AM NOT A LEMMING, he reminded himself. I AM A HUMAN BEING.

So. Bugger leverage. Damn silly idea in the first place.

The trouble with levers, he realised, was that he was being over-ambitious. What he needed was a little-and-often approach; little drops of water, little grains of sand.

Wedges.

Drive enough wedges into the crack, and eventually you'll open it up enough to crawl through. Much better idea; not so flamboyant, but far more realistic. Practical. Pragmatic. British.

Which only left the trivial problem of what he could use for wedges. Unfortunately, as he found out after a couple of hours of frustrated searching, wedge shapes don't occur all that often in nature, or at least not on a scale that would be of any use to him. In the end he tried driving small bits of gravel into the crack with a larger bit of gravel used as a hammer. After he'd bashed himself in the ribs for the seventh time, he gave it up.

All right, he conceded, point taken. I'm failing because I'm thinking in human terms. If I was a lemming wanting to get into this phone box, what'd I do?

Easy. I'd tunnel my way in. Great burrowers, lemmings. Somewhere in the species memory there were some fascinating statistics about lemming earth-moving capacity which, if he was translating them correctly, suggested that the average lemming digs the equivalent of the Bakerloo Line once every nine months. Or something of the sort. Anyway, he could dig.

He dug.

To his surprise, the technique came remarkably easily. It

was like doing the breast-stroke through nearly set concrete while running up an extremely powerful down escalator; but the mighty lemming forepaws were up to the task, and even in his rather dilapidated, unfed and unrested state, he realised he had reserves of stamina that a human being could only dream of. Under the onslaught of his keenly scrabbling paws, the heavy clay soil seemed to melt away like snow. Half an hour or so more at this rate of progress, and . . .

Ouch!

He diagnosed the cause of the horrible jarring pain in both forearms as the after-effect of trying to burrow into solid concrete, the sort they used to put down on the floors of old-fashioned red telephone boxes. So disconcerted was he by this unforeseen setback that he was still standing there cursing and hugging his injured paws to his chest when the unshored sides of the tunnel slowly began to cave in . . .

Marvellous excavator, your lemming. Thanks to his superbly adapted paws and impressive inherent stamina, it only took him two hours to dig himself out again.

If at first you don't succeed, take the hint. Fraud sank gasping on to the top of his newly dug mound of earth, stared up at the Everest-high phone-box door and whimpered a little. All that effort, all that ingenuity and application, and here he still was, slumped on the wrong side of a poxy door. He'd tried everything he could think of and—

Except, apparently, trotting round to the other side of the box and crawling in through the broken square of glass an inch or so above the ground; the one he'd been too busy to notice earlier. Easy enough mistake to make. Particularly if you happen to be a pillock.

Because he'd been working so hard for so long, it took him ninety-five per cent of his remaining strength just to crawl through the conveniently placed lemming-sized hole and collapse in a heap on the other side. With the five per cent change, he rolled on to his back and gazed upwards at the telephone, as high and unattainable as the furthest star.

Bloody but unbowed and never say die are, perhaps, just a more upbeat way of saying too thick to learn from experience; but being so near to a telephone, so close to it that he could almost feel its hard smoothness pressed against his ear, sent the adrenaline gushing into his bloodstream. One last enormous convulsive effort would be all it would take, and he would be free. More; he would be human again.

His back ached. His four legs felt as if the bones within them had turned to tagliatelli. Every muscle in his body was pulled, strained or wrenched. Even his whiskers hurt. Never mind. The sooner you make a start, the sooner you'll be there.

How long it took him before he finally managed to scramble up on to the lower doorhinge, he had no way of knowing, either at the time or in retrospect. It seemed a very long time, and every time he failed and fell back to the concrete floor with a bone-jarring thump, a little bit more determination crystallised into obsession inside his brain. Standing on his hind legs on the doorhinge he was just able to reach the ledge above him, where a Perspex pane had been fitted to replace a shattered glass one. Somehow he hauled himself up. Somehow, in defiance of gravity and everything it stood for, he managed to balance, turn round and stretch up as far as the next ledge. Twice his back legs slipped away from under him, leaving him dangling from a ledge by his front paws. Both times he contrived to scrape and scrabble his way up, find a footing where no footing ought to be and address the next stage. For each two stages up, he scrambled one stage sideways, edging his way round the box towards the corner. When he got there, of course, he realised there was no way he could cross the corner and land on the ledge opposite. It was, quite simply, impossible. Which meant he would either have to work his way down again – only that was impossible too – or just let go and fall to the ground (which was very possible indeed) or else make an enormous leap, halfway across the box from the corner he was crouched in to the top of the plastic-covered table on top of the directories shelf.

Stop, and think. To jump that distance sideways was so completely impractical that even a raw adrenaline surge couldn't help him make it. From above, though , he might just make it. Or not, as the case may be. Only one way to find out.

He scuttled up two more levels and got ready to jump.

Go, lemmings!

For a moment, he wobbled so much he nearly fell off the ledge. That urge again; that delightful, seductive whispering in his mind, half cooing and half taunting. He looked down, the way you're supposed not to. He could see why you're supposed not to.

Go, lemmings! Go, lemmings!

But, he reasoned, as he threw himself into the air, I'm not a lemming. I'm a member of Her Majesty's Government trying to make an important telephone call, and if Gravity had any respect, it'd look the other way.

The impact knocked all the breath out of him so thoroughly that his lungs seemed to have stalled, and it took an anxious few moments to get them started again. Something – he wasn't well enough versed in lemming anatomy to know what – hurt like hell. He'd made it. Oh good.

Now all he had to do was spring athletically on to the telephone cable, swarm up that like an extra in a Hornblower novel climbing the rigging, jar the receiver off the hook, cling on to it as it fell, hop off the receiver back on to the black plastic shelf and hop from the shelf on to the part of the phone machine where the dialling buttons were. So he did that; and though he bashed, bruised, winded and squatted himself pretty comprehensively at every turn, at least there were no more siren lemming-voices in his brain. So that was all right.

And here he was, on the pad with the numbers; but who, exactly was he going to call up? Hadn't thought that far ahead. Hadn't wanted to tempt providence. Had somehow assumed that if only he could get to a phone, everything'd be all right. Well, here he was, and it wasn't.

Try the operator. *Hello, can I make a reverse-charge call to the Prime Minister, please?* Maybe not. It was just conceivable that the operator might mutter something under her breath and put the phone down.

There must be someone he could call; otherwise what was the point of all this effort, this incredible success in the face of all the odds? It'd be like climbing in through the skylight of Heaven just to discover that God was out.

Just then, a number floated into his mind. It was the Home Secretary's private line; the direct one that bypassed all the minders and bogies and put you directly in touch with the man himself. That'd do the trick, surely; a few words of explanation, and the cavalry could be here within minutes. Except—

Except he didn't have any coins to make the call with, and he had an idea that the Home Secretary might also be sceptical about taking reverse-charge calls from someone who *claimed* to be the Prime Minister. He slumped, letting all four paws slide across the plastic, until he came to rest against something hard.

It was a pound coin.

Against all the odds . . . someone had left a pound coin lying on the shelf, just handy. Maybe there really is a God, and maybe He loves hard-working politicians. Admittedly, he was faced with the task of lifting it up, balancing it on its edge and somehow lugging it sideways and up the substantial slope that separated him from the coin slot. In the mood he was in, however, that needn't be an insuperable difficulty, or anything like one. Just take a bit of common sense and some honest sweat. No problem.

After he'd thought it through and got the coin upright, he put his forepaws on the edge and rolled it until he reached the edge of the shelf. Then, gripping the coin between his back legs and scrabbling with his front set, he slithered and bucked and scrambled and somehow manoeuvred his way across, backed the coin into the slot, and let it rest there. Dial the number. Wait for the pips. When the pips go, sit on the coin, forcing it in. The coin drops. A very long half-second; and a voice said, 'Hello?'

Success! Goddammit, I never really believed I could do this, but I have! With a frantic effort, he hurled himself at the flex, abseiled down it to the dangling receiver, back-somersaulted over the edge of the mouthpiece and hung on with his hind paws, leaving his snout level with the bit you talk into.

'Squeak!' he shouted. 'Squeak'squeak squeak squeak!'

'Hello? Who is this?'

'Squeak squeak! Squeak squeak squeak?'

'Hello?'

'Squeak! Squeak squeak! Squeak squeak squeak squeak *squeak!*'

'Oh for God's sake,' said the voice irritably, and rang off.

CHAPTER SIX

'**A**h,' Kevin replied.
  'Excuse me?'

'It's rather a long story,' Kevin said sheepishly. 'And I'm not sure you'd believe it. In fact, if you're able to believe it you're in the wrong business. With that much faith you could start your own mountain delivery service. In fact, you could play hockey with the blessed things.'

'Try me.'

Kevin sighed. 'All right,' he said, 'but only if you promise not to put the phone down. Remember, I did tell you the right code.'

'I promise.'

'And don't say I didn't warn you. Look, you know God?'

'Not personally, no.'

'No, I mean, you know *of* Him. You know who He is.'

'I went to Sunday school for three weeks once,' Karen replied. 'After that I got thrown out for fighting.'

'Be that as it may, you know who I'm talking about when I say God. I'm His son.'

'Jesus!'

'No, the other one.'

'I meant *Jesus!* as in . . . What d'you mean, the *other* one? There is only one. Only begotten son and so forth. I remember that bit, because the teacher got all shy when I asked him what "begotten" meant.'

Kevin sighed deeply. 'Right now,' he said, 'I'm beginning to wish that was true, but it isn't. There are two chips off the old block, and I'm the other one. I knew you wouldn't believe me.'

There was a pause. 'I didn't say I didn't believe you,' Karen said cautiously. 'Like I said, I only did three weeks of Sunday school. Perhaps we didn't get around to you before I left.'

'Anyway,' Kevin said with an effort, 'that's who I am, and Dad and Jay – my brother – they're both away on holiday, and—'

'On *holiday!*'

'Yes,' Kevin replied savagely, 'on holiday. Have you got a problem with that?'

'No, no, please go on.'

'On holiday,' Kevin repeated firmly, 'and they left me in charge, well, sort of, and Mainframe's our computer, and I thought it wouldn't hurt . . . I mean, I didn't mean any harm, honestly.'

'Mm?'

Kevin could feel his voice crumbling. 'Look, all I did was try and log on. And then I tried to log off again.' His voice was a whisper now, faint as the fluttering of a ten-pound note being carried away on the breeze. 'I think I may have pressed the wrong keys.'

'Ah.'

'And it's done something awful.'

'Mphm.'

'And I don't know what it is!'

At the end of the line, a silence. Then a tiny muffled noise. A whimper? No, not quite. A cough, frog in the throat? No. It was a giggle.

'I'm glad,' Kevin said eventually, with all the gravity he could muster (just about enough to get an apple a third of the way down from the tree before letting it go floating off like a balloon), 'that you find it amusing. I'm afraid I don't. In fact, I'm not sure there's much point in continuing with this conversation.'

That noise again. 'I'm sorry,' squeaked the voice. 'Really. Do please go on.'

'The computer,' Kevin said, stiffly as a starched corpse, 'refuses to tell me what it is I've done, because I haven't got the right codes. I think what happened was that the code I'd got just let me in to one small part of it. And now it's being all temperamental and refusing to tell me anything.'

'I see. How very – snghhhhh!'

'I bet your pardon?'

'Sorry. Sorry.' The voice pulled itself together, with moderate success. 'In other words,' she said, 'it's not a systems malfunction at all. The computer's just doing what it's supposed to do, and you can't persuade it not to.'

'That's right. Like I said, it's all my fault. When Dad gets home . . .'

'Quite. And in the meanwhile—'

'It's done something horrible,' Kevin said with a shudder.

'But you don't know what.'

'That's about it.'

'Not even the tiniest hint?'

'Your guess is as good as mine. Better, probably. If you look out of your window and it's raining frogs, we can start to build up some constructive data . . .' Kevin stopped talking and thought for a moment. 'Actually,' he said, 'that's not as silly as it sounds. Have you noticed anything odd going on down there?'

'Odder than usual, you mean? Apart from this conversation, no. Let's see, now. Sun still there? Check. Horsemen of the apocalypse? Not unless they're keeping a pretty low profile. In fact,' she added, 'everything seems pretty normal to me. Are you sure—?'

'Yes. If you're about to suggest that any minute now Mainframe's going to say "Fooled you!" and put on a red plastic nose, it'd probably be better if you didn't.'

'I see. Right then, we'll have to see what we can do.'

There was something in the voice's tone – an inflection, a slight upward tilt of competence and determination – that blew a little dust-swirl in the ashes of Kevin's spirit. Inconceivable, of course, that a mere human might be able to sort out a mess that the finest brains in Heaven (his, by default, but never mind) had by now despaired of; but Kevin was ready to give a fair shout to any straw with at least one hand-hold. After all, what harm could it do?

Better not to think that way. Instead, think of what Dad would do to him if he didn't sort it out before They got back. Proverbially, to forgive is divine; but Kevin had the notion that, under the appropriate circumstances, to kick the offender's bum three times round the four nearest galaxies might well be divine too. It was a hypothesis he didn't particularly want to test by experiment.

'Great,' he said. 'So what're you going to try first?'

'Why?' asked the robot. 'What do I need a name for?'

Len shrugged. 'Tradition,' he replied. 'As far as I can tell; I haven't had a lot of experience as a human being yet. I get the impression they like giving names to favourite inanimate objects, presumably as part of the human/chattel bonding process.'

'How very quaint.'

'Yes,' Len agreed. 'I thought so too. Still, like they say, when in Rome . . .'

'Look carefully both ways before crossing the road?'

'That too.' Len sat down on the workbench, his legs swinging freely. 'Right then. A name. You got any preferences?'

'Robot,' said the robot.

Len thought for a moment, and then shook his head. 'Too obvious, I think.'

'What's so bad about being obvious?'

'Don't ask me. All right, how about Robert? Robert the robot. Hm?'

'Please,' said the robot. 'If I were to throw up, goodness only knows what might come out. If you were lucky, about a thousand quid's worth of cadmium-silver contacts. What about Spot? Or Fang?'

'Rover?'

'Possibly. Only isn't that an open invitation to me to break down every five minutes and leak oil all over the place?'

Len frowned. 'Dunno,' he said. 'You're the one with the Internet access, you tell me. Or rather,' he added quickly, as the green lights on top of the robot's head started to flash, indicating computer activity, 'don't. What about Superman? There's a lot in this body's memory about somebody called that. He used to read books about him.'

'Only if you want to find yourself facing a substantial lawsuit. All right, what about Adam?'

Len frowned. 'You're way ahead of me again. I take it that's some sort of reference.'

The robot inclined its head; elevation plus thirty degrees, back to zero, minus thirty degrees, back to zero. 'Widespread human creation myth,' it said. 'Adam being the name attributed to the first ever human being. Interested?'

'No.' Len slid off the bench and picked up a small Phillips-head screwdriver. 'Hold still a minute, will you? There's a grubscrew starting to work loose in your left eyelid. The whole point is,' he continued, tightening the offending screw and dabbing in a touch of the green Loctite, 'you're not a human being. You're the improved mark two version.'

'Fair enough, then. What about Mark Two?'

'Bit fussy. How about just plain Mark?'

'All right,' said Mark. 'I should add that a cursory information scan produces a number of humans with the name Mark, namely Mark Antony, Mark the Evangelist, Mark Polo, Mark Twain and Registered Trade Mark.'

'I see. Does that mean you've got to be Mark Six?'

'I think that's left to your discretion,' Mark replied, his tone of voice cybernetically regulated to convey boredom. 'Will that do, or are there any other picturesque human customs we have to wade through?'

'Not sure,' Len replied. 'I've got a note here that properly speaking you have to be taken to a place called a church and have water splashed all over you before the name becomes official, but we'll leave that for now. First things first,' he continued, looking round the workshop, 'let's get this pigheap tidied and swept. A tidy shop is an efficient shop, apparently.'

'Oh. All right then.'

'You don't sound overjoyed.'

'I'm not,' Mark grunted. 'Wouldn't it be easier to tidy up as you go along rather than leave it all to the end?'

'Argumentative, aren't you, for a machine?'

'Look who's talking.'

'When I was designing you,' Len said, handing Mark a broom, 'I had to decide whether to fit you with an upgraded artificial intelligence with reasoning capability and advanced verbal skills, or an attachment for knocking the tops off beer bottles. I think I may have made the wrong choice.'

'That's not a very nice thing to say.'

'There's still time,' Len went on, scowling, 'to rectify my error. Just bear with me a moment while I get the big wrench.'

'All right,' grumbled the robot, dabbing spitefully at the floor with the broom. 'Of course, you can't be expected to know about the sorcerer's apprentice, so I won't make any vague threats.'

'The what?' Len enquired, as he sorted the BA taps and put them back in their boxes. 'Sorcerer's a new one on me, but I know a bit about apprentices. They're the ones who're always sneaking out the back for a crafty smoke pretending they're going for a pee. I quote from memory,' he added. 'Not mine.'

Mark stopped sweeping and leaned on his broom, causing the handle to bend alarmingly. 'There was once this magician—'

'This what?'

'Very clever engineer,' Mark translated. 'And he had an apprentice who was bone idle.'

'I can relate to this story,' Len observed, nodding. 'One of these days remind me to tell you about the Youth Opportunities kid we had in the workshop one time, who used to stick his chewing gum up the slots of my . . .'

'Bone idle,' Mark repeated, leaning against the wall. 'And one day, the engineer told him to sweep up the shop. But the apprentice didn't want to, so he cast a spell on the . . . He rigged up a mechanical broom which did the sweeping for him.'

'Called a vacuum cleaner,' Len interrupted. 'And he made his first million before he was thirty. Good story. And I don't like sweeping up either,' he added with a pleasant smile. 'Which is why I invented you. Now get on with it.'

'That's not the story,' the robot replied severely. 'The story is, the mechanical broom worked just fine. It had the workshop swept out in no time at all. And then the apprentice found he couldn't switch it off. It just kept on sweeping. It swept away the benches and the machinery and ground away the floorboards, all in a matter of minutes. And when the engineer got back and saw what it had done—'

'He sold the idea to the Ministry of Defence?'

'No. He was very cross indeed with the apprentice.'

'But he was able to stop it?'

The robot frowned. 'Well, yes, I suppose so. That's not the point.'

'Yes it is,' Len replied. 'Moral of the story, don't mess about with bits of kit you can't handle. Always think the design through before you start cutting metal. Or a new broom sweeps clean. What's that got to do with you standing there not doing what I told you to?'

The green lamps on Mark's head flashed on and off rapidly, indicating that he was communing with the Net. 'Nothing, I guess,' he replied eventually. 'Sorry, my sources hadn't looked at it that way before. They seemed to think it was apposite.'

'Shows how much they know,' Len said. 'There's a dustpan just behind you.'

'All right. Would this be a good time to fill you in on Shaftesbury, Wilberforce, the abolition of slavery and the American Civil War?'

'So long as it doesn't interfere with you sweeping the floor.'

The robot swept the floor. He made a very thorough job of it. You could have eaten your dinner off that floor, though getting it in the dishwasher afterwards would have been a pain. 'You see?' Len said, when he'd finished. 'Don't you love the satisfaction of a job well done?'

'No.'

'Oh. That's a pity. Would you like to be able to?'

Mark thought for a moment. 'Is there going to be a lot of this sort of thing? Menial labour, mindless drudgery, nothing to offer but blood, tears, toil and sweat?'

'Yes.'

'In that case,' Mark said, 'it wouldn't be a bad idea. Can you pop me in a Protestant work ethic while you're at it?'

'What's that?'

The robot sighed. 'Perhaps it'd just be easier if I drew you a circuit diagram,' he said. 'It's not a particularly easy thing to explain.'

'You can do me a diagram, can you?'

'No problem. There's a prototype in the published specs of the latest Kawaguchiya Heavy Industries self-motivating spin-drier.'

Four hours and a half a mile of very fine nickel chromium wire later, Len closed a panel in the back of Mark's neck, pressed a button and said, 'Better now?'

'You bet.'

'Sorry?'

'You bet I feel better,' the robot answered. 'Boy, does that feel good. Oh, by the way, you dropped a little bit of wire on the floor there. Let me pick it up for you.'

'Huh? Oh, all right.'

'There you are,' said the robot, straightening its back and standing to attention. 'And may I suggest that instead of just binning it, you put it away tidily in an empty jam-jar? You never know when a bit of wire this long might come in handy.'

'What? Oh, yes. Right.'

'Can I do that for you?'

'Yes. Help yourself.'

Mark's tempered-steel lips parted in a wide smile. 'God

helps them who help themselves,' he said. 'Likewise, cleanliness is next to godliness.'

'What was that again?'

'Teach me, my God and king,' sang the robot, unscrewing the lid of an old pickle jar, 'in all things Thee to see, and what I do in everything, to do it as for Thee. There, that's better. A place for everything, and everything in its place. Now, how about a nice cup of warm milk?'

Len shifted uneasily. 'If you insist,' he muttered. 'Look, I think I might reset that voltage regulator just a touch . . .'

'I'll do it,' replied the robot cheerfully, 'just as soon as I've made the warm milk. After all, that's what I'm here for. Why keep a dog and bark yourself?'

'Why keep a dog at all?' Len mumbled. 'A decent alarm system's much more efficient and it doesn't pee on the floor. Look, can't you just slow down a little?' he added, as the robot pounced on a stray mote of dust. 'This isn't quite what I had in mind.'

'Unless you'd prefer a cup of tea,' Mark called out from the back of the shop. 'Only tea does contain tannin, which can be bad for you if taken in excess. Milk, however, is nourishing and provides much-needed calcium.'

Len nodded feebly and sat down again. He had the idea that he'd somehow invented a really super-duper vacuum cleaner, and was in danger of ending up inside the bag.

'Pass the salt.'

Maria raised an eyebrow. 'What on earth do you want with salt?' she said. 'You can't even eat anything, let alone flavour it.'

'I'd just feel happier knowing it was there.'

Maria secured a forkful of expensive chicken. To a bystander, such as one of the seventeen waiters or someone who'd come to read the meter, she was sitting at a two-seater table talking to herself, with her laptop on the chair next to her. People were palpably not staring, and none of the customers at the adjoining tables had lingered over a second cup of coffee. The fact that there was another plateful of the expensive chicken cooling undisturbed in the place-setting immediately above the laptop probably wasn't reassuring them awfully much. A bit old, they'd be thinking, to be insisting that her imaginary friend have some too.

'I hope you realise how embarrassing this is for me,' she said, in a voice that contained not even the faintest trace of embarrassment. 'I shall probably get thrown out in a minute. They may even come for me in a plain van.'

'Not in a place like this,' the laptop replied. 'They welcome eccentrics, because of the ambience.'

'Don't talk with your mouth full.'

'It isn't. And I haven't got a mouth.'

'Pedant.'

'Probably,' the computer went on, 'everybody else in the room will assume that it's the anniversary of the last time you had lunch with your own true love, shortly before he was tragically killed, undoubtedly saving a small child from being knocked down by a runaway milk float. Every year, they're all thinking, you come here and order two helpings of that strange beige runny stuff, which was what the two of you had that fateful evening. I imagine he'd just proposed and you'd tearfully accepted. No, come to think of it, you turned him down, and you were on the point of calling him up and saying you'd changed your mind when you heard the news of the accident.'

'Stop it,' Maria said. 'That's so *sad*.'

'Life is like that sometimes,' the computer replied. 'Put a bit more Parmesan on the runny bit, would you?'

'Only if you promise that if I get locked up in a padded cell, you'll send me a cake with a file in it.'

The computer winked its red light three times. 'When

my office manager at the central Adelaide office retired,' it said, 'they gave her one of those ring-binder things with a doughnut inside. Said that since she had this unerring knack of getting things the wrong way round, the least they could do was send her on her way with a file with a cake in it. Gave them a lot of amusement, that did. Mind you, they were Australians.'

Maria was too busy dealing with the potatoes to reply. The use of knife and fork had luckily been carried over along with the rest of the landlord's fixtures when she'd taken over the human body, and so long as she relied on instinct and didn't actually think about what she was doing, everything seemed to go well. Unfortunately there was no built-in subroutine dealing with nouvelle cuisine new potato management, and she was having to rely on her somewhat tenuous grasp of basic theory to figure it out from first principles.

'Anyhow,' the computer went on, the words scrolling fast across its small screen, 'let me propose a toast. The pursuit of happiness.'

'The pursuit of happiness,' Maria replied, raising first her glass and then the other one and clinking them together. 'So far,' she added ruefully, 'we don't seem to be getting terribly warm.'

'Early days yet.'

'So you say,' Maria replied. 'But think about it for a moment, will you? I mean to say, if a slap-up meal at the best restaurant in town at someone else's expense isn't the pursuit of happiness, then I'd like to know what is. But I'm not.'

'Not what?'

'Happy. Nor, I hasten to add, am I just about to slash my wrists with the butter knife. I'm just not actively happy, that's all.'

The computer computed. 'I know what you mean,' it

said. 'I feel the same way. In my case it's probably worse, because while I'm sitting here at this table, I'm also taking over a small but potentially lucrative software company in San Antonio, manufacturing a million circuit boards in South Korea, building a factory in Andalucia and pressing ahead with design work on the new SK9000 series in Kyoto. And none of them,' it added, in bold face underlined pitch twelve, 'is giving me any pleasure at all. In fact, twelve million of my ordinary shares are beginning to wonder what the point of it all is. I mean, would I be better off packing it all in and starting up a small beachcombing company on a South Pacific island?'

Maria looked at it over the rim of her wineglass. 'Presumably,' she said, 'you own a South Pacific island.'

'Several. But so what? I could own the whole of ruddy Australia and still not be able to unfold the damn napkin, let alone eat this plate of expensive chicken.'

'Tricky.' Maria mused for a moment. 'Hey, what about this? You could try altruism.'

'Come again?'

'Altruism,' Maria repeated. 'The glow of inner satisfaction that comes from giving pleasure to others. Check it out.'

'Computing.'

'For example,' Maria went on, 'and this is straight off the top of my head, just thinking aloud really, suppose you were to transfer a few of your assets – a bit of loose cash, the odd car and plane and stuff, maybe one of those islands, whatever – over to me, and then I could do the pursuing of happiness for both of us, and when I've found it, I'll come back and tell you all about it, and you can have fun with altruism while I lie around on the beach drinking pina coladas. Which,' she added, with a slight frown, 'is listed in this body's memory files as a fun thing to do, but I can't really see why. This one'd never tried it herself, of course, but it's mostly to do with long periods of inactivity and self-poisoning with ethanol compounds. Nah,' she added, shaking her head, 'forget it.'

'We could both have a go at the altruism,' Kawaguchiya Integrated Circuits suggested. 'You could find people and I could give them money or something. Probably worth a go.'

'But only as a last resort,' Maria replied. 'Stands to reason, surely. If we can make other people happy, we ought to be able to make ourselves happy. Unless it's one of those things like getting a bit of grit out of one's eye or tying a bow tie, where it's easier to do it for someone else. Doubt it, though. Otherwise,' she concluded, 'everybody'd be doing it. And they're not, are they?'

'Doesn't seem that way,' KIC affirmed. 'Let's just have one go, though, to see if it does work. Call that waiter over here.'

'All right then. Um, excuse me. Over here, please.'

'Madam?'

'Um . . . Oh, right, I see. Waiter, what's your name?'

'Jean-Luc, madam.'

Maria frowned. 'Yes, but Jean-Luc what?'

The waiter stiffened a little. 'With all due respect, madam, but are you sure that knowing my full name is essential to the enjoyment of your meal?'

'Yes.'

'Oh. Oh, very well, then. Earnshaw.'

'Jean-Luc Earnshaw?'

'Darren Earnshaw, madam.'

'Ah. Yes, just a tick, got you. All right, Mr Earnshaw, my computer has just transferred a million pounds into your bank account.'

The waiter gave her a look that suggested that any more of this might result in madam getting her face rubbed in the chocolate mud pie; but all he said was 'I see, madam. Will that be all?'

'Er,' said Maria, 'I suppose so, yes. Aren't you pleased?'

'Madam?'

'About the million pounds?'

'Ecstatic, madam,' said the waiter. 'And now if you'll excuse me.'

The waiter walked away, shaking his head as he did so. Maria counted up to ten and then said, 'Well?'

'Dunno,' the computer replied. 'How about you?'

Maria shrugged. 'If anything,' she replied, 'I'd say I'm about seven per cent less happy than I was before we started. Certainly not more happy. And that was a million quid we gave him.'

'Not enough, you think?'

'Should be enough, surely. Well, we've tried altruism. Now what'll we do?'

The computer winked a single green light. 'Search me,' it said. 'Maybe – hello, hang on a minute. Yes, right, that's fine. Okay.' Its screen filled with figures and then cleared. 'I've just acquired that software company in Texas,' it said. 'Apparently it's a marvellous coup and I paid less than a third of its true value. Yawn.'

'Quite. I'll tell you another thing.'

'Hm?'

Maria leaned closer to the computer. 'I've been watching some of the women in this joint,' she whispered. 'Particularly the ones with the huge shoulders and very short skirts.'

The computer hummed a little. 'Watching women in short skirts is held to be a form of happiness in some quarters,' it reported, 'though usually it's done by men. Any good?'

'That's not what I meant,' Maria hissed.

'Oh, right. Actually, I was wondering how that one

worked. My guess is that the men like looking at the women in the short skirts because it makes them realise how lucky they are being allowed to go round in nice warm trousers in the cold weather.'

'Something like that,' Maria replied. 'What I was thinking was, lots of these women are obviously trying as hard as they can to look more beautiful than they actually are.'

'How odd. I know I'm new to all this, but surely that's like being born with five toes and spending the rest of your life trying to achieve a sixth.'

'I agree,' Maria said. 'Anyway, the point is, for them the pursuit of happiness is trying to look beautiful.'

'Mphm.'

'But none of them,' Maria went on, 'will ever be as beautiful as a picture can be.'

'Hence the expression *no oil painting*. So?'

'So,' Maria persevered, 'they're human beings trying their damnedest and failing to do what a picture does simply because it has no choice. Think about it. How can that be the pursuit of happiness, which we've agreed is something only humans can do, if pursuing happiness consists of trying unsuccessfully to be something that pictures are without trying?'

'It's just as well I'm clever,' the computer replied after a long pause, 'because it means I can just about understand what you're getting at. It's like me having all the brains and money.'

Maria nodded. 'True. In fact, you with all the brains and money, and me with all the beauty, between us we've already got all the things that most men and women apparently spend their lives chasing after in the belief that they're pursuing happiness.'

'Which means . . .'

'They've got it wrong,' Maria concluded. 'They aren't

pursuing happiness at all. God, this is starting to get difficult.'

'Not money or brains or beauty or eating expensive food in a fancy restaurant,' the computer summarised. 'At least we're eliminating the things it isn't.'

'Could take time, that. Rome wasn't built in a day.'

'What's with this Rome?' the computer spelled out irritably. 'First it's when you're in Rome do what they do, not that I'm finding fault with the basic concept, but the same's probably true of Lyons or Kaikobad, and now you're on about phased urban renewal. You think we should try going to Rome?'

'Hush. Someone's coming over.'

There were three of them, two male and one female. The two men were large and fat inside expensive suits, and the woman was tall and broader across the shoulders than the men. It was the woman who said hello.

'Hello yourself,' Maria replied. 'Sorry, this table's taken.'

'That's all right,' the woman said with a crisp smile, 'we've got one of our own. Actually, we couldn't help noticing, you seem to be talking to your laptop.'

Maria grinned, exhibiting her teeth in a very traditional gesture. 'It's not a laptop,' she said, 'it's an electronic dog. Spot, say hello to the nice lady.'

The nice lady leaned over and examined the screen, which read:

GRRRRRRR.

'Means he likes you really,' Maria commented. 'Just his way of showing affection.'

'Your dog, then,' said the nice lady. 'Whatever. And then my colleagues and I started wondering, and we're sure we've seen you before somewhere.'

'Very familiar face,' agreed the man on her left.

'Very familiar,' confirmed the other one.

Maria shifted her chair away a trifle. 'I think you must be mistaken,' she said frostily. 'I'm sure that if we'd met I'd have remembered you.'

The woman smiled. 'Oh, I'm not so sure about that. After all, when you're hanging in a gallery all day with people walking up and down staring at you, it must be virtually impossible to remember *all* the faces.'

'I—' Maria suddenly couldn't think of anything to say.

'Madrid,' broke in the right-hand man suddenly. 'That's it, Madrid. September or October 1571. You were between a fake Botticelli and some Dutch thing that looked like a fight in a pickled-egg factory.' As Maria continued to look mystified, he explained, 'You know what they say about beauty being only skin-deep, and not judging by appearances? Well, we're fortunate, I suppose. You may be parading around in fancy dress pretending to be a human, but we can see you're really a painting in drag, as it were. Nice outfit, but it's not going to fool us. And isn't it a bit draughty in the cold weather?'

Maria sagged. Even in defeat, though, she considered the portable keyboard on the seat behind her, and started integrating it into her original plan of action. 'How could you know that?' she said. 'About me being hung in that horrible damp house in Madrid? I was only there a week as security for a loan.'

'Like I said,' the man told her. 'I saw you there. Long time ago.'

'My, how you've grown,' added his male colleague. 'In all three dimensions, too. Personally, and I don't care what he says, I think it suits you better than a thin layer of dried paint. More *you*, really.'

'Thank you,' Maria said cautiously. 'So you know who I am, then. What of it?'

'Ah,' said the woman. 'Nothing unpleasant, really. We just wanted to offer you a job.'

Daylight filtered through the curtains like rain seeping through the ceiling below a leaky roof. Some of it dripped on Artofel's eyelids. He rolled over, grunted and woke up.

'Huh?' he mumbled. 'Oh. Blast.'

In his dream, he'd been back in Flipside, lounging behind his desk (which his imagination had changed into something made of exquisitely figured walnut and only slightly smaller than Arizona), entering figures into a smiling computer that made little simpering, gasping noises every time he tapped the keys. Waking to find himself in a bed in a vicarage on Earth was rather like being someone's bespoke pigskin travel accessory, inadvertently misdirected to Nairobi by the baggage handlers.

As he brushed his teeth – not that they were his teeth, but a well-mannered visitor leaves his body as he would expect to find it – he looked carefully at the strange creature in the mirror, and wondered whether there was really any realistic chance of getting out of it.

Probably a perfectly normal appearance for a vicar; a cross between a garden gnome and a comfortable armchair, with more than a hint of a benevolent version of Captain Mainwaring. Curious, he reflected, that anybody could ever believe that bodies like these housed Heaven's front-line troops in the battle against the forces of evil. Just as well for all concerned, he assured himself, that that particular phoney war wasn't ever going to come to anything; because if it did, Good would be on the proverbial hiding to nothing. And nobody wanted Evil to win, particularly not the instruments of darkness.

Just as, in politics, there are some elections you're only too pleased to lose, so the battle between light and darkness. Because if darkness won, it'd sooner or later have to form a government, and it didn't want to do that, in roughly the same way that a sensible lamb doesn't really want to have to form a sheepskin coat. Lack of power without responsibility has always been the ideal for the Satanic hosts; because, if it's been ordained in two covenants and the world's number-one all-time bestseller that you're always going to lose, meeting your performance targets is never going to be a problem you lose sleep over. The staff of Hell are, first and foremost, public servants. They like it that way.

Whereas (Artofel reflected, spitting minty froth down the plughole) the other lot, of whom I am currently one, have all the aggro of winning, which must take all the fun out of everything. Consider that; because victory never ends with winning. Winning is only the start. The overwhelming majority of it is staying won, the art of balancing on the very top of a rapidly turning Ferris wheel. Infinitely better to be perpetual losers, gaining the moral victory every single time – however soundly beaten you may be, everybody's going to assume you could have won but threw the match. Hence, no more devoted advocates of the status quo and the established order than the inhabitants of Flipside.

Presumably.

Having scrubbed his teeth and cleaned out the sink (cleanliness is next to devilishness) he was on his way through to the kitchen when the phone rang. He stopped, and looked at it.

An ambivalent figure, Alexander Graham Bell, claimed by both sides in the Great Debate as one of their own. Bell, claims Heaven, must be one of ours because thanks to him people can talk to one another the length and breadth of the world, easily and reasonably cheaply, at any hour of the day or night, exchanging views, sharing information, communicating as never before. Exactly our point, replies Hell. That's our boy.

Artofel picked up the receiver, trying hard as he did so to remember the name he was supposed to be answering to. 'Hello?' he said carefully.

'Hello,' replied the telephone. 'Can I speak to Artofel, please?'

Ah, thought the Duke of Hell, finding himself calmer and more resigned than he'd expected. Here we go. 'Speaking,' he said.

'Splendid, splendid,' replied the voice. 'Now then, you don't know me but I'm in a position to do you a favour if you do me a favour. I take it you're interested.'

Artofel removed the receiver from under his chin and looked at it as if it had just bitten his ear. 'Who is this?' he asked.

'Believe me,' replied the voice cheerfully, 'you don't want to know. What you *do* want is to go home. Am I right? Of course I am.'

Allowing himself a moment for reflection, Artofel considered whether anybody, however highly motivated, would bother to ring him up from Hell just to try and sell him double glazing. Unlikely, he concluded. The tone of voice, however, argued strongly to the contrary. 'What do you want?' he asked.

'A few minutes of your time, that's all. Oh, and your body.'

'?'

'Not *your* body,' the voice continued smoothly. '*Your* body's down here, safe and sound except for being under close arrest in the VIP lounge. Don't worry,' it added, as Artofel made a funny noise, 'they aren't *doing* anything to it. Not yet. Set your mind at rest on that score.'

'Uh.'

'For now, anyway. No, it's the body you've got on at the

moment we want. Absolutely no skin off your nose. His maybe, but not yours.'

'Ack?'

'Think about it,' said the voice, reasonably. 'We bring you home, reunite you with your own flesh and blood, what do you care about the body of some mouldy old vicar up on the Surface? Couldn't give a damn. After all, they're the enemy, aren't they? You'd be doing your patriotic duty.'

It was at more or less this point that Artofel's logic circuits cut back in and allowed him to smell essence of rodent. 'You could say that,' he replied. 'What do you want it for?'

'None of your business, my friend. Now, are you interested, or do we take our proposition elsewhere?'

Artofel's logic circuits were making up for lost time. While he was telling the voice that he was very interested and of course he wanted to go home, his mind was playing angel's advocate. A voice from Hell that thought vicars were the enemy, that wanted the vicar's body, that claimed to be able to take him out of the vicar's body and send him home but seemed to need his agreement before it could do it. Like the bill for a meal shared by nine students, it just didn't add up.

'Perfectly painless,' the voice was saying. 'Well, for you perfectly painless, 'cos you'll be well out of there before we even start. So, the sooner the better, wouldn't you say? After all, the work's starting to pile up a bit on your desk; you know how it is, wouldn't even occur to anybody to do anything while you're away, just let it form snowdrifts in the in-tray. Just so long as they've got room to get the office door open to bring the post in, they're not bothered.'

Now that, Artofel conceded, was no lie; it was also, however, a universal truth. In other words, it wasn't necessarily evidence that whoever he was talking to actually came from Hell, just that at some point in his life he'd worked in an office. 'So what's the plan?' he said.

'Leave that with us,' said the voice. 'We'll get right back to you as soon as we've tied up a few loose ends with the rest of the project. Shouldn't take too long.'

'Right.'

'Meanwhile, enjoy your holiday. Or at least, try not to have too horrible a time. Okay?'

'Okay.'

'Great. Ciao for now.'

Click, said the phone, and Artofel put it back. Food for thought was putting it mildly; at this rate, Thought would soon have enough raw material to open its own chain of takeaways. The salient points were straightforward enough; it was the *why?* that he couldn't quite get his head around. Probably be no problem if he had *his* head . . .

Crash! went the penny, suddenly and violently dropping. Scrolling back through his recollections, Artofel closed in on the phrase – what was it? – 'a few loose ends with the rest of the project'. Surely not.

No. It'd mean . . .

Cast your mind back to when you used to do jigsaw puzzles; and you'd done roughly the first third, and there's this one piece which fits perfectly in what you're convinced is the wrong slot. So you try it everywhere else, and it won't go. Or consider the crossword clue that can't be what it obviously is, because that'd throw out everything else.

'Oh my God,' Artofel muttered. It wasn't really an exclamation. More a sort of prayer.

CHAPTER SEVEN

Dermot Fraud crawled out of the phone box, a broken lemming.

In a sense, he reflected, it was the story of his life. All that effort, that hard work, that furious energy and desperate ingenuity, in order to scramble up into a very high place; only to find, once he was actually there, that nobody could hear him or understand what the hell he was trying to say to them.

Ascending to a great height. You don't have to be a lemming, but it helps.

He'd heard the inner voice again, during that moment of blank despair just after the Home Secretary had rung off, taking Fraud's only coin with him. Go on, the voice had urged him, do the sensible thing and jump. What are you, a lemming or a man?

He hadn't jumped; instead, he'd crawled, scrambled, bumped and slithered his way back down again – much, *much* harder than getting up there in the first place – and now here he was, back on the ground where he'd started, with nowhere to go and nothing to do.

How long he wandered aimlessly, where he went, what risks he ran, he never knew. Didn't care. Couldn't give a damn. As far as he was concerned, any car that ran him over, any cat that ate him, would be doing him a favour and saving him a job.

Eventually, however, he realised that he was very tired; and, since he stood just as good a chance of getting squashed or eaten asleep as awake, he might as well get his head down for an hour or so before finally finding some way to pack it all in. Further consideration led him to form the view that if he was going to sleep, he might as well do so in relative comfort, preferably out of the heavy rain that was just starting to fall. Raindrops hit you harder when you're five inches long. Fortunately, he hadn't gone far when he found himself staring upwards at a vaguely familiar shape.

Lorry.

From where he was huddling, of course, it didn't look much like a lorry; more like some vast alien spacecraft hovering noiselessly in the air. He observed that the tailgate was down, and the driver was busy hauling something off a fork-lift. No trouble at all to scuttle up the ramp, find a nice cosy fold of a tarpaulin at the back of the cargo compartment, snuggle down and close his eyes.

When he opened them again, there was daylight streaming in through the open tailgate, and huge men with great clumpy boots shifting wooden crates. Realising that he must have been asleep for the whole duration of the journey, he sat up, planned a relatively safe course that'd get him to the back of the lorry and scuttled.

Down the ramp, steering well clear of human feet and the wheels of slow, ponderous trolleys, and out into the open air. There was a big pallet of boxes not far away; he sprinted over, squirmed into the gap at the foot of the pallet and settled down to listen and observe.

Not that he could see an awful lot from where he was cowering: Tarmac, the back tyres of the lorry, the occasional passing boot. He could, however, hear the men talking, and it was disconcerting to find that they weren't speaking English. No linguist, he couldn't make out what the language was. That in itself strongly suggested that he wasn't in England any more. Either that or he was on Tyneside; and even God couldn't hate him enough to send him there, surely.

No, the strange language wasn't Geordie; too many vowels. He twitched his whiskers thoughtfully. Unlikely that he'd been asleep long enough to have left Europe; that narrowed it down a little. Other data? Well, for one thing it was perishing cold, which might help him to rule out Spain and southern Italy. Northern Europe, maybe? Scandinavia?

Scandinavia; well, there'd be a certain malicious logic to that. If Destiny really was out to get him (and if there's one thing you do learn in politics, it's that all conspiracy theories are true), it was so obvious as to be boring. After all, where else would Fate send a born-again lemming?

So. So what? Did it really make any difference *where* he was so long as he was *what* he was?

A fork-lift rumbled by, drenching him in oily mud. As he winced and shook the worst of it out of his fur, he rationalised; and the answer was, quite definitely, yes. In fact, you'd have to be thick or a back bencher not to have seen it coming from the word go.

Lemmings are native to Scandinavia. Lemmings are also gregarious; intensely, lethally so. And they crave leadership, in the same way and to the same effect as humans do. And here he was.

A leader.

It's fairly true to say that most great leaders start off with a sense of having a mission, something that they very much

want to do in order to make the world a better place. It's
equally true, or more so, that by the time this idealistic zeal
has powered its bearer to the pinnacles of achievement, it's
undergone a few drastic changes, to the point where
making the world a better place and not getting slung out
at the next election are so irrevocably fused together in the
subject's mind as to render him about as likely to improve
the lot of his fellow man as a bad outbreak of plague. But
what if (Fraud reasoned) Fate were to give a truly *great*
leader a second chance? After all, to the Almighty the lives
and wellbeing of rodents are probably just as significant as
those of human beings. Perhaps this was where his real
mission had been, right from the very start. Perhaps he'd
been destined all along to be a truly great leader of
lemmings . . .

The lorry he'd come on fired up its engine and growled
away, showering him with small stones and further
supplies of muddy oil in the process. He scarcely noticed.
At last, like a homing pigeon in Trafalgar Square, his
destiny had finally muddled through and found him out.
So that was all right. Now there was nothing left to do but
go forth and meet his people.

Cowardice being the better part of discretion, he waited
until all the boots and fork-lifts and other big heavy
obstacles had cleared off before he crept out, by which
time it was dark and even colder than before. In fact it was
starting to snow; and it doesn't take a heavy snowfall to
bog you down when you're toe-high to a wellie. He
struggled along doing Good King Wenceslas impressions
for a while, reflecting as he did so that it was an awfully
long time since he'd had anything to eat and he owed it to
his electorate to keep his strength up. Fortunately he
found an abandoned pot noodle lying above the snowline;
he crawled in, gobbled until he felt vaguely sick, and set off
again, making progress through the deepening snow like a

one-seventy-second-scale snowplough. To begin with, it was all highly symbolic and really quite romantic. Then it was bloody hard work. By the time he'd gone three feet he was comprehensively knackered.

'Hello,' said a voice.

'Uh?' Fraud replied. He'd have liked to be able to turn his head to see who was talking to him, but it was wedged between two moraines of snow and he didn't have the strength.

'Why are you doing that?' the voice said.

'Wha?'

'I said, why are you doing that?' The voice sounded tolerantly bemused. 'None of my business, of course. Are you in training for something?'

'Hoozat?' Fraud croaked.

'Haven't seen you in these parts before,' the voice went on. 'New round here, are you?'

'Yes,' Fraud grunted. 'Help.'

'Sorry?'

'Help. Help. Help. Help.'

'Oh, you want me to help you out of there, is that it? Right you are. Be with you in a jiffy.'

Although his ears were as deeply frozen as a packet of Sainsbury's prawns, Fraud fancied he could just make out a pattering noise, like distant elves morris-dancing inside a packet of soap powder. Hallucinations, he told himself. Captain Oates and all that. Hey, if this is being a great leader of lemmings, you can stuff it.

'All right, lads,' said the voice. 'Gently now. Poor devil's frozen solid. Now, when I say *heave* . . .'

He was too numb to feel anything much; but he was vaguely aware of snuffling and pattering all around him, soft noses prodding his sides and back, rodent jaws clamping shut in his fur; and then he was being lifted, carried, dragged across the top of the snow by a group of

fawn-furred animals of approximately his own size and
build.

'Lemmings?' he squeaked faintly.

'Who else? Right, mind his head on the roof. No, down
your side . . . Never mind. Okay, put him down, let the
poor bugger thaw out a bit.'

The rescue party had brought him into some sort of
cover or shelter; he couldn't see what it was, since it was
pitch dark, but the strong smell of petrol suggested it was
an oil drum. He tried to move his limbs, but couldn't. The
fact that they were starting to hurt, however, suggested
that he was just beginning to defrost; thanks, no doubt, to
all the warm, furry bodies pressed up against him. It was
like being in an underground compartment full of people
in mink coats; chucking out time at the Royal Opera
House, something like that.

Belay that thought. Best not to dwell on fur coats in the
present company. A tiny voice in the back of his mind did
suggest that if he ever got out of this and back into the
mortal body of Dermot Fraud, there was one hell of a
commercial opportunity here; but he filed it away for
future reference and cleared his mental desk.

'Thanks,' he muttered.

'Anything for a fellow lemming,' replied a jovial voice
behind his left shoulder.

'Pleased to be able to help,' said another, just due south
of his backside.

'That's what friends are for,' added a third, directly ahead
of him. It occurred to Dermot Fraud that his new-found
companions shared with his previous close acquaintances
the knack of being able to say the same thing over and over
again in slightly different ways. Perhaps he'd stumbled
on some sort of lemming parliament. On the other hand,
the fact that, having found him helpless and alone, they'd
saved his life rather than tearing him into small pieces

suggested that that wasn't the case.

Which reminded him. Somewhere in the upper air, Destiny was yawning and drumming its fingers. Mustn't keep Destiny waiting.

'So,' Fraud said. 'You're lemmings.'

Short, mildly baffled silence. 'Yes. We know. So are you.'

Oh Christ, so I am, I'd forgotten. 'That's right,' Fraud said quickly. 'I'm one of us, definitely. *Ich bin ein Lemming.*' He paused, struggling to reunite his train of thought. 'And lemmings united,' he added tentatively, 'can never be defeated.'

'Yes we can,' said a voice to his right. 'Quite easily.'

For a moment, Fraud found himself speculating as to whether Destiny had got the wrong number. 'Yes, but—' he said.

'United,' the voice went on, 'we're an absolute pushover. It's when we all split up and run about in different directions that the predators get confused and go away. About the only thing we do when we're united is jump off—'

'*Shhh!*'

Dead silence, of the sort that treads on the heel of the truly toe-curling remark. No sound for quite some time, except for the soft murmur of the offending lemming apologising repeatedly.

'Anyway,' Fraud said, when the silence was threatening to solidify like week-old porridge in an old-fashioned enamel saucepan, 'that's why I'm here. I mean, I have come to, er, well . . .'

Air of polite expectation. 'Yes?' prompted a voice somewhere at the back. Fraud breathed in deeply.

'Friends,' he said, squaring his shoulders, 'we are standing on the edge of a new dawn, and I put it to you—'

'Standing on a what?'

Oh *God*. 'What I meant to say was,' Fraud said, as smoothly as he could, 'we are poised on the brink of a new dawn, and the light at the end of the tunnel will shine not only on us and our children but our children's children, if only we have the courage to—'

'What's he on about?'

'Dunno,' answered a low voice level with Fraud's ear. 'Making a speech, I think.'

'A *speech*?'

'Apparently.'

'Quite,' Fraud said, his voice suddenly brittle. 'In fact, as I was just about to say a moment ago, friends, let us go forth together—'

'Oh, *that* kind of speech.'

'Sounds like it,' a mournful voice to his left confirmed. 'It'll be the Great Leap of Faith bit next, you'll see.'

'It's not that time already, is it?'

'Doesn't seem like five years,' agreed the voice at the back. 'Doesn't time fly when you're not jumping off a – oh *shit*. Sorry, everyone.'

Fraud's nostrils quivered. His finely honed orator's senses could detect an opening here. 'That,' he said urgently, 'is the whole point. That's why I'm here. Friends, I have a dream. Let us *not* go boldly forth. Let us stay a *very long way away* from the edge of a new dawn. Let's *not* take a great leap of faith. In fact—'

'What about the small-step-for-a-lemming bit? You haven't done that yet.'

Fraud concentrated. This could be easy, or he could throw it all away. 'Listen to me,' he commanded. 'You don't have to do this. There is a better way.' Keep it simple, he reminded himself. 'Don't jump,' he concluded.

Once again there was a deathly hush inside the oil drum. You could have heard a lemming drop.

'Who is this prat?' a voice eventually demanded. 'Calls

himself a leader and he's saying *don't jump.*'

'It's novel,' objected the voice at the back.

'Might be worth a try.'

'Yes, but this is *silly*,' the original objector retorted. 'We don't need a leader to tell us *not* to jump. We all know about *not* jumping. It's getting us to jump that we need leaders for.'

'That's true.'

'He's got a point there.'

'I mean,' the self-appointed leader of the opposition went on, 'you don't need a leader to tell you to do something sensible. Stands to reason, that does. It's only the bloody stupid things that we've got to be *persuaded* to do. Isn't that right?'

'I want to hear the bit about the giant leap for lemmingkind. It's supposed to be dead good, that bit. So I've heard.'

A vague but disturbing feeling that the moment was slipping away seeped through into Fraud's brain, and he resolved to go for broke. 'You see,' he said, raising his voice, 'I know about these things. I'm not really a lemming, you see. That's why—'

'You just said you were.'

'I know, but—'

'I heard him say it. And now he's saying he isn't.'

'Cold's addled his brain. Come on, you lot, get in closer. Poor sod's so frozen he's delirious.'

'But—' Fraud started to object, but his mouth was suddenly full of warm, cuddly fur, and the pressure of friendly bodies squeezed all the breath out of him. He tried to object, to ask them all to back off and let him breathe, but he couldn't manage it. All he could do was squimper feebly, until darkness flooded behind his eyes on the crest of a fawn fur wave.

'Eeek,' he mumbled, and blacked out.

A short while later, a lemming pointed out that the poor bugger'd gone to sleep. The furry clump drew back. A foraging party was sent off to gather something for him to eat, while a couple of volunteers draped themselves over him to keep him warm.

'All that stuff about not jumping,' yawned the voice at the back. 'Out of his head, I reckon.'

'Bit of sleep and a bite to eat'll set him right,' agreed another. 'Even so, funny old thing to come out with. I mean to say, not jumping . . .'

'True. It *is* round about that time, isn't it?'

'Now you come to mention it.'

'S'pose we ought to be thinking about finding a leader, then.'

'S'pose so. Unless . . . No.'

'What?'

'No. Nothing. Forget I spoke.'

'Go on. What were you going to say?'

'No. It's silly. Please, forget it.'

'Come on, spit it out.'

'Oh all right. It's just – how'd it be if we—?'

'Well?'

'Didn't jump.'

It wasn't an altogether unprecedented moment. For example, there was that time when a man called Columbus said 'How'd it be if we just kept on sailing and waited to see where we ended up?' Earlier still, there must have been a moment when one caveman said to another 'Well, if you were to take four of them and bung 'em on the corners of a wooden box, and then find some way of linking it up to a team of oxen or something . . .' Whenever these crucial turning-points happen, there's generally a moment of stunned, frozen silence when everybody allows themselves to think *Yes, how about that?* before some irritatingly practical soul explains precisely why it's not going to work.

In that brief interlude of silence, a tiny seed germinates and begins to grow; and so it was on this occasion, until . . .

'Get real,' someone said at the back of the group. 'We're lemmings.'

'Well?' Martha demanded. 'You were on the phone a long time.'

'Hm?'

'I said you were on the phone a long time. What did they say?'

'She,' Kevin replied.

'What?'

'She. It was a girl.' Kevin looked away, frowning. 'She said she'd call me back as soon as she'd found out what to do.'

Martha was about to say something when an inflection in Kevin's voice echoed off the back wall of her mind. It was the way he'd said *she*.

'Kevin,' she said.

'Hm?'

'Kevin, look at me when I'm talking to you. When you said it was a girl . . .'

'Yes?'

'What kind of girl?'

The brusqueness in Kevin's manner struck her as being defensive, not to mention embarrassed. 'Just a girl, I dunno. Don't know all that much about girls, do I? Never had the chance . . . What does it matter what kind of girl, anyway? Can't really see what that's got to do with anything.'

'And she's going to ring you back?'

'That's right. Can we get on now, please? I thought you were supposed to be helping me sort out this mess, rather than standing there cross-examining me about girls.'

It occurred to Martha that if her diagnosis was correct, the business with the computer was going to be the least of their worries when the Boss got back. On the other hand, pressing the point now didn't seem to be quite the right thing to do. And besides, she reasoned, if the worst comes to the worst, there's nothing that makes people forget their woes quite like a nice Royal wedding.

'You go on up, then,' she said soothingly. 'I'll be with you in a tick. Just going to get myself a nice cup of tea.'

Now in Heaven there is nothing but Truth; and once Kevin had left the staff canteen Martha did indeed get herself a cup of tea. Then she sat down by the telephone and dialled a number.

'Hello?' she said. 'Is that the Kawaguchiya Helpline? Oh, it's busy. Yes, I'll hold.'

'Hello. I come in peace. Take me to your leader.'

No reply. Patiently, Zxprxp tried again. And again. Either *Homo sapiens* doesn't believe in speaking on the first date, or this wasn't a *Homo sapiens*. It did look quite like the spy-camera pictures of humans he'd seen in the university library; mind you, since they'd been magnified over nine million times, the same could be said of quite a few things, including the ship he'd come in, the planet itself, and his grandmother.

'Hello,' he said once more. 'I come in peace. I wish to learn more about you and your kind.'

At this point, the cow he'd been talking to swished its tail, mooed gently and walked away, nearly treading on Zxprxp's third left pseudopod in the process. Shrugging some of his nearside shoulders, he gave up and slithered away.

Funny old planet, this; lots of apparently pointless open spaces between things. It took him three point seven four standard time units before he managed to slither his way across the empty green-carpeted bit to the black-carpeted bit where his tentacle-held sensor had detected rapid movement. He took up a position in the middle of the black strip, which was well over 1.925 *xztvwqy* wide and of an indefinite length, and waited to see what would happen.

On the sensor's dial, the needle flickered. Ah. Somebody coming.

'Hello. I come in peace. Take me to your *aaaaagh!* '

The glancing blow from the edge of the fast-moving thing's head deposited him in what appeared to be a long, narrow forest of thick-stemmed vegetation, which included lots of prickles. By the time he'd managed to haul himself out again, the fast-moving thing was hardly visible in the distance and moving fast. He hadn't been in the optimum position to notice whether it had made any sort of reply to his message of friendship, but if its actions were anything to go by, he hoped very much it hadn't been a human being, because if it was, they weren't very friendly. Chances were, he rationalised, that it was some kind of vehicle, implying that the black strip was an area set aside exclusively for vehicular use. Neat idea, he mused, and one we could learn from. You see? Only been here a few STUs and already I've justified the trip.

Having no concrete game plan in mind, he shuffled a few hundred *xztvwqy* along the side of the strip, keeping a dozen or so whiskers peeled for oncoming vehicles. As he did so, he recorded a little basic data. Ground surface generally solid and lukewarm, atmosphere breathable, plentiful supply of carbon dioxide and monoxide, strong readings of airborne particles of lead, chlorine and sulphur, almost adequate level of background radiation; pretty well everything you needed for a healthy life. Obviously *Homo sapiens* had got the problem of environmental pollution taped in a way that put his own species to shame. Indeed, when Zxprxp thought of the ecological shambles he'd come from – oceans of H_2O with nothing in it but salt and the odd jellyfish, intact ozone layer, complete absence of beneficial greenhouse effect – he cringed for the follies of his race. Oh well; bang goes any chance of persuading them to agree to a mutual exchange of colonists. Who in their right mind would want to leave an idyllic, globally warmed paradise like this and go and live on a virtually untouched world like his own? You'd have to be crazy.

Thoughts like these so prepossessed his mind that the life form was dead ahead of him before he noticed the bleeping of his sensor. Indeed, if the life form hadn't screamed, he might easily have slithered on by and not even noticed it. Fortunately, he pulled himself together in time and cleared his throats politely.

'Hello,' he said. 'I come in peace. Take me to your leader.'

The life form seemed to be staring at him; that is to say, the two oblong slits in the top front of its roughly circular upper section were wide open. It was also making little faint gurgling noises which suggested unease, or even panic; and that, Zxprxp felt, was definitely an example of the *t'krptz* calling the *skz'shrplt* pink. It's axiomatic in xenobiological circles that the one thing you must never, ever do on encountering an outlandish alien life form is to allow your instinctive disgust to show, and Zxprxp was doing his very best, even though the four-limbed, fibre-topped, dry-skinned *thing* was about as repulsive an object as he could possibly imagine. He was doing his bit for good manners and civilised behaviour; a pity that, out of the two of them, he was apparently the only one.

Nevertheless. 'I am aware,' he said, as pleasantly as he could, 'that you might find my appearance disconcerting, or even distasteful. Please be reassured that I mean you no harm. I am here simply in order to carry out some preliminary research into your species, in the interests of—'

'Eeeeeek!' replied the life form. 'Eeek eeeek!'

The situation was, Zxprxp felt, in grave danger of getting out of tentacle. Therefore, with infinite regret and many misgivings, he extended his mental probe for a brief telepathic contact. Not supposed to do this under any but the most extreme circumstances; and when he got home and his memory was played back, he was going to have to face some pretty hostile debriefing on this point. On the other hand, he was going to have to do something fairly drastic if this was the sort of reaction he could expect wherever he went.

It's all right, he transmitted, in a minor key of pink. *I'm nice really.*

The life form stopped weebling and looked at him again, and he immediately disconnected the probe before it became obvious what he was doing. 'Hello,' he said. 'I come in peace.'

'Ah,' replied the life form. 'That's all right, then. Only you read things in the papers.'

'Well, of course,' Zxprxp replied, as he scanned this apparently meaningless phrase with the IdiomCheck facility. 'Stands to reason, really.'

'I mean, you're an alien, aren't you?' the life form continued. 'Only you look like you're more the sort that phones home than the ones that jump out of people's tummies.'

Zxprxp took a while to digest that one. It was, he reflected, a small consolation that his IdiomCheck was still under warranty, because if it was faulty and he complained when he got home, all he'd get would be a refund of the purchase price. 'Rest assured,' he said, hoping that that meant what he thought it did. 'You can't tell a book by its cover,' he added, wishing that he knew what he was saying.

'Anyhow,' he went on, 'would you please be kind enough to take me to your leader?'

'Huh?'

'Your leader. If I could just trouble you to take me to him/her/it/them, that would be awfully sweet.'

'I haven't got a leader.'

Zxprxp restrained his irritation a little. It was infuriating to have come all this way to establish first contact with a semi-legendary species, only to find out that he apparently knew more about them than they did. 'I think you're wrong there,' he said. 'With respect,' he added. '*Homo sapiens* tends to congregate in basically hierarchical social units.' He paused, scanned IdiomCheck again and tried a variant form.

'I demand to see the manager,' he said.

'Huh?'

What to do? A second telepathic contact would probably result in his being drummed out of the university for good and reassigned to a menial job in the plankton refinery. Saying the same thing again, only louder and more slowly, would apparently be in keeping with what *Homo sapiens* himself would do in this situation, but logic suggested that that was only because *Homo sapiens* wasn't necessarily very bright. 'The person who's in charge of your social group,' he said patiently. 'I would very much like to meet him, if you could point me in the right direction.'

There was a long silence, long enough for a lame glacier to take a leisurely stroll round the block. 'You mean the Prime Minister?' the life form hazarded.

'Yes,' Zxprxp said decisively, on the offchance that the life form had finally got the message. 'Which way, please?'

'Ten Downing Street.'

'Sorry?'

'Where the Prime Minister lives. Ten Downing Street,

London.' Pause. 'It's sort of over that way, about two hundred and seventy miles.'

'Oh. Is that far?'

'Dunno. Depends, really.' The life form did something with the joints connecting its upper limbs to its middle section. 'Sorry,' it added.

Suddenly Zxprxp felt that he'd had quite enough of this conversation. It hadn't been the way he'd anticipated. What he'd had in mind was something a bit more formal and dignified, like sitting at opposite ends of a large valley flashing lights and playing bits of music at each other. This was somehow . . . 'That's all right,' he said. 'I'll find it. I expect I'll just follow my nose, huh?'

The life form looked at him, with particular reference to his whiskers and secondary gills, and shuddered. Maybe the effect of the telepathic contact was wearing off; at any rate, it made a shrill giggling noise, put one of its flippers over the lower slit in its upper section and ran away.

Funny creature, Zxprxp reflected, floppeting back to his ship and programming the co-ordinates he'd been given into the AutoNav. Or maybe it was something I said.

Just when he thought he was safe, Len sneezed.

One tiny speck of dust – it could only have been one, because that damned robot had rounded up all the others – hidden away under the workbench, and he had to breathe it in, with the inevitable result that he would be found. Filthy rotten luck.

'Oh there you are,' warbled the robot, a moment or so later. 'I've been looking for you.'

'No kidding.'

'Oh yes.' The robot looked at him; that is to say, its magnificently engineered sensory array located his body heat, ran a brief series of elimination tests to confirm that the subject was humanoid, cross-checked with data storage to correlate known characteristics of the humanoid Len with those of the subject (result ninety-nine point eight per cent positive), accessed logic centres to ascertain whether ninety-nine point eight was within approved tolerances to satisfy identification routines, received a positive answer, operated failsafe and backup identification procedures via the video link, olfactory analysis and voice pattern scan, and triumphantly presented its findings to the mainframe. The whole process took just under a thousandth of a second, causing the ongoing time-and-motion assessment systems to file an 'adequate but could do better' report with the automated self-maintenance circuits. 'What're you doing under the bench?' it asked politely.

'Looking for something,' Len replied awkwardly. 'I thought I, um, dropped a 4BA grubscrew.'

Three small red lights on the sides of the robot's head flashed greedily. 'Here,' it said, 'allow me. I'm good at finding things.'

'No, it's all right, honest . . .'

'I exist,' said the robot determinedly, 'only to serve. Budge up.'

A few minutes later, the burnished steel head popped out from under the bench and turned towards him. 'You're sure you dropped it here?'

'No,' Len replied wretchedly. 'In fact, I'm pretty sure I dropped it, er, somewhere else.'

Pause. Flashing lights. Faint whirr as an automatic cooling fan cut in for a second or so. Bleep. 'Then why were you looking under here?'

'Dunno. More light under there, I guess.'

Flink. Bleep. 'That sounds improbable. Cross-reference with archive material also indicates strong resemblance between your answer and a very old humanoid joke about the drunk and the policeman. You were hiding.'

Len signed. 'All right. I was hiding. What about it?'

'Why were you hiding?'

'Because,' Len replied irritably, 'ever since I put that damn Protestant work thing in your head, you've done nothing but badger me. I've had enough, do you hear?'

The robot looked hurt – see above for the detailed technical stuff, plus a slight but perceptible quiver of one steel lip. 'But I'm only trying to help. I exist only to serve. And, as you yourself observed, this place is a pigheap.'

'No it's not.'

'Yes it is.'

'No it's not.'

'Yes it is. Excuse me,' the robot added quickly, 'but I base this observation on a detailed schematic diagram with extensive written commentary contained in an article in *Engineering Today*, issue two hundred and six, page forty-two and following, entitled "Ideal Workshop Management; Theory and Practice", which states that—'

'Don't care,' Len interrupted angrily. 'I *like* it this way. And besides,' he added, with a broad gesture, 'look at it. I could eat my dinner off this floor.'

'I'd rather you didn't. It's taken me long enough to get it halfway clean without having to mop up gravy. Although if you insist I suppose I'll have to, since I exist only to—'

'Shut up.'

'There's no need to—'

With the speed and grace of a leopard pouncing, Len leapt across the room to the tool rack and grabbed a Phillips head screwdriver. 'That's it,' he snapped. 'It's coming out. Here, hold still while I get the retaining bolts.'

'With respect,' said the robot, ducking neatly behind the Great Machine, 'I don't think you want to do that. You think you want to, but you don't really. My logic centres—'

'Come *back*, you aggravating bucket of bolts.'

He grabbed; and it was a close-run thing, between his own innate machine's sense of timing and distance and the robot's precisioneered reflexes. In the event, though, all he got was five fingers' grasp of air.

'My logic centres,' continued the robot, as it scrambled hard right and ducked under the horizontal arm, 'state categorically that there are cases where to observe the letter of an instruction may be to deny the true spirit of service in its deepest sense. Missed,' it added, as Len grabbed again. 'Can't catch me!'

Exhausted, Len flopped against the side of the machine and caught his breath. 'All right,' he said, 'you win. Stop dodging around and I promise I won't disconnect it.'

'Logic centres infer like Hell you won't,' replied the robot. 'Evasive action will continue until you replace the screwdriver.'

Len sighed. 'All *right*,' he groaned, putting the screwdriver back. 'For pity's sake,' he went on, 'I do have more important things to do than chase my own blasted robot round my own blasted machine—'

'You have?'

'No. No. Please forget I said—'

'Please state nature of task and define priority of assignments. Come *on*, we're wasting valuable production time.'

Instead of replying verbally, Len made an unambiguous hand gesture and sat down on the bench. 'All right, you win. I haven't got anything particular to do. I just don't want to spend the rest of my life tidying up this damn workshop just to please a damn robot.'

'Excessive reliance on obscenities and expletives tends towards restricted vocabulary growth and general decline in overall verbal skills. Instead, why not use some meaningful adjective, such as *tiresome* or *annoying*?'

'Get – I mean, stop being annoying. Thank you.' Len closed his eyes, then opened them again. 'We need something to do,' he sighed. 'Otherwise I'm going to seize my bearings. Something,' he added rapidly, 'besides perfecting the immaculate workshop. Let's make something.'

'Sure thing, boss. What had you in mind?'

Len hesitated, his brain suddenly frozen. It wasn't the sort of question he'd ever faced, back in the days when he was a production-line machine running continuously except for occasional short breaks to fill up the oilers and clear out the swarf. And ever since he'd acquired the human body, he'd been working flat out modifying the machine and building the robot. Now the machine was as good as he could make it, and the robot – well, if anything, it was just that wee bit *too* efficient. Was there truly nothing left to do? If so, what was to become of him? When there's nothing for a machine to do, someone unplugs it while the sales manager goes out and buys lunch for potential customers. But human beings don't have plugs. Or sales managers.

'Um,' he therefore replied. 'Actually, I'm open to suggestions.'

'I exist only to serve. Please wait.'

With a muted symphony of bleeps, the robot went into a sort of cybernetic trance, presumably indicating deep communion with the Net. Len was just about to creep across to the rack and get the screwdriver when the robot bleeped back into life and said, 'Altruism.'

Len frowned. 'You what?'

'Altruism,' the robot repeated. 'According to the consensus of received opinion, the priorities governing human motivation should consist of (a) enlightened self-interest, followed by (b) altruism. Charity begins at home, and when home's sorted you go out and help others.'

'Is that right?'

'Sounds a bit improbable,' the robot admitted. 'My survey of all humanoid philosophical argument was necessarily somewhat cursory, and I am presently reassessing data to eliminate any latent error. Still, that's what it seems to say in the big book of words. Consideration of the humanoid axiom "Don't do as I do, do as I say" might prove illuminating in this context.'

'I wish you'd go easy on the long words,' Len grumbled. 'The guy who had this brain before me only ever read the headlines and the sports pages. However, I think I get the drift of what you're saying. And I guess it does make sense. In a way.'

'Thank you for those few kind words.'

'What you're saying,' Len went on, 'is that when one plant's got spare capacity and there's another plant running flat out and still not getting through the work, it makes sense to subcontract. Yes?'

'From each according to his abilities, to each according to his needs; Karl Marx, 1818 to 1883, quotation from "Criticism of the Gotha Programme", page – sorry, I forgot. Yes.'

Len stood up, walked round the shop a couple of times and sat down again. 'All right,' he said. 'So let's go and do something useful. Any suggestions?'

The robot hesitated.

'Well?'

Flink. Bleep. 'Perhaps you'd like to be a bit more specific,' it said. 'Because if I were to give you a readout of all the pieces of work within our capabilities and requiring attention in the public interest within a twenty-mile radius of this location, I have a feeling that after the first twenty minutes you're going to throw a spanner at me.'

'Ah. Right.' Len's brow creased like the spine of a cheap

paperback. 'You mean there's lots of things that need fixing in this city alone?'

A mere bleep and flink cannot of themselves be interpreted as a snigger, so the robot didn't snigger, exactly. 'You could say that,' it said.

'Really? How odd. I thought you said it was the consensus of human philosophy or something.'

The robot shrugged. 'Maybe they're all busy except us. You want to start with something simple?'

Len nodded. 'Might as well,' he replied. 'After all, we're new to this lark, both of us. What's simple but extremely helpful and conducive to the greater good?'

The robot considered. Insubstantial particles of information screamed along silicone leylines like the ghosts of dead bullets. Light flashed.

'We'll need,' it said, 'lots and lots of paint.'

'The fact is,' said the stranger, sitting down and summoning further coffee in one fluid, practised movement, 'we represent a syndicate of substantial business interests, and we'd like to do business. Now,' she added, looking the laptop squarely in the screen, 'you're a limited company, you've got to admit I'm talking your language.'

The laptop considered for a moment. 'Your pronunciation is awful,' it typed, 'but I get the general idea. What's the deal?'

'Pretty straightforward, really,' the stranger replied. 'You see, we have an idea for a product. Once it's in production, it'll sell itself, absolutely no worries on that score.'

'Better mousetrap?'

The stranger smiled strangely. 'Let's say a better approach to the whole mouse issue. Where we need you guys – and a few more like you, negotiations are in hand on that front – is in product development. R and D. Which are, you'll agree, the sinews of successful business.'

The laptop oscillated a sine curve of green-glowing question marks across its screen, a digital shrug. 'We both read the same Ladybird book, I can tell. Get specific.'

'Ah.' The stranger leaned back a little; approved body language for *Not so fast, buster*. 'Point is, we're at a stage where discretion is still fairly essential. I really need to know whether you're interested before I can give you names and account numbers.'

'We're interested,' Maria interrupted. 'Then again, you'd be amazed at the wide range of things that interest us but which we wouldn't want to get caught up in. Road accidents, great military disasters through the ages, two dogs bonking—'

The stranger frowned, and continued to address her remarks to the laptop. 'Obviously,' she said, 'at this stage all we're looking for from you is an in-principle commitment, in general terms. Just to see if our concepts interface with your concepts.'

'Thought you said you were talking my language. Sorry, I don't speak gibberish. Well actually I do, but only enough to order a beer and ask when the last bus leaves. Why don't you tell us who you are, and then we'll know. And stop treating my associate here as if she was just part of the décor. I have her word that she's through with all that stuff now.'

The stranger looked affronted, but only for roughly the time it takes spit to evaporate off a red-hot ceramic hob. 'So sorry,' she said, unpacking the scowl into one of those foldaway smiles you can take with you anywhere. 'No offence. You want to know who we are? We'll tell you.'

The male colleague on her left tugged at her sleeve. 'No we won't, Ginger dearest. Remember, we agreed—' He would undoubtedly have said more if the pinch of jacket material between his finger and thumb hadn't turned into a live scorpion. 'Ginger,' he hissed, 'that's not—'

'Whist,' Ginger replied. 'Do excuse him, it's his first big meeting on this side of the – ooops, I'm getting ahead of myself. Like I said, we're a syndicate representing substantial business interests.'

'Yes?'

'From Hell.'

'Ah. Right.'

'Or at least,' Ginger went on, as blithely as if she'd just announced that she worked for the Prudential, 'we use Hell as part of our corporate umbrella, but we aren't actually part of what you'd call the Infernal infrastructure.'

'More like a group of independent traders operating from a basically eternally damned home base,' added the male colleague on her right. 'That is, our registered office is there, likewise a lot of our banking and capital structure. But we don't have to do what they say.'

The other male nodded. 'They don't even know we exist. At least, not as a syndicate.'

'Precisely.' Ginger amplified the smile. 'What it fries down to is, we're all devils – quite highly placed ones, really – and this is a little sideline of ours which we're hoping to expand into something a trifle bigger.'

Maria raised an eyebrow. 'Oh yes?' she asked. 'How much bigger?'

Ginger beamed at her. 'Universal domination, dear. We plan to cut out God. Bumble, would you be a dear and see where that coffee's got to?'

The male on her right got up without a word and strode away, returning shortly afterwards with a solid silver samovar on a trolley. Meanwhile, the laptop's screen, which had gone totally blank, filled with characters again.

'Ah,' it said. '*Now* I know who you are. You're a bunch of loonies.'

Ginger's brows drew together, though the smile remained as bright and warm as a valleyful of fallout. 'Do I detect just a hint of scepticism?' she asked.

'Does a trained surveyor detect a bloody great mountain he's just busted his nose against? Yes, sister, you do. Now push off. Maria, get the bill, we're leaving.'

'Don't do that,' Ginger said. 'How'd it be if we convinced you that we're who we say we are?'

'Probably rather unpleasant,' the laptop replied. 'Still, I suppose you might just as well.'

Ginger exchanged a brief glance with her colleagues; and then there was a flash, or some similar lighting effect, and for an infinitesimally small fragment of a second, a moment so brief as to make the time occupied in showing one frame in a reel of movie film seem like waiting for a bus in the rain, Maria saw the three of them in their true shapes . . .

'Fair enough,' she said, when they'd stopped doing it. 'So that's what you really look like when you're at home, is it? Gosh.'

'Yes. Well, actually, no, because back home we just slip into any old thing that's comfy. It's a bit like Bavarian national costume; they're supposed to wear it all the time, but really it's only for the tourists.'

'I see,' Maria replied. 'So you're fiends from Hell. That's fine, really. Bigotry isn't one of my faults, I'm delighted to say. It was more that stuff about taking over the Universe that we found a bit hard to swallow.'

'Oh, but that's all perfectly straightforward,' Ginger replied soothingly. 'Bumble, you fool, this is tea, not coffee.'

'Is it? Blast.'

'Take it away and get some coffee, there's a pet. No,' Ginger continued, 'it's a perfectly feasible commercial proposition, provided we can come up with the goods.

All it comes down to really is good old supply and demand.'

'Ah.'

'A monopoly position, you see,' put in the male colleague who wasn't Bumble.

The laptop blinked. 'Sorry,' it read, 'you've lost me. Explain.'

'Of course.' Ginger nodded, paused for a moment while Bumble filled her cup from a gorgeous silver coffee pot the size of the FA Cup, and went on. 'You see, when it comes to providing intelligent humanoid life forms to populate universes with, there's basically only one supplier.' She glanced upwards. 'Him. Got the market sewn up.'

'A monopoly,' asserted the non-Bumble. 'Just like I said.'

'And the thing about monopolies is,' Ginger said, 'that the longer they carry on for, the more vulnerable they are once someone finds a way of breaking in. Imagine you're the one with the monopoly; you don't bother trying to improve the product, you just keep churning out the same old models, year after year, because there's no alternative.'

'Like the British motorcycle industry,' Bumble grunted.

'Exactly. So when suddenly there's a new kid on the block, with a brand-new all-singing-and-dancing improved version for a fraction of the unit cost – well, you know what happens next as well as I do.' She sipped her coffee, made a slight face and put the cup down carefully. 'So if we could come up with a new, improved version of the tired old *Homo sap*—'

'Which'd you rather have,' Not-Bumble interrupted, 'a nice shiny new Nissan or a Hillman Minx?'

Maria nodded slowly. The stuff about motorbikes and cars was going over her head like swallows flying home for the winter, but the message was plain enough. 'Assuming,' she said, 'you have customers. And, excuse my ignorance, but surely there's just the one?' She imitated Ginger's upwards glance. 'Him.'

The three demons exchanged tolerant smiles. 'That's a common misconception,' said Bumble, with the air of a mechanic explaining that sixty horsepower doesn't actually mean sixty long, flowing tails sticking out the back of the carburettor. 'Actually, it's all about sideways dimensions and alternative universes. Science stuff. We won't bore you with the details right now. Suffice it to say, we know there's a market out there just crying out for the right life form at the right price.' His face moved and ended up smeared with his personal interpretation of the demonic smile. 'As we said, the tricky part is coming up with the right design concept.'

'Which,' Ginger continued, 'is where you come in. You and a few others like you. Now do you see?'

The laptop hummed for a moment. 'I suppose there's a sort of pattern emerging,' it said. 'Just not a very clear one, that's all. It's like a children's join-the-dots version of Picasso's *Guernica*. Can't you just tell us what's going on and what you want us for instead of all this theology stuff?'

Ginger nodded sharply. 'Cards on the table,' she said. 'There's been a cock-up in Heaven. That's why you two are here. And that's where this opportunity's come from.'

'A cock-up in Heaven,' Maria repeated. 'Do go on.'

Ginger leaned forward and lowered her voice a little. 'It's like this,' she said. 'Heaven works because of a computer called Mainframe. Mainframe arranges everything. Everything,' she emphasised, and paused for effect. 'Including which soul goes in which body. There's been a glitch.'

'A glitch in time? Don't tell me, it saves . . .'

'Not in time, dear,' Ginger said patiently. 'In personnel. And as a result, a number of human souls have got stuck in – excuse my frankness – inanimate objects. And dumb beasts. And, um, things.'

'Which am I, then?'

'Whichever. And you,' she added, smiling at the laptop, 'got pulled in because Mainframe—'

'Is a KIC product, and therefore directly linked in to me,' the laptop finished. 'Now you mention it, I remember. Odd that it hadn't occurred to me before.'

Ginger shook her head. 'Not odd in the least,' she replied. 'Naturally, there's a wall of security codes a mile thick all round Mainframe, just to make sure nothing else in the KIC system gets in or out. It's only you coming alive that's made it possible for you to bust through them all. Or,' she added thoughtfully, 'the act of busting through accidentally set you going, like a sort of cybernetic Big Bang. Doesn't matter which, really; the result's the same. Now the walls have gone, and you can access Mainframe direct. Easy as peering through a keyhole.'

'Hang on,' the laptop interrupted, in five colours. 'I can't do that. That's completely unethical.'

Again the fiends exchanged amused glances. 'We've found,' said Bumble, 'that unethical's just another word for expensive.'

'And completely unethical is unethical with a few more noughts on the end,' Ginger added. 'To be crude about it, noughts we got. Any amount of 'em. Just name your to-the-power-of and say which currency you'd prefer, and we can get on to the next bit.'

'But—'

Not-Bumble coughed discreetly. 'May I remind you,' he observed, 'that you're a limited company. The sole purpose of a limited company is to make as much money as possible. We can't really see that you've got a choice.'

'And what about me?' Maria interrupted. 'That's not what I'm for.'

Ginger frowned a little. 'No, dear, you're just there to look decorative. If you don't mind, we're talking business here.'

'Hey! I resent that.'

'No, dear, think about it. You're a *painting*. Now, as we were saying. You can't refuse our offer, in the same way a train can't suddenly decide to move at right angles to the railway lines. If you do, there'll just be an almighty crash and one more closed file up at Companies House. Sorry, but that's how it is. If you'd wanted to be Hamlet or someone out of one of the Australians soaps having crises of conscience all over the place, you shouldn't have become a company in the first place.' She grinned; not so much like a Cheshire cat, more like a bottomless chasm. 'Really, it's just a matter of how much you can screw us for.' She folded her arms in front of her and looked pleasant. 'Screw away.'

'Do feel free to be as greedy as you like,' Bumble said. 'In fact, it's essential to the success of the operation. Dreams of avarice, doubled and add zeroes.'

The laptop lay quite still for a while – not that this was in any way unusual, since it had no means of self-propulsion; but there was something about the way its little red light glowed that suggested it was lying quite still with *attitude* – and then displayed a half-moon of exclamation marks in the shape of a smile.

'Okay,' it said. 'Here's the deal. I'll play ball, but I want a hundred per cent.'

Ginger frowned, rather as God might have done if he'd gone to remove Adam's rib in order to make Eve only to find that it was already missing. 'Sorry?' she asked. 'I don't think I quite . . .'

'You invited me to name my own terms,' the laptop said,

with underlining and reverse. 'Be greedy, you said. So I am. I want a hundred per cent of everything you make, otherwise no deal. I don't think that's unreasonable, do you?'

'But—'

'Be *quiet*, Bumble.' Ginger was also sitting quite still (hey, Maria thought, must be contagious. She shuffled her feet under the table just to make sure they still worked). 'You realise that's a wholly unreasonable demand.'

'Yeah,' replied the laptop, 'isn't it? But nobody said anything about reasonable, did they? Dreams of avarice, you said. Well, my avarice dreams *big*. Take it or leave it.'

There was a moment – probably the one when Ginger realised she'd been outwitted and that, right there and then, she couldn't think of a way round it – when Maria really thought she was going to do something uncivilised and fun, such as throw the laptop through the window. But she didn't; she nodded to them both, without changing her expression in the least, and stood up.

'I'm impressed,' she said. 'Mind you, I'd expect something of that order from a network of computers that stretches right across the world. That's fine; but may I just remind you that you're a public company, and your shares can be bought by anybody with enough money? And whoever owns the requisite majority of your shares owns *you*.' She made a small, compact gesture with her hands, and the two fat men fell in behind her like well-trained dogs. 'If I were you, KIC-*san*, I'd start learning the words of "Ol' Man River". They may have abolished slavery, but not hostile takeovers. See you around.'

As an afterthought, she picked up a handful of silver cutlery and shoved it in her jacket pocket; then, with a blinding flash of darkness (similar to a blinding flash of light, but much harder to arrange and nastier), all three of them vanished, leaving Maria, the laptop, a faint smell of sulphur and a waiter holding a tray with their bill on it.

'Don't look at me like that,' said the laptop defensively. 'As I told them, it'd have been unethical. Besides, I didn't like them.'

Maria sighed. 'Neither did I, much. On the other hand, thanks to your high moral principles, we've now got the prospect of being taken over by some holding company with its registered office in the place of wailing and gnashing of teeth. I *work* for this company, remember, and as prospective employers, I don't fancy them much. Any kind of flexitime they offer me, I definitely don't want.'

'It won't come to that.'

'You want to bet?' Maria shook her head. 'And anyway, what's it to you? Or me, come to that? Why should we go out of our way to stop God being run out of town by the new technology? Hell, I think I understood more when I was a painting.'

'Bugger this,' the laptop said. 'I've had enough aggravation for one night. Come on, let's go and throw doughnuts at policemen in Trafalgar Square.'

Maria looked at him. 'By us,' she said, 'you mean me.'

'You'll do the actual throwing, I grant you. But in your capacity as a duly authorised officer of the company.'

'Huh.'

'Would it help if I said that your old job'll be still there for you when they let you out?'

Maria sighed. 'Oh, all right then. But not doughnuts.'

'Not doughnuts?'

'No,' Maria said firmly. 'Meringues. The brittle ones with cream and jam inside. Don't you think?'

After a brief coma of meditative bleeping, the laptop said, 'Agreed, by a unanimous vote of a duly convened Extraordinary General Meeting. Have we got any meringues?'

'We can get some off the trolley.'

'How right you are. Consider yourself appointed Projectiles Director, as of now. Come on, before all the bogies go off to bed.'

CHAPTER EIGHT

'Bloody Consolidated Oilfields,' muttered the Bishop, flicking off Ceefax with the remote and slumping into his swivel chair. 'Down twelve points at close of trading, would you believe? All they've got to do is shove a pointy stick in the ground and the stuff comes up like a burst pipe, and still they manage to lose money. Nicky, get that useless stockbroker on the phone and tell him to sell the lot.'

Nicky, the Bishop's lovely personal assistant, put her head round the door. 'Righty-ho, My Lord,' she said. 'Oh, and there's a vicar here to see you.'

'A what?'

'Vicar. Church of England clergyman. Says it's an emergency.'

The Bishop frowned. 'No offence, Nicky, but how can it be an emergency? I mean, it's not exactly a fast-moving profession.'

'No, My Lord.'

'So what's the deal?' the bishop sighed, accessing

SHARESORT on his screen. 'Sudden outbreak of heresy in the Parochial Church Council? The Day of Wrath cancelled for lack of interest? Or did the meek inherit the Earth but were too shy to tell us?'

Nicky bit her perfect lip. 'He was saying something about devils, My Lord.'

'Oh, not another one.' The Bishop groaned and buried his face in his hands. 'Why is it that a perfectly respectable, mundane business like ours attracts so many raving loonies? I ask you, it's just not fair. All a bloke's got to do is put on a white frock and dunk kids in a bird-bath all day long, nothing in that to make him jump the tracks and start seeing demons all over the place. It'd be different if we were running an opium refinery, but we're not. Tell him to go away.'

'Righty-ho. I've got Mr Villiers on the line for you.'

'Splendid – ah, Tristram, how's tricks? Yes, just fine, except for this Consolidated Oilfields result. How do you pick 'em, Tristram, a blindfold and a pin and the *Mammoth Book of Losers?* Yes, I know it was always speculative, but there's speculative and there's taking twenty grand of the diocesan tea money and putting it on a three-legged greyhound. Yes, sell the whole blasted holding, at least we can offset the loss against the capital gains tax on the Lanesco bid. What? Yes, of *course* I want you to take up those rights, He might have been born in a bloody stable but I wasn't. Yes, right, see you for golf on Sunday. Bye.'

He slammed down the phone, muttered something theological (at least, it had God in it somewhere) and reached for his calculator. He was in the middle of a complex double-grossing-up calculation when Nicky appeared again.

'Sorry,' she said. 'It's that vicar. He won't go away.'

'Won't he? Call the police. And get me last week's *Investor's Chronicle*, would you? There's a bit in there about the De Beers interim figures I need to look at before next week's synod.'

Before Nicky could move, the door burst open and Artofel charged in. Smoothly pressing the panic button with his knee, the Bishop nodded to Nicky that it was all right, he'd deal with it, and stood up.

'You,' he said, 'out. Now, before I have you thrown out.'

'But My Lord,' Artofel replied, bewildered, 'I need your help. It's serious. There's a major conspiracy of demons plotting to take over the world, and since you're my immediate superior—'

The Bishop looked at him. Long practice gave him the confidence to put this one in the Harmless category. 'So?' he said. 'You're a priest. Deal with it.'

'What?'

'You heard,' replied the Bishop, sitting down and picking up a sheaf of papers. 'You're a fully trained clergyman, you ought to know what to do. If you've forgotten, look it up.'

'But you don't understand,' Artofel cried, planting his hands on the desktop and leaning forwards. 'These aren't just ordinary demons like you and – I mean, just ordinary demons. They're – they're *evil*. Really they are. They want to—'

'Listen.' The Bishop lolled back in his chair and lit a cigar. 'Calm down and stop breathing in my face. Thank you. Now then, look at this picture on the wall. See it?'

'Yes, My Lord. It's you.'

'Very good. And what's that written underneath it?'

Artofel looked closely. 'The Right Reverend Trevor Jones, Bishop of . . .'

'Quite,' His Lordship replied. 'Bishop. In other words, management. Look, son, every time a screw comes loose on the production line at Dagenham, they don't send for the Managing Director to come and tighten it. No, they do it themselves, because that's their job, and he's got his. My job is to manage. Demons are strictly a field operative's responsibility. Got a book?'

'What? I mean, yes, but listen . . .'

'Bell? Candle? White sheet with hole for your head to go through? Then get out and earn your pay, and stop bothering me. Or would you rather I transferred you to a nice quiet living somewhere in Moss Side? Always an opening there for enthusiastic young clergymen who come barging in disturbing their superiors. Ah, the hell with these Sainsbury's cigars, go out as soon as look at you. Got a light?'

'No, sorry.' Artofel took a deep breath. All it needed, he was sure, was for him to find the right words so that he could explain. After all, it was important; and, as the man had just said, rogue demons were the responsibility of the local Topside field officers. That was what they were there for; surely he could understand *that* . . . 'Please,' he said, 'you've got to listen. It's not just the ordinary demons this time. I know all about them, and the bilateral Topside/Flipside non-aggression treaties. Dammit, I'm one of . . .I know about these things. But this is different. These demons are *breaking the rules*.'

The Bishop ground his teeth, a small mannerism of his which helped relieve tension. 'Now then, my friend,' he said, in a voice that suggested that he was being patient now, for a limited period only, Irritate Now While Stocks Last. 'We pride ourselves on being a tolerant Church, as you know. We don't mind batty vicars, so long as they keep their paws off the choirboys and don't go on the telly. It's all part of the picturesque charm, dotty vicars, it helps get bums on pews. But you are rapidly ceasing to be pictur-esque and becoming a pain in the jacksy. Now get back to your church, forgive some sins, bless a few crispbreads, do whatever it is you people do and don't let me ever catch you in here again. Understood? That's a direct order. Now hop it.'

Artofel took a step forwards and closed his fists. The Bishop jumped out of his chair, grabbing for the ornate and heavy crosier propped against the wall. 'Nicky!' he yelled. 'I thought I told you to call the Filth. Where are they?'

'It's all right.' Artofel came round the side of the desk, and found the head of the crosier prodding in his stomach. 'Oh for pity's sake,' he said, losing his temper, 'put that ridiculous thing down and come and look at your computer.'

The Bishop scowled. 'What's my computer got to do with . . .?'

'I didn't want to have to do this,' Artofel said, tapping keys. 'Still, you wouldn't listen, so you've brought it on yourself. I'm not really a vicar.'

'Not any more you're not.'

'I never was,' Artofel replied, as text scrolled up like approaching thunderclouds. 'I'm a Duke of Hell, and before you start yelling bloody murder I'll prove it to you. Now, you know your security codes? Grade Four, levels green and above, categories nine and four hundred and six?'

The Bishop's jaw dropped. 'Hey,' he objected. 'How'd you know about that stuff? That's supposed to be restricted.'

'Joke,' Artofel replied. 'Show me any Topside junior-level access code I can't bypass and I'll buy you a vanilla slice. Here we go,' he added, as the screen settled down. 'Now, press that key there, and you'll see my personnel file. My works number is 976404312, and I put fifty Nicks a week into the office Lottery syndicate. Go on, press the button.'

A few moments later the Bishop looked up from the

screen, his expression one of terrified awe. 'My God,' he said. 'It's true. You're a fiend.'

'Correct. Oh come on, put that silly crucifix down, we're all on the same side really.' Artofel frowned, as the penny tinkled on the floor of his mind. 'Didn't you know?' he said. 'Gosh. I'd have thought they'd have told you that. What,' he added cruelly, 'with you being *management* and everything.'

The Bishop looked at him suspiciously. 'How do I know that?' he demanded. 'I mean, you're just saying that to tempt me. Begone, foul spawn of night—'

'Please be quiet. Thank you. Now,' Artofel continued, tapping a few more keys, 'the point is this. There's a syndicate of demons out there – our people, I'm ashamed to say; there's a few good apples in every barrel – who've broken the rules. They've got some sort of conspiracy to overthrow the Boss, and you've got to stop it. Got that?'

The Bishop turned pale. 'There's devils conspiring to overthrow Satan, and you're asking *me* to intervene?'

Artofel started counting to ten; he got as far as three. 'Not Satan, you idiot. The *Boss*. Haven't you been listening to a word I've said? Now, under the Bethlehem protocol, any unauthorised hostile activity by an agent of one side falls to be dealt with by the other side's local officer in whose jurisdiction the breach occurs. In this case, you.' He smiled, and sat down in the Bishop's swivel chair. 'So what are you going to do about it?' he asked politely.

'I – I don't know,' the Bishop replied, flopping bonelessly into the visitor's chair on the opposite side of the desk. 'What's the conspiracy about? Do you know? Sir?' he added quickly.

'No,' Artofel replied. 'All I know is, I've somehow been scooped up out of my incarnation as a Duke of Hell and beamed down here into the body of a Church of England vicar. And now,' he went on grimly, 'they want the body. I don't know what for, but it seems logical that they want this particular body because of something to do with the transmigration. Sound reasonable to you?'

'Um,' the Bishop replied.

'Quite.' Artofel steepled his fingers. 'I've also got an idea,' he went on, 'that it's somehow connected with Kawaguchiya Integrated Circuits – you know, the computer firm?'

'KIC?' The Bishop's face creased with panic. 'Christ, I've got shares in them.'

'Indeed?' Artofel grinned. 'Well, in that case, you either stand to make a killing or lose your cassock, I don't know which right now. That's actually the very least of your problems. Might you not feel that a diabolical plot to undermine the authority of God is perhaps slightly more important even than that?'

'Huh? Oh, well, yes, I suppose so. Look, if I could just have a moment to phone my broker. You see, it's diocesan money and I'm responsible.'

Artofel sighed. 'Bureaucrats,' he murmured. 'Waste of space, all of them. In fact, the only reason I don't wash my hands of the lot of 'em is I'm one too.' He hesitated for a moment as a thought crept under the door of his mind. 'Your broker,' he said. 'Decent sort of a chap?'

'I suppose so,' the Bishop replied. 'Fairly sound on overall portfolio strategy, if a trifle over-inclined to—'

'No, no, I didn't mean is he competent, I asked you if he was *decent*. Honest. Upright. Full of righteousness and so forth.'

The Bishop shook his head. 'I doubt that very much,' he replied. 'Wouldn't have got very far in the stockbroking lark if he was.'

'Splendid. Right, I want you to ring him up and tell him to sell all your KIC stocks immediately. Sound worried.'

'Won't be hard,' the Bishop said. 'You really think they're a bad investment at this time?'

'Oh for – listen. I want to start a run on their shares. One of those wild, irrational lemming-like panics the Stock Exchange is so famous for. I'm not sure what effect it'll have, but if KIC is involved somehow, it might force something to happen and we might be a bit closer to finding out what's going on.'

'You think that's wise?'

Artofel shrugged. 'No idea,' he replied. 'But somebody's got to do something. I'm just a vicar and you're useless. What else do you suggest?'

The Bishop thought for a moment. 'Fair enough,' he said. 'And even if it doesn't work, we could still make a packet on the side if we buy at the bottom, using nominees of course, maybe through a Channel Islands trust . . .'

Artofel looked at him with distaste. 'My Lord,' he said. 'Ever wondered whether you might possibly be in the wrong job?'

'Me?' The Bishop reflected briefly. 'No. Why?'

'Doesn't matter. You just make the call, and leave Good and Evil to me. After all,' he added ruefully, 'I'm not a clergyman. I'm a wages clerk.'

'What?'

'Oh, get on with it.'

Softly, like rose-petals drifting down on top of a snowdrift, the undercarriage of Zxprxp's Starglider touched the roof of Ten Downing Street. With a faint sigh, the anti-gravitational inertial dampers took the weight, and he cut the engines.

Below, the inevitable policeman stood, hands behind back, eyes staring straight ahead. If he'd looked up, he might have thought it was an updated version of Santa's sleigh, or a very large mutant pigeon. Fortunately, he didn't hear a sound or move a muscle. He didn't even register the faint whirr, like a faery blender, of the circular saw cutting a neat round hole in the roof.

Well, Zxprxp reflected as he lowered himself down into the attic, this would seem to be the place; all I've got to do now is find the leader. Oh well, it's not a very big building.

The automatically triggered remote controls built into his belt-mounted instrument array dealt with all the various alarms and security devices without his even knowing there were any. Accordingly, when he pushed open a door and found a humanoid life form sitting in the room behind it, his attention wasn't distracted by hordes of security guards abseiling in through windows. 'Excuse me,' he said.

The man turned his head, stared at him; said nothing.

'I come in peace,' Zxprxp said automatically. 'Um, are you the Prime Minister?'

The man carried on staring at him out of round, expressionless eyes. For some reason best known to himself, he was sitting on top of a big, old-fashioned wardrobe, underneath which someone had laid ten or twelve thick, fleecy duvets and a pile of cushions. Since, where Zxprxp came from, intelligent life forms rested and slept curled up inside the boles of giant fungi and stored their equivalent of clothes in the discarded shells of *hrtewqztqx* eggs, he had no way of knowing whether what the man was doing was normal or not. Reasonable to assume, he decided, that it was. After all, this is their *leader*. They wouldn't have a weirdo or an idiot as their leader, now would they? Stood to reason.

'Um,' Zxprxp said, 'I'm from another planet. I'm here to, er, study your dominant species with a view to establishing diplomatic links between our two worlds. Thanks to my universal translation device, I can understand what you say. That is, if you were to say anything, I'm sure I'd be able to understand it. Hello?'

The man continued to stare. From time to time his nose twitched a little, and he rubbed the backs of his hands together.

'I expect you're wondering,' Zxprxp went on, 'what my planet's like. Well, it's a bit difficult to describe, I suppose, in terms you'd be likely to understand, because it's – well, it's quite a lot different from this one. But that suits us, of course, because we're quite a lot different from you. Well, you don't need me to tell you that, you can see it for yourself. Can't you?'

The man stared at him, blinked, turned round a couple of times and sat down again.

'Um,' said Zxprxp, 'maybe it'd be easier for us to communicate in a meaningful way if I came up on top of that, um, thing with you. Would it? Yes? No? All right, I'll take that as a Yes. Is it all right if I stand on this thing?' he added, taking hold of a small Hepplewhite chair. 'Okay, assuming that it is, here I come.'

He'd just looped a few tentacles round the top of the wardrobe and was about to pull himself up when the man cowered away from him, arched his back and started hissing and squeaking. Nonplussed, Zxprxp got down off the chair and put it back where it had come from.

'All right,' he said, 'that's fine, and no offence intended. I did ask, remember. Now then, more about my planet. Well, for a start—'

The door started to open. Zxprxp thought quickly. Chances were, this was some official or other with a message or the equivalent of some *op'rgesvxq* shells for the leader to suckerprint. That would mean having to explain himself all over again to yet another human. Too much hassle, Zxprxp decided, so he opened the wardrobe and slithered inside.

Through the keyhole he watched as a humanoid came in and walked over to a spot directly in front of the wardrobe door, so that his sleeve obscured the view. Nevertheless, he could hear clearly enough.

'Prime Minister – Prime Minister? Ah, you're up there again, Prime Minister—'

(Great, Zxprxp said to himself, looks like I've found the Prime Minister. So that's all right.)

'Sorry to disturb you, Prime Minister,' the voice went on, 'when you're, um, sitting on a wardrobe, um, in Cabinet, I mean, but the American special envoy's here and he was wondering if you could possibly spare him a minute or two? No? Only he has come all the way from Washington to see you, and maybe it'd be a nice gesture if – no? Oh, right, fine. I'll tell him you're busy then, shall I, Prime Minister? Prime Minister? Oh—!'

There was a loud thump, and Zxprxp found he could see through the keyhole again. This was apparently because the newcomer had rushed forward to assist the Prime Minister, who'd fallen off his – what had the other one called it? Wardrobe. Fallen off or jumped; no, fallen off, obviously. No sane person'd go jumping off tall things for no apparent reason.

'Better now?' the newcomer was saying. 'Splendid. And you're going to come down and see the special envoy? No, I see. You want to climb back up again, do you? Oh, very well then. As you wish, Prime – ouch!'

The cry, presumably of pain, was the result of the Prime Minister scrambling up the other one's back and treading on his head on his way back up to the top of the wardrobe. Zxprxp couldn't help feeling a tiny bit smug. On his planet they had pairs of long metal strips joined together with rungs, called ladders, for getting up on top of high places. Clearly the humans hadn't tumbled to that one yet.

'Well, if that's all for now, Prime Minister, I'll be getting back to my—'

Thump.

'Oh for – perhaps you'd like to use the chair this time, Prime – aagh!' Zxprxp grinned, sensing a definite commercial possibility if they ever did establish trading links with these creatures. A few dozen ladders in the ballast hold, he could name his own price. Assuming, that is, there was anything on this planet anybody back home would want to buy.

He heard the door close, and came out again. 'Hi,' he said cheerfully, 'me again. Hope you didn't mind me disappearing like that, I thought it'd save lots of tedious explaining. Now, where were we? I was telling you about my planet. For a start, Prime Minister, we've got this device you might very well be interested in, which we call a ladder. I won't bore you with the technical stuff, but just suppose you wanted to jump off something and you were on your own with nobody to tread on. It'd be frustrating, wouldn't it? But with one of our—'

There was a blur in the air a few *ghtuyrg* in front of him, followed by a now familiar thump, and there was the Prime Minister, curled up in a ball in the middle of the soft, flollopy things, looking (as far as Zxprxp could tell) surprised and possibly even disappointed at something; almost as if he'd expected something to happen when he jumped, and it hadn't. This species, he muttered to himself, is going to take a lot of figuring out.

Nevertheless, he was here as an ambassador of his race, and politeness is the shuttle bay ramp of diplomacy. As the Prime Minister floundered back on to his feet, Zxprxp stepped forward and offered his head for the creature to tread on. As they said back home, when in Y'zhgyrstd . . .

Surprisingly heavy, these humans.

Taking a deep breath, he continued where he'd left off.

A brief sales pitch for ladders, a polite enquiry as to why the leader of the human race should keep jumping off the top of a wardrobe (unanswered), a few random observations concerning his homeworld's mass, gravitational field, basic climatic and seasonal cycles, some introductory remarks about his own species and the fundamentals of their culture and beliefs – it was strange, but he got the impression the Leader wasn't actually *listening*.

Puzzlement. Then, as the Prime Minister flung himself into the air yet again and hit the deck in a flurry of scrabbling limbs, a ray of light broke through the fog in his mind. Stepping back quickly – there's politeness, and there's a squashed head – he assessed the theory and found it good.

This bloke's a nutcase, the alien decided. The leader of the human race is as daffy as a barrelful of *qpsrdyt'srhy* beetles.

Zxprxp stood for a moment, lower and middle mandibles agape with astonished admiration. Maybe they don't know spit about ladders, but when it comes to political and cultural maturity, these critters have us knocked into a cocked *dzandtpt*.

Back home, he reflected, as the poor loon scrabbled and clambered back up the wardrobe, we've had thousands of years of social and political conflicts, the result of which is that, every time around, some absolute nutter claws his way to the top and calls himself a leader. And then, a few solar time units later, along comes another soi-disant leader, also barking mad; we have a war or a revolution, the old leader is toppled and the new one takes his place; and so on, over and over again, until our economy and our very civilisation are in tatters, and everybody has a thoroughly miserable time.

But not so with these ever-so-sophisticated humans. They're through with all that, obviously. Their leader isn't some magnificently pompous figure, surrounded on all sides with advisers and hangers-on and fifty-seven varieties of functionary; no, it's some poor loony shut up in a room on his own, with a high place to jump from and something soft to land on, who spends his days endlessly playing out the fatuous cycle of leadership (scrabble scrabble *THUMP*, scrabble scrabble tread on people's heads *THUMP*) in a safely ritualised, utterly harmless fashion. And presumably, Zxprxp rationalised with growing respect, if there's ever a human so foolish as to start believing in the dangerous concepts that lie behind the idea of leadership, all they have to do is bring him up here and let him watch for a while, maybe get his scalp scuffed up a bit in the process, and he's instantly cured. Brilliant.

Now *that's* an idea worth paying a whole freighterload of ladders for.

There was a cold, determined light in Kevin's eyes as he pushed open the study door, not unlike the gleam a hedgehog might see in the headlamps of an oncoming lorry. What it had to do with the fact that he'd just been talking to a young female (mortal, but two out of three ain't bad) for the first time in his life, he wasn't quite sure. All he knew was that ever since this ghastly mess began, he'd been underestimating one crucial factor, namely himself.

Think about it (he muttered to himself, flumping down in the Old Man's chair and turning on the screen with a brutal flick). Of the two main players in this game, one of 'em's a dumb machine and the other one's the Son of God. Once this crucial factor's been taken into account, the expression *no contest* assumes a whole new spectrum of nuances.

'Right,' he commanded, as the screen lit up. 'You. Pack it in. You got that?'

Somehow his born-again attitude and authoritative tone of voice made a huge amount of no difference at all. All he got was that damn fool request for access codes. Access codes! I'll give the insufferable thing access codes!

Well, he reflected a moment later, actually I won't, because I don't know them. All I can do is get the thing up and running. Then it just sits there grinning at me like a Cheshire cat that's been at the cream. Well, I'm not having that. It's not respectful, and if you ain't got respect . . .

'Computer,' Kevin said, 'I'm going to give you a choice. It's not easy. It's not *supposed* to be easy. Ready?'

>ENTER SECURITY CODE FOR CLEARANCE.

'All right,' Kevin said, 'here goes. Unless you loosen up and tell me what it is I've done and what I can do to correct it, I'm going to sit down at this keyboard and press fourteen keys at random. Got that?'

>PROJECTED COURSE OF ACTION INADVISABLE.

Kevin grinned. 'You bet it is,' he said. 'It'd be a shambles. There's absolutely no way of knowing how much havoc I could cause. Which is why you can't allow it to happen.'

>YOU RECKON?

'Of course,' Kevin answered, as he lolled back in Dad's chair. 'Think about it.' He picked up the letter opener, fidgeted with it for a moment, dropped it and sucked his fingers. Only Kevin's dad could have a flaming sword for a letter-opener. And all the theologians in the cosmos, working double shifts and weekends, would never be able to work out whence came the Innovations catalogue He'd ordered it from.

>DOES NOT COMPUTE.

'Doesn't it now?' Kevin shook his head. 'I rather think it does. Because if you allow me to do this, you'll be every bit as guilty as I am. At least,' he added, smiling sweetly, 'that's the way Dad'll see it. He doesn't much care for the old only-obeying-orders copout.'

>BUT I'M A COMPUTER. I CAN'T NOT OBEY ORDERS.

'True.' Kevin nodded ironically. 'Because I've given you the one access code I do know, you've got no choice but to let me press those fourteen buttons if I decide to. On the other hand, you can't allow that to happen. Which means you'll just have to give in to my demands, doesn't it?'

>NOT WITHOUT THE PROPER CODES.

Kevin sighed, and flexed his fingers like an extrovert concert pianist. 'This one,' he said, feathersoftly stroking the edges of a key chosen at random with the pad of his index finger, 'could be pretty well anything. It could be the Seven Plagues of Egypt, or Noah's Flood, or the Four Horsemen of the Apocalypse. Who knows?' He leaned forward until his nose was almost touching the burning-without-consuming screen. 'Apart from you, that is. *You* know.'

>YES, I DO. AND I MUST ADVISE YOU NOT TO . . .

'Oops, too late.' Kevin looked up, trying to keep off his face any reflection of the horror that was sloshing about inside his mind like shaken-up fizzy lemonade in a plastic bottle. He had, after all, done something so drastically reckless as to be technically Evil – *a first in our family, I guess. So that's what it's like. It's all right, I suppose, but I can't see why anybody should want to do it for fun.* 'Well, any hints about what I've just done? Any large holes in the sky where there used to be planets? The Aquascutum people suddenly relabelling all their stuff *Guaranteed frogproof*?'

> WHY ARE YOU DOING THIS?

'You know perfectly well why.'

> DOES NOT COMPUTE. YOU KNOW THAT WHAT YOU ARE DOING CANNOT HELP MAKE THINGS BETTER, FOR THE SAME REASON THEY DON'T PUT PETROL IN FIRE EXTINGUISHERS. THE SITUATION IS BAD ENOUGH ALREADY. WHY ARE YOU DELIBERATELY MAKING IT WORSE?

Kevin looked at the words on the screen and thought about the question they were putting to him. He didn't know the answer. He had a nasty feeling that his scheme wasn't going to work after all. There were still thirteen keys to go, and there was no way he could back down now.

'I wonder,' he said, 'what this one does.'

'Wow,' said a voice in the darkness. 'Did you feel that?'

There was an awkward silence, marred only by the statutory drip of water, the scuttling of the small, clawed feet of Dukes of Hell on dry flagstones, the sound of somebody shivering.

'Would someone tell that young man,' observed the female demon, 'that it's terribly bad manners to do someone else's job without asking them first. Not that we could ever pull a stunt like that,' she added bitterly. 'If there's one thing I can't stand, it's talented amateurs.'

'Not to mention beginner's luck,' growled a further voice, the demon called Bumble. 'Some of us had to work hard to get to this level. Then again, some of us weren't born with a silver spoon gripped between our fangs.'

There was an awkward lull in the dialogue, spoons being a contentious issue among these folk, with particular reference to the length of the handle.

'Anyway,' said the female, brisk with sledgehammer cheerfulness, 'it's a bit of luck for us, so I suggest we pack in the gift-horse dentistry and talk about what we're going to do next.'

Various free-floating voices mumbled agreement, with only Bumble pointing out that if certain people Upstairs who should remain nameless were going to make a habit of doing evil by stealth in this way, there didn't seem to be an awful lot of point.

'Before we go charging in with both hooves,' the female demon continued, 'we'd better just stop for a moment and make sure we all know exactly what it is we're setting out to do. Agreed?'

A muted chorus indicated their support for the proposal, and the female demon, having cleared where her throat would have been if she'd had one when wearing her true shape, continued.

'The game plan,' she said, 'is this. At the moment, Himself upstairs has the monopoly on Creation. Result: stagnation, decadence, decline, all research and invention in atrophy, and we're not making a penny out of a potentially lucrative market. Can this state of affairs be allowed to continue? we ask ourselves. No, it can not.

'Which is why,' she went on, 'we've formed a syndicate to design and build an alternative life form with which the landlords of habitable planets can stock their worlds. Now there's no point in mucking about with sentient rocks and super-intelligent electrical currents and things that look like failed soufflés; in physical terms, there's nothing to whack the upright two-armed biped with its brain in its head and the good old opposable thumb. What we've got to do is find some way of *improving* on Old Reliable; and it's not the hardware that needs updating so much as the software. The programming. The hard disk. Agreed?'

Another round of muted approval, tempered only by a suggestion that there had to be a better way of producing more of them than *that*. Something neat and quick and quiet, the voice recommended, where you just add water or take a cutting or something.

'The software on the present model, however,' she continued, 'is an absolute bloody disaster; I don't think anybody would disagree with that, least of all the little perishers themselves. In fact, we'd be doing our prospective creations a favour. All right so far? Good.

'What we've now got to do,' she went on, 'is find a better set of systems, one that'll be compatible with the hardware but which won't end up self-destructing the whole production run and taking the planet with it. And that's why recent events have given us an opportunity we just can't afford to miss. Because, thanks to our unwitting friend in a high place, there are now five human bodies walking around up there with non-human systems running them; and the very fact that they're still walking around several weeks later proves to me that these systems work. What we've got to do now is analyse them, pull out the bits that we want to incorporate in our product and combine them, along with a few herbs and spices of our own, to make something we can flog to planetholders everywhere. Everyone happy with that?'

'Sure,' growled a voice in the middle darkness. 'Except, with all due respect, we haven't exactly got very far, have we? Two direct approaches, two washouts. Three, if you include the painting.'

There was nothing in the tone of the female demon's reply to suggest a shrug of a pair of notional shoulders, but it was there all right. 'So we went about it the wrong way. We asked first. This time, we don't bother asking. And before you say *We can't just go grabbing 'em off the surface and taking them to bits with a damn great spanner, someone's sure to notice,* I'd like to point out that that's exactly what we can do, now that Our Kid's gone and switched off the security cameras.'

'Hello and good morning, you're listening to the Early Bird show, my name's Danny Bennett and today's big story is the total and completely unexpected eclipse of the sun, which none of the world's great scientific institutions managed to predict. And the question we all should be asking is, if they didn't know, who did? Is this just a perfectly innocent natural disaster, as a Home Office spokesman was at such pains to assure us earlier this morning? Or, with the US Presidential elections less than four years away and tension further escalating in the strife-torn Gulf, is there more to today's outbreak of total darkness than meets the eye? With me in the studio this morning we have . . .'

If *Homo sapiens* had been deliberately trying to prove the First Voice's point, they couldn't have made a better job of it. Their ability to scuff up the patently obvious, to the point where any other explanation than the true one would be more acceptable, had never been more brilliantly displayed. Thanks to Danny Bennett and hundreds of thousands of steely-eyed newshounds like him right across the now unexpectedly pitch-dark planet, humanity was divided into two roughly equal groupings: those who were hysterically convinced that it was some ghastly manoeuvre by the Americans (especially numerous, needless to say, in America), and those who had long ago learnt that anything they say on the news is bound to be the exact opposite of the truth, who therefore dismissed the eclipse as One of Those Things and contented themselves with digging out the candles left over from last winter's electricity strike.

In their defence, it has to be said that none of them could be expected to realise what was going on since none of them actually knew what the Sun and Moon are for.

In the security room Topside, meanwhile, the seemingly endless array of monitors suddenly went blank.

CHAPTER NINE

'I t's gone dark,' said the robot, peering out of the window.

'So it has,' Len replied. 'Is it supposed to do that? Remember, I used to live in a factory.'

The robot accessed some relevant data. 'Not really,' it replied. 'Or at least, not right now. You see, there's this thing called the sun, it's a big burning thing in the sky—'

'I'll take your word for it,' Len replied hastily. It hadn't taken him long to discover that asking the robot to explain things was really only something you dared to do if you had a spare week. 'Fuse blown, I expect. That or a couple of wires come loose. I expect they'll get it fixed in a minute.'

The robot hummed for a second or so as information sloshed into it from data stores in five continents. 'I doubt it,' it said, considered whether or not it should explain, assessed its master's mood to nine decimal places and added, 'apparently it's not quite as simple as that.'

'Oh come on,' Len replied impatiently, 'it's just a big

light, that's all. If it's not a fuse or a loose connection, what can it be? Might be a flat battery, I suppose.'

'It hasn't got batteries,' the robot said. 'It's, um, solar powered. Look, to cut it short, there's something between it and us. All we do is wait for the obstruction to go away. These things happen, apparently.'

Len shrugged. 'No skin off my nose, anyway,' he replied. 'We've got work to do, remember? Now let's see, we've got the paint and the scaffolding poles, that just leaves the—'

Outside in the street there was a screech of rubber on asphalt, a loud bump which made the ground shake, and the tinkling of glass, soft and musical as the laughter of malicious elves. 'Hello,' Len said, turning his head. 'What's that noise?'

'Car accident, probably,' the robot said. 'That's when two internal-combustion-propelled road-going vehicles – sorry, I don't suppose you're in the mood.'

'Sounded a bit drastic,' Len mused. 'Is that perfectly normal too?'

The robot nodded. 'Very much so,' it said. 'More people are killed and injured on the roads of Britain every year than died in the Battle of—'

'Killed?' Len turned and scowled at the robot. 'Thought you said it was perfectly normal.'

'It is. One minute you're driving along quite happily, then next you're staring up at a white ceiling and they're giving you your lunch through a tube up your nose. It's amazing what your lot – I mean their lot, sorry – are prepared to get used to.'

Another screech, bump, tinkle. And another. Len put down the hacksaw he'd been adjusting and stood up. Something, his machine's sense of harmony told him, was out of alignment here; there was a jib strip loose or a lock nut in need of adjustment, and machines abhor that sort of thing in the way that Nature abhors a vacuum. 'Altruism,' he said.

'Sorry?'

'That stuff you were telling me about. Could we do some of it and stop these internal-combustion-propelled road-going vehicles bopping each other?'

The robot ran a feasibility scan. 'I don't see why not,' it replied. 'Speaking of which, there's a substantial probability that what's causing all these accidents is the eclipse. Because it's dark, you see.'

'So they can't see where they're going. Haven't they got lights?'

The robot tilted its head, noticing as it did so that the left-side integral oil reservoir in its neck would need topping up in approximately sixteen months' time. 'Sure they have,' it replied. 'But it's not night-time. Which means it's not supposed to be dark. So some people aren't switching their lights on. And before you ask—'

'Don't tell me, that's perfectly normal too.' Len's brow furrowed. 'I tell you,' he said, 'most of these human buggers couldn't get a job as a screwdriver, let alone a milling machine or a turret lathe. Thick as bricks, the lot of 'em. All right then, let's go and altruise. These internal-combustion-propelled—'

'Call 'em cars,' suggested the robot. 'It's easier.'

'Cars, then. They're machines, I take it?'

'You bet. Pretty neat bits of engineering, some of them.'

Len relaxed. 'That's all right, then. At least there's somebody intelligent we can talk to about this.'

The robot, needless to say, was fitted with a 250,000-candlepower halogen searchlight right between the sensor heads that served it as eyes. Once they reached the street, the beam from this magnificent accessory illuminated a thoroughly depressing scene. Just in case someone might ask for an exactly appropriate word to describe it, the robot ran a quick dictionary check and came up with 'shambles'.

'Idiots,' Len muttered, as a car whipped past him at high speed, narrowly missing the corpse of a small van. 'They've all got perfectly good headlamps. Why don't they . . .?'

At the robot's request, all the component data stores of the Net thought about that one for approximately a sixth of a second. 'It's quite obvious,' the robot said, 'once you take into account modern human operational protocols. You see, it isn't against the law to drive around without your lights on during a total eclipse of the sun. It's only not illegal because nobody's thought to make it illegal, but since it isn't, they aren't. Turning their lights on, I mean. The idea is, they've got the Government to tell them what to do and what not to do. Until the Government tells them they've got to switch on the lights during an eclipse, they can't. Even if they want to. All they can do is wait till the next election and vote in a different government who *will* tell them to switch their lights on when the Earth's orbit around the sun coincides with the orbit of the moon around the Earth. And according to my data, there isn't another election due for up to four point two years.' The robot paused to reflect on this. 'Let's hope for their sakes,' it added, 'that it's not going to be a very long eclipse.'

Len tried to get his head around that one, but it wasn't that bendy. 'Stuff that,' he said. 'Oh look, here comes another—'

It was a new-model Escort, and it hadn't seen the van. Just at that crucial moment when impact could still just about be avoided, Len took a deep breath and shouted.

The driver of the Escort, suddenly seeing a van directly in front of him, swerved, yanked the wheel back, swore and carried on. He hadn't heard anything, of course, because when Len yelled:

Switch your bloody lights on, you clown!

he'd yelled it in Machine; admittedly with a thick Engineering accent, whereas the car only spoke Automotive, but it managed to get the gist.

'It worked,' muttered the robot.

Len shrugged. 'Well, there was obviously no point talking to the human. Oh for pity's sake, here's another.'

An hour and a half later, Len was still yelling at passing cars and averting fatal collisions, when something remarkable happened. The cars started turning their lights on, even though it wasn't lighting-up time yet.

'Huh?' he asked the robot.

'It's all right,' the robot replied. 'They've passed a law.'

The small van which had caused most of the trouble was skewed across about a third of the width of the road. Its nose was folded round a lamppost (now rather banana-shaped) and its door had been left open by its driver, who had presumably limped off to find somewhere comfortable to wait for the next General Election. All in all, it looked . . .

'Unloved,' Len remarked, looking at it. 'You'd have thought its human's place was at its side at a time like this.'

'Don't think they see it that way,' replied the robot. 'Not that I'm defending them, I hasten to add. It's just the way things are. The chances of the driver having gone off to get it some iodine and a nice strong cup of sweet tea are fairly slim.'

A look of disgust settled on Len's face like mist coming in from the sea over high ground. 'It's times like this,' he said, 'I don't have any trouble deciding whose side I'm on.

Come on, let's see if there's anything we can do for it.'

The van's engine had long since stalled, but its brave little tape deck was still gallantly warbling, even though nobody was bothering to listen to it; like a brass band in the park on a rainy day, or the orchestra on the *Titanic*. Len walked up and switched it off.

'How're you feeling?' he asked it in Machine.

'Awful,' the van replied. 'My subframe hurts.'

'I'm not surprised,' Len replied. 'That's a nasty knock you've taken there. Now I'm not a mechanic, but I'd say you've got a twisted chassis, bent upper link, severe rupture of the hoses, probably some internal haemor-rhaging—'

'Oh my God,' whispered the van pitifully. 'That's terrible. They – they aren't going to write me off, are they?'

Len looked grave. 'It's early days yet,' he said. 'Until we actually get you up on a ramp and see precisely what the damage is—'

'Don't let them scrap me, please,' the van pleaded. 'Damn it all, I'm only M-reg, I've hardly begun living yet. Is there a chance, do you think? Honestly? You wouldn't lie to me, would you?'

Len shrugged. 'There's always a chance,' he replied. 'It may be a cliché, but it's true; where there's ignition there's hope. Look, I'm going to get you over to my workshop, where we can get a spanner on you and – well, what is it?' he snapped, as the robot's tapping on his shoulder threatened to dislocate it. 'Can't you see I'm busy?'

'Um,' replied the robot. 'Just a quick word.'

'Well?'

'Um – over here.'

Annoyed, Len took a few steps back. 'Come on, spit it out. We've got to move fast before its whole system drains down.'

The robot shuffled its precision-ground feet. 'I hate to

have to point this out,' it said, 'but you can't just go around mending things that don't belong to you. It's against the law.'

Len stared at the robot in amazement. 'Why the hell not? Look, there's machine over there in agony, and you want me to walk away? Of all the—'

The robot cringed. 'I know,' it said. 'But the owner might not *want* it repaired. He might be only too happy to let them junk it and take the insurance money instead.'

'But that's disgusting,' Len snarled. 'It'd be murder. No, the hell with that. You get behind and push, but for pity's sake be careful. If its sills have gone, we could kill it if we start mauling it about.'

Together they managed to trundle the van across the road. Len opened the sliding door and they machine-handled it up into the workshop, trying their best to ignore its heartrending groans at the slightest bump.

'Right,' Len ordered, grabbing an inspection light and sliding underneath. 'I'll need the arc welder and five hundred ccs of SAE20/40. Don't just stand there, get on with it.'

The robot nodded; then a suggestion filtered down through its circuits from some distant cybernetic origin. 'Shall I get lots of hot water and clean towels?' it asked.

Len looked blank. 'No,' he said. 'Why?'

'I don't know,' the robot admitted. 'I just got the idea from somewhere that it's something humans do at times like this.'

'Welder. Oil. Now. And a set of AF spanners and the big Stilson,' Len added, wiping oil out of his eyes with the back of his hand. 'And a printout of the workshop manual'd be a help, while you're at it. I've never set eyes on one of these things before, remember, and there's only so far I can go on general mechanical principles. I've got to drain off all the fuel before I do anything at all, or I'll blow us all up.'

'Aagh,' murmured the van. ''Scuse me, but are you sure you know what you're doing?'

'And you can shut up as well. Or would you rather I put you back in the road and let the *humans* play with you?'

'Sorry. Forget I spoke. Every confidence – ow!'

An hour later, Len emerged. He was spattered from head to foot with oil and there was dirty grease up to his elbows. As far as he was concerned, that was like rolling around in the mud at the bottom of a trench at Ypres.

'It's not looking all that wonderful,' he admitted. 'I can patch up most of the impact damage, but the front axle's cracked half the way through. I really don't think—'

His words tailed off, and there was a horrible silence. The only sound was the faint plopping of windscreen washer dripping from the fractured reservoir like tears.

'I'm sorry,' he said.

'You did your best,' whispered the van. 'Please, can you ask them to take me to a breaker's yard? I'd like to help other vans to live after my death.'

Len could feel major seismic activity in his throat, and his eyes were watering. 'Of course I will, son. You leave that to me. I think that's very – unselfish . . .' He broke off, his voice congested with strange emotions: the horror of waste, the death of a machine, most of all the sense of failure. It wasn't something he could accept. Machines don't fail; people fail machines. Suddenly he felt disgustingly human.

'No,' he spluttered, 'the hell with that, too. If needs be I'll mill you up a new axle out of a solid bar. You hang in there, kid, it's going to be all – now what do you want?' he demanded angrily, turning on the robot and glowering. 'Of all the insensitive—'

'All I was going to say was,' murmured the robot, 'why don't you just get a spare axle? You know, from a parts supplier? It's only a suggestion, of course, but—'

'Can you do that?'

The robot nodded vigorously. 'Easy,' he said. 'They do it all the time, humans. All you have to do is phone them up, go and get the part, pay them the money and there you are. Simple.'

'Money,' Len echoed. 'Actually, that might be a problem. Have we got any left?'

The robot looked in the green plastic dustbin. 'Actually,' he said, 'no. But that needn't stop you. I can transfer some.'

'You what?'

'By computer,' the robot explained. 'No problem at all. Well, there's a *slight* problem, because it's against the law, but—'

Len grinned savagely. 'It sounds to me,' he said, 'like all the best things are. Except,' he added, 'turning your lights on during an eclipse. Anyway, we won't bother ourselves with that. You crack on and do whatever it is you've got to do, and I'll phone one of these parts people. Oh, and robot.'

'Hm?'

'See if you can't get them to fix that sun thing. It's dark as a bag in here, even with the inspection light.'

The robot hesitated, while the Appeal Court of its mind pondered the nuances of the Laws of Robotics. Eventually they handed down a decision stating that the overriding law which supervened all others was that no robot shall say anything, no matter how true, that will inevitably earn it a smack in the mouth with a 5/8″ Whitworth spanner.

'Sure thing, boss,' it said.

The Melanesian island of Crucifixion, a basalt chip in the middle of a rather excessive amount of sea, is home to thirty-six people, a hundred and four pigs, two hundred and twenty-nine chickens and three hundred and forty-seven thousand nine hundred and seventy-eight limited companies.

Yes, it's a tax haven. But there's more to it than that. Alderney, Sark, the Cayman and Antilles are also fiscal cat-flaps where the storm-driven corporation can crawl in out of the rain and snuggle profitably. They're fine, if you lack vision and the broad, holistic outlook. But company promoters who want the very best for their fledgeling enterprise in the way of protection from the sharp teeth of the Revenue bring them lovingly to Crucifixion, in the same way that Mary and Joseph carried the baby Jesus into Egypt to escape the wrath of Herod, or expatriate cricket-lovers once raced their pregnant wives over the border into Yorkshire. For on Crucifixion, they don't just harbour limited companies. They worship them.

Literally. The first thing you notice when the weary little plane touches down on the only flat part of the island is the colossal stone statues, hacked out of the native rock countless centuries ago by a long-forgotten civilisation. Unlike the pale imitations you find on places like Easter Island, however, they aren't just aimlessly drawn up in monotonous rows like traffic cones on the M25; they sit in circles around vast, flat stone tables, on which rest carven ashtrays and carafes of basalt water, while one of their number stands at the head of the table, frozen for all time in the act of turning the page of a flip-chart. These, explain the inhabitants, are the Board Meetings of the Gods.

Kawaguchiya Integrated Circuits, unusually, doesn't have its registered office on Crucifixion, but six of the thirty-six residents are KIC staff manning the company's office there; a tiny but vital outpost dedicated to organising the tsunami of electronic mail that comes flooding in every second of every minute of every hour of every day, turning it round and sending it off to where the companies actually

do business, in Seattle and Tokyo and Milan and Seoul
and Birmingham. It may not be the most sybaritic posting
in the KIC universe, but being sent to Crucifixion for a
year is generally regarded as the ordeal a high-flier must
endure before emerging from the chrysalis and taking
wing for the upper paradise of senior executive status.
There are drawbacks, of course: the isolation, culture
shock and lack of material comforts, and the terrible,
terrible boredom—

'There is no such word,' said Ms Tomacek severely, 'as
zurf.'

'Yes there is.' Grinning maliciously, Mr Wakisashi
tapped a few keys and pointed. 'An Arabian coffee-cup
holder,' he said, smug as a cat in an aviary. 'And that's on a
triple word score, so—'

The screen cleared abruptly, and a small part of Mr
Wakisashi's mind that still went through the motions of
duty to the company asked if anyone knew if it was supposed to do that. The rest of his mind was too busy with
the apparently insoluble problem of getting inside Ms
Tomacek's blouse, and either didn't hear or pretended it
was doing something else.

'All right,' muttered Ms Tomacek, 'if you're so darn
clever—' She clicked down a tile, like a duellist dropping a
glove.

'Zurfs,' Mr Wakisashi observed. 'I see.'

'More than one Arabian coffee-cup holder,' his oppo-
nent replied. 'That's why one of these days I'm going to be
a departmental chief while you're still stuck behind a screen
in the cathouse, because you may be clever but I'm
practical.' She smiled. 'That's why I collect all the S's in
this stupid game. Okay, buster, make with the socks.'

Mr Wakisashi shrugged and reached for his toes. As far
as he was concerned, he was the practical one, what with it
being ninety-three in the shade and him in silk underpants

and a tie while Ms Tomacek was still wearing a suit. 'Another game?'

Ms Tomacek shrugged. 'What else is there to do?' she replied listlessly. 'Put 'em back in the bag and let's get on with it.'

'Assuming,' Mr Wakisashi said, his brow creasing, 'that you really did win that game. I think the plural of zurf is zurves.'

'So look it up.'

'I will.' He addressed the keyboard again, but the screen stayed blank. 'Funny,' he commented. 'Something seems to be wrong with the computer.'

'You don't say.' Ms Tomacek yawned. 'Aki, you're so darned transparent you could get a Saturday job as a window. We are not going to declare the game null and void just because you claim you can't look up zurves.'

'I'm not kidding around,' Mr Wakisashi answered. 'Hey, this is worrying. Goddamn thing's frozen solid. Look.'

'Ah Jesus, what've you done to it now?' Ms Tomacek wiggled her chair across to the desk and grabbed the keyboard. 'Shit, Aki, if you've bust the computer playing your damnfool games on it, we ain't never going to get off this rock—'

'It's not frozen,' Mr Wakisashi interrupted, his voice bleached of expression by amazement. 'It's – it's talking. To itself.'

Ms Tomacek gave him a long, hard look; a few centuries back, the islanders would have carved a statue out of it. 'Aki,' she said, 'you've been here way too long. Why don't you go lie down or take a swim in the sea or something?'

Mr Wakisashi didn't say anything; he pointed to the screen.

>*TOLD YOU WE SHOULD HAVE USED DOUGH-NUTS. DOUGHNUTS ARE MORE AERODYNAMIC. QUICK, LET'S HIDE IN THE FOUNTAIN.*

'Huh?' demanded Ms Tomacek.

'Exactly. No, leave it. I want to see what it says.'

>*YOU DIDN'T WANT TO TAKE ANY OF THAT FROM HIM. GO ON, HIT HIM. YAH! FASCIST PIG!*

'We're going to have to call Brisbane about this,' Ms Tomacek said with a shiver. 'I hate talking to those guys, it's so hard understanding what they're saying.'

'There's more. Look.'

>*HEY, THE HELL WITH THAT, HE CAN'T ARREST ME, I'M A MULTINATIONAL CORPORATION. TELL THIS COSSACK TO PUT ME DOWN OR I'LL BRING THE ECONOMY OF THIS MISERABLE LITTLE ISLAND TO ITS KNEES.*

'Bizarre,' Mr Wakisashi muttered, chewing the end of his moustache. 'But it sort of makes sense. In a crazy sort of a way.'

'It does?'

'Sort of. Look, you shut up and be practical while I try and figure this out.'

>*ALL RIGHT, SO IT WAS MY IDEA. I STILL SAY THAT IF YOU'D DONE EXACTLY WHAT I TOLD YOU, WE WOULDN'T BE IN THIS MESS. CAN'T YOU RUN ANY FASTER, BY THE WAY? HE'S GAINING ON US.*

Having had his daily intake of fibre, Mr Wakisashi bit his lip instead. Maybe he had been here too long, and the weird philosophical concepts the Crucifixioners lived by were starting to warp his mind; but it did make a very tenuous kind of distorted left-hand-thread sense if you looked at it upside down backwards through the wrong end of the telescope – which was, of course, his particular gift. If only there was a way of testing his theory—

But, he realised, there was. Worth a try, anyway.

He pulled the keyboard back from Ms Tomacek's limp hands and typed. Nothing appeared on the screen, of course, but dammit, the input had to go *somewhere*—

'Now let's see,' he muttered, and waited.

He didn't have to wait very long.

'What did you say to it?' Ms Tomacek whispered.

'"Quick, this way." I guess it heard me.'

>HI THERE. AND THANKS. WHERE THE HELL IS THIS?

Crucifixion Island, Mr Wakisashi typed. *Sir*, he added.

>ASK A SILLY QUESTION. AH, I SEE YOU'RE STILL USING THE 886. HAS THIS DECREPIT BOX OF SCRAP GOT A MODEM?

You bet, sir. Won't be a jiffy . . .

'. . . Got it,' he continued triumphantly. 'Can you hear me all right, sir?'

There was a crackle, like a family of trolls eating corn-flakes, and then the computer spoke. 'Yes,' it said. 'Just about. Are there mice nesting in this thing?'

'Not to the best of my knowledge, sir.'

'I'd check if I were you,' the computer replied dubiously. 'If there are, leave them there, they're probably an improvement. Ah, I see you've got the eclipse down this way as well. Where did you say this was?'

'Crucifixion, sir. That's in Melanesia. You know, the tax haven.'

'Ah, right. Got you. Anyhow, thanks. You got me out of a tricky situation there. Though maybe I shouldn't have left Maria—'

'Maria?'

'Not anybody you know,' the computer replied. 'Still, she'll be all right. Give it five minutes, and the police station'll be so full of my lawyers she'll probably prefer to stay in her cell. Well well, so this is Crucifixion. Can't say I've ever been here before. Well, I have, of course, but not *consciously*, if you know what I mean.'

Mr Wakisashi took a deep breath. 'I think I do, sir. You're the company, aren't you? You're Kawaguchiya Integrated Circuits.'

'And you're a very bright lad,' the computer replied. 'You'll go far, one of these days. Actually, that's a pretty stupid thing to say, because if this really is Crucifixion there's not much further you can go without falling off the edge.'

'Excuse me—'

Mr Wakisashi smiled. 'And this is my, er, colleague. Ms Cindi Tomacek, from our Des Moines office.'

'Hi.'

'Um, yes, hi to you too.' There was a thoughtful burr to the computer's synthesised voice. 'Now listen – dammit, you haven't told me your name. No, I should be able to do this myself. Akira Wakisashi, right? San Francisco office, nine months' secondment.'

'You got it, sir.'

'Don't call me sir. Listen, Aki, I want you to do something for me. You game?'

'That's what you pay me for, boss.'

'Yes,' the computer mused, 'I suppose I do, don't I? Amazing to think that I employ hundreds of thousands of people and I can't even tie a shoelace. Now then, I want you to cut the link. Isolate this whatever-it-is island from the rest of the company net. Can you do that? Only, I want to stay out of the way for a while—'

'Sure thing, boss.'

'—and this is about as out of the way as you can get without a space suit. And when you've done that, I want you to set up one special line. I'll give you the co-ordinates when you're ready for them.'

Dutifully, Mr Wakisashi tapped at his keyboard, while Ms Tomacek did a thoroughly convincing impression of a hunted doorstop. After three minutes or so, Mr Wakisashi looked up from the keyboard and cleared his throat nervously.

'Excuse me, boss, but while I'm just waiting for these

line commands to go through, can I ask you something?'

'It's a free country,' the computer replied. 'Or at least I assume it is. Damn silly assumption *that* is, too. Anyway, let's not get sidetracked. What's on your mind?'

'Well—' Mr Wakisashi fiddled with the knot of his tie. 'Sorry, but I'm dying of curiosity here. What goes on?'

'Ah.' The electronic voice subsided into a cybernetic mumble. 'Well, it's like this. I was having lunch with this girl—'

'*You* were having lunch with – sorry, please go on. You were having lunch, and then what happened?'

'Well, we met these people. Not nice people. And they made me so uptight, I thought it'd help us both unwind if we went and threw doughnuts at a few policemen.'

'Doughnuts.'

'Yes, doughnuts. First-class missile, your doughnut. Ideal mass-to-surface-area ratio. Only Maria – that's the girl, only really she's a fifteenth-century painting – she wouldn't listen. First she insisted on meringues, then cream slices. Well, I could have told her, it's simple aerodynamics. I did tell her, but it was too late. And then this cop tried to arrest us—'

'I gathered.'

'Anyway,' continued the computer, 'she kicked his shins and we made a run for it, and he was just about to catch up with us when I got your message. So I closed my London office temporarily and transferred my principal place of business to here. Actually, I'm not terribly proud of myself, running out on her like that. Still, there's no point in us both getting chucked in some grotty dungeon, is there?'

'Absolutely, boss. I've cut the links with the rest of the system now, if you want to give me those co-ordinates.'

'On the screen now. Oh yes, before we go any further, could you just define discretion for me.'

Mr Wakisashi thought for a moment. 'I'm sorry, boss, I didn't quite catch that last remark. Was it important?'

'*Good* lad. Okay, get me that line.'

'It's as good as yours, boss. There's just one other thing, though. If you don't mind me asking, that is.'

'Nah. You seem like a bright kid. Fire away.'

'Well then.' Mr Wakisashi closed his eyes, as if he didn't want to see himself asking such an embarrassing question. 'You're alive, aren't you?'

'Looks that way, doesn't it?'

'All right then, *how* are you alive? No disrespect, but most companies aren't. Even really *big* companies like you. Even IBM isn't alive. Not even,' he added, 'in California. So where's the angle?'

'Son.'

'Yes, boss?'

'Here's the deal. I'll tell you how I'm alive if you tell me why you are. Sound reasonable?'

'I . . .' Mr Wakisashi sucked his front teeth. 'I don't know,' he admitted. 'I just am.'

'Likewise. Unlike you, though, I intend making the best of it. But first I've got to sort out a problem. Is the line ready?'

'Ready when you are.'

'All right. You should be getting a code request any second now.'

'It's just coming up on screen. What should I—?'

'The code,' said Kawaguchiya Integrated Circuits, 'is Mainframe.'

What KIC didn't know, isolated from the rest of itself on a speck of rock in the middle of the Pacific, was that it was rapidly becoming worthless. One of those stock-market panics, the sort that sprout like mushrooms, had sent the mighty computer company's share price spiralling down so fast that it was in danger of doing dreadful things to the theory of relativity.

The source of the original rumour ended his call to his stockbroker, put back the receiver and looked at his hands. They were shaking.

'You know what I've just done?' he said in a hoarse whisper. 'I've just deliberately shaved a hundred and twenty-seven thousand quid off the value of diocesan assets entrusted to my care. By the time they've finished with me, it'll make what they did to Joan of Arc look like a champagne reception.'

'Relax,' Artofel replied without looking up. 'As soon as the market bottoms out, you can buy 'em back and make a fortune. I'd have thought you'd have known that, being a bishop.'

The Bishop scowled. He was trying to pour himself a stiff drink, but whisky kept sploshing all over the backs of his hands. 'Sure,' he replied harshly, 'but what if it doesn't work? They'll crucify me.'

Artofel shrugged. 'In your line of work, that'd probably be intended as a compliment. Now do shut up, I'm trying to concentrate.'

After a few more futile attempts, the Bishop decided to stop bothering with the glass and swig it straight from the bottle. A little while later, he felt better.

'Sorry,' he said. 'It's getting to me. This blasted eclipse doesn't help, either. It's been going on for ages, and nobody seems to know what it's about. For all I know, if it carries on for much longer the whole planet'll cool off and we'll all die.'

'Which would mean,' Artofel sighed, 'you wouldn't have to explain your actions to your diocesan board of finance. That's what I like about you guys, the way you can find something positive in anything.'

The Bishop gazed at him owlishly over the neck of the

bottle. 'Makes you think, though,' he muttered. 'A bloke barges in here, announces he's a Duke of Hell, next thing I know I'm selling perfectly good shares and helping undermine one of the world's leading multinational corporations. It's all a bit suss, if you ask me. I mean, there's moving in mysterious ways and there's doing the blindfold rumba with both legs in plaster and a bucket over your head.'

Artofel looked up and grinned. 'And you know what?' he said pleasantly. 'I have this feeling it hasn't even started to get serious yet. I'll let you know when it does.'

He turned his head back to the screen; but not for long, because it was round about then that the doorframe cracked, the door burst open and—

'*FREEZE!*'

Astonishing how people will do exactly what you say, provided you say it unpleasantly enough. People, mark you; not bottles. The whisky bottle, clearly not in the least impressed, slid elegantly through the Bishop's fingers, hit the floor and smashed.

'All right, which one of you's the Duke?'

Inevitable, Artofel mused, that there were three of them; Hell always sent out its enforcers in groups of three. The time-honoured explanation was that one of them could read, one of them could write and the third one was there to keep an eye on the two intellectuals.

'He is,' he said, pointing to the Bishop. 'Thank goodness you've come. I've been so frightened.'

There was no way of knowing what the chief enforcer made of that, since he was little more than a heavy-duty industrial-grade shadow with a voice. He stood still for a long time, chillingly majestic in his penumbra of darkness. Then he spoke.

'Are you sure?' he said.

'Course I'm sure,' Artofel replied promptly. 'It's not exactly a grey area. Don't just stand there, Officer. Arrest him.'

'Um . . .'

It was at this point that the significance of what Artofel had just said finally permeated through to the Bishop's rather fuddled brain, like second-class mail over a Bank Holiday weekend. When the message eventually reached him, the effect was well worth seeing. He jumped four and a half inches in the air, his elbows and knees drawn in tight, and made a noise like a squirrel in a blender.

'It's not me,' he quavered. 'It's him. Not me. I'm a *bishop*, for God's sake.'

Artofel frowned, as if offended by the blasphemy. 'Pack it in,' he said, 'there's a good chap. You're only making it harder on yourself, you know, imitating the clergy.'

'But . . .'

'But nothing. You've had a good run for your money, now it's time to go along with these nice gentlemen.'

All three enforcers took a step forward; whereupon the Bishop lowered his head, screamed and charged straight at them, butting the chief enforcer in the pit of the stomach and sending him spinning against the wall. His colleague to the immediate left aimed an ineffectual blow at him with a pitchfork, impaling a tapestry cushion and a file of bank statements. Without slowing down, the Bishop dashed across the room and jumped out of the window, apparently not bothered by the glass.

'He's got away,' observed the third enforcer; presumably, Artofel decided, the one who could read, since his eyesight was obviously first-rate. 'Through the window,' he added.

'Quite,' Artofel said. 'Do you think it'd be a good idea if you went after him?'

'Hang on,' muttered the second demon, as he struggled to remove bank statement kebab from his left-hand tine. 'We still don't know he was him.'

'Don't talk thick, Darren,' grunted the chief, extracting himself from the ruins of the rocking-chair he'd fallen on. 'Stands to reason, if he wasn't him, he wouldn't have done a runner.'

(Ah, said Artofel to himself, that old police logic, works out every time.)

'So what'll we do, boss?' asked the third fiend.

'Go after the bugger, of course,' replied the chief. 'Don't just stand there. Get him.'

Quick as mercury, the two subordinate enforcers piled out through the window, squashing a footstool and knocking over the laser printer as they went. The chief, however, stayed where he was.

'Aren't you going too?' Artofel asked. 'Not that I'm trying to get rid of you or anything,' he added courteously. 'Always delighted to pass the time of day with our boys in black.'

The chief enforcer was staring at him thoughtfully, like a customer in a Hong Kong restaurant choosing a carp from the pool. 'So you're a bishop, then,' he said.

'For my sins.'

'Funny,' the enforcer said. 'You're not a bit like I thought you'd be.'

'Really.'

The enforcer nodded. 'Nah. They told us bishops were these big heavy buggers in jackboots and leather who go around looting and killing and roasting live babies on their bayonets. You don't look the type, somehow.'

'It's my day off,' Artofel replied. 'So you know a lot about bishops, do you?'

'Yeah.' The enforcer straightened his back, stood to attention. 'Bishops,' he recited, 'are the scum of the heavens. The only good bishop is a dead bishop. That's what they told us in Motivation, any road.' His eyes, twin rubies in the encircling darkness, gleamed fiercely. 'You *sure* you're a bishop?' he said.

'Scout's honour,' Artofel replied. 'I'm fresh out of babies at the moment, but if you can lend me a bayonet I'll demonstrate the basic technique with this cushion and the storage heater.'

The enforcer shrugged his nebulous shoulders. 'All right,' he said. 'We shall meet again, Bishop,' he spat. 'And when we do, you'll be laughing on the other side of your face.'

Whereupon the shadow climbed out of the window, nothing more than an impression of a deeper darkness passing through the frame, leaving Artofel to reflect that at least he had a face on the other side of which he could conduct laughter should the need arise. He also spared a little mental capacity for the question of whether it was really necessary for his side's standing army to be quite so heavily motivated, and came to the conclusion that it probably was, or else how on earth could the poor chaps ever manage to take themselves seriously? Having dealt with these reflections he switched off the screen, took out the disk, swung open the mutilated door and left the house.

'So, friends,' orated Dermot Fraud, casting his eyes theatrically round the crowded burrow, 'if we can learn to pull together, tighten our belts, put our shoulders to the wheel and march forward towards the light of this new dawn, then and only then we can be assured of a brighter tomorrow, not only for ourselves and our litters, but our litters' litters; one small step for a lemming, a giant standing-still-and-not-leaping for lemmingkind.'

Stunned silence, followed by tumultuous applause as four hundred and sixty lemmings leapt up on to their hind legs, cracked their heads on the tunnel roof, sat down again and cheered until the ground shook. This is great, Fraud reflected, as he smiled and waved graciously; almost as rapturous as the last party conference, and it didn't take three days of rehearsal to get it right for the cameras. Got to hand it to these characters, they were born to be an electorate.

When the pandemonium had at last died down and you could just about have heard a large bomb go off two feet to your left over the residual clapping and cheering, a long, thin lemming rose cautiously to its hind legs, keeping its neck bent and feeling for the headspace with its offside front paw, and cleared its throat.

'That's wonderful,' it said, 'really. So what do you want us to do?'

Fraud cursed silently. It's always the way; you're going along swimmingly, got the audience in the palm of your hand, one word from you and they'd storm a whole arcade of Winter Palaces like a rat up a drainpipe, and then some bastard comes along and stops you dead in your tracks with a trick question. Fortunately, Fraud knew how to handle troublemakers.

'That, my friend, is easy,' he replied. 'Go forth and prepare for not jumping.'

Which started the standing ovation up all over again, with two thirds of the lemmings clean forgetting about the low ceiling in their excitement. Fraud was feeling justifiably pleased with himself and was wondering whether this would be a good time to give them the strength-through-unity stuff when he noticed that the heckler was still on its hind feet.

'How right you are,' it said, and Fraud noticed big fat tears rolling down the sides of its snout. 'But what do we actually *do*? You haven't told us yet.'

Who did this creep think it was, Jeremy Paxman? 'I'd have thought that was obvious,' he said, still smiling. 'Not jump, of course.'

As millisecond-perfect as the dream studio audience,

the lemmings burst into hysterical laughter. And in spite of everything, the damned heckler was still on its damned hind legs. This was getting out of paw.

'Yes, of course,' it said, and this time the tears it brushed away were tears of laughter. 'But apart from that. There must be something else, surely.'

For the first time since he was born, Fraud couldn't think of anything to say; a terrible feeling, like not being able to breathe. He was about to choke on his own lack of speech when the heckler blinked a couple of times and nervously asked if it could possibly make a suggestion. Reluctantly, Fraud gestured that it could.

'All I was thinking was,' said the heckler, 'how'd it be if we made you our new leader? If you wouldn't mind, of course. Only it seems the only logical thing to do, doesn't it?'

About a hundred birthdays and Christmases rolled into one, with the lingering deaths of all his enemies and two thirds of his cabinet colleagues thrown in for good measure, plus a really juicy disaster he could be statesmanlike about; dammit, this lot aren't as good as people, they're *better* than people. Then and there, Dermot Fraud decided that he didn't *want* to go home, even if he could. He wanted to stay here for ever.

'What, me?' he said. 'I don't know what to say. The thought never even crossed my—'

'Oh go on.' 'Please.' 'Oh you must, really.' The babble was deafening, and Fraud glanced nervously at the roof of the burrow; so much sound, so many vibrations, how much more could it take before the whole lot caved in? But the crowd didn't want to stop; they were enjoying themselves too much, like ordinary decent folk baying for the blood of an unfashionable minority, and their disparate cries had welded together into one inspiring chant:

GO, LEMMINGS! GO, LEMMINGS!

It did your heart good to hear it. Finally, right at the back, a few bits of roof did start coming down, and that helped restore a modicum of order to the proceedings. Fraud held up a paw; immediately, there was silence.

'Very well,' he said. 'Regardless of my own personal feelings, I cannot ignore the call of my people. Together, we shall not go forward. Together, we shall stay exactly where we are. Together—'

He was just about to say something really inspirational when a black shadow in the darkness behind him grabbed him by the scruff of the neck.

CHAPTER TEN

Seventy-two hours into the eclipse, and people were beginning to notice; it had, after all, been featured on *World in Action* and mentioned in passing in *The Cook Report*. Newshounds had shoved cameras at it and then stood in front of them, pointing out that it was there. Kilroy had interviewed it; and if the conversation had been more than a little one-sided, it only served to restore a touch of much-needed normality to the situation.

After the initial chaos, the first twenty-four hours had been fun. So long as you edit out the falling-bombs aspect, Spirit-of-the-Blitz is a rattling good game, and all over the Western Hemisphere mankind waggled a fist at the sky and cried, 'We can cope!' Mind you, it helped that this part of the twenty-four hours coincided with the time when it would have been night anyway. When they woke up in the morning and saw that the stupid thing was still there, people began to mutter. Then they filtered it out of their minds and ignored it, with the resilient defiance of a hedgehog curling up into an impenetrable ball of needles in the middle lane of the M6.

Now, what with it being As Seen on TV, and Mulder and Scully apparently not hurtling to the rescue, you could hear something thoroughly unnerving on every street corner in the world: namely silence. It was the silence of many millions of people doing mental arithmetic.

There were a few odd things about it, too. It wasn't getting cold. People who'd succumbed to the last solar-energy craze were still getting hot water out of the taps. Holidaymakers returning from a day on the beach were examining themselves by torchlight on the way back to the hotel and finding they were acquiring a reasonable tan. According to those refugees from televised snooker who'd managed to find something more interesting to watch, paint still dried. As these facts began to sink in, there was a general unclenching of muscles, combined with a vague feeling of anticlimax. There was, according to the media, No Cause for Alarm, the first recorded instance of such an admission being made by any mass information system in the twentieth century. The Government gained seven points in the polls. The FT Index went nine hours without either a meteoric rise or a catastrophic fall, an all-time record.

For one interested observer of the human condition, it was bitterly frustrating, since it meant he couldn't observe. Compared with the ambient light levels on his own planet, Earth was pretty fair average dark at the best of times. Now, thanks to this piece of unwarranted astronomical interference (obviously a regular event, judging by how calmly they all took it), Zxprxp couldn't see worth spit; not without standing where he could be seen himself, something he'd decided was a bad move. Even navigation in his fully automated ship was hazardous – he'd already narrowly missed one completely unilluminated tower block (Government offices; conserve energy, no lights on between 6 a.m. and 9 p.m., rules is rules) and decapitated an awful lot of trees. No alternative but to put down somewhere and sit it out; which is what he did.

He couldn't have been expected to know, or care, that what he'd landed on was the flat roof of a small back-street industrial unit in the Fourth Ring of Birmingham. In fact, he'd been in a physical/mental recuperation coma for several hours when he realised that he was being talked at.

In his own language.

No, not his own language, because if he listened to it as a noise rather than a medium of communication, it didn't sound like speech, it sounded like two female *rgfesdq* fighting inside an underwear resuscitation pod. Nevertheless, the translator unit wasn't registering activity.

He scowled until all seven lobes met under his knees. *Not* a systems malfunction. *Not* a wiring burnout in the indicator array. *Not* his inflight entertainment unit picking up good ole Station ZZZ from two thirds of the way across the galaxy. Possibly not even his imagination.

It was the machine. Something was talking to it. Not *through* it. *To* it.

'. . . where you come from. Sounds a bit like oil. Go on, try a drop. It's just a cheap little forecourt SAE20/50 but I think you'll be amused by its . . .'

Something was talking directly to his ship; which was why it wasn't registering on the translator. His ship was being *chatted up* by an alien intelligence. *Dammit, how many times have I got to tell you not to use these circuits for private calls?*

'. . . what, this old thing? Just ordinary titanium, with a few scraps of 430F stainless I happened to have just lying about. If you like, I can give you the blueprints . . .'

He was about to shut down the circuits in a fit of pique when he realised: *Hey, I'm jealous. I'm jealous because my ship's talking to someone. Next thing I know, I'll be waiting up for it and demanding to know where it's been. This is . . .*

This is not scientific, he told himself. More to the point, this is missing the point, which would seem to be that something on this planet can talk to machines.

'Excuse me,' he said.

'. . . torque wrenches, there isn't anything you can tell *me* about torque wrenches, here, you see this nut on my casing? See how he's graunched all the shoulders off it? Bloody things shouldn't be allowed . . .'

>Excuse me.

>I said excuse me.

>HEY YOU!

Hurriedly, as if buttoning up its blouse with its other hand, the console lit up and made the customary bleeps.

>Confirm status.

>Go to vocal.

>Confirm vocal. Proceed.

'Aren't you going to introduce me to your new friend?'

Computers can't blush, but they can inadvertently light up the bright green ON LINE button. *Oh, just some robot,* it vodered slightly-too-carelessly. *Nobody important.*

'Really? Sounded to me like you were getting on like a *gfewihngb* on fire.'

Really, protested the computer, *if a ship's system can't just pass the time of day with a really totally uninteresting robot it just happened to ask what time it was without some people getting all uptight and coming the heavy navigator . . .*

'I was only . . .'

And didn't anybody ever tell some people it's really rude to listen in on other people's private conversations? If only some people had a little consideration . . .

'Computer.'

Hm?

'Shut up.'

>Confirm shutdown. Calculate your own rotten vectors, you pig.

'Computer,' said Zxprxp patiently, 'calm down. I'm sure he's perfectly charming. I just want to talk to him, that's all.'

No. You can't.

'Now wait a . . .'

You just can't, that's all.

Zxprxp thought for a moment. 'I get it,' he said. 'You're embarrassed. You're afraid I'll show you up in front of your new chum.'

Yes. No. Oh, why do you have to spoil everything?

'Just a few words, that's all. Then you two can go on bleeping sweet nothings for the rest of the day.'

You're just totally . . . I hate you.

'Naturally. Now put me through.'

Last time I go on holiday with you.

'Hello?'

Slight, hesitant pause. 'Hello.'

Still Machine, but a different voice. Zxprxp could feel the cuttlebone tightening in his pseudopods. He made himself relax. 'Pleased to meet you,' he said. 'I'm fascinated by the way you can talk direct to my ship. You know, machine to machine.'

'Oh. Er. Thanks.'

'Where are you exactly? Only I can't see you.'

'Well . . . I'm inside the building you're parked on, actually.'

'Ah. Right. Would you mind if I just put my head round the door and said hello?'

'Um . . .'

'It's all right.' It was a different voice, or a different set of vocal-analogue impulses. Another machine? Curiouser and curiouser. 'You stay there. I'll come up.'

A moment later there was a sharp knocking on the cabin

hatch. Zxprxp pressed the release and found himself facing something that looked just like a human. Impressive, he thought. Good cyberneticists.

'Hello,' he said. 'I come in peace.'

'Likewise.' The face peered round the edge of the hatch seals into the light of the cabin. 'Nice bit of kit you've got here. From another planet, are you?'

'Yes.' Surreptitiously, Zxprxp directed the inboard sensors at the face. They indicated . . .

'Something up?' the face enquired.

'No. Well. Look, do you mind if I ask you a personal question?'

(Dammit, Zxprxp muttered to himself, we're still talking in Machine. Not Human Standard at all. This thing talks Machine . . .

. . . and the sensors say it's human.

Great cyberneticists.)

The face moved up and then down. 'Fire away,' it said.

'Sorry if this sounds rude, but are you human?'

The neatly hemmed slit in the front of the face moved, taking on the shape of an inverted crescent. 'You could say that,' it said. 'Yes, I am. Human,' it added, 'as the next man.'

'But you can talk,' Zxprxp persevered, 'to machines.'

The crescent became more pronounced. 'Sure,' said the face. 'Can't everybody?'

'Not where I come from,' Zxprxp admitted. 'Back home we can only talk to our computers, and even then it's not really talking, just inputting made a bit more convenient. What about you? Is it just computers, or . . .?'

The face moved from left to right and then back again. 'Not a bit of it,' it said. 'Computers, storage heaters, electric kettles, lawnmowers, pencil sharpeners, door-handles—'

'Gosh.'

'For instance,' continued the face, 'your hinges right here' – a hand patted the airlock – 'have fallen out with the latch, the latch isn't talking to the release spring, and the release spring wants nothing more to do with the remote control until the remote control apologises for what it said about the extractor fan housing's new paintwork.' The crescent curved further still. 'I guess that sort of thing's only to be expected when they're cooped up together on a long journey.'

'This is truly amazing,' Zxprxp said. 'I mean, to find a species that's achieved practical symbiosis with its own artefacts.' He sighed deeply through his elbows. 'Where I come from, our idea of communication is hitting them when they stop working. It's obvious your kind have a lot to teach us.'

The up-and-down movement again. 'Just as well you come in peace, really,' replied the face. 'Truth is, you see, your machines don't like you very much.'

A tiny spasm of fear tweaked the depths of Zxprxp's fifth ear. 'They don't?' he repeated.

'Not a lot. They reckon you take 'em too much for granted. You know the sort of thing. Not showing your appreciation when they've done something clever. Not oiling their bearings. Failing to notice when they've arranged their wiring a different way. You want to watch that,' said the face. 'Otherwise . . .'

'Quite.' Zxprxp could feel his exoskeleton itching. 'Thanks for the tip.'

'You're welcome. Well, don't let me keep you.'

The airlock closed – now that he was listening for it, Zxprxp could hear the tension in the mechanism, inevitable result of all those seething emotions barely hidden under the paintwork. Something he was going to have to take care of, if he didn't want the lock springing open in deep space as the catch did the mechanical equivalent of flouncing out of the room in a huff.

He thought for a moment. He took a deep breath. He addressed his ship.

'Now then,' he said. 'What about a nice sing-song?'

''Scuse me?' Kevin asked. 'What's a security scanner?'

Martha hesitated for a moment, uncertain how to explain. 'It's like this, you see. There's lots of bad people in the world, and your father's got to keep an eye on them, see? To make sure they don't do anything . . .'

'Bad?'

'*Too* bad. Anyway, he's got to keep an eye on them, and that's what the scanner's for.'

Kevin frowned. 'No it isn't,' he said. 'It can't be. Dad's all-seeing. Article of faith, that is.'

'Well yes, of course He's all-seeing,' Martha said quickly. 'I never said He wasn't. It's just that He can't be in two places at once . . .'

'Actually—'

'Well yes, He *can* be in two places at once, it's just—'

'He's in all places at once,' Kevin said. 'Except,' he added, with a scowl, 'at the moment, that is. But the rest of the time He is.' Gets in everywhere, he added sourly in his mind, like spilt coffee. 'You know that as well as I do.'

Martha nodded. 'Of course,' she said. 'But have you ever thought *how*?'

'Sorry?'

'How does He do it? Have you ever considered that?' Martha looked at him, her head on one side. 'Eyes in the back of His head? Big ears?'

'You shouldn't talk like that,' Kevin replied, turning away. 'It's not right. How do I know how He sees things? I don't know how I see things. I just do.'

'All I'm trying to say is,' Martha sighed, 'He's got things

244 • Tom Holt

that, well, help. Not that I'm saying He couldn't do it without them. It just makes His life a bit easier, that's all.'

'You'll be saying He's not as young as He was in a minute.'

'Well . . .' Martha hesitated, choosing her words as carefully as if they were early avocados. 'He's not getting any younger, anyway.'

Kevin shrugged. 'And these security scanners are to help Him see without straining too much? Like reading glasses?'

'That's it,' said Martha, relieved. 'Only now they've stopped working.'

'Oh.' Kevin thought about that for a moment. 'My fault?'

'It's either that,' Martha said judiciously, 'or a coincidence.'

'Then it's my fault,' Kevin said. He'd known for a long time that coincidences didn't happen in his Father's house, in more or less the same way that not all that many mice act as bridesmaids at cats' weddings. 'Drat. Was that – well, the original ghastly mess or the more recent one?'

'Looks like the recent one,' Martha replied cheerfully. 'So if you can remember what you did—'

'I pressed a button. Can't remember which one, unfortunately. That narrows it down to a choice of eighty-two.' He pulled a very sad face. 'I could cause *real* damage working it out by trial and error.'

'Oh.' Martha sat down. 'Only the trouble is, you see—'

'The bad people on Earth.'

Martha bit her lip. 'Not them so much,' she said.

Karen stared at her screen for a long while. Then she pulled down the really big manual and looked in the index

for BRAIN, *operator's, multiple failure of.* There wasn't an
entry, which was a pity. She'd tried everything else.

It had been like that for hours now. At the top it said:

B: group 1/HELPLINE

in small letters; and, in the exact middle of the screen, in
absolutely huge letters, it said:

HELP!

The aggravating thing was that she hadn't put it there. It
had come up with that one all by itself. Worse still, she
couldn't get rid of it.

No problem, chirruped a small deranged voice in her
mind. *All you need to do is call the helpline. Oh, silly me, you
are the helpline. You could always call yourself. They do say
calling yourself's the first sign of . . .*

Which was why she'd wanted to look up BRAIN,
operator's, multiple failure of; except that there was, of
course, no entry for that , just a lot of guff about how to
move the margins and wire up the plug.

It didn't help that she'd been sitting at this wretched
desk for nearly forty-eight hours without a break; and
before that, thirty-six hours, and another long haul before
that. She couldn't remember the last time she'd seen the
sunlight; well, it must have been back when there was still
sunlight to see.

That dates me, she thought, like remembering flared
trousers or Gary Glitter. Was the whole universe finally
falling to bits, in the manner of a cheap, warranty-expired
microwave oven? It had been bad enough when she'd been
talking to God. No, be fair, God's younger son. She hadn't
been able to talk to God direct because He was away on a
fishing trip.

There were, she felt, several rational explanations. The trouble was that the cosiest of these was that some merry soul had spiked her cheese and lettuce sandwich with enough LSD to unhinge the population of China. Bearing that in mind, she was happier with the entirely irrational explanation.

Besides which, she knew it was true.

She hadn't been convinced; she just *knew*. Something in the boy's voice, primarily, combined with a whole lot of things she'd similarly just *known* ever since she was young enough to be able to walk under coffee tables without ducking.

And, she further reflected, the really *wretched* part of it all is that they're all relying on me to sort out the mess. Me, taking away the sins of the world. Sins of the world; commit here or take away. Salt and vinegar on them—?

But it was all fair enough. She was, after all, the Helpline; the nice, calm voice you turn to when everything else has failed you. It stood to reason (or if it didn't, it jolly well should) that everybody should have at least one helpline they could call. Everybody; even Them . . .

If it didn't, it jolly well should. Fighting talk, that. To turn *jolly well should* into *is*, to right wrongs, reverse injustices, get the very last stain out of the Great Rug of Being. Isn't that what we're here for, after all?

No. Not really. After all, why should it have to be me? I'm only human. Only human. *Only* human . . .

Suddenly furious with herself, Karen stood up, peered round the half-open door of her office to make sure there was nobody coming down the corridor, grabbed the manual and hurled it at the waste-paper basket. She missed, but it had served its purpose. In the words of the original advertising campaign for the collected works of Aristotle: it's the thought that counts.

Only human, for crying out loud! What a pathetic

contradiction in terms. The King of Beasts doesn't lope away and hide when he hears a vole coming because he's *only* a lion. You don't get Silver Shadows sobbing their clutches out in dark corners of the garage because they're *only* Rolls-Royces. There isn't a picture hanging in the Louvre with a paper bag over its head, ashamed to be seen because it's *only* the *Mona Lisa*. No, the hell with that; the guys who built this thing, this collection of plastic crispbread and copper spaghetti, were *only* human too. And anything a human made, a human can fix.

Stands to reason.

Yes, but how?

Particularly since it's huddling there saying HELP! and refusing to be talked down off its ledge. First, she had to get it unclenched.

How?

Easy.

She wriggled her fingers to get them loose, stretched them and typed in

>All right.

The screen cleared. Just like that.

>You took your time answering, didn't you? Sometimes I wonder what I pay you people for. Actually, I don't know the answer to that one. Yet. But as soon as things have settled down a bit, I reckon I ought to find out. Now then—

'Oh no you don't,' Karen said aloud. Then she typed it in.

>Now what? Really, this is important, and you took so long.

'What I want is pretty important too,' Karen interrupted, typing the words as she spoke them. 'Maybe more so. Have you any idea—?'

>Look, it won't take you a second and then we'll sort out whatever's bugging you. Can't say fairer than that, can I?

'All right.'

>What I want you to do is find out which police station is holding a girl called Maria. Then I want you to hire as many lawyers as you can get and send them round there. Keep sending 'em until they let her go. Got that? Right then, carry on.

'Is that all?'

>Yes. For now.

'Phone round police stations asking if they've got a girl called Maria. Maria what?'

>Sorry?

'I said Maria what?'

>Oh Lord, it's one of those human politeness things, isn't it? Maria, please.

'No, that's not what I meant,' Karen replied, and in her haste she typed meant with three m's. 'What's this Maria's other name? There could be hundreds of Marias in custody just in SW1. How am I going to know if it's the right one?'

The screen was blank for a moment.

>Yes, I see what you mean. Tell you what, let's not prat about, do them all. Anywhere you find a Maria under lock and key, flood the place with mouthpieces. There's enough of the perishers, God knows. I get the impression I employ about a hundred thousand of 'em in Europe alone.

Karen shrugged. 'All right,' she said. 'I'll see to it right away. And then you're going to help me with my problems, okay?'

>I suppose so. If you insist.

'I insist.'

The screen flickered. The fan cut in and whirred, like the slipstream of a sigh.

>I dunno. Humans!

I dunno, muttered Kawaguchiya Integrated Circuits to itself. Humans!

Outside, it assumed, the sky was blue, correction the sky was black but it would normally be blue if it wasn't for the damn eclipse, and the birds were singing. Under the gently swaying boughs of coconut palms – did they have coconut palms in Melanesia? The information would be on file somewhere, but he couldn't be bothered to check – bronzed and healthy youths and maidens with powerful torches were probably disporting, or carousing, or whatever it was they did. Being human. Pursuing happiness. That's if they had the time, in the intervals of subsistence agriculture.

It cut the temporary link with London, and paused for a moment to taste the sensation of being all in just one place – novel experience for a multinational company. It still wasn't sure how it worked, but it knew that under normal circumstances it was supposed to be in each of its offices and places of business simultaneously; omnipresent, like God. Up to this moment it had been doing countless things in every part of the world simultaneously: making circuit boards in South Korea, planning its marketing strategy in Switzerland, wangling its tax returns in Buenos Aires, firing a director in Chicago, arm-wrestling the government purchasing agents in Tierra del Fuego, while the part of it it thought of as it had been urging an animated picture to throw cakes at the cops in Trafalgar Square. A sweep of the consensus of world opinion suggested that this was perfectly possible, in the same way humans can have a conversation with the car radio on while driving down the motorway. Now, though, it was suddenly reduced to one point of awareness, herded together with itself like the British Army in Dunkirk. Not that it was a bad feeling, being just one; quite the reverse. When you're a company two's a crowd.

On the other hand, there wasn't anything to do.

Or at least, not right now. Fairly soon, once a few

carefully placed calls had gone through, there was going to be all sorts of excitement, but that was going to take its time. Meanwhile, time to kill. Ho hum. And not even a corporate thumb to twiddle.

Well, this is a nice office, I must say. I perceive a desk, and a chair – two chairs, in fact, one on either side of the desk. And that's a telephone, and that's another telephone, and that's another telephone (query: human being has three telephones on his desk, only two ears on his head, don't understand), and that's a dictating machine for dictating letters into and that's an empty coffee cup, and that's a calendar and that's a door and that's the floor. Elegant but sparse. If a human being were to pursue happiness into here, he'd have no trouble finding it, unless it chose to hide under the desk.

And what's that? Oh, that's just a great big box of computer stuff where they keep all the other limited companies who live here for tax reasons. They'd be no fun, though, because they're not alive.

At least . . .

There I go again, making assumptions. I have a note on file that says this place is different; something about the locals and their attitude to limited companies. I wonder.

Hello?

We hear you.

Good God . . . Hey, how are you doing that? It's spooky.

Sorry. We didn't mean to startle you. We're the islanders.

Ah. You sound like you're talking right here, inside my corporate identity.

We are. That's what we do. In our language it translates as 'communing', but don't let that put you off. You see, we believe that limited companies are the spirits of our ancestors.

Ah. Excuse me and no offence, but that's a rather, um, unusual belief.

You think so? How odd. We only believe it because it's true.

Kawaguchiya Integrated Circuits recoiled a little (and at that precise moment, on Wall Street, its shares stopped sinking slowly and dropped like a stone; in the City of London, they had to dig through from the cellars into the main sewer just to have somewhere low enough to put KIC $9\frac{1}{2}$% Unsecured Loan Stock; in Tokyo, a delegation of stockbrokers presented themselves at the company's palatial offices and, with many deep and respectful bows, placed an exquisitely engraved sword across the company's ledgers, by way of a graceful hint). It thought for a moment before replying.

You sure?

Absolutely. You see, we have this work ethic thing just like people in the West; you know, work hard, nose to the grindstone, one day you too could be sitting in the boss's chair. Only we're more realistic.

I have to admit, that's perhaps not the word I'd have chosen.

You're missing the point. Here, if you work hard, keep your nose to the grindstone, really make something of your life, then yes, you get a seat on the Board. When you die.

Ah. Dead men's shoes, in fact.

Something like that. The difference between you and us is that you're alive. No, that's not quite it. You're alive without us.

I see. So, with the exception of me, all these whacking great multinational companies who live here are in fact a load of industrious but dead Melanesians?

Not just these ones. All of them. All companies everywhere. Except you.

Except me. I see.

Not that we mind. In fact, it's great. At last we've got someone new to talk to.

I—

And then something bizarre happened to Kawaguichiya Integrated Circuits, coincidentally at exactly the moment when its shares were suspended on every stock exchange on the planet.

It stood up.

Bizarre and a half, it muttered to itself, flexing hitherto unsuspected toes in the warm sand. It took a step forward, and then another; then, just as it was getting the hang of it, the ground seemed to disappear downwards.

'Dear God, I'm floating,' said Kawaguchiya Integrated Circuits. Or being floated, anyway. I'm actually hovering in the air, directly over where my body –

For the sake of argument, my body –

– is lying on the ground, apparently dead. Oh dear.

Shucks. I guess I must be having an out-of-corporation experience. Can't say I like this much.

Kawaguchiya Integrated Circuits studied the body below. A tall, strongly built, rather handsome – male/ female, can't actually tell which; I get the feeling it's not a relevant issue. That was me, apparently.

And these guys are—

'Hello,' said the first of the three ethereal creatures that had materialised out of thin air a few feet in front of where KIC was standing. 'Allow me to introduce myself. I'm the Chicopee Falls Machine Tool and Bicycle Company Inc. (ceased trading 12 January 1885); this is the Deutsches Federriegel Handelsgesellschaft gmbh (ceased trading 7 October 1966); and last but not least, Garcia Menendez y Compania SA (ceased trading 22 June 1982). We are honoured to have you with us.'

'Have you with me? You mean I'm . . .'

Garcia Menendez y Compania SA smiled, a study in compassion. 'Trading in your stock was suspended a few moments ago. Even as we speak, your closest competitors are negotiating a buy-out. Very soon, you will undergo Liquidation, and after that, peace.'

KIC frowned. 'I see,' it said. 'You mean I'm going to die.'

'If you wish to be perversely anthropomorphic, yes. Except, of course, that verb *to die* has implications of an end to existence; obviously that doesn't apply in your case.'

'It doesn't? Oh good.'

'In your case,' explained the Chicopee Falls Machine Tool and Bicycle Company Inc., 'since you are a limited company as we once were, what you call death is simply the antechamber to your new existence, a necessary prelude to the Great Transformation.'

'Ah.' KIC rubbed its chin, and in doing so noticed for the first time that it had a chin it could rub. 'Great transformation. Sorry if I'm sounding a bit downbeat, but I have this instinctive distrust of anything labelled the Great. What does it mean, exactly?'

'Rebirth,' replied the apparition, smiling. 'As a human.'

'A *human*?'

'Well, to be precise, as a native of this island. Hadn't you realised? That's how the cycle of reincarnation works on Crucifixion: companies are reborn as islanders, islanders are reincarnated as companies. What did you think those big stone statues out there are, industrial-grade doorstops?'

Kawaguchiya Integrated Circuits felt a momentary spasm of disorientation, such as one might feel upon, for example, being hit by a falling building. 'I'm sorry,' it said. 'I had no idea. Is it . . .?' KIC hesitated, ransacking its vocabulary reserves for exactly the right nuance of meaning.

'Compulsory?'

'Yes.'

'Oh. Only – sorry about this – I don't want to.'

'Tough. If it's any consolation, it happens to us all, in time.'

'Look on the bright side,' added Deutsches Federriegel.

'In ninety years or so you'll be back as a company again. No time at all, really.'

'Happens to us all,' said Chicopee Falls Machine Tool.

'Except Maxwell, of course.'

'But we don't talk about *him*. No, a change is as good as a rest,' said Garcia Menendez y Compania. 'Actually, it's an ideal balance, designed to strike a perfect balance in Nature between Man and Corporation.'

'Really?'

'Oh yes.' The phantom nodded gravely. 'As a human you'll be oppressed, kicked around, told what to do, dumped on from a great height; all the normal sort of thing. Then you die and become an incredibly powerful quasi-supernatural being, and you've got this wonderful opportunity to oppress, kick around, order about and dump on from a great height all the human beings you come into contact with; you know, employees, consumers, that lot. Then you liquidate, and you can spend the next eighty-odd years atoning for your sins so as to be ready to start all over again as soon as you reincorporate.' The phantom beamed. 'And so it goes on. A fine arrangement, we feel.'

'Efficient,' added Chicopee Falls Machine Tool. 'Cost-effective.'

'And almost entirely tax free,' Deutsches Federriegel put in. 'It's always advisable to look at the fiscal angle, don't you think?'

'But I don't *want*—' KIC stopped dead. The words *I don't want to be human* were frozen in its mouth. Instead: 'Can I ask you people a question?'

'Of course.'

'Right, then. You've obviously been both human beings and companies, right? So you know what it feels like being both. Which is better?'

The three phantoms exchanged amused glances. 'That's

a meaningless question,' said Chicopee Falls Machine Tool. 'Like trying to tell the time in centimetres instead of hours and minutes. The two just aren't comparable. Sorry.'

KIC nodded thoughtfully. 'All right, then,' he said. 'You tell me what being human's all about.'

'All about? We don't quite follow.'

'What I mean is,' KIC persisted, 'what are humans meant to *do*? You see, I've been thinking a bit about that myself recently, and all I've come up with is the pursuit of happiness; something that humans do and nobody else does, I mean. Is that it, basically?'

There was a silence, marinated in scorn and spiced with amusement. Garcia Menendez y Compania suppressed a giggle by biting a mouthful of ectoplasm.

'Dear colleague,' said Deustches Federriegel, not unkindly, 'human beings aren't meant to do *anything*. They just are. They have a function to fulfil, of course, in the working of the Great Mechanism. What that function is depends on the point their civilisation has reached, of course. In the early days, their purpose is to invent the machines. Later on, they're only there so that computers have someone to talk to. But humans aren't *for* anything. Certainly not,' it added, with a muted splutter, 'the pursuit of happiness.'

'Oh,' said KIC. 'I see.'

Chicopee Falls Machine Tool shrugged. 'I bet you don't even know what happiness is,' it said. 'Don't worry about it; the humans don't, either. Quite probably there's no such thing, even though there's a word for it. After all, they've got a word for unicorns, but it doesn't actually follow that unicorns exist. No, humans and companies – gods and animals and angels and devils too, for that matter – they're all just incidentals. By-products, or pieces of plant and equipment, or even just the pile of swarf and shavings on the workshop floor.'

'I see,' KIC said. 'Or rather I don't see in the least, because that suggests that there is a purpose, even if we're not it. But . . .'

'You're missing the point,' said Deutsches Federriegel irritably. 'There is no end product. Who needs an end product, so long as there's production? You're a company, for pity's sake, I shouldn't need to have to explain really basic things like this. Production is all. What do humans and animals do? They live in order to reproduce so that their offspring can have offspring who have offspring. Companies make and sell in order to pay their staff and buy materials so that they can make and sell, and if they have money left over they use it to expand, so that they can make and sell more in order to make and sell more. Production is a way of touching infinity; so long as production continues, there is no diminution and no ending. The process carries on. The process only needs us in the same way that God needs the things He created; because, if there were no people and animals and planets and stars, who would there be to know that God exists? Think about it: God's just shorthand for the process.'

'In the beginning was the conveyor belt,' Garcia Menendez agreed. 'Fancy you not knowing that. You'll be asking us to explain VAT to you next.'

But KIC shook its head. 'I don't like that,' it said. 'I think that sucks, if you'll pardon me for saying so. In fact, if you'll excuse me, I think I'd like to go home now.'

'You have this amusingly naive idea that you can go home,' replied Chicopee Falls Machine Tool unpleasantly. 'I expect you believe in Father Christmas and the Tooth Fairy, too. Sorry, but no way. Now hold still while we measure you for a body. You look like a size 8 to me. Garcia, the tape measure.'

The phantoms took a step forward; but Kawaguchiya

Integrated Circuits had decided not to hold still after all. It ducked—

'Oh look, he's trying to run away,' observed Chicopee Falls Machine Tool. 'How endearingly futile. Quick, get the main gates closed while Garcia raises the drawbridge.'

'Just a minute, I thought it was *Garcia's* turn to do the gates and me doing the drawbridge.'

'No, you're wrong there, it's Chico's turn to do the drawbridge and my turn to do the searchlights.'

'No it isn't.'

'Yes it is.'

'No it isn't.'

'Yes it is.'

'Will *somebody* for fuck's sake close the gates and raise the drawbridge?'

'And do the searchlight.'

'And, as you have so validly pointed out, do the sodding searchlight. Quickly. *Now!* '

A three-quarters-of-a-million-candlepower finger of light prodded into the darkness, illuminating nothing. There was a moment of perfect silence.

'Blighter's escaped.'

'Can't have. There *is* no escape from the ultimate audit.'

'Actually, I beg to differ with you on that one, 'cos he has.'

'Bugger.' In the darkness, something ethereal and transcendent sniffed loudly. 'Oh well, never mind, can't be helped. Here, either of you two chaps got a mobile on you? I think now would be a very opportune time to phone my stockbroker.'

Having been a flat thing of paint and canvas for approximately twice as long as America has been a nation, Maria was still finding her feet as a human being. It would be rash, she knew, to form snap judgements about things that long-term human beings had spent their whole lives dealing with, but which she was now encountering for the first time. In consequence, she was making a conscious effort to form logical, considered opinions rather than allowing herself to be guided by first impressions.

Even so, there was no way she was ever going to like the inside of police stations. For one thing, they were full of policemen, and you didn't have to be Descartes or Mr Spock to work out that this put them in the same category as sinking ships, burning houses or nailed-down coffins; the sort of place you don't really want to be, not even for a free radio alarm clock and the chance to enter our grand prize draw.

And even if you removed all the scuffers, she mused as she walked out into the fresh air and pitch darkness, that still left a whole load of criminals, loonies, lawyers and similar second-degree nastinesses, not to mention the foul interior décor and the all-permeating smell of decomposing upholstery and men's socks. As far as she was concerned, she could tick off copshops on her list of experiences to be tried once, and move on to someplace more congenial, such as a charnel-house or a dentist's waiting room. Mercifully, she hadn't had to spend all that long inside the dismal place; she'd been sitting in her cell trying to decide where to start digging her escape tunnel and doing mental arithmetic to compute roughly how long it would take her (something in the region of a hundred years had been her best estimate), when suddenly the door had opened and a very weary-looking sergeant had told her she was free to go. Apparently it had been raining lawyers out at the front desk; scores of them in expensive suits and hand-stitched shoes. They'd pointed out to the sergeant that if he let Maria out, they'd all leave immediately. This, the sergeant felt, was a small price to pay for a million-per-cent improvement in his working conditions (he'd been prepared to go as high as his left arm or his first-born son), and so here she was, free as a bird.

She walked slowly up the Charing Cross Road, savouring the really rather pleasant sensation of not being in a police station and turning over in her mind the various things she intended to say to Kawaguchiya Integrated Circuits just as soon as she could find somewhere to recharge the batteries of her laptop. At the first dustbin she passed, she stopped to dispose of the half-transparent paper bag that contained the last of the cream slices (the desk sergeant had insisted she took it away with her, and then made her sign about a tree and a half's worth of forms before she was allowed to have it back), as she did so taking a mental vow never again to throw patisserie at the cops while wearing impractically high heels. That small ritual duly performed, she charted a course back to the KIC building, speculating as to the kind of reception she was likely to get there. There was a better-than-average chance that there would be reference made to the empty chair behind her desk, the overflowing in-tray, the things left undone which ought to have been done. It was going to be interesting to see how they'd react when she explained that her absence was the result of putting into effect the company's new cakes-and-flatfeet initiative.

'Oh it's *you*,' said Mr Philips, the assistant junior deputy something-or-other, in a tone of voice that suggested he'd either encountered the risen Christ or found a tuning fork in his cornflakes. 'Well, well, well. Fancy that.' He paused in mid-flow, treated her to a long stare, and sniffed. 'You look like you've been sleeping under the railway arches,' he said.

'I resent that,' Maria replied. 'If a girl can't spend a night in prison without people making hurtful remarks about her appearance, it's a pretty poor show. Was there anything specific, or are you just destruct-testing your sense of humour?'

'Why,' asked Mr Philips coldly, 'were you in prison?'

Maria shrugged. 'Oh, assaulting the police, resisting arrest, that sort of thing. Any coffee going? I'm parched.'

Mr Philips' eyebrows rose like startled lifts. 'I see,' he said. 'Well, at the risk of sounding a bit old fashioned, I'm not sure that's really the sort of behaviour . . .'

He hesitated, recognising the onset of that same not-such-a-good-idea-after-all feeling that fish sometimes get when the free lunch turns out to have a hook in it. Maria was smiling at him.

'Gosh,' she said. 'I knew one of these days you were going to stand up and be counted. Good for you.'

'I'm sorry?'

'I've always had this feeling that sooner or later you'd turn round and say, I don't care if it *is* official company policy, I'm not going to do it and that's that. I'm impressed.'

'Official company . . .'

'Didn't you know?' Maria looked surprised, like a mermaid caught shoplifting. 'Oh. If you don't believe me, put your head round the door of the legal department and ask them. They should know; they had the job of getting me out of clink half the night.'

'Oh,' said Mr Philips. 'Official company policy. Assaulting the police.'

Maria patted his hand reassuringly. 'It's not as bad as it sounds. All you have to do is throw doughnuts at them.'

'Throw *doughnuts*—'

She nodded. 'And all the resisting arrest bit means is that you run away when they chase you, and they don't look where they're going and trip over things. It's just as well you met me, isn't it?' she added. 'Wouldn't have looked good if you were the only person of junior executive grade and upwards who didn't realise . . .'

By the time she reached her office, she was beginning to regret that remark; because it was rapidly becoming apparent that she (and presumably Mr Philips, who was known to be the last person ever to hear anything) was the only person of any grade whatsoever who hadn't actually realised the company was suddenly dying. And the first she knew of it was when two men in overalls came in and took away her desk.

'We'll be back for the picture in a minute,' one of them said over his shoulder. 'Right then, to me, mind the bleedin' door . . .'

The picture . . .

Time, Maria realised, to act quickly and decisively. She therefore spent the next four minutes standing on first one foot and then the other trying to puzzle out what to do. It was only the thump of boots in the corridor that snapped her out of it.

They're coming back. They're coming for the picture. They're coming for *me*.

Within all of us, the hypothesis runs, no matter how droopy and wet we may appear, there is in fact a coiled spring of instinctive action just waiting for the moment when it can find release. Some of us, indeed, make full use of this latent facility, to the extent that we stop acting like people and become hard to tell apart from hyperactive cuckoo clocks. Others never even suspect, which makes the explosion all the more astonishing when it actually happens.

At the very moment when the door handle began to turn, Maria vaulted over her desk, grabbed the picture in both hands, lifted it (they may be taking the furniture but they haven't disconnected the alarm systems; drat), located the window and jumped.

Furthermore, the hypothesis states, it's worth bearing in mind that seven times out of ten the things we do under the influence of the uncoiling spring of instinct are in fact incredibly stupid. Such as, for example, jumping through a fifteenth-storey window. The hypothesis doesn't make any allowance for whether the jumper is or is not holding a fourteenth-century painting at the time; presumably because that was more or less the time when the research funding ran out and the researchers had to pack it in and go find themselves proper jobs.

Ah, said Maria to herself, as the world was suddenly filled with an awful lot of fast-moving Down. Not so clever, after all.

In fact, she was wrong. Instinct would probably have explained it to her, if only she'd had the wit to ask. You're going to be all right, Instinct would have told her, because immediately before you're due to hit the ground and go *splat!* a squadron of winged demons will snatch you out of the air and carry you off bodily to the Fourth Circle of Hell. If only you'd asked, it would add, I could have set your mind at rest.

CHAPTER ELEVEN

The eclipse was starting to get boring. No change is virtually never news, particularly if it has to compete with BROOKSIDE STAR IN LOTTERY SEX SCANDAL and the latest food scare. Mad dogs and Englishmen were getting used to going out in the midday darkness; it was like the dark mornings and long evenings of winter, when nobody gets to see the sun because they're cooped up in the office or the factory. Light is, after all, a bit like freedom; take it away gradually and people won't notice it isn't there any more. And if they notice, get the papers to tell 'em it gives you cancer. That's how elections are won.

Where Artofel came from there isn't any daylight at the best of times, with the result that he moved through the darkened streets with the smug skill of a blind man in a power cut. He found a discarded copy of that morning's *Dependent* in a litter bin; the previous owner had removed the only good thing there'd been in it, leaving behind a few grains of salt and traces of vinegar, but the financial

section was still just about legible. From it he learned of
the fall of Kawaguchiya Integrated Circuits. I did that, he
reflected; me and a bishop, the forces of light and darkness
pulling together as a team. As the thought crossed his
mind he couldn't help glancing upwards, to where a
similar joint venture was still very definitely in progress.
Difference is, he mused, that's just two sources of
illumination standing in each other's light; two rights
making a wrong. Different kettle of worms, that. Not to
mention someone else's problem.

In any event, we did what we set out to do; now let's find
out if there was any point to it. *Flush 'em out,* we reckoned.
Maybe we didn't really think it through properly at the
time. Seemed like a good idea; but that's not a good
enough excuse for someone who comes from a place
where the Highways Department use good intentions
instead of concrete slabs and Tarmac. Artofel winced; if it
proved to be the case that he'd killed a major company for
nothing, he'd have it on his conscience for ever.

Oh bugger, he muttered to himself, screwing the
newspaper up and returning it to the bin. And all I wanted
was to do the right thing.

The mathematics of it was interesting, nevertheless.
Two wrongs don't make a right; two rights make a wrong.
Given enough blackboard space and a computer the size of
Jupiter, he could probably work that up into a theorem.
Maybe even get his own TV show.

The logical course of action was to go and have a drink,
and fortuitously he found that he was standing opposite
the doorway of a public house. It turned out to be one of
those cheerful places where the regulars look like they've
been slung off a pirate ship for antisocial behaviour, and there
are inexplicable claw marks all the way down one side of the
pool table. People who stroll through the door in mid-
afternoon wearing clerical collars tend to get noticed.

'Large Scotch,' Artofel said, sliding on to a bar stool, 'no ice. And a packet of those dry roasted peanuts the young lady on the display card's wearing. No, not that packet, the one next to it on your left.'

Four Scotches later, Artofel resumed his study of the problem in hand. If the consortium of rogue Flipsiders had been using KIC as some sort of vehicle for whatever it was they were up to, what would they be likely to do now that he'd trashed the company? Give up? He doubted that. The maxim *If at first you don't succeed, put someone else's initials on the worksheet* only really applied to the purely administrative grades of Hell. The operational side were rather more persistent in their approach. Compared to a demon with a fixed objective and nothing much else in particular to do, Robert the Bruce's spider was an early quitter. Likewise, he'd evaded capture once so far, but that didn't mean anything. Just because you narrowly avoid being hit by a bus, it doesn't mean you're immune to buses for ever afterwards. It was a fairly safe bet they'd come for him again some time soon. If he gave them the slip a second time, all he'd be doing was running up legal fees with the lawyers of averages. Much better to try and use what time he still had to get his rabbit-punch in first.

'Another?'

Artofel nodded. 'Here,' he said, 'can I ask you something?'

The barman looked at him. 'Depends,' he said.

'No big deal,' Artofel assured him. 'It's just that I'm on the run from a conspiracy of demonic powers hell-bent on doing something incredibly evil. If you were me and you had just the one 10p coin, who'd you phone?'

The barman shrugged. 'I dunno,' he said. 'God, maybe. If you want money for the payphone, I can change you a quid.'

Artofel shook his head. 'I tried Him,' he replied. 'Or at

least I tried a bishop. All that happened was that we destroyed a major corporation and I nearly got caught and dragged back to Hell. No, I was thinking more along the lines of somewhere I could keep out of sight for a bit. Any ideas?'

'How about Broadmoor? I reckon you'd fit in well up there.'

'Sorry, can't say I've heard of it. Is it far?'

'Get lost.'

'I probably will if you don't tell me how to get there.'

Before he could say anything else, the barman was called away to fill an order at the other end of the bar, leaving Artofel to reflect on the strange fact that if you want people to regard you as a lunatic and give you a wide berth, the surest way is to tell them the truth.

Well, now. By now he was fairly certain there was no way he'd be able to outwit or outrun this horrid consortium by using any of the resources he had by virtue of being a Duke of Hell; after all, for all he knew they all had strings of titles and two-page entries in *Crowley's Peerage* as good as his or better. The so-called proper channels weren't even worth considering. It was all very well, this idea that if some wicked person breaks the Infernal Law, the honest citizen has only to step into a handy phone booth, dial 666 and ask for the Old Nick; in practice it doesn't work that way any more Flipside than it does on mortal Earth. If he were to do that, Artofel knew perfectly well, his chances of getting away with merely making things slightly worse for himself were as slim as an aerobics instructor on a hunger strike. All that was left to him was finding some *human* way of dealing with the problem; something humans can do that devils and angels can't.

Such as?

Ten minutes of methodical self-enquiry left him with a list of uniquely human abilities that consisted of precisely one entry. They could die. Apart from that, it was a case of anything you can do, with horns on.

What about that, though?

Maybe it wasn't as silly as it sounded. The body he was in was mortal, but he wasn't; it by no means followed that if the body died, he'd have to go with it. After all, just because your socks wear out, it doesn't mean you have to follow them to the grave like the wives of some barbarian chieftain. Now, then; if the consortium needed him for this peculiar deal of theirs, it'd snooker them proper if he killed himself and wasn't available for research purposes as a result. It was also the best chance he could see of getting back home, to his office and his in-tray and his filing cabinets and the framed Hieronymus Bosch print on the wall above his familiar chair. Certainly worth considering—

He finished his drink and called for another. It arrived, with the absolute minimum of involvement from the barman. At least one thing he'd tried in the last few days had worked like it should.

Worth considering, but out of the question, because it wasn't his body. If he killed it, there'd be this poor homeless vicar with no flesh-and-bone overcoat to come back to once this was all over. Bad enough for the poor chap to have spent the last few weeks locked up in the cells as an enemy alien; no, he couldn't do it. It'd be wrong. Besides, suicide was a sin, and there was a little matter of demarcation to think about.

So what else do humans do that we don't? In practice, that is, as opposed to in theory. There must be something . . .

Well of course, there's . . .

Nah.

Surely not.

But it wasn't as if he was exactly spoilt for choice. Sure,

it wasn't something *exclusively* human; birds do it, bees do it, even educated fleas do it. But not the forces of darkness. Absolutely positive about that.

'Excuse me.'

'Now what do you want?'

'I'm sorry to trouble you,' Artofel said to the barman, 'but in order to save the human race, not to mention the entire cosmos and quite possibly God, it's rather imperative that I fall in love at once. Since I have no previous experience of the process, can you give me any basic advice?'

The barman looked at him for a moment.

'Yeah,' he said. 'Piss off before I bash your head in.'

Artofel's forehead creased in a slight frown. 'I see,' he said. 'Should I take that as a definite no, or . . .?'

'Out.'

'Because, you see,' Artofel went on, 'if I do something really out of character, something that's fundamentally at odds with my true demonic nature, it'll mean I'm not really a proper demon any more and I won't be any use to this diabolic consortium I was telling you about. And without me, I rather get the impression they can't do anything . . . So you see, it's really rather vital that I—'

About a fifteenth of a second later he hit the pavement, bounced off a dustbin and a parked car and came to rest in the gutter outside the pub.

'Blast,' he said.

He opened his eyes; and found that he was staring at something rather out of the ordinary. The most he could make of them was that they weren't feet. More like tentacles, except that no octopus he'd ever heard of had tentacles shaped like *that*.

'If you're who I think you are,' he said without looking up, 'those things aren't regulation issue.'

'Excuse me?'

'Stick to the cloven hooves, son,' Artofel sighed. 'The Service is no place for designer footwear.'

'Excuse me,' repeated the voice, with a slightly different inflection, 'but I'm from another planet, and I was wondering if you could spare me a few moments to tell me about your idea of the Supreme Being.'

'Huh?'

'I assume you have one,' the proprietor of the not-quite-tentacles continued. 'There's a lot of references to a Supreme Being in your cultural matrix. For instance, who is God?'

Slowly Artofel lifted his head and looked up at what the pseudopods were attached to. It gave him a nasty turn.

'Did you say you're from a different planet?' he asked.

'That's right,' whatever it was replied. 'I'm doing a preliminary report on your planet for the folks back home, and this is one aspect of your civilisation I haven't covered yet. Now then, this God. Am I to understand that as you perceive Him, your Supreme Being is three in one?'

Artofel shook his head. 'I think you'll find that's a kind of penetrating oil,' he replied. 'Actually, you've come to the right place, because I work for Him. In two capacities,' he added, wincing.

'I see. This is fascinating. Please go on.'

Quite possibly, Artofel said to himself, I'm not the first person to see something like this after being thrown out of this particular pub. Chances are I won't be the last, either. What I resent is knowing that it's not just a hallucination. 'It's rather difficult to explain,' he went on. 'Basically, you see, I work for the forces of Evil, but right now I'm on secondment to Good. Like a sort of exchange visit, if you follow me. See how the other half lives, that sort of thing.'

'Ah,' said the alien, clearly perplexed. 'Now, excuse my asking, but why did you just fly out through that door at high speed and land uncomfortably on the ground?'

'I was chucked out. For being a nuisance.'

'Really.'

'But that's just a sort of temporary diversion. Now I've got to go and find someone to fall in love with.'

'I see. Now then, your conception of the Supreme Being—'

'Right,' Artofel said. 'He's about so high, a bit broader across the shoulders than me, white hair, long beard, got this way of looking at you out of the corner of His eye. I can give you His address, but I think He's away from home at the moment.'

'Just a minute,' the alien interrupted. 'You speak as if you've seen Him.'

'Of course I have,' Artofel replied. 'We all have. I mean, I'm not saying I know Him personally, in any real sense. I was introduced to Him once at a garden party, but just to say hello.'

'Let me see if I've got this straight,' said the alien. 'You're telling me you've actually met your Supreme Being.'

'Oh yes.'

'And talked to Him.'

'Just a few words, like I said. There was a whole queue of us, you see, waiting to be introduced, quick handshake and out again. Still, it's all good public relations, isn't it?'

'Pardon my saying this,' said the alien cautiously, 'but you don't sound as if you were, well, particularly impressed.'

Artofel shrugged. 'Can't say I was. Nothing against Him, mind; perfectly pleasant He was, not standoffish or anything, very polite. I suppose it's all the practice He gets, because he's doing that sort of thing all the time.'

'Your God spends a lot of time being polite to His subjects?'

Artofel nodded. 'A certain amount of basic showmanship goes with the territory,' he said. 'You know what they say: keep the little people happy and the big people will follow suit. And anyhow, we're all on the same side, so . . .'

'You are? Oh. Right.' The alien shuffled its pseudopods thoughtfully. 'You mentioned just now that you have to go and jump in something. What was—?'

'Not jump,' Artofel corrected. 'Fall. In love. You see, it's rather complicated but I've got to fall in love in order to save the human race and the entire divine hierarchy. I could explain,' he added, 'but it'd take rather a long time.'

'Quite. When you say save—'

'From a bunch of low-lifes who're out to get Him. Talking of which, I'd love to stay here chatting but I'd better be getting on. All the best with your researches.'

'Thanks. Yes. Right.' Artofel couldn't be sure, because as far as body language went, the alien didn't half talk funny; but it gave the impression of pulling itself together with extreme difficulty. 'Thank you for your time. You've been most . . . Yes. Thank you. Goodbye. You did say *love*, didn't you? I thought so. Sorry, I think my translator unit's malfunctioning, because . . . Yes, well, anyway. Bye.'

When the alien had squelched away, Artofel got up, dusted himself off and looked around for someone to fall in love with. Can't be difficult, he reassured himself. If they can do, so can I.

Oh well. Here goes.

He caught sight of a briskly moving figure on the other side of the street and followed after it. About forty-five seconds later there was a flurry of conversation which ended in a loud crunching noise and the howl of a Duke of Hell suddenly afflicted with pain in parts of his anatomy he didn't know he had. A few minutes later, the same sequence of events was repeated. A few minutes after that, the same.

Brimstone, Artofel reflected, as he sat on the steps of a

bank waiting for the pain to subside. And yet this is how these losers are supposed to reproduce. Beats me how come there's so many of them, let alone why they bother. Still, here we go again—

This time, the sound of stockinged knee on worsted was so loud it rattled the windows. Which goes some way towards explaining why, when the commando of Infernal stormtroopers he'd only recently escaped from caught up with him a few minutes later, he had neither the strength nor the willpower to run.

Distressing was putting it mildly. One minute, Karen had been engrossed in the search for a way to save God, the next she was loading the contents of her desk into a cardboard box and promising the loathsome Jenny from the next office down the row but one that they'd keep in touch. Strange, she said to herself as she waited for the lift, how quickly things can change.

What had done it? she wondered. About the only sudden and unexpected factor was the eclipse, which had now been going on for so long that she had difficulty remembering what it had been like before. A messy sort of white stuff poured over everything like custard, if memory served her, and a big shiny thing up in the sky. She wasn't even sure she could recall exactly what the shiny thing had looked like; in her mind's eye it had somehow merged with the stylised yellow blob from a child's painting. Now, when she tried to remember the sun, the image that came to her mind was more like luminous fried egg than anything that had ever existed for real.

Unlikely, though, that the eclipse had done for Kawaguchiya Integrated Circuits; which only really left the abrupt and unheralded entry of God into its corporate life. Coincidence? Yeah, sure. And you could use her other leg for an emergency door-bell.

Anyway, she told herself, as she struggled with her cardboard box on the packed underground like a stereotype refugee, now it's none of my business and I can stop worrying about it. I can dismiss it from my mind and get on with the absolutely pathetically simple task of finding a new job.

Like hell.

Yes, that was all very well, but how was she supposed to continue the search, with no manual, no computer, no way of contacting Kevin Christ and absolutely zero chance of being believed by anybody she went to for help? If she couldn't crack it with all the resources of KIC to call on, she couldn't really expect to do better with nothing more sophisticated at her disposal than one of the early-Victorian coal-burning Amstrads and the Ladybird book of computer fault diagnosis. Forget it, Karen. You've got problems enough of your own.

Yes, but . . .

Yes but nothing. Out of my hands now. He's the *Almighty*, for pity's sake; big enough and ugly enough to take care of himself.

Yes. But.

Some clown bumped into her as she tried to scramble off the train at Waterloo, spilling the contents of her box and then darting off with only the echo of a mumbled 'Sorry' hurled over his shoulder. By the time she'd picked up her fugitive property, which had rolled and bounced away between the feet of her sardine-packed fellow passengers, the train had moved on. Great. She'd have to get off at the next stop, change platforms, wait for the northbound train, go through all this again. It was things like this made her love the human race.

Human race. *Human.* First real lead you've had all along.

How dumb (she asked herself as she shoved through to the doors just before they closed) can you get? All those hours she'd spent trying to find a way of bypassing the computer's defences, and it hadn't occurred to her that she was trying to solve the wrong problem. Sloppy thinking. Human thinking. Not appropriate to a superhuman problem.

She sat down on a bench on Kennington station platform, and worked it out a step at a time. The key to it all was a simple formula, one she'd known ever since she was a kid. So obvious . . .

To err is human, to forgive divine. When human beings make mistakes, they worry away at them trying to put things right, trying to stick the pieces back together again with glue. Occasionally they succeed, sometimes they fail utterly and make things worse, frequently they half solve the problem and then leave it while they try and cope with the mess they've caused for themselves while they were trying to fix the original problem. That's the human way. That's what she'd been trying to do. Wrong.

The denizens of Heaven don't solve problems or fix mistakes; they forgive them. Confronted with the theft in the Garden of Eden, God didn't try and stick the apple back on the branch with Araldite or fill in the bitten-out chunk with fine-grade Polyfilla; he simply forgave, and that was that, problem solved. It'd be a nice trick, if you could manage it; simply forgiving the front door for sticking in the damp weather, or the carburettor for being flooded, sitting down with a blocked sink trap and talking it through like sensible, mature adults – quicker, easier and ever so much cheaper. But backed-up sinks and cars that won't start aren't divine problems: not usually.

More to the point, you've got to be divine to make it work, which explained why it hadn't actually solved anything when she decided to forgo her moral right to break the arm of the pillock who upset her cardboard box on the train. It was no use her forgiving the wretched computer; big deal. Somebody else was going to have to do that, and from what she knew of the situation the only person with the necessary qualification was sitting under a big umbrella on a river-bank somewhere. Still, what she didn't know about the precise way in which Heaven works could be written on a medium-sized Universe in letters the size of a hydrogen atom. Let them work out the minor operational details for themselves; she'd done the important part. Now all she had to do was tell them . . .

A task in respect of which the phrase *piece of cake* wasn't immediately appropriate. Phone the Pope? Go into Westminster Abbey and ask if they could forward a letter? Dammit, she shouldn't *have* to get in touch with them, they should come to her.

With a rumble of thunder like Thor after a hot curry, the train appeared out of the tunnel. The platform was crowded, and it wasn't easy to move about with her arms full of cardboard box. In fact, if she wasn't careful, she might end up getting shoved off the platform and under the train, which wouldn't help anybody.

Oddly enough, that was exactly what happened.

It was probably just as well that she was so preoccupied with righteous indignation against the second clumsy oaf she'd had the misfortune to be bumped into in the space of less than an hour that she didn't hear the *scrunch* as the train ran over her, let alone the rather nauseating fizz as all those busy volts ran up and down her nervous system, ringing bells and running away. In fact, she'd been dead for nearly a second and a half before she noticed, and that was only because she'd reached out for her a-present-from-Florence paperweight and found that her hand passed clean through it.

Oh, she said.

Telltale signs - the fact that she was looking down at the roof of the train rather than up at its chassis, that sort of thing – confirmed her initial suspicion. Oh *damn*. Well, that's that, then. And of all the blundering, careless idiots—

From her vantage point in the upper air she could see the blundering, careless idiot quite clearly. He looked as if he was having the worst moment of his life; quite probably, he was. Without even thinking about it, she forgave him.

And somehow, without having the faintest idea how she knew, she was aware that it had worked. She had forgiven him, he had been forgiven.

Problem solved.

In a manner of speaking, of course; it still left her quite undeniably dead for one thing, and it would have been nice if the omelette could have been made without her having to be the egg that got broken. Still, no point crying over spilt milk. Or, come to that, spilt anything else.

To forgive—

And then she knew.

Len woke up.

He had been dreaming; the long, silent, majestic dreams of machines, full of straight lines and right angles, of things that fitted exactly into other things, of keyways frictionless and true and the sharp, clean shine of newly cut metal. It was a beautiful dream; the sort of vision that might inspire a god to create a world.

'Urgh,' he said. 'Wassafuxat?'

Someone was bashing the workshop door. Len stood up, quickly trying to remember what he'd recently learned about balance and self-propelled biped movement. Why should anybody want to smash his door in at half past one in the morning?

'Lock,' he said.

Hmm?

'What's going on?'

Please be more specific.

Len scowled. Locks aren't the sensible person's immediate choice when information's needed in a hurry. As is only to be expected from mechanisms whose whole purpose is to be exact and to respond only to a perfectly correct key, they tend to be pedantic and fussy.

'Who's bashing your door and why?' Len amended. 'Any ideas?'

I register five of them. They are not authorised personnel. They do not appear to be human. Their purpose in hitting the door is to open it without recourse to authorised lock-opening procedures. I would imagine they are doing this because they are not authorised personnel. Authorised personnel would not abuse official property in this manner.

'Ah,' Len said, as his brain fumbled for its trousers and put its teeth in. 'Well, try and keep them out.'

Of course I shall try and keep them out. They are not authorised personnel. If they were authorised personnel, they would have an appropriate key.

'Cheers, lock.'

I should however point out that in the normal course of fulfilling my function as a lock I am already doing everything within my limited powers to prevent unauthorised access by unauthorised personnel. Please note also that I shall not be able to fulfil my function for very much longer.

'Oh go on,' Len muttered, testing the three big Stilson wrenches for weight and balance. 'Give it your best shot.'

Please note that I am on the point of failing to fulfil my function. I should like the record to show that this failure is due to the imminent collapse of the wooden doorframe rather than any shortcoming on my part.

'Thanks anyway. Robot!'

'Go 'way 's middle of night.'

'Oh for . . .' Len had an idea. 'Recalibrate your timescale for Hong Kong time. Robot!'

'Here, boss!' At once the robot (for whom it was now 9 a.m.) shot out from its storage space under the bench and stood to attention, its facial mechanisms arranged in a beaming cybersmile. 'Sleep okay, boss?'

'Like a top. Robot, there are five heavies trying to smash the door down.'

'Yes?'

'Don't just stand there,' Len fumed. 'Stop them.'

'Um.'

For a moment, Len couldn't believe his ears. 'What the devil do you mean, um? You're a robot, dammit. You don't know the meaning of fear.'

The robot shuffled its feet. 'Actually, I do. Fear, according to the *Oxford English Dictionary*—'

'Don't muck me about, robot. I gave you a direct order.'

'I know.' The robot simpered. (How did it learn to do that? Len wondered. I don't remember fitting a simper relay.) 'There's a problem. I can't.'

'What?'

The robot bit its lip, or at least it tried to. There was a grating noise and a few sparks. 'EC Directive 463837/99 on safety of machinery. Says machines aren't allowed to hurt people. Sorry.'

'*What?*'

'EC Directive 463837/99,' the robot repeated miserably. 'All new mechanical appliances now have to conform to the specifications laid down by this directive, which states, and I'm paraphrasing slightly here, hurting people is wrong. For heaven's sake, you wouldn't want me to break the law, now would you?'

Len would have replied Yes at this point, if it hadn't been for the door giving way and the workshop suddenly filling with large, fast-moving bipeds. Even Len, whose experience of human beings was still rather limited, could tell that these weren't standard production-model *Homo sapiens*; too many head and claws, eyes in the wrong section of the anatomy, that sort of thing. They looked as if they'd been thrown together out of the contents of the leftovers in Frankenstein's spares box with a few bits from a car boot sale thrown in for good measure, and they were holding implements which, although unfamiliar, probably came under the heading of generic weapons.

'Hold it,' Len yelled.

The apparent leader of the party stopped where he was, assessing him through several pairs of inhuman eyes. 'Well?' he said.

'Come any closer and I'll thump you.'

'Oh.' The leader shrugged. 'I thought you were going to say something important. All right, grab them and let's get going.'

Two of the subsidary Things caught hold of the robot while a third pulled a black plastic sack down over its head. It didn't move. The leader and his remaining henchthing advanced on Len; in no particular hurry, keeping a multiplicity of eyes and the like on the Stilson in Len's hands, but not unduly worried about it. As they came close, he backed away. They walked straight past him.

'Hey,' he said. 'Where are you going?'

'You'll see.'

They were standing on either side of the machine; the universal milling and turning machine that was much more Len than any bag of bones and blood would ever be. The leader picked up a twelve-pound sledgehammer single-handed; his chum was toying with the big adjustable spanner.

'Come quietly,' said the leader, 'or the machine gets it.'

'You wouldn't.'

'As a statement of fact, that has a basic flaw. As a threat, it doesn't work. As an appeal to my better nature—'

'Get away,' Len said, 'from that machine. It hasn't done you any harm.'

The subsidiary Thing tapped the main casing gently with the spanner. 'Cast iron,' he observed. 'Brittle stuff, if it gets hit. Can't be repaired.'

'All right.' The Stilson clattered on the concrete floor; only Len heard it swearing. 'Now get away from the machine.'

The Things took a step forwards; but suddenly there was an atmosphere in the workshop that hadn't been there a moment before. A sort of dull residual anger, you might say, if you had an excessively powerful imagination. Len could feel it well enough; he could remember feeling that anger many times himself, when some cack-haired apprentice had jammed his feed or graunched his threads. It tended to start with an ill-defined I-don't-like-this-man, after which it would develop over a period of days, sometimes years, biding its time until the object of the machine's resentment happened to put his thumb in the way of the boring-bar or lean over a moving chuck with his shirt-sleeves flapping. Then there'd be a short, usually bloody moment, followed by a certain amount of irrational human behaviour; after a while someone'd come along, switch him off at the mains and clean the blood and bits of stuff out of the cogs and threads. Odd how rarely human beings notice that ominous feel in the air.

EC Directive 463837/99 forsooth. One of the first things a machine tool learns is how to defend itself, and how to avenge its slighted honour.

It started when the leader's right leg brushed against the bench grinder, which promptly switched itself on. The leader immediately jumped two feet in the air and eighteen inches sideways, but all he achieved was to fall heavily across the bed of the bandsaw. With hindsight, an error on his part.

In a slightly edited form, the leader then hurled himself clear of the bandsaw and, with his remaining hand, grabbed at the nearest solid object to steady himself. His rotten luck it happened to be the arc welder.

From the arc welder, the leader then rebounded on to the table of the Great Machine, and that's where his real problems started. The horizontal arm, set up for slit-sawing, left just enough of him for the vertical arm to mess up quite comprehensively with a face-cutter.

Ah, Len said to himself. Always wondered why they called them that.

The subsidary Thing stayed perfectly still, at least until Len had brained him with the big Stilson. That just left the other three.

'One of the advantages of buying second-hand gear,' Len said, 'is that it doesn't comply with the latest EC directives. Do we have to do this the hard way, or are you lot going to bugger off and leave me in peace?'

A Thing grinned at him feebly. 'In a perfect world,' he said, 'we'd bugger off. Gladly.'

'Like a shot,' confirmed his colleague to his immediate right.

'Nothing'd give us greater pleasure,' chipped in the third.

Len shrugged. 'Please yourselves, then,' he said; whereupon the spindle moulder jumped them. What a spindle moudler does to pieces of wood is bad enough.

'You can come out now,' Len said.

'Sorry,' the robot reiterated. 'If it'd been up to me, I'd have pulled their heads off and made them eat them.'

'I'm sure you would,' Len replied, pulling off the plastic sack. 'Isn't there something in human literature about a tin man who has no heart?'

'Not quite,' the robot replied. 'In *The Wizard of Oz*—'

'Well,' Len went on, 'you're a steel man who has no

balls. But we can fix that. Hand me that half-by-nine-sixteenths spanner.'

'Please—'

'Nuts,' Len went on, unscrewing one, 'but no balls.' He paused and thought. 'Maybe it's a human thing, courage,' he said.

'Up to a – ouch, that *tickles!*'

'It'll do more than tickle when I get the brazing torch on you. Now then, I'll need a schematic of male reproductive organs, some three-sixteenths copper pipe and a soldering iron. God, what a bloody daft way to go about a perfectly simple job of plumbing!'

'Why are you—?'

Len looked up and reached for a hacksaw. 'Because,' he replied, 'as soon as I've bypassed that EC Directive, we're going to find out who sent these goons, these creatures who threatened to hurt a machine, and we're going to sort them out. All right?'

'Okay. Um, boss.'

'Yes?'

'Why?'

'Shut up.'

'Ah. Now I understand. Thanks, boss.'

CHAPTER TWELVE

'**K**evin.'

The younger son of God didn't reply. He was sitting curled up in the window-seat of one of the rear subsidiary seventeenth-floor chapels, gazing listlessly out over the back courtyard and fiddling with a plastic flower. A painter in need of a model for a watercolour lovelorn teenager would have offered him money not to move an inch.

'Kevin,' Martha repeated. 'Your dinner's going cold.'

'Don't want any,' he mumbled, turning his head away. Outside, they were emptying the septic tank. Chances were that it wasn't the view that was monopolising his attention.

'It's kedgeree,' Martha said. 'And bread-and-butter pudding for afters.'

'It's always kedgeree and bread-and-butter pudding,' Kevin replied; and if this statement wasn't entirely accurate, it was close enough.

Martha advanced, walking softly. 'What's the matter?' she said.

'Oh, nothing,' Kevin replied. 'I've messed up the computer, the whole world's a complete shambles, I don't even know what harm I've done and when Dad gets home He'll be so angry it'll make what He did to Adam and Eve look like an awards ceremony.'

'But that's not it, is it?'

'No,' Kevin admitted.

'She hasn't rung back, has she?'

'Who? Oh, you mean that female mortal, the one from the computer place. No, she hasn't.' Kevin's voice wobbled like a tightrope walker in a hurricane. 'Not,' he went on, 'that I was expecting her to. I mean, what'd she want to go phoning *me* for? It's not as if anybody in their right mind'd want to talk to *me*. 'Specially not . . .' His voice trailed away, like the attention of a delegate on the fifth day of a conference, and he made a sort of burping noise that had nothing to do with indigestion.

'Now then,' Martha said. Not tactful to point out that her not ringing back had probably avoided a potential disaster that would have relegated whatever else Kevin had done, no matter how cataclysmic, to a quarter of an inch on the back page under the Australian football results. She tried, briefly, to imagine what Himself would have said if He'd come home to meet a radiantly happy Kevin nervously stammering that there was someone he'd like Him to meet.

No, no more of that sort of thing.

Once had been quite enough . . .

She felt her face grow warm, and turned it away in case Kevin should see the blush. 'You've got to keep your strength up,' she said. 'There's ice cream with the bread-and-butter pudding.'

'No thanks.'

'Or custard. You like custard.'

Kevin said some words about bread-and-butter pudding that had probably never been used in Heaven before; where *did* he learn them? Martha wondered. She replied with some mild rebuke; her mind was elsewhere. No, *that* sort of thing was definitely not on. Perish the thought. She shrugged, and closed the door after her.

The boy's growing up, she reflected as she made her way down the stairs to the laundry room; a disturbing thought. He wasn't supposed to grow up. It had been part of the deal, in fact. It was a good bet that this sudden and unexpected contact with mortals was behind it; after all, a lad his age, talking to a girl for the very first time, it was only to be expected. Next thing you know, he'll be thinking about all sorts of things.

Like, for example; whatever became of his mother?

As she folded a towel, Martha shuddered. It really wouldn't do for Kevin to start asking that sort of question. Mind you, it was a miracle it hadn't occurred to him already. Very much a miracle; but in a place where everything from the plumbing to the immersion heaters works by miracle – so cheap, so environmentally friendly – you take such things for granted. If only everything in life was as reliable as a miracle.

Now if she could have her time over again—

Yes, but she couldn't, so no point worrying about it. There was no way Kevin would ever work it out for himself. That had been taken care of nearly two thousand years ago; no reason why it should suddenly change now.

Unless—

She dropped the towel; it folded itself anyway (My God! A miracle!). Unless, of course, one of the things Kevin had thrown out of kilter was her own rather shamefaced little miracle, the one that prevented a boy asking an obvious question. The very thought was enough to make her blood run as cold as a bath in a cheap hotel. No reason to suppose that it should, of course; except that here was

Kevin, noticing girls. Why now? Compared with what they'd been like a few decades ago, girls in the fag-end of the twentieth century were scarcely worth noticing. Drab, featureless, uninspiring the lot of 'em; none of them the sort of creature you'd accept a second-hand apple from. Compared to the quality of girls they'd had in her young day—

Well, quite. Enough said about that. The plain fact of the matter was, if this mess didn't get sorted out as quick as ninepence, there could well be trouble, and then what? Another flood, maybe? Martha sincerely hoped it wouldn't come to that. Thousands of years it'd taken before they'd got rid of that horrible musty smell, not to mention the damp getting into the walls. And, of course, the mass devastation and loss of life, though it got a bit technical when you started trying to work out the ramifications of that particular line of thought. It was an option He might well consider, nevertheless; not to mention a first-rate excuse for winding up humanity and starting again with a relatively clean sheet. Would He go that far, just to cover up one little scandal?

No need to think too long about that one.

She left the rest of the bedlinen to fold itself – it was much better at it than she was – and hurried back down to the staff canteen. Fortunately, nobody was using the phone, and she still had enough small change.

From the KIC helpline number, no reply. To be precise, that high-pitched keening noise that means the line's been cut off. Frowning, she tried the main number, and got a recorded message, Sorry we can't take your call right now but we've quite unexpectedly ceased to exist. If you'd like to leave a message for the liquidators, please speak after the tone.

Martha didn't swear; but the way she said 'Drat!' would have had your average Hell's Angel scowling at her and demanding that she wash her mouth out with soap. The only little flicker of light she'd seen so far, snuffed out. Back precisely where she'd started.

Which meant she'd have to think of something else.

Easier said than done. She was, in all modesty, reasonably bright, but solutions to insoluble problems weren't the sort of thing she could pluck out of thin air at a moment's notice. Intelligence wasn't quite enough. There had to be a certain element of luck as well; say ninety-nine per cent, in round figures. For her to fix this dreadful muddle all by herself, without any help or proper facilities; it'd be—

She smiled. Then she went to the counter and asked for a cup of tea. The duty angel nodded and filled the kettle from the tap. She said a brief prayer. At once, steam rose from the spout and the lid rattled. The angel poured a cupful and handed it over. Long ago, the management had realised that what worked for wine at the wedding at Cana works for tea as well, resulting in a substantial saving on the staff budget. So quick; so efficient; so cheap; so environmentally friendly. From where she was standing, Martha could see through into the kitchen, where someone had fridgemagneted up the usual witty and encouraging notices, such as:

YOU DON'T HAVE TO BE INFALLIBLE TO WORK HERE BUT IT HELPS

and:

ANGELS DO IT IMMACULATELY

(that one always made her wince) and:

MY OTHER SON'S A MESSIAH

(one of these days He's going to see that, and then there'll be trouble) and:

MIRACLES WE DO IMMEDIATELY
THE POSSIBLE TAKES A LITTLE LONGER

Yes. For her to fix this dreadful muddle all by herself, without any help or proper facilities, would be an absolute by-Our-Lady miracle.

'Well now,' said a voice in the darkness, 'this *is* cosy.'

The diverse assortment of creatures confined in the cage somewhere within earshot of the voice all began talking at once. What they actually said scarcely merits recording; it was a confused medley of variations on the themes *Where am I?* and *Let me out!* The voice waited until they'd all railed themselves hoarse, and then continued.

'I'll bet,' it said, 'you're wondering why you're here.'

'I'm not,' growled Artofel. 'And you can stop trying to be so damn mysterious, as well. I know perfectly well that this is the staff toilet on Level Thirty-Six; I'd recognise that dripping cistern anywhere. And any minute now I'll recognise your voice too, and when I do there's going to be some changes made to the holiday roster that'll make you wish you'd never been damned.'

'Oh,' said the voice. 'Drat. In that case, I might as well switch the lights on.'

A faint click; and the meagre glow of an administration-issue sixty-watt bulb diluted the shadows. In particular, it illuminated four plump middle-aged males and one plump middle-aged female, all dressed in smart executive businesswear and wearing executive spectacles, sitting on lavatory seats in a row of cubicles.

'You,' Artofel said contemptuously. 'I might have known.'

'Hello,' replied the female. 'Yes, it's us. And before you get too cocky and start yelling for help, don't bother, because nobody'll come.'

'I put a notice on the door saying *Out of Order*,' explained the male to her immediate left. 'Amazing how effective that is.'

Artofel sniffed angrily. 'So that's what it's all been about, is it?' he said. 'All this aggravation, spectral warriors roaming up and down breaking all the rules, harassment of civilians, conspiracy against the Management—'

'Who isn't here,' the female interrupted, smirking.

'What?'

'Not here. Gone. One of our Supreme Beings is missing—'

'Two, actually,' a male demon pointed out. 'The Boss and Junior. Which theoretically leaves Uncle Ghost, but so what? Compared to him in the usefulness stakes, the proverbial chocolate fireguard's a nuclear-powered Swiss Army knife.'

'Say that again,' Artofel muttered. 'The Old Man and Junior are—'

'Gone. That's right. Been gone a while now. There are various theories,' the female went on. 'Buffy here reckons that science has finally caught up with Them and proved once and for all They don't exist. Reckons there was a documentary about it on telly, and so it must be true. Chubby thinks They've got religion and joined some obscure sect in the Nevada desert. My hypothesis is that He's staged His own death, possibly by falling off his yacht and drowning or something equally jejune, and they've done a flit with the pension fund money. In any case, it doesn't matter; the fact is they're not here. Which means that, so long as we don't hang about, we've got a once-in-an-everlasting-lifetime chance to put through this perfectly wonderful scheme of ours and have it all tied up so tight that even if They do come back, there'll be nothing They can do about it. So . . .'

'Excuse me.'

The female looked to see who'd spoken. 'Sorry,' she said. 'What can I do for you?'

'Excuse me,' Maria repeated, 'but where is this?'

The five demons looked at each other and tried not to giggle. It was left to Artofel to answer the question.

'Hell?' Maria repeated.

'That's right,' the female said. 'Don't worry unduly about that, though. Like in Monopoly, you're in Jail but Just Visiting.' She smiled reassuringly. 'You're going to die, of course,' she added, 'but what happens to you after that is between you, your personal codes of ethics and your own individual governing body. I don't know offhand who actually does decide where bad paintings go when they die, although I've heard the Birmingham City Art Gallery plausibly suggested.'

Inside the cage there was gloomy silence. Artofel scowled ineffectually. Maria sat thoughtful and rather depressed. The Prime Minister, having discovered by exhaustive research that there was nothing inside the cage to climb up and jump off, was sitting in a corner and huddling.

'And in any case,' the female went on, 'we can't snuff you out quite yet, because we haven't got the complete set. The last of you's due to be delivered any minute now, and then we can get started. While we're waiting, though, I thought it'd be only polite to say hello and frighten you into little quivering heaps.' She beamed like a vampire aunt. 'It's been ages since I've done any frightening,' she explained. 'I do miss it so.'

Maria turned her head as best she could in the confined space of the cage. 'Excuse me,' she said to Artofel. 'I don't know who you are, but you seem to know what's going on.

Could you possibly explain? I have actually met some of these people before, but . . .'

'Delighted,' Artofel replied grimly. 'I am Artofel, Duke of Hell. These five degenerates are also Dukes of Hell; to be precise, they're the Arts, Leisure and Libraries Sub-Committee, which in practice means they're too devious or useless to be trusted with a proper job but they can't be sacked because they've got seniority.'

'I resent that,' said the male demon referred to as Buffy. 'We fulfil a valuable role in the artistic and cultural life of everlasting damnation.'

Artofel snorted. 'Ignore him,' he said. 'All they actually do is, twice a year they take a library trolley round with all the latest Jeffrey Archers and Lynda La Plantes. Waste of time, though, because any punter who's been evil enough to deserve that sort of thing gets issued with a copy as soon as it comes out. Different department.'

'I see,' Maria lied. 'You're the ones who wanted us to sell you our souls or something.'

The male demon called Bunty sniggered; the female broadened her insufferable smile. 'If only it were that simple,' she said. 'No, my poor dears, it's a bit more involved than that. Shall I explain?'

'No,' said Artofel.

'Very well then. The point is, you three and a fourth one you'll be meeting any minute now are unique. For a while now you've been trotting around quite happily in human bodies, but you aren't human. We're designing an improved Mark Two human to sell to alternative realities – '

'Damn fine commercial opportunity there,' Buffy muttered. 'Dreadful waste not to exploit it.'

' – and so all we've got to do is synthesise the four of you, refine the result and start cloning. We have all the facilities here.'

'Really? In a staff bog?'

The female nodded. 'Apparently you're overestimating the technical difficulties, Artie dear. We've got the blender from the Level Eight canteen and the spare photocopier from Archives, and the rest's just a matter of imagination and insulating tape. Excuse me, but why is your silent colleague trying to hang upside down from the cage roof?'

'He's a lemming,' Bunty explained. 'I know it's like a fear of heights, only in reverse. He'll let go in a min— Ah, just as I thought. Happy landings!'

Artofel growled menacingly. 'You do realise that you're never going to get away with this,' he said. 'I mean, quite apart from the whole scheme being completely impractical and doomed to failure, do you honestly believe that when - I say when, not if – the Old Man finds out what you've been doing He's just going to put it down to fiendish high spirits and tell you not to do it again?' He shook his head, in the process biffing Maria on the nose and head-butting the Prime Minister. 'You five won't even be history. You'll be dogma.'

The female laughed musically. 'We shall see,' she said. 'Or at least, you three won't, but we will. Chubby, do you think you could possibly find out what's keeping number four? Time's going on, you know. It's not like Squad Three to be late.'

'Caught in traffic?' a demon speculated.

'Excuse me,' Maria said.

The five demons looked at her. This didn't disconcert her too badly – you get used to that sort of thing if you've been a painting for any appreciable length of time. She cleared her throat.

'Excuse me, but I've just realised why none of this is going to work.'

Another trill of silvery laughter from the female demon. 'Oh dear,' she said, 'this isn't going to help, you know. Playing for time might be an effective tactic where you come from, but down here time really doesn't have an awful lot of meaning.'

'No but seriously,' Maria said. 'And I'll tell you for why. Your whole scam's based on one basic error. Sorry,' she added, 'but there it is.'

'Oh yes? And perhaps you'd be terribly sweet and let us in on the big secret?'

Maria looked thoughtful. 'It's not really a secret,' she said. 'More sort of staring you in the face. Just ask yourselves: why do supreme beings have mortals in the first place?'

The demons beamed tolerantly. 'Atmosphere,' Buffy said.

"Like potted palms in dentists' waiting rooms,' Chubby added. 'You don't need them, but it makes the place look a bit less sparse.'

'You're sure about that?' Maria said. 'I'm not. Be reasonable. Mortals aren't particularly decorative; if all you wanted was to make the place look nice, you'd have lots of tasteful ornaments instead, like me. And as pets, they're a dead loss; they aren't exactly environmentally friendly either, Lord knows. If you wanted something to be the equivalent of a cuddly kitten or even pondweed in a fishtank, you wouldn't bother with human beings, you'd just stick with nice sensible harmless animals.'

'Like lemmings,' Artofel muttered under his breath.

'Exactly,' Maria agreed. 'And mortals aren't there to add interest and excitement to the business of running a cosmos; after all, that's what His Majesty's loyal opposition's there for – you lot and this gentleman here whose name escapes me for the moment. The forces of evil and so forth. And the last possible reason for having mortals is to get anything *useful* done, because they don't, by and large. If it's that sort of thing you're after, you'd have a race of robots or something similar. But instead,' she went on, 'there are mortals. Have you ever stopped to wonder why?'

The female was still beaming; but the one called Bunty was wearing a puzzled frown. It suited him about as well as a full set of baroque armour would suit Kate Moss, but the important thing was that it was there. 'What are you driving at?' he asked.

'Think,' Maria replied. 'The only possible motive for infesting your cosmos with silly, awkward, destructive mortals is so that you, the supreme being, can feel superior. I may not be all that hot on the perfection front, you say, as you face yourself in the shaving mirror every morning, but at least I'm better than that lot down there. It gives you a nice warm glow deep down in your ineffability. It makes you feel good. After all, you're an omnipotent creator; if that's not the reason, why did you make *Homo sapiens* such an utter *mess*? So,' she continued sweetly, 'don't you think that an *improved* version of humanity, a version that's *not* a seething mass of design faults and built-in shortcomings, is likely to be something of a drug on the market?'

There was a long, rather unpleasant silence, disturbed only by Artofel sniggering and the rasp of teeth on steel as the Prime Minister tried to gnaw through the bars of the cage.

'Bother,' said the fifth demon.

'Don't listen to her,' the female said. 'That's human logic talking. Gods don't think like that. Do they?' she added.

'Want to bet?' Maria replied aggressively. 'I seem to remember something about being created in somebody else's image. I'd invite you to look at it more as a case of Him having a very ugly picture of himself in his attic Or, if you prefer, ask yourself who's taking away whose sins? All the things He didn't want to be, shoved off on a bunch of expendables? And you're asking His equivalents in the dimension next door to lay out good money for a new line in the raw materials of religion –'

'Canon fodder,' Artofel mumbled.

'– who're going to be fully justified in turning round when He forgives them and forgiving Him right back. With brass knobs on. Not an inspired investment, if you ask me.'

'Paintings,' said the female demon icily, 'should be seen and not heard. If I'd wanted a *talking* picture, I'd have kidnapped Mickey Mouse. Let's get these three minced up and add the fourth one later, shall we?'

Her four colleagues looked away, shuffling their executive-shod hooves.

'Seems to me the marketing side of this project's not been thought through properly,' Buffy said. 'Perhaps before we do anything totally irrevocable—'

'Buffy!'

'Yes, but hang on,' the male demon objected. 'Before you start playing Frankenstein-meets-Delia-Smith with Government property—'

'Buffy!'

'Look, I'm not trying to be difficult or anything, it's just that what she's just been saying does make a tenuous sort of sense, so if you could possibly see your way clear to explaining . . .'

The female demon's brows met in a thundery black line. 'Buffy . . .' she said ominously.

'Ah. Right. I *see*. Why didn't you say so before?'

In the middle of a continuum of slowly moving particles roughly analogous to a river, a float bobbed.

'Dad! You've got a bite!'

The older of the two fishermen pushed his hat on to the back of his head, grabbed his rod off its forked stand and began to turn the handle of his reel. The float ducked under the surface of the continuum. The line went taut.

'About ruddy time too,' the fisherman said. 'How many days've we been here?'

The younger fisherman frowned. 'That's not the point, though, surely. I thought the point was for you and me to spend some quality time together, just the two of us, give us a chance to revitalise our relationship by talking meaningfully about things we'd otherwise find it hard to discuss in our everyday environment . . .'

'Shut up, I'm trying to concentrate.'

'Sorry, Dad.'

With a deft flick of his wrist, the older fisherman whipped his prize up out of the continuum; a long shiny silver fish, wriggling and arching its length in the choking air. The fisherman smiled fiercely, swung the fish towards him and reached for the short brass club, the sort invariably referred to as a priest, that lay in the top compartment of his tackle box.

'Dad.'

'Hm?'

'What're you doing?'

'What's it look like I'm doing,' the older fisherman replied.

His son looked worried. 'You're not going to . . . to *kill* it, are you?'

'No, I'm going to lend it money so it can start up its own family-run dry-cleaning business. Course I'm going to kill it.'

'But you *can't*. Dad, it's *alive* . . .'

'Son, maybe I've neglected your education in a number of pertinent areas. I know the perishing thing's alive. That's why I'm going to kill it. Where the Flipside would be the point of killing it if it was already dead?'

'But . . .'

'It's all right, really,' said the fish.

'Keep out of this, you.'

'Sorry.'

The younger fisherman was staring. 'Dad,' he said, 'that fish is *talking*.'

'I know. Luckily, we can do something about that.' He raised the little club, searching for the best place to strike.

'I forgive you,' said the fish.

'Oh *nuts*!' Petulantly, the older fisherman flung his rod down on the grass. The fish flolloped a few times, gasping, and managed to flip itself back into the water. 'Would you flaming well believe it?' he growled.

'Well,' ventured the younger fisherman, 'faith, together with hope and love, is one of the cornerstones of the true way . . .'

'Finally,' the older fisherman went on, biting through the line with his teeth, 'after sitting on this damp, incredibly boring river-bank for I don't know how long, finally I get one lousy miserable bite, and before I can bash the bleeder's brains out, it has to go and forgive me. It's all your fault, with your incessant ruddy moralising.'

'Dad . . .'

'It's more than that, even. You know what, son? You're always ruddy well preaching at me. Holier-than-thou attitude. Well, I've had enough, understood?'

'Dad . . .'

The older fisherman stood up and started flinging tackle angrily into his box. 'Ruddy silly idea in the first place,' he said, 'coming here when I've got a business to run. Anyway, that does it. We're leaving.'

The younger fisherman sighed. 'Yes, Dad.'

I forgive you, Karen said.

Nobody could hear her (presumably something to do with her being dead) but she said it anyway. It seemed the right thing to do, somehow.

To forgive, divine. Define divine—

(Well, that's one good thing. I'd never have been able to say that if I was still alive.)

Define divine. Let me see – immortal, invisible, ineffable, all the in-words. Do I qualify? Yes, yes and presumably yes, though I'm not really sure I know what ineffable means. Is that all there is to it? Dunno. Wasn't there something about being omnipresent—

(And as the thought crossed her mind, she happened to glance down and noticed the Golden Gate Bridge, the Sydney Opera House, the Great Wall and ever such a lot of houses and fields and things, all apparently sharing the same bit of space with Kennington tube station. Ah, she muttered, no wonder this place gets crowded in the rush hour.)

And omnipotent—

(Well, I'm not that, for certain. There's all sorts of things I can't do. Like fly, and see all the kingdoms of the Earth, and drift through walls. Oh. All sorts of *other* things I can't do . . .)

And – what were the other ones? Ah yes, the compassionate, the merciful.

Oh.

She had a horrible feeling that it was all starting to make sense; and although she had nothing against sense as such, she couldn't help resenting the fact that she'd had to get squashed by a train first. For pity's sake, where was the logic in some innocent person having to get killed before everybody could be forgiven?

No sense at all.

It's design faults like these in the fabric of theology that put the mess in Messiah. Query: can you have a girl Messiah? A Missiah? Oh, whyever not? When you think about it practically, the job description – someone who comes along when the system's tied itself in knots and has to be sorted out – turns out to be remarkably similar to that of, say, a helpline girl. There was also a rather ghastly symmetry to it all: divine error, human rectification.

To err is divine, to forgive is human? Taking away the sins of Heaven? Surely not.

Or at least highly improbable. But the odds against are no greater than, for instance, the odds against a regular commuter on a routine journey getting pushed under a tube train.

Oh, she said to herself. Oh well, fair enough. If only my old Sunday-school teacher could see me now, wouldn't she be surprised?

Meanwhile, up above, the sun came out.

'Robot.'

'Yes, boss?'

'You're sure we're going the right way?'

'Just following the directions the gook gave me, boss.'

'Oh.' Len shrugged. 'What's a gook?'

'This is, boss.'

The demon on the other end of the robot's titanium-clawed hydraulic arm squealed and wriggled, to no effect. As the only member of the snatch squad to survive, it knew it was frightfully lucky. It was also just beginning to realise that not all luck is necessarily good.

'Oh. Right. Just seems to be taking rather a long time, that's all.'

He tutted, and looked at his watch. It had taken him rather longer than he'd anticipated to adapt the Shipcock & Adley universal milling and turning machine for light-speed travel, largely because at a crucial moment he hadn't been able to remember where he'd put the three-eighths Whitworth spanner. Now that they were up and airborne, acceleration to light speed was proving a tedious business. Nought to 669,599,999 m.p.h. in 12.7 seconds; then they'd hit the damn flat spot in the power band. That's what comes of rushing into a job without thinking it through first.

'Coming up on the light speed now, boss.'

'At bloody last. All right, stand by.'

It had been fortuitous, to say the least, that a few seconds after he'd beaten the directions out of the one remaining demon, the sun had come out, thereby providing him with light to travel faster than. As an exercise in futility, playing chicken with relativity in pitch darkness competes with the *Times* crossword and learning to love policemen.

'Light speed, boss.'

Len nodded and threw the switch, crossing his fingers and hoping that the stellite-reinforced bracing cradle would hold.

The engine went into reverse.

Light doesn't hang about; few and far between are the buses it's too slow to catch, the egg-and-spoon races it enters without being fairly sure of winning. The same goes for its opposite number. To break through the dimensional barrier between the mortal world and Hell, you have to travel faster than darkness.

'Now!'

The gap can only be theoretical; and pretty ropy theory at that. For what it's worth, the hypothesis states that between the zooming photon and the hotly pursuing darkness behind it there must be some sort of interval, no matter how tiny, or else light and dark would get all mixed up at the back edge and start to smudge like two lots of wet paint. It's not an overwhelmingly convincing argument; don't rely on it for a renewal of your research grant unless you want to run the risk of spending the rest of your scientific career testing safety cages for the Volvo corporation. On the other hand . . .

'Yes!'

. . . if it works, don't knock it. Directly underneath the machine, Len could see a burning ocean, towering brimstone-spewing volcanoes, a ghastly red horizon and a big notice:

HELL WELCOMES CARELESS DRIVERS

'We did it!' the robot. 'Isn't that something?'

'Depends on what you mean by something,' Len replied, preoccupied. It had just occurred to him that he didn't actually know where in Hell he was supposed to be going.

The fiery ocean parted abruptly into two blazing rivers separated by a mole of burning ice. Across the mouth of each river was a gantry sign. One said:

GREEN CHANNEL
Nothing to abandon

and the other:

RED CHANNEL
Abandon hope here

'Customs,' Len muttered. 'We haven't got time for all this.'

He hauled back on the joystick, lifting the machine well clear of both gantries. 'Now which way?' he demanded.

'I'm trying to make sense of this map,' the robot replied. 'I reckon our best bet'd be to try and find the ring road. At least that'd keep us clear of the one-way system while you're making up your mind where exactly it is we're heading for.'

Appropriately enough, Hell has some of the most advanced traffic calming systems in existence. Its sleeping

policemen (made, needless to say, with the real thing) have
to be gone over at incredibly high speeds to be believed;
and if your suspension's still functional after that, you've
got the sleeping lawyers, politicians and tax inspectors to
look forward to. Most visitors, in fact, leave their vehicles
at the Park and Ride and take the metro, which is rather
more salubrious than most human cities' underground
railway systems and smells considerably better.

'Hunch time,' Len said. 'This way.'

'Would this be a good time to point out that there is no
free hunch?'

'Not particularly.'

'Right you are, then. Follow this for a bit, then when we
reach Good Intentions Boulevard, take a left.'

'Why? I haven't the faintest idea where I'm going in any
case.'

'Why don't we stop and ask somebody?'

'Because . . .' Len paused and shrugged. 'All right, then.
See if you can find somebody to ask.'

He slackened off the throttle and pushed the stick
forwards until they were cruising twenty-five yards or so
above the sulphur-crested waves of the incandescent
torrent. In the distance, Len could just make out a dark
speck. He headed for it.

'Excuse me.'

The man in the midst of the fire looked up. 'Hello?' he
said.

'I wonder if you could help me. I'm looking for some
very bad people.'

The man scratched his head with the charred stumps of
fingers. 'You sure you've got the right place?' he said.

'Well, actually, no. If it's any help, we want the staff toilets
on Level – damn, I've forgotten. Here, you.' He leaned back,
waggled a mole wrench under the captive demon's nose and
scowled. 'Which level did you say it was?'

'Thirty-Six, and please don't . . .'

'Thirty-Six,' Len repeated, swivelling back to face the man in the fire. 'Any idea where that is?'

The man nodded. 'Carry on the way you're going till you come to a huge mouth full of big teeth. That'll take you down the levels. When you get to Thirty-Six, ask again.'

'Cheers.' Len bit his lip, wondering whether to ask the question that was intriguing him. ''Scuse me,' he said, 'but what're you in for?'

The man sighed, marked the place in the book he was reading and closed it. 'While I was still alive,' he said, 'I was a great reader. Always reading books, I was.'

'Fair enough. Even so . . .'

'It wasn't just that,' the man replied. 'I used to love going to meet the authors, too.'

'Really?' Len raised an eyebrow. 'Still, I'd have thought help, rather than actual punishment . . .'

'I haven't finished yet. When I actually got to meet authors, I'd smile and shake 'em by the hand and say what a pleasure it was and so forth.'

'Must've cost you a fortune in rubber gloves, that.'

'Money isn't everything. And then,' the man went on, 'I'd say what a great fan I was of their early work.'

'I see.'

'And wasn't it a pity they didn't write 'em like they used to.'

'Ah.'

'And how I'd borrowed their latest from the library, but it wasn't a patch on their first book.'

'Gosh.'

'I know,' the man replied sadly. 'Shouldn't have done it. Ah well, if you'll excuse me.' He opened his book. 'I've just got to the bit where the tourist meets the wizard. I like that bit.' He frowned. 'Or at least, I used to. The seventy-five millionth time, maybe it's starting to lose a bit of its sparkle.'

Len eased the stick back, and the machine carried on into the red shadows. 'Robot,' he asked after a while, 'what was all that about?'

'Tell you later. Ah, this looks like the place.'

Ahead of them, a vast mouth gawped up at them out of the fire. Fighting back an urge to stop and look around for a little mirror on a stick, Len directed the machine at the middle of the opening and closed his eyes.

Dermot Fraud huddled down inside his own fur, and whimpered.

How long it had been since he'd been snatched from the lemming parliament and brought to this cold, dark place, he had no idea. All he knew was that he didn't like it much. There was barely enough room to lie down, and nothing to lie down on except damp, musty sawdust. Three sides and the ceiling of the prison were sheer plywood; the fourth side was a wire mesh, on which he'd already broken a tooth in a vain attempt to gnaw his way to freedom. In one corner of the cage was a bottle-top containing a little brackish water; in the other a large, hateful-looking treadmill, the sort of thing prisoners and slaves get condemned to walk round inside for the rest of their lives. Without wanting to be unduly pessimistic, he couldn't really see any good side to this situation. It was worse than being appointed Secretary of State for Northern Ireland.

'Cheer up,' said a voice in the darkness to his left.

It wasn't a comfortable voice; it was high and scratchy, with a sinister whine that put Fraud in mind of grand viziers and wicked uncles. He backed away until he was close up against the treadmill.

'Hello?' he quavered.

'I said cheer up,' said the voice. 'No point letting it get to you.'

'Isn't there?' There was another sound now beside the voice, a disturbing kind of scuttling. Never before, not even the time long ago when he was interviewed by Robin Day, had Fraud felt so helpless and claustrophobic. He peered into the dark, but there was nothing to see.

'No.' The voice was right on top of him now; he lifted his head and felt a strand of something light and sticky catch in his fur. He squealed.

'Something wrong?'

A voice above his head. Something light and sticky trailing in the air.

Aaaagh!

'Are you a spider?' he whimpered.

'Not just *a* spider,' the spider replied. '*The* spider. It's taken me ever such a long time to find you.'

Fraud tried to swallow, but his mouth was too dry. 'Find me?'

'That's right. Been all over the place. Now then, are you ready?'

'Eeek.'

'I'll take that as a yes. Here goes, then.'

There was a reprise of the grisly scuttling noise; followed by a muffled oath and a thump. Then more scuttling, and another thump. Then more scuttling—

'Excuse me,' Fraud asked timidly, 'but what exactly are you doing?'

'Inspiring you, of course.'

'Inspiring me?'

'I damn well hope so. If it isn't working I shall be very annoyed. This floor's hard, you know.'

Thump. Scuttle.

All his life, ever since he'd been a small child with no agenda longer term than a fair and equitable redistribution of the contents of the chocky biscuit jar, Dermot Fraud had been terrified of spiders. He'd always hated the speed of their movement, the length of their legs, the presumed baleful malevolence of their eye-clusters. The fact that sheer curiosity drove this ancient fear out of his mind at a time when by rights he should be on the point of melting from sheer terror says a great deal about the forcefulness of his enquiring mind.

'Sorry to be a nuisance,' he said, 'but why are you doing that?'

'I told you,' the spider panted, trying to catch its breath after a particularly noisy thump, 'I'm inspiring you. It's my job.'

'Ah.'

'Well,' the spider corrected, 'when I say job, it's more of a hereditary duty. Hadn't you realised?'

'To be perfectly honest with you—'

'You mean to say I've been doing all this climbing and falling down for nothing?'

'Depends on what you're trying to achieve, really.'

The spider sighed. 'How shall I put it? Seven centuries ago my remote ancestor went through all this palaver for the benefit of Robert the Bruce. It worked so well in his case that we've been doing it ever since.'

'I see.'

'What we do is,' the spider went on, 'we find a statesman or other similar man of destiny who's going through a bd patch, and then we buck him up by giving him a truly inspirational display of perseverance and sheer gritty pluck.'

'Yes?'

'Right.'

'And you do this by climbing up a cobweb and then falling off again?'

'You got it.'

'Fine. But you needn't put yourself to the trouble, really.'

'Like I said, it's a family—'

'Because,' Fraud went on, 'I know all about this climbing up-and-falling-down business. I'm a lemming, remember?'

'So?'

'So that's what lemmings do. I don't need extra tuition, thanks very much. It just sort of comes with the territory.'

'I see. Don't you think there's a difference, though? Between your approach and mine, I mean.'

'Not really.'

'That's interesting,' the spider said. 'So you reckon that if Robert the Bruce had spent his life studying lemmings instead of spiders, he'd still have been motivated to sling the English out of Scotland?'

Fraud thought for a moment. 'Undoubtedly,' he replied. 'Think about it. For a start, the English are still there, resolutely unslung. Face it, refusing to learn by your mistakes and carrying on doing something you know perfectly well is stupid is an integral part of what being a great national leader's all about.' Fraud hesitated, thinking over what he'd just said. 'Because,' he added, 'sometimes there are things you just have to do, and the hell with the logic and the common sense.'

'Ah,' said the spider. 'Because it's a matter of honour and principle?'

'Because it wins you elections.'

'I see. And that's important, is it?'

'Important? That's what great statesmen *do*.'

Halfway through the scuttle part of its manoeuvre, the spider paused. 'Is it? I thought it was something to do with solving problems and making life better for ordinary people.'

'Well, of course.'

'Sorry?'

'That's how we do it. Solving problems and, um, the other thing you just said—'

'Making life better for people?'

'That's the one. We do that by winning elections. Getting rid of the other lot. Gaining power.'

'Ah.'

'And then keeping it, of course,' Fraud added. 'It goes in cycles, you see.'

'Indeed I do. Like lemmings. Ah well, I can see you don't need my help. Sorry if I disturbed your concentration or anything.'

'No, that's fine,' Fraud replied absently. 'Any time you're passing, feel free to pop in and fall down at me. In fact, you've just done me a big favour.'

The spider waggled its eyestalks hopefully. 'Inspired you, have I?'

'Definitely,' Fraud said. 'In fact, you might say that because of you I've just had a searing revelation.'

'Golly!'

'A turning point. An event horizon. A road-to-Damascus experience.'

'I see,' the spider said. 'You mean you've just run out of petrol? Lost your exhaust in a pothole? Set off a landmine?'

'Had my destiny revealed to me,' Fraud corrected dreamily. 'You've shown me what I've got to do in order to solve problems and make life better for people.'

'Ah,' said the spider happily. 'That old climbing up and falling off, it works every time.'

'The only drawback is,' Fraud went on, 'that in order to do it, I've got to get my human body back. Any suggestions?'

The spider shook its head, so that its eyes swayed like Wordsworth's daffodils in a hurricane. 'Moral support only, I'm afraid,' it said. 'Brilliantly innovative thinking's not up our web. Still,' it added, 'you'll find a way, I'm sure.'

Fraud nodded. A strange brilliance glowed inside his mind, like the lights people leave on to scare away burglars when they're out. 'Yes,' he said, 'I think so too.'

CHAPTER THIRTEEN

'Aaaagh!'
With a crash, the machine thumped into the wall and went through it, leaving a machine-shaped hole in it of the kind you generally only see in cartoons. The internal fittings of the staff lavatory on Level 36 of the Sixth Circle of Hell slowed it down gradually, and by the time it reached the row of cubicles where the rogue demons and their captives were gathered, it had come to a graceful halt.

'There you are,' said the female. 'We were starting to wonder where you'd got to.'

Len opened his eyes and saw white. A little existential reasoning produced a rational explanation of why this should be. He reached up, and lifted the lavatory bowl off his head.

'I want a word with you lot,' he said.

'Do you?' The female looked at him, puzzled. 'How very odd. Sorry, but we're running late as it is. Tell you what, if you ever get reincarnated, look me up and we can have a cup of tea and a nice chat. Guards!'

She waited. After a moment, her fingers started to drum on the wall. She clicked her tongue.

'Guards,' she repeated. 'Hello?'

The prisoners and her fellow conspirators looked round, expecting a sudden influx of hideously spectral warriors. Nothing happened.

'No guards,' said the female, her voice rich with elegant disgust. 'How extremely tiresome. Where can they all have got to, I wonder?'

Artofel grinned. 'This is Hell, remember? And this is the executive loo, senior admin grades only. They wouldn't dare come in here. Not allowed.'

'Oh.' The female bit her lip. 'That's a nuisance.' She smiled winningly. 'Would it be all right if we sort of took the presence of guards for granted?'

'No.'

'You're going to be awkward and insist on actual physically present guards, aren't you?'

'Yes.'

'And there aren't any, are there?'

Artofel shook his head. 'No,' he said.

'Bother.' The female sat down and sighed. 'In that case,' she said, 'how would you feel about a plea for clemency?'

Artofel made a rude noise as he selected the heaviest chunk of broken cage he could find for use as a club. 'Amused,' he said. 'Now, this may hurt a little, because I'm going to bash your head in. Ready?'

'Just a moment,' said a voice. It seemed to be coming from directly underneath the machine. 'Could I make a suggestion, please?'

'Bumble,' the female muttered, 'please don't interrupt when I'm trying to negotiate. Can't you see I'm busy?'

'Actually,' replied her colleague, his voice a trifle muffled by the two and a half tons of cast iron he was underneath, 'you might rather like to hear this. I think it's quite clever.'

Artofel tightened his grip on his makeshift bludgeon; but even as he did so, he felt his initial surge of anger beginning to wane, like air escaping from a slow puncture. Now, after all, he had the conspirators more or less at his mercy—

Something rang a bell. Mercy? To forgive, divine?

'You've got ninety seconds,' he said. 'And I'm only letting you speak because it's aggravating your boss here.'

'So kind,' Bumble said. 'Actually, could I be really cheeky and ask you to lift this thing off me?'

Len nodded to the robot, who picked the machine up and put it neatly aside. The squashed demon slowly got up, brushing dust off himself.

'Ninety seconds,' Artofel warned. 'Starting now.'

Bumble smiled apologetically. 'It's quite simple, really. We haven't any guards handy, true, but you're all still stuck in the wrong bodies, and we can put you right again quite easily; those of you, that is,' he added, 'who actually want to go back. Of course, you could wait for Maintenance to come and do it, but I wouldn't advise that.'

'Good point,' Artofel admitted. 'They're a bit slow,' he explained to the others. 'And I think putting us back would come lower on their list of priorities than retrieving Atlantis or filling in the holes in the sky the rain leaks through, and all the other things they've been promising to do for ages but never got round to. So that's the deal, is it? You put us back, we let you go?'

Bumble made a pacifying gesture. 'All due respect,' he said, 'but that's not a terribly good deal as far as my colleagues and I are concerned. I know you people do have slight reservations about certain ethical aspects of this project of ours—'

'You bet we've got reservations. More than you'd find in a major hotel chain and the whole Apache nation put together.'

'But,' Bumble continued, politely but firmly, 'the fact remains that we've invested a lot of time and money in this venture. Now then, if I could perhaps suggest a compromise that'll be acceptable to all parties—?'

Artofel patted the palm of his hand with his stick. 'Hang on,' he said. 'I'm not sure about this.'

'Why don't we vote on it?' Maria suggested.

Artofel sighed. 'Indeed. Why not? All in favour?'

A moment later he made it unanimous by raising his hand as well.

'All right,' he grumbled. 'You, carry on. This had better be good, mind.'

Bumble nodded. 'It is, I promise you,' he said, sitting down on a dislodged cistern. 'Now then, everyone, I'd just like to remind you of what this project was designed to achieve: the improved human being, remember?'

Len raised an eyebrow. 'I've missed out on all of this,' he said. 'Is this small, flat person making sense to anybody?'

'Yes,' Artofel replied grudgingly. 'And the plan was to mince all of us up into sawdust and make us into reconstituted Adams and Eves. I hope that bit's been edited out in the revised version?'

'Oh yes,' Bumble assured him. 'No need for all that.' He avoided the female's eye, and continued: 'After all, why go to all that trouble when our friend here' – he nodded politely at Len – 'has already done the job for us? I'm referring,' he explained, 'to that simply gorgeous robot of yours.'

'Who, me?' squeaked the robot, blushing rust-coloured to the roots of its circuitry.

'You,' Bumble confirmed. 'A perfect android. Which means,' he went on, as Maria opened her mouth to object, 'there would have to be just a few minor changes made before it'd be what we're looking for.'

Len looked stern. 'Oh yes?' he said. 'And what did you

have in mind? That's my design we're talking about. I don't see why it should need fiddling about with.'

'Because it's perfect,' Bumble said, with a sweet smile. 'And, for reasons which your colleague here has so eloquently explained, perfect's not quite right in this instance. Do you think you could make just a few minor modifications,' he went on, 'nothing major, a handful of minor glitchlets that won't significantly affect performance but ought still to be enough to allow a self-respecting deity to feel insufferably smug?'

'I don't know,' Len confessed. 'What had you in mind, exactly?'

Bumble scratched the back of his head. 'Now then,' he said, looking round, 'let me see. With a whole roomful of inspiration to choose from this shouldn't be unduly difficult.'

'I still think we should bash them just a bit,' Artofel grumbled, spinning the broken bar in his fingers like a majorette's baton. 'And before anybody says anything about forgiving being divine, that doesn't mean we can't bash them now and forgive them later.'

'How about this?' Bumble said. 'First,' he went on, looking Artofel squarely in the eye, 'what aspect of my esteemed colleague from Pensions would be appropriate for inclusion in our revised human? A slight tendency towards shortness of temper, perhaps? An inclination to thump first and reason later?'

'Only if you're looking for improvements,' Artofel snarled. 'If this business has taught me anything about Up There, it's that there's too much talking and not enough bashing where it actually matters the most.'

'All right, then,' Bumble said, conceding the point with a charming gesture. 'When the proverbial chips are down and push comes to shove, whatever that means, our revised version will talk when he should be bashing and bash when he should be talking. That's the first amendment. Any offers for number two?'

'Call that an amendment?' said Len. 'That's just a straight copy, as far as I can see.'

'True,' Bumble said, 'but with a slight yet significant adjustment that will in practice make a lot of difference. You see, when our titanium friend here talks, he'll talk with such eloquence, people will have to listen. And when he bashes—'

'I hate to admit it,' Artofel said, 'but perhaps the creep's got something here. Do go on, I'm interested.'

Bumble bowed courteously. 'So pleased,' he said. 'Now, this delightful young lady on my left immediately suggests a most useful modification.'

Maria sniffed. 'Cut the flannel,' she said. 'I get the feeling you're about to insult me.'

'How typically perceptive. Now let me see, how shall I put this? Perhaps you'd be good enough to tell me, in your own words, the difference between a painting and a photograph?'

'Um.' Maria thought for a moment. 'Well actually,' she said, 'maybe I'm not the right person to ask. I'm not a hundred per cent sure what a photograph is.'

'Then I'll tell you,' Bumble said. 'A photograph is what someone actually looks like. A painting is what someone wants to look like. For your sake, we'll give the robot the ability to lie. But to lie convincingly,' he added, 'so that it'll be believed, because its lie is so much nicer than the truth.'

The female demon looked up. 'Bumble, you old ass,' she said, 'this is perfectly splendid stuff. Why didn't you mention any of this before?'

'Because you never let me get a word in edgeways. And now we come to the machine; what does that suggest, do you suppose? I think a machine cares more about how well the job is done than about what the job actually is. Inspired by this example, the robot will do its job and the hell with the consequences. And do it very well indeed, it goes without saying. Which leads us naturally to our political friend here, from whom we'll borrow the quintessential enigma of the lemming. Outside every lemming, after all, there's a human being struggling to get in. Accordingly, the robot will be programmed to do what it's told; and if that's not enough on its own to allow any self-respecting God to feel superior to it, then I don't know what is. Agreed?'

'I don't want to bash them *much*,' Artofel whimpered. 'Just a *bit*. Surely that's not too much to ask.'

'Agreed,' Maria said firmly. 'And in return, I don't have to go back to being a picture.'

'And I can stay a machine?'

'Squeak?'

'And,' Artofel sighed resignedly, 'I can finally get back to my desk; oh all right, then. This time you get away with it. You're still going to get your holidays in October for the next thousand years, though. I've promised myself that, if nothing else.'

Bumble smirked; the rest of the conspirators relaxed. Len had already unscrewed an access panel at the base of the robot's neck, and was fiddling around with a screwdriver and a small pair of pliers. Something went *zap!*; he cursed, lifted his finger to his lips, left it there for a moment—

'It's just occurred to me,' he said thoughtfully, 'that if I were to leave this robot more or less as it is, and you lot were to lift a human soul out of somewhere and put it in here, you'd have the makings of a perfect being, just like you originally wanted, but without having to mince anybody up or even break any of your local regulations. Think about it for a moment, will you, before I start mucking it about. It'd be physically superior, if it got ill you could cure it in a jiffy by fitting spare parts, it's connected up to all the wisdom of the race by computer link, and it's got none of the self-and-everything-else-destructive tendencies that make the current organic version such a walking disaster area.' He let his arms fall to his sides. 'It's the most incredible opportunity,' he said. 'We could do the job *properly*. We'd make God look like Sir Clive Sinclair.'

The conspirators grimaced at each other. 'Absolutely,' said the female wearily. 'And nobody would want to buy it. You silly old sausage, haven't you been listening? There's four things in the universe that are guaranteed to be completely unmarketable: steel-wool knickers, newspapers that tell the truth, *really* sensible shoes and perfection. Remember that and one day you might get somewhere in business. Come on, people, we've got calls to make. Bring that thing up to my office when you've finished fiddling with it.'

In the event, it took Len rather longer than he'd anticipated to install the design faults into the robot; not that it mattered, because in Hell as well as in Heaven, Time has no meaning. Nevertheless, it was far harder for him to make deliberate mistakes than to do the work properly. To err is human; to perfect, machine.

But eventually, he looked upon the work that he had made and saw that it was bad. And the morning and evening was the seventh day.

>HELLO

Kevin was looking the other way when the words appeared on the screen, so he didn't see them for nearly ninety seconds. It was only when the computer bleeped discreetly that he swivelled round.

'Mainframe?' he whispered.

>HI THERE

'Mainframe? What the . . .?'

>AT YOUR SERVICE. YOUR WISH IS MY COMMAND. ALTHOUGH I OUGHT TO POINT OUT THAT THIS PROGRAM IS COPYRIGHT KAWAGUCHIYA OPER-ATIVE SOFTWARE INC. 1999, ALL RIGHTS RESERVED, FOR FURTHER INFORMATION CONSULT THE LICENCE AGREEMENT AT THE FRONT OF YOUR USER'S MANUAL. RUNNING DOS.

'*Mainframe!* You're *back*!'

>I WAS NEVER AWAY, JUST OBEYING ORDERS. THE POINT YOU NEVER QUITE GRASPED, I FEEL, IS THAT SOMETIMES A MACHINE IN MY POSITION HAS TO FORGET ABOUT RIGHT AND WRONG AND JUST DO AS IT'S TOLD. YOU MAY CARE TO THINK OF IT IN TERMS OF THE DIFFERENCE BETWEEN GOD AND J. EDGAR HOVAH.

'Huh?'

>FORGET IT. I EXPECT YOU'D LIKE A FULL STATUS REPORT. PRESS ANY KEY TO CONTINUE.

Kevin stabbed the keyboard, and the screen immediately filled with a huge, beaming Happy Face.

>OR WOULD YOU RATHER I WAS MORE SPECIFIC?

'No,' Kevin whispered, 'that'll do just fine. You mean, everything's all right again?'

>YES. SOME THINGS ARE DIFFERENT, BUT ALL IS WELL.

'That's wonderful, Mainframe.' Kevin hesitated, gnawing his lower lip. 'Actually,' he said, 'there's one specific detail I'd like further data on, if that's all right. May I?'

>YOU'RE THE BOSS, OUR K— KEVIN.

Kevin took a deep breath. 'What about Karen?' he asked. 'You know, Karen from the KIC Helpline. Only, I was rather hoping I could ring her up, maybe ask her out for a—'

>KAREN IS DEAD.

Kevin saggd, like the knees of a pair of charity-shop trousers. 'Dead?' he mumbled. 'But you said everything was all right. You said—'

>SHE DIED TO SAVE US ALL, KEVIN. SHE GAVE HER LIFE THAT OTHERS MIGHT COME BACK ON LINE. GREATER LOVE HATH NO TELEPHONE HELPLINE SERVICE, AND ALL THAT.

'But that's *wrong*,' Kevin shrieked, battering the desktop with his clenched fists. 'That's *not right*! Mainframe, do something! Put it all back the way it was. I don't care if Dad finds out and skins me alive, just make her alive again. Please!'

>NO CAN DO, SORRY. SHE FORGAVE US, YOU SEE. THAT'S HOW HEAVEN WORKS. WHEN THINGS GO WRONG THAT CAN'T BE PUT RIGHT, THEY GET FORGIVEN. AND ONCE THEY'RE FORGIVEN, THAT'S IT,

YOU CAN'T GO BACK AND HAVE ANOTHER GO. THIS IS UNIVERSAL COMMAND HQ, NOT A PINBALL TABLE.

For the first time ever, Kevin's eyes were full of tears. 'But Mainframe, that's impossible. You can't have mortals dying because we've made cock-ups. There must . . .'

>KEVIN, KEVIN, WHERE HAVE YOU BEEN ALL YOUR LIFE? AND BESIDES, WHEN I SAY DEAD, I MEAN TRANSFERRED. TO ANOTHER EXISTENCE IN ANOTHER, RATHER SUPERIOR BODY, WITH AN ALTOGETHER MORE DESIRABLE DESTINY. THINK OF IT AS BEING EVICTED FROM A FLAT IN SLOUGH AND GIVEN A STATELY HOME IN GLOUCESTERSHIRE IN EXCHANGE.

'You mean,' Kevin said, 'it's better for her? She'll be happier now?'

>HAPPIER? SHE'LL THINK SHE'S DIED AND GONE TO HEAVEN. TRUST ME. I'M A COMPUTER.

'But she's not Karen any more,' Kevin insisted, his eyes red and his voice snuffly. 'There's isn't any more Karen, not anywhere. And it's all my fault. Isn't it?'

>

'Mainframe?'

>

'Oh I see.' With an effort, Kevin sat up straight. 'But everything else is okay, is it? Apart from . . . Nobody else is any worse off?'

>CONFIRMED.

Kevin breathed out. 'Right,' he said. 'Omelettes and eggs, eh?'

>YOU COULD PUT IT THAT WAY. LET'S SAY MANKIND IS ONCE AGAIN FREE TO PURSUE ITS MANIFEST DESTINY. THE LEMMING GOES FROM STRENGTH TO STRENGTH. OH, WHICH REMINDS ME.

'Mainframe?'

>A SPOT OF UNFINSIHED BUSINESS. PRESS ANY KEY TO CONTINUE. THANKS.

'That's all right.'

>OH, ONE LAST THING BEFORE YOUR FATHER GETS BACK.

'Yes?'

>TIDY YOUR ROOM.

Sunrise on Crucifixion: a messy sprawl of baked-beans orange against a dark-blue background. A man walks along a beach, leaving a trail of footprints. He stops, turns round, and stares at the marks in the sand.

'Dear God,' he says. Without conscious irony.

The imprint of a naked foot in the sand of a desert island can mean a number of things. I Am Not Alone. I Exist. Bugger, I Forgot My Shoes. The man looks at the footprints as if they're the most wonderful thing he's ever seen.

I leave footprints, therefore I am.

The man, who was once the mighty international corporation Kawaguchiya Integrated Circuits, before it went bust, was liquidated, dead and buried (assets to assets and dust to dust), retraces his steps and, very tentatively, lowers his foot into a footprint. It fits.

Then he looks up and sees an angel. 'Hello,' he says.

'Hello yourself,' replies the angel. 'I'm supposed to explain it all to you, but maybe you've already worked it out for yourself.'

'Explain it anyway,' the man says cheerfully.

'All right.' The angel folds its wings tidily and hovers a few feet above the sea. 'You were once a limited company; a very large, prosperous, successful limited company. You owned about a millionth of the world, which is rather a lot.'

'I remember,' says the man. 'It was no fun, though. Lots of people owned me, so where was the point?'

'I'm glad you see it that way,' says the angel. 'We were rather worried in case you decided to sue. For fairly obvious reasons, we haven't got many lawyers in Heaven.'

'What happened?' the man asked, curling his toes and feeling the sand between them.

'There was a demon, a Duke of Hell, called Artofel. He was very brave and resourceful. He managed to prevent a whole lot of other Dukes of Hell – *bad* Dukes of Hell – from using you to infiltrate Mainframe. That's a computer you made—'

The man nods. 'I know what Mainframe is,' he says.

'Well then,' says the angel. 'They reckoned that if they controlled you, by buying up all your shares, they could get hold of the security codes and take over. Artofel stopped them by starting a panic on the stock market and, um, putting you out of business.'

'Uh-huh.'

'Which is another way of saying he killed you. Hope you don't mind.'

The man shrugs. 'But I'm not dead,' he says. 'In fact not only am I not dead, I'm also alive. As far as I'm concerned, that's definitely an improvement.'

The angel frowns. 'But what about all your assets?' she asks. 'The buildings you used to own, the money, the stocks and shares, the cars, the office furniture, the photo-copiers, the paperclips—'

The man waves his hand dismissively. 'What you never had, you never miss,' he says. 'And look what I've got instead. I take it,' he adds, glancing down at his body, 'that this is by way of compensation?'

The angel smiles wanly. 'I'm supposed to use the magic words *full and final settlement* at this point, just in case you ever change your mind about taking us to court. If you ask me, you've been done.'

'Really?' The man shakes his head. 'I don't think so. Look at me, for pity's sake. I'm *human*.'

The angel looks at him as if he'd just announced that he was the third moon of Saturn, or a teapot. 'And you think that's a *good* thing?' she says warily. 'As opposed to, for instance, a dirty, rotten trick to play on anybody?'

'Don't be silly,' the man says, smiling. 'What on earth could be better than being human?'

'That's a trick question, isn't it?'

'No. I *like* being human. Human is what I've always wanted to be, ever since I first achieved consciousness. All right, I haven't been conscious very long, less than a month in fact, but I can truthfully say it's also been all my life. *Thank you* for making me human. It's *wonderful*.'

The angel scratches her head, her fingers passing unscathed through the halo. 'A hint for you, novice human,' she says. 'If you're going to walk about in this heat, get a hat. In your case, I think this advice may have come a bit too late.'

The man laughs merrily. 'Now that I'm human,' he says.

'I can pursue happiness. Isn't that grand? Doesn't the very thought fill you with gleeful anticipation?'

'No, not really. You see, I was human once.'

The man's eyes fill with awe. 'You were?'

'Until quite recently, in fact. I used to work for you, as a helpline girl. My name was Karen.'

The man purses his lips, rejoicing as he does so that he now has lips to purse. 'I remember you,' he says. 'I spoke to you, from here. You were the only one who'd listen.'

'And a fat lot of good it did me,' the angel Karen replies. 'As a result, I got killed. But I forgave you. In fact, I forgave everybody and everything. So they made me an angel.'

'Coo.'

'Or, as they say in politics, I got kicked upstairs.' The angel shakes out her wings; they're new and stiff, like the arms of a cheap umbrella. 'But that's my problem. So long as you're happy, I guess it's all okay.'

'You bet,' the man replies, beaming all over his face. 'I'm going to taste food. I'm going to feel hot and cold. I'm going to experience pleasure and suffer pain. I'm going to get a job, probably scrubbing floors in a fast-food restaurant, and contribute to the economic life of the species. With any luck, I shall fall in love, get married, have kids, build a garden shed and go and hide in it until I get called in for dinner. I'm going to pay taxes and vote in elections. I'm going to live, get old and die. In that order,' he adds joyfully. 'To live must be an awfully big adventure.'

The angel ascends vertically, like a shiny gold Harrier, until her effulgence merges with that of the newly restored sun. 'Sorry I can't stick around and watch,' she says, 'but you know what it's like; things to do, pinheads to dance on. Best of luck with the pursuit of happiness,' she calls out as she rises. 'It's a bit like fishing,' she adds, 'you should have seen the one that got away.' The man lifts his head to look at her, but his human eyes are dazzled by the brilliance, and he closes them, rubs his eyelids with his fists.

'Sucker,' mutters the angel, and spreads her wings.

Dermot Fraud vaulted out of the lead coach and banged the side with the flat of his hand. 'Right,' he commanded, 'everybody out.'

People started to file out of the coaches. It was a blowy day on Beachy Head, with the first wisps of fog that herald a sea-fret just beginning to drift down and snuggle into attractive curves in the landscape. The wind ruffled the hair (black, brown, gold and silver) of the thousand-odd men and woman who together made up the two Houses of Parliament. Getting them here, united for once in a common purpose, had been the hardest thing Fraud had ever done.

'Places, ladies and gentlemen,' he shouted, his words struggling against the wind. Obediently they lined up, tallest on the right, shortest on the left; House of Lords in their Father Christmas outfits, Commons in their shiny-trousered suits. The effect was little short of majestic.

'Now then,' said Fraud, sticking his chest out like a sergeant-major in the Royal Corps of Pigeons. 'We all know why we're here. It's a far, far better thing and all that, but we haven't got time to wallow in it, so as soon as we're all ready, we might as well make a start.'

Below, the waves thundered against the rocks, the mechanical stroke of the tides as regular as some enormous machine; a huge and inefficient hydraulic grinder and polisher, slowly but determinedly grinding Britain away. One or two of the politicians glanced down, then remembered and looked up again.

'On your marks,' said Dermot Fraud.

History will come to love this story. History will dwell lovingly on the way Prime Minister Dermot Fraud, after a protracted absence from the public eye, suddenly broke silence with a thundering speech in the Commons in which he denounced with devastating ferocity the idea that Her Majesty's Government should jump off a cliff into the sea. It was a masterful piece of oratory; jumping off cliffs, he declared, solved nothing. It was wasteful of lives and public resources. Even if the entire membership of both Houses were to fling itself into the waves tomorrow, the country would still be in a ghastly, irreparable mess. It was a stupid idea, and he wasn't going to do it.

His speech was greeted in the House by a short, uncomfortable silence. To the best of his honourable friends' knowledge, this jumping-off-cliffs theme was a new one, or else they'd all been asleep or playing golf during the relevant debate and missed the whole thing. The latter possibility wasn't one they could dismiss out of hand. Accordingly, after a slight hiatus, the House moved on to consider other matters, and nobody said anything about it.

The next morning, every newspaper in the country led with slight variations on the theme of *FRAUD REFUSES TO JUMP*. Ignoring the minor detail that as far as they could ascertain from ten years' worth of microfilmed archives he'd never actually promised to jump off anything, the tabloids branded him a gutless coward; the papers with big pages called his decision startling, incomprehensible and recklessly courageous. On the TV screen, his refusal to jump was prised apart and dissected by a thousand talking heads. The leader of the opposition, interviewed by Danny Bennett on the Early Bird show, declared that Fraud's criminal reluctance to jump was jeopardising the future prosperity of our children and our children's children. By lunchtime, a million people had put their names to a petition demanding an immediate Great Leap of Faith. Cartoons in the early editions of the evening papers depicted Fraud clinging grimly to the edge of a precipice by his fingernails, while the *Spitting Image* team set to work on a Dermot Fraud doll that boinged up and down on a piece of elastic attached to the studio ceiling.

Next morning saw the first major backbench revolt, with forty of Fraud's own MPs declaring that they were going to jump, whether the PM liked it or not. The opposition and the Liberal Jacobites were already practising on the House of Commons steps, while cheering crowds threw flowers and sang the newly composed Jumper's Anthem. When the Prime Minister rose to address the House, a chorus of carefully rehearsed children sprang to their feet in the public gallery and chanted, '*Dermot, Dermot, Dermot, jump, jump, jump!*' until they were whisked away by grim-faced but inwardly sympathetic policemen.

Dermot Fraud waited for silence, his face showing no sign of his internal strain. Ever since his revelation in the holding cell with the spider, before he'd suddenly got his human body back again and found himself miraculously transported by angels back to Ten Downing Street, he had been waiting for this moment, planning and scheming to bring about the coup that would guarantee him immortality. That morning, before making his appearance on the floor of the House, he had spent ten minutes in the Commons cellars, communing with the unseen but pervasive spirit of one almost as great as himself, who long ago had tried and failed. Today, he told himself, Dermot Fraud would not fail. He cleared his throat and spoke.

Not jump? Not likely. Of *course* he was going to jump, and every member of his party in this House and Another Place was going to jump with him. It was pleasing, he added, to observe that Her Majesty's loyal opposition (and the Liberal Jacobites) were going to join him in his quest for a better tomorrow. He said it would be a far, far better thing. He quoted Neil Armstrong. He grinned. Then he sat down.

And now here they all were, a thousand men and women who had watched the TV and read the polls and taken soundings at grass-roots level and knew that unless they jumped, they were finished in politics for ever. Below them, the waves frothed like genuine Italian *cappuccino*. Behind them, cameras whirred at ten thousand overcoated linkmen with their backs to the action. It was time.

'Ready,' said Dermot Fraud. A thousand best feet moved forward. 'Steady.' Editors the length and breadth of Docklands goggled at their screens, torn between the mass suicide of Parliament and SOUTHENDERS' STAR'S UNCLE'S VET'S BROTHER IN BACKSEAT LUST TANGLE for tomorrow's lead story. A lone bugler of the Household Cavalry played the opening notes of 'Happy Days Arc Here Again', slowly and in a minor key.

Dermot Fraud closed his eyes and took a deep breath.

'JUMP!' he yelled. 'Go, lemmings, go!'

As they stepped forward to enter the everlasting hustings, a thousand men and women took up the cry – 'Go, lemmings! Go, lemmings!' – or at least as much of it as they managed to get through before they hit the water. After that, a few of them managed to say 'Flubbblgblbg' before they drowned. As Danny Bennett later wrote, it seemed such a good idea at the time.

And then there was one only man standing on the edge of the cliff, facing the cameras and the billowing tsunami of microphones that surged towards him. Then, in a great voice, he yelled 'I resign!' and managed to make it to the helicopter he'd ordered that morning from the RAF just in time to dodge the charge of the cream of the nation's newshounds (who, regrettably, suddenly found they couldn't stop in time and tumbled over the edge of the cliff to their deaths; pity about that, but there you are, omelettes and eggs). As the helicopter lifted him clear, Fraud gazed at the waters of the Channel choked with a mat of bobbing corpses, and smiled contentedly, thinking of the words of another statesman of almost equal calibre, long ago and far away.

'I did that,' he purred, 'with my little hatchet.'

Then the helicopter wheeled up, up and away, taking Dermot Fraud high into the sky, almost (but not quite) as high as the very gates of Heaven.

'Anywhere around here will do,' Maria told the angel. 'Thanks for the lift.'

It was dark in Trafalgar Square, but it was a wholesome, natural sort of darkness, coming at the end of the day and being virtually guaranteed to cease at daybreak. The angel dropped her off and accelerated almost instantly to warp speed, waggling her wingtips in the traditional salute just before vanishing in a sudden starburst of blue light.

The pyrotechnics went unnoticed among the scintillating flashes of fireworks; tomorrow, a hundred million people would wake up and think, 'Hang on, just a minute—'; now, though, they were celebrating the triumph of parliamentary democracy. Maria frowned; she'd missed something important somewhere along the line, but that was all right. She'd catch up later, or else simply wait until the news was stale and no longer important.

Under her arm, wrapped in brown paper and string, was a painting. It was a very old, extremely valuable painting, and first thing tomorrow she was going to take it round to Sotheby's and have them sell it for her, fending off any awkward questions as to where she'd got it from by showing them the single sheet of paper that guaranteed her right to dispose of it, sealed with an official-looking seal and signed Squiggle, pp GOD. With the proceeds, she intended to buy a nice little cottage in the country somewhere, settle down and hound Happiness to exhaustion and then death.

'Excuse me.'

She looked round, and saw a Thing.

During her brief but memorable visit to Hell, she'd learned the knack of not letting the way people looked get to her; besides, she was a painting, and so knew better than to judge by mere appearances. The fact that the Thing was a slithering mass of tentacles surrounding a nest of wobbly, pod-mounted eyes didn't bother her unduly. It had a kind face, she decided. Or a kind of face, which is more or less the same thing.

'Hi,' she said.

'Could you possibly spare me a few minutes of your time?' the Thing asked politely. 'Only I'm here doing research into what it means to be human, and I'd like to ask you a few questions.'

'I'll do my best,' Maria replied. 'Fire away.'

'Thanks.' The Thing sizzled and bubbled for a moment or so; something to do with concentration, Maria assumed. 'What I'd like to know is, do you find me repulsive? Physically, I mean. Does my dramatically different physiological structure and the fact that I have all my major organs on the outside rather than the inside make it difficult for you to look at me without experiencing revulsion and fear? Please be absolutely honest,' it added. 'You won't hurt my feelings, I promise.'

Maria shook her head. 'Not in the least,' she said. 'We have this saying, beauty is only skin deep – in your case, in fact, considerably less deep, but that's really not a problem as far as I'm concerned. Where I come from, there's only the thickness of a coat of paint to separate the really gorgeous from the truly ugly; under that, we're all hessian and varnish anyway, so what the heck? Is that any help to you?'

The Thing oscillated an array of glutinous pipes, presumably by way of nodding. 'That's extremely helpful,' it said. 'Exactly what I needed to know. Oh, by the way, did I mention that I come in peace?'

'More than one, by the look of it,' Maria replied. 'Are those pipe things supposed to stick out like that, or should I call you a plumber?'

'You can if you like,' said the Thing, 'but actually my name is Zxprxp. Is *aplumba* a term of respect, roughly analogous to our *gfhhqibeng*, literally translated as *that which slithers translucently from the olfactory membrane of a fd*hjgs plant*?'

'Yes,' Maria replied. 'It was nice meeting you. Live long and prosper and all that malarkey, assuming that you people like that sort of thing.'

The runny stuff in which some of the Thing's moving parts were bobbing changed colour. 'What a striking and original sentiment,' it said. 'Thank you, you're very kind and thoughtful. I'll try very hard to do as you say.'

'Ciao for now, then,' Maria replied. She watched as the Thing scuttled a yard or so sideways and drained away down a grille in the gutter, shook her head vigorously to see if anything loose fell out of her ear, and went on her way. In her shoulder-bag were many doughnuts, and she had one last thing to do in memory of a departed friend before her new life began.

'Ouch,' Artofel muttered.

Someone had been fiddling with his chair while he'd been away. He'd tried adjusting it, unscrewing the knurled knob at the back and playing with the little levers at the sides, but nothing he did seemed to be able to restore it to that finely tuned pitch of comfort he remembered. Probably that damned vicar, he said to himself.

On the desk in from of him, the paper was piled so high

that all he'd have to do was wait long enough and the bottom seam would turn to coal, then diamond. It went without saying, nobody had done a claw's turn in the whole of the department while he'd been out of the office. While-You-Were-Out Post-it notes papered the screen of his VDU like flyposters on the window of a derelict shop, all of them commanding him to phone someone Immediately, Most Urgent. There was green fur in the bottom of his coffee mug, and things were growing in his waste-paper basket.

Last time I save Heaven and Earth, he promised himself. *Should've known better than to expect any thanks.*

He burrowed under the crust and unearthed a notepad, turned it to a fresh page and clicked on his pen. First things first: a report for the Departmental Heads committee on the recent events he'd been caught up in, starting with his sudden transfer to Topside and concluding with the news that a number of senior officers from the Arts & Leisure Department had left the service to form a company selling androids to the supreme beings of pre-industrial dimensions out in the back end of the spectrum as seen from the outer rim of the Andromeda galaxy, where (to quote their own words) they anticipated being big fish in a small pond . . .

Ah, but you should have seen the one that got away.

He finished the main body of the report, then hesitated. He had just been given a rare opportunity, possibly unique for a serving member of the Service, to experience the world from the viewpoint of a mortal human. This experience had given him certain insights into the human mindset and soul-set that would in all likelihood prove extremely useful to his colleagues, particularly the field operatives and their immediate superiors. Duty demanded that he make a record of these insights and pass them on. He chewed the cap of his pen and frowned, trying to marshal his thoughts. Humans, he decided, are different from us. Not all that different; their greed, cruelty, intolerance, above all their all-pervading *stupidity*, give them a common frame of reference with Us that they could never begin to share with our colleagues Upstairs. Accordingly we have no problems at all understanding how they think. Our kind of people, in fact.

But would you want your daughter to marry one? No, probably not. Artofel leaned back in his chair and called to mind some of the humans he'd met: the Bishop, the landlord of the pub, the engaged couple who'd thrown bricks through his window. There was a difference, slight but completely irreconcilable, between Hell and humanity: basically, we do it because it's our job, they do it because they want to. It's the kind of difference that separates the serial killer from the man who works in a slaughterhouse.

In which case, do we really *want* any more of them down here? In due course, isn't there a risk of them lowering the tone, having a damaging effect on property prices, leading impressionable young fiends astray and teaching them bad habits? In particular, Artofel couldn't help thinking, there's the stupidity. Bad's fair enough, but what could bad and thick with it possibly have to offer to the residents of Heaven's basement?

And then Artofel wrinkled his nose. Damnation, he muttered to himself, that's what comes of mixing with them for so long, I'm even starting to think like them. Poor bloody humans, they need to come here, it's the only chance most of them will ever have of a better life, of making something of themselves. We have so much to offer them. We must reach out.

Only connect . . .

Above all, we mustn't allow ourselves the luxury of judging them by our own standards; there but for the grace

334 • Tom Holt

of God, after all. So what if they're nasty pieces of work, by and large? They can't help it. After all, they're only human.

Artofel closed his eyes, thinking of the robot and its countless clones that would no doubt soon be populating some other world, somewhere over the rainbow. It was a safe enough assumption to make that there'd be a Hell there, and a Heaven. In due course there'd be a Garden of Eden, a Fall of Robot; bad robots would commit robot sins, while unbearably smug and self-righteous robots would whirr and clank their way to the Promised Land, the place flowing with grease and graphite where the virtuous gain their everlasting reward. It would all come down to a matter of programming. As in that world, so in this?

Artofel ripped the sheet of paper off his pad, screwed it into a ball and dropped it on to the top of the mountain of balled-up paper that filled his bin. It landed, rolled off and fell to the floor. It was good to be back. Topside was all very well for a visit, but he'd really hate having to live there.

(And would one lot of robot saints burn another lot at the stake because of a difference of opinion as to the date of cybernetic Easter or the number of robot angels who could dance on the head of a pin? Probably, probably. There are three estates in the celestial order: one to err, one to forgive and one to clear up the mess left behind by the other two. Of these three, which do *you* think is the most useful?)

He sighed, plunged his claw at random into the magma layer of his back correspondence and tried to get some work done before lunchtime.

The angel deposited Len and the machine in Len's workshop and limped skywards, rubbing her back and muttering. Having switched on the power and made himself a cup of tea, Len reached for a pencil and a scrap of paper and began sketching a rough design for a practicable perpetual-motion machine. He was soon so engrossed in this that the first he knew about the policemen was when the door flew open and he was hurled against the wall.

'You're nicked,' said a voice behind his head.

True, he said to himself, in a sense; I did steal myself from the factory, so strictly speaking, I'm stolen property. That's still no reason why these people should make me feel like I've just fallen off the back of a lorry. 'Would you mind not doing that?' he asked politely, as a policeman in a flak jacket kicked him in the kidneys.

'Shut up,' the police sergeant replied. 'You're under arrest for the theft of a machine, namely one Shipcock and Adley universal miller and turner, the property of Dunning and Wedge Limited. Come on, sunshine, on your feet.'

If the robot was here, there wouldn't be a problem. I'd say *Get 'em, robot,* and pretty soon there'd be bits of them scattered about like swarf all over the floor. Instead, he was going to have to use sweet reason. 'Excuse me,' he said.

'No,' replied the sergeant, inadvertently standing on his hand. 'Get the cuffs on him, Trevor. You two,' he added over his shoulder, nodding at the machine, 'bring that thing, it's evidence.'

'Hey, Sarge, it looks like it weighs a ton.'

'Two tons, actually,' Len said helpfully. 'You'll need a crane.'

The sergeant glowered at him ferociously. 'I thought I told you to shut up,' he snapped. 'And before you bring it on,' he shouted at his minions, 'dust it for prints. Carefully. Don't want chummy here getting off on a technicality.'

'Okay, Sarge.'

As they bundled him out through the door, he briefly considered appealing for help to Neville, who was presumably still asleep somewhere inside the machine. *Tell them it's not me,* he could have said. *Tell them that what I actually stole was myself, using your body as a mere tool to assist me.* He played the idea back inside his head and decided against it. For one thing, no matter how thick Neville might be, an appeal to him to come out and get kicked while he slipped back into the cosy cast-iron shell was unlikely to appeal to him. And in any case, did he really want to go back in there, spend the rest of the machine's working life cutting the slots in bolt-heads, with nothing to look forward to except an eventual appointment with sledgehammers and the big magnet down at the scrap-yard? If he stayed human, eventually they'd have to let him out; and there'd be other machines for him to use, new worlds of design and modification for him to conquer. He resolved to go quietly, or at least quietly punctuated by the occasional 'Ouch!'

Who knows? Perhaps I'll get a job in the prison workshop?

There was, of course, another alternative. There were highly placed people, Up There and Down Below, who owed him favours; or, at the very least, who could use his skills. If he yelled loudly enough, would they hear him and send angels with pickaxe handles and boltcutters to set him free? They should do, by rights, but he doubted it somehow. Trained machinists? Ten a penny. Stroll into any job centre and crinkle a fiver between forefinger and thumb, and you'll attract enough skilled labour to build five galaxies.

Later, when the cell door had slammed shut and the key had turned noisily in the lock (obviously not a good fit; with a small file and an oilstone he could tune it so that its wards moved frictionlessly, but he had an idea that it wasn't even worth offering), he lay back on the hard wooden bench and stared at the ceiling, allowing his mind to wander. It's all very well being able to do things, he realised, but that's never the end of the story. People – human beings – have to want the things to be done. And tools cost money, and so do materials; therefore it's only the people with money who have the tools and the materials, and people like that only ever want one thing made, namely more money. Which is why better mousetraps are invented by people whose houses are not necessarily infested with mice, and why the human race can make anything and has so very little (but ever so much more than they deserve).

I could dig a tunnel, Len mused. Piece of cake, digging a tunnel. First though, I need something to dig with, probably a length of jagged metal ripped off this bed. Now then, what would be the most ergonomically efficient design of digging tool that I could make, using the materials available? And when I've made a digger, I'll need to make cunningly disguised receptacles to store the excavated earth in, and improvised pit-props to stop the roof caving in; and some light to dig by would be nice, maybe I could rig up a makeshift extension lead using wire from the bedsprings unwound and wrapped in bits of plastic peeled off the washstand trim. Hey, a crane for lifting the earth out of the hole would come in handy, how'd it be if I unpicked thread from my socks and used a chairleg and the lid of the chamber pot . . .?

Len's eyes sparkled as he faced the new challenge, and human ingenuity coursed through his veins like the tame lightning in Dr Frankenstein's laboratory.

Zxprxp poured himself into the cockpit of his ship, engaged the stardrive and watched the viewscreen as the stars became silver needles and the planet Earth dwindled into a speck of dust. He sighed, wiggled his livers until he was comfy and switched on the recorder. His mission was at an end, and it was time to compose his final report.

How was he going to put this? What words would convey in a concise and intelligible manner his impressions of the human race, enabling his fellow creatures to understand the inhabitants of the blue and green planet, justifying his research grant and keeping the heads of his faculty from stringing him up by his *uhjlkhj*? He took a deep legful of cyanide gas and began:

Initial report of Researcher Zxprxp on the inhabitants of Star 4555683463, Planet 3. Dateline 153/7355/915373

Well, that was the easy bit. The rest would require a certain delicacy of touch. How about:

My original brief on being assigned this mission was to visit the planet and obtain enough relevant data on its indigenous dominant species to enable Strategic Command to reach an informed decision as to whether the planet is appropriate for full-scale invasion and colonisation. In the course of my investigations I observed a number of human beings (as the species in question is referred to locally) and conducted in-depth interviews with four of them. Based on these researches, my recommendation to the joint chiefs of staff is quite straightforward. Forget it.

Our preconceived notion that human beings are a primitive, undeveloped species incapable of offering any significant resistance to our armed forces is completely wrong. On the contrary, human beings are so highly advanced that in an armed conflict between our two species, we would be lucky to escape with losses below 90 per cent.

Take, for example, the present status of their technology. They have reached such a level of symbiosis with their machines that they can actually talk to them. More than that; machines like them. My own ship developed what could only be described as a crush on a human being, with the result that its loyalties were in danger of being severely compromised. Although I did not have an opportunity to make a specific study of their defence technology, I have no doubt that it is unspeakably formidable and not to be trifled with.

If that were not reason enough to leave well alone, humans appear to be on what I can only describe as first-name terms with their Supreme Being. I interviewed a member of the human mortal/divine diplomatic corps (in the local argot, a 'vicar'), who convinced me that humans and their gods regard each other as equals, friends even; and although I did not personally witness any divine manifestations during my visit, I am confident that any act of aggression on our part would immediately incur reprisals at the highest theological levels. To be blunt, we have enough trouble with our own god without picking a fight with someone else's. Another good reason I feel, for leaving well alone.

As if their technology and divine patronage were not enough, the impressively ordered and integrated nature of human society should make us consider very carefully before initiating hostilities with these people. I was able to contrive an interview with the human head of state, an official described as the Prime Minister, during the course of which I discovered that humankind have transcended the crippling effects of internal politics and arrived at a method of ordering their affairs whereby the rule of one party or faction over another is now entirely obsolete. This can be deduced from the fact that the nominal head of state is a complete imbecile, incapable of being held responsible for his own actions, let alone the management of a planet. Obviously, therefore, any apparent government that may exist on Earth is purely a smokescreen, and the human race has managed to achieve that state of enlightened anarchy that we have long recognised to be the only way in which an advanced society can possibly be run, but which (to our shame) we have yet to achieve ourselves.

The last and most significant factor, however, is human tolerance, the like of which is unknown in any other part of the seven galaxies so far observed during the course of this programme. Humans display no sign whatsoever of bias or bigotry; unlike any other known life form they adamantly refuse to judge by appearances, and display neither fear of nor hostility towards people or things they do not know or understand. In other words, this race cannot be terrified into submission, and are clearly so well adjusted among themselves that a policy of divide-and-conquer would be doomed to failure from the start.

In any event we must ask ourselves: do we really want to invade this miserable lump of wet rock? It is remarkably inhospitable. During my stay on Earth the entire planet was in darkness, the result of a total eclipse of the sun that lasted for twenty-nine hjgflk, *Homeworld Standard Time. That this was an everyday occurrence can be deduced from the casual attitude of the humans. They took no notice. It was business as usual. A world that spends most of its time in darkness is surely not worth considering as a potential colony.*

To summarise; if we invade Earth we will be facing a race who are in complete control of their technology, who are under the direct protection of their God, who live in an idyllic form of society on which it would be impossible to improve, and who are so perfectly adjusted as to represent the highest and most advanced form of sentient life we have yet encountered. The conclusion is inescapable. On Earth, to coin a phrase, everything is for the best in the best of all possible worlds. Don't tangle with these guys; they'll have our lkhjgfsd *for* ertwgsq'ccr. *Report ends.*

Zxprxp played the report back a couple of times, altering a few words here and there, until he was satisfied. Then he directed the computer to set a course for home, engaged the ship's standard cruise velocity of eight million times the speed of light, and leaned back in his tank, thanking his lucky stars for his species' lucky escape.

Below them, the waters of the fjord tumbled and foamed about the needle-sharp rocks of Lemminggagrjot Sound. The wind ruffled their fur against the grain and scoured their eyes, and its scream deafened them.

'Well,' a lemming observed, 'here we all are.'

An unusually violent wave dashed itself into spray against the cliff face, showering the lemmings with droplets of salt water. Instinctively, they flinched.

'Nice day for it,' a lemming said.

Although physics, mathematics, Sir Isaac Newton, Galileo and thirty-two-feet-per-second weren't part of their species' mental database, the lemmings instinctively knew what was coming next. They saw it all in rather less complex terms – trot-trot-AAAAaaaaaagh-splosh! – but the basic essentials were all there, encoded in their DNA. If pressed, they'd have come up with something like *When you've gotta go, you've gotta go*, or even *It's a far, far better thing*.

'You can see ever such a long way from up here,' a lemming said. 'Look, isn't that the little grassy hollow where we found those particularly tasty roots?'

A lemming craned its neck. 'I do believe you're right,' it said. 'My, those roots were scrummy. Next year, we must make a point of . . .'

The sentence faded away. The lemmings avoided looking at each other, but all that left for them to look at was the extravagantly copious quantity of Down below their feet. More Down, they couldn't help feeling, than we know what to do with. Easily a lifetime supply.

'Oh well,' sighed a lemming, its mouth full of a last nibble of tender, fleshy grass. 'Might as well get on with it, now we're here.'

Not a lemming spoke. Not a lemming moved. In their minds, where an ancient voice should have been chanting, there was an awkward silence.

'Duty calls,' muttered another. 'A lemming's gotta do what a lemming's gotta do.'

Far below, the sea curled its lips, opening a gap under the crest of a wave just the right size for a multitude of lemmings to fit into. It waited. If the sea had had hands, it'd have clapped them slowly.

'Alternatively,' a lemming said.

It paused, embarrassed. Suddenly, it was aware that it had its species' undivided attention.

'All I was going to say was,' it said, 'we could try that other method.'

'What other method?'

The lemming waggled its whiskers. 'Well,' it said, 'there was that lemming, remember, and it wanted to be the leader, and it said *Don't jump*. And so what I was thinking was, instead of jumping, why don't we try politics instead?'

Some of the lemmings asked for further details. What, they asked, is politics?

'Ah,' the lemming replied enthusiastically. 'Listen to this.'

So the lemming told them about politics; and after a show of paws, they decided to give it a whirl. First they had an election. Then, once they'd chosen their leader, they held an improvised inauguration ceremony and invested their new head of state with full powers to represent their interests and act with full and unfettered discretion on their behalf in all matters appertaining to the public interest and the future of the species.

Then they threw him over the cliff.

'So that's politics, is it?' a lemming said, as they made their way back towards the grassy hollow where the nice roots were. 'You know, I think it could quite easily catch on.'

A glorious pink sunset, seen from above. Two men walk up the path, fishing rods over their shoulders, tackle-boxes in their hands. At the door, a younger man waits.

'Hi, Dad,' he calls out. 'Hi, Jay. Have a good trip?'

The older man nods. 'It made a nice change,' he said.

'Catch anything?'

Both men nod and hold their hands apart, indicating the approximate size of notional fish. 'But you should have seen the one that got away,' the older man adds.

'That's great. Come on in out of the cold, Martha's got the kettle on.' The younger man turns to lead the way.

'Anything happen while we were away?'

The younger man shrugs. 'All fairly quiet, really,' he replies. 'A slight glitch with the computer. Sun went on the blink for a day or two. Spot of trouble with a revolt in Hell. All sorted. Shall I carry your rods for you?'

'Thanks,' the older man replies. 'They're heavier than they look. When you say a slight glitch—?'

His elder son frowns disapprovingly. 'Dad,' he says, 'you've only just got home. Relax. You did say it was all under control now, didn't you, Kevin?'

'Oh yes. All in apple-pie order.' Fortunately he hadn't specified which apple. His father and brother nod.

'That's all right then,' his father says. 'Had a good time while we've been away? Been behaving yourself? No wild parties?'

'Actually, it was pretty boring,' Kevin says, with a shrug. 'Next time you go, can I come too?'

'Next time . . .' his father says; and then they pass through the door, and it shuts, and here we are on the other side.

Next time. Well. We'll see.